KENNETH KAPPE

The RETURN of the DRAGONS

HIDDEN MAGIC VOLUME I

© 2017 by Kenneth Kappelmann
All rights reserved. No part of this book may be reproduced, stored in a retrieval system or transmitted in any form or by any means without the prior written permission of the publishers, except by a reviewer who may quote brief passages in a review to be printed in a newspaper, magazine or journal.

The final approval for this literary material is granted by the author.

First printing

This is a work of fiction. Names, characters, businesses, places, events and incidents are either the products of the author's imagination or used in a fictitious manner. Any resemblance to actual persons, living or dead, or actual events is purely coincidental.

ISBN: 978-1-61296-847-6
PUBLISHED BY BLACK ROSE WRITING
www.blackrosewriting.com

Printed in the United States of America
Suggested retail price $22.95

The Return of Dragons is printed in Adobe Caslon Pro

The RETURN of the DRAGONS

This book is dedicated to
the one person who took the time to read it
and in turn, forced me to publish it,
Denise Kappelmann

For Kyle, Kaylie, and Max.

In memory of Ronald Kleinke, a man I never
met but see every day in my son.

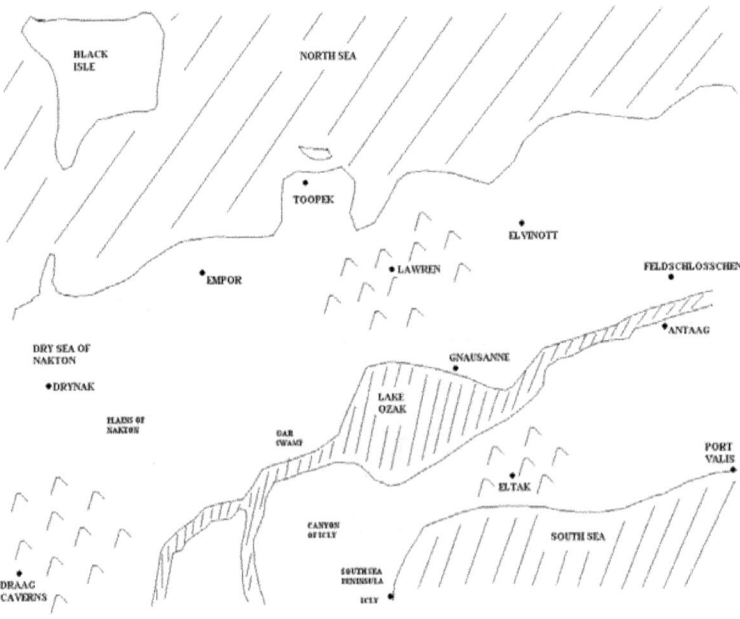

Map of Troyf

Prologue

In every world, there is good and there is evil. It is the balance of those forces which allows life to flourish. On Troyf, that balance has been challenged many times in the past but never as deeply as during the Dragon Oppression. During those dark times, behind the guidance of one very young and disturbed black dragon, the dragon forces raged war across the land. With fire and magic, they dispensed their wrath over all of Troyf, attempting in one sweep to assert their rule, making all other creatures their servants. They began their oppression by attacking those races who had powers, which carried the greatest possibilities of defeating their own, specifically the canoks and the human magi. The attacks were brutal and designed not to wear the groups down to servantship, but to strip every ounce of their life from them. They knew that these groups would never truly serve, only patiently wait for the opportunity to seek their revenge.

That opportunity came when the dragons turned their attention from the nearly destroyed groups to center on the other populations. In this they underestimated the magicians, and it proved to be their undoing. The remaining canoks and magis pooled their resources and delivered a massive attack on the dragon homeland while it was left relatively unprotected. The dragons used their lands as the focus of power for their magic. When it was destroyed, so was their oppression. The humans and canoks believed they had won the war, but time would tell a different story. Time may even tell that although young, Slayne, the large and powerful black dragon, developed a plan that went much deeper than what it appeared.

It is now two hundred years later, and peace has ruled across Troyf for the entire period. However, although all other races were able to recover, the dragon oppression left the canoks divided. The once proud four-legged creatures of peace were permanently scarred. The fierce magic unleashed by the dragons divided the red-coated canok nation into two opposing forces: the black reign, which fought for their own self-interests, usually joining forces with goblins, dark dwarves, dragons, or the like, and the white reign who held to their old ideals and worked to reseal the bonds that had been severed by the darkest of dragon magic.

The times again seem to be changing. Now there are tremors in the forests. Large evil forces are gathering and leaving bloodshed in their wake. Goblin armies of immense size are active throughout many forests that for two hundred years have been considered friendly. Is there a new enemy on Troyf which seeks to gather those it can to serve and blanket the country with its wrath, or have the enemies of the past returned to complete their plan and seek total domination? Unknowingly, one human, with his strange assortment of companions, must learn everything about himself before those questions can be answered and the enemies become known with the hidden magic.

CHAPTER 1

Return to Toopek

"You did well, Kirven," Schram stated as he pulled his body up to put weight on his tired legs. With tiny beads of sweat rolling down his cheeks beneath his curly brown hair, he walked over toward his companion.

Kirven's body swayed under his dizziness; then, his four legs regained their balance, and he replied strongly, "Thank you, Schram, and might I return the compliment to you as well?" The two smiled and turned, and after spreading some elven dust across the area, they headed out of the clearing, leaving the scorched and blackened body of the canok and the slain-bloodied remains of its goblin cohort in their wake slowly being taken by the forest.

"What do you think goblins are doing in the forests so close to Toopek?" began Schram. "I can't believe that he was only a drifter, especially with the obvious strength his canok possessed when wielding its magic." The young warrior bent down and stroked his friend's crisp white fur and patted the black diamond spot, which appeared between his upright ears, as he waited for his response.

Kirven himself was a canok, but not like the black creature which had attacked them with the goblin only moments earlier. He was of the white reign. His body, including his ears, eyes, tongue, and claws, was all completely white. Kirven's black diamond spot on his fore brow was unique to him, and its existence was a topic never discussed, even with Schram. The young man, now into his twenty-fifth year, had known the canok since he was only a child, and throughout their lives together, he had learned two things about his closest friend. First, he was the only canok in the white reign that had the mysterious black spot and probing into its existence had meant death to many in the past, and second, Kirven was by far the most powerful canok he had ever encountered.

There was a slight pause in the discussion as a frown began to curl over Kirven's face clearly being carried to his voice. "That canok was indeed powerful, and by no means the goblin's possession as your statement implied. With one twitch from its opaque blackened eye, he could have reduced that weak-minded goblin to nothing more powerful than a bandicoot. He chose to walk with the goblin as I chose to walk with you."

The shrewdness in his tone was one which Schram had not heard for a long while. Schram looked down in shame because he knew his one misspoken word had struck Kirven deeply. Canoks, whether black or white, are their own individuals. They are not pets to be used by some master but instead act under their own guidance and control, using magic when only they alone deem it necessary, never for any purpose other than one they believe to be sound. Schram's words carried his sad apologetic feelings as he said, "I'm sorry, Kirven. I did not mean—"

"I do not know what they were doing here," he interrupted, answering Schram's previous question. "The black would not tell me, and all the goblin spoke was gibberish because he knew your blade had struck true," he paused, then added, "And I am sorry that I was harsh. Sometimes I forget that it is you that I am talking to. Now, let's get on to Toopek." His voice was becoming lighter as he added, "Perhaps someone there can tell us what has happened that would bring goblins into the forests, but regardless, the city will welcome the return of its only prince."

Schram grimaced a bit, not liking being referred to by title and knowing that he would be more pleased to see his mother and father, the king and queen, than they would be to see him. They did not hold to the idea that the prince of the largest human city in all of Troyf should be parading about the countryside with a four-legged magician from a history best forgotten, but Schram felt differently. Something inside him pushed him to explore the world, to place himself against that which was unknown.

They had only been gone this time for about two months, but something said when he left had caused the prince to wish to return as soon as they could. His mother, Queen Suzanne, had come to him the night before their leave and pleaded with him not to go, saying she felt great evil in the air. The statement had seemed odd coming from her as she held no beliefs in any magical senses or found any comfort in her son's relationship with Kirven. Schram had told her all would be fine and the trip was a necessity because Kirven needed to return to his homeland to explain to the other canoks the ideas the humans had for the future. Through his companionship with Schram, the canok had become an ambassador to both nations, trusted beyond measure by each. When Suzanne realized that she would not be able to sway her son from his motives, she had issued one final comment, "Trust in yourself what you are about to undertake. The knowledge within you is great and save you it can."

Schram had thought the entire scene to be quite strange, but knowing that they would face few dangers on this journey, he had passed it off as nothing more than an overly worried mother. However, as the trip had taken over thirty days longer than it should have and they had run into so many odd occurrences, Schram began to feel his mother's statement eating at his mind. They had seen dwarves running scared through the forests, elves and humans left for dead with no memory of what had happened to them, and such a high number of goblins and trolls in supposedly friendly lands. All of these had added many days to their travels and a new wonder, stemming on fear, about what was happening to their minds. Schram had thought that maybe the canoks would have some answers, but when he mentioned his mother's comment to Kirven, he replied saying only that she was a very wise woman with many mysteries about her. Finally, even the other canoks in Kirven's homeland seemed to be on edge as if they knew that something was wrong but were afraid to talk about it, or at least would not talk about it with Schram. That was the other thing about canoks. They had a magical language all to themselves, always changing it, but still keeping it the same. They could make themselves understood by only those who they chose to let understand, and that understanding could be turned off at an instant. Two people could be hearing the exact same thing, but one would recognize nothing but gibberish while the other would hear the words clearly in whatever language they spoke. During this visit to Kirven's home, Schram understood little.

With all the oddities taking place along the journey, Schram was ready to be home, and his pace now displayed it. Though it was a gloomy day with rolling clouds shaded even more by the tall tree cover, the two seemed content and happy as the newfound coolness was a refreshing replacement compared to some of the sweltering humid days they had faced when they began. The mild air pushed Schram's long legs forward, and Kirven, who stood half the human's height at the shoulder, repeatedly added slight skips to his pace to stay beside his friend.

Schram was fairly tall, even for a human, standing nearly six-and-a-half feet tall. However, it was not only his height which gave him his powerful demeanor, but he also stood broad shouldered with well-developed muscles in both his arms and legs. He wore the armor of the royal family of Toopek, silver and white with a golden family crest on the breastplate, though now it was stained with so much goblin blood that barely anything showed through its blackness. Schram's brown hair hung near shoulder length and curled with small waves about his head. As he walked at his quick step, his senses taking in all occurring around him equal to most elf's abilities, he began to get the feeling that something was not right. He could not place where the discrepancy was, but he could feel that one was present. He glanced down to Kirven whose expression showed the same idea but also appeared not to be able to identify it.

With the new mood of worry around them, the two seemed to increase their pace that rivaled a slow run. They did not speak as they moved, leaving their total concentration free to absorb their surroundings. It was nearly an hour later when they finally cleared the trees and entered the western outskirts of Schram's home, Toopek. However, the Toopek they arrived to was not the same one they had left only a short time ago.

Schram's face was blank while he fought to regain his breath, and again he looked down to his companion but saw that his white eyes held no answers. The usually merchant-crowded streets stood desolate and bare, giving an almost dead appearance. The few people Schram could see walked swiftly and directly to their destinations, never talking or even looking around. Then, it came to him. What he could barely sense as they approached now bit him like the teeth of a viper. That scent. In the air was the distant smell of fire, but from where he could not tell. He glanced upward to see the gray smoke-covered skies, the gentle wind pushing the clouds over the city from the harbor. Kneeling down, he began to speak to Kirven, not realizing the canok had vanished. Swinging his head around, he saw the small white creature with his front legs lifted up onto a ledge peering into a shop window.

"What is it?" he asked in a somewhat hushed tone.

"*Shh!*" Kirven replied telepathically. Instantly, Schram froze, knowing his friend would only speak that way if there was extreme danger. "Come on quickly. Get out of the middle of the street."

Schram hurried over to his friend, not questioning his judgment but also not understanding the danger they faced in his own home. The residents of Toopek never even locked their doors because there was so little crime, but still, the eeriness of the situation and the warning in Kirven's actions sent a shiver down the human's spine.

Worry, excitement, and fear were all growing within the young man as he cautiously followed the canok down the side of the street. They were on the main road through the city, and even the coldest winter day late at night would bring about more activity than they were now witnessing. At most, maybe two individuals could be seen, and they were only eyes peeking through closed drapes. Schram thought about what Kirven had said while they were still in the forest and quickly came to the realization that Toopek was not about to welcome anyone home, even their prince.

Suddenly, Kirven's ears shot upward, and he began to run down the street, ducking into a dark alley, hollering at Schram to follow. They both found some loose rubble to hide behind and peered back out onto the road.

"What is…" Schram began to whisper, stopping as he tried to absorb what he now saw appearing around the corner ahead of him. Parading down the street was what looked to be about two hundred goblins being led by a handful of black canoks. Behind them, they dragged something, something Schram could not identify. "Going on?" he finished hesitantly.

Kirven could only shake his head as he too had only questions. Softly he spoke a few short chants, which Schram knew was to protect them from being discovered by the blacks at the lead in the parade-like formation.

Both looked on, trying to gain some sort of insight regarding the scene but gaining nothing from what they observed. Suddenly, they heard a rustling behind them, and Schram spun, drawing his sword in the same motion. However, his joints quickly relaxed as Kirven had already released a spell, freezing their adversary where he stood. Schram stared blankly at the statue with sword drawn. It was Tomas Sherblade, a head member of the Toopekian council and chief advisor to Keith Starland, Schram's father.

"Zah poh," rang Kirven's deep voice, lifting the spell and causing Tomas to fall to his knees.

Without delay, they grabbed the weakened man and pulled him over behind the cover they had assembled from the rubble. However, the goblin party had begun passing the alley now, and the protection behind which they sat actually gave little comfort. Schram knelt down next to his still groggy friend, whispering, "Tomas, are you all right? It is me, Schram, the Prince."

A smile gradually formed across Tomas's face as he slowly seemed to be regaining his senses.

"Schram? Really, is it you?" The two hugged, each regarding the other's presence with speculation, but both still pleased to see them. "And, Kirven, how have you been?" Kirven nodded while the human reached up to pat his head. "I guess you both can see what has happened since you left."

Schram leaned back. "We can see it, but we don't understand it."

His eyes were filled with despair. As he began to brush himself off, checking the parade in front of him as he did, it became obvious that the things he was about to speak of would prove difficult for him to say. He kept his voice low, but it did not damper the hardships he was feeling.

"The truth is, nobody knows exactly what happened." Again he looked around as if guarding against the fear of a sudden ambush. "Three days ago, loud explosions were heard across the bay at the Tower of Council. We could see fire and smoke bellowing upward from the castle and surrounding mountain, so I authorized sending a heavily armored ship across with more than a hundred men to investigate the disturbance and see to the king and queen's safety. The ship returned the next day with nearly the entire crew slain, burned, or missing. The few that were still alive could remember nothing, their comments sounding like psychotic outbursts." His voice trailed off as he heard something from the street that drew his attention.

Ignoring the sound, Kirven asked, "But what about the goblins and the black canoks we now see in the city? When did they arrive?"

He looked back to stare into the flat white eyes of the canok.

"They arrived the following day." His voice became cold, and now he seemed to be reliving the story in his mind rather than simply retelling it. "Thirty ships, each carrying uncountable numbers of goblins and trolls mixed thoroughly with those you call relatives. Anyone who resisted was killed. Even some of those who did not resist were killed. Last night, we held a secret council for all who would come to discuss what could be done, and the majority of the people who attended that meeting are now being displayed in the goblin's parade before us." Tomas motioned toward the street where it now had become apparent what they were dragging in their wake.

"The bodies," Schram said to himself grabbing his sword hilt as he spoke. "My friends."

"Take it easy, Schram," Kirven gently interjected. "There is nothing you can do now. Our time to act will be later."

A tear joined the beads of sweat on Schram's cheek as he replied, "But what about the Tower of Council, the castle, and, and…" his voice began to fade and crack, "my parents?"

Tomas's face saddened. "We do not know. Nobody knows."

The prince fell to his knees, burying his face in his arms. A silence ensued until Kirven inserted, "Did the secret council decide anything?"

"We decided that we would seek out the aid of—"

"Istak matak," interrupted Kirven.

Schram leaped to his feet, grabbing Tomas in one arm and his sword in the other, all but forgetting his sadness for the moment as he paid heed to Kirven's warning. "Come on, Tomas!"

"What? What is it? What did he say?!" Tomas asked adamantly as he was pulled down the alley away from the street.

Schram, now completely back to his senses, had not realized that Tomas had not understood Kirven's words, which had sounded perfectly clear to him. He wondered why the canok had not given both of them the same warning, but due to its content, he had no time to try to evaluate Kirven's reasoning. "He said that magic is after us."

Tomas shrugged as he turned and ran hard behind them, trusting what they said. Sarcastically and mostly to himself, he added, "Oh, that clears it up."

"Shut up and run! I cannot stop it!" Kirven demanded; now his words clear to both.

The three ran down the alley as fast as they possibly could. Both Tomas and Schram looked back in horror to see a glowing orb floating quickly through the air in the trail behind them. They had fixed some distance between them, but the globe seemed to be adjusting its pace as it neared, and quickly, their lead was evaporating.

They reached the end of the alley and had to go right, leading out of town, or left and head toward the harbor. Tomas asked, panting as he spoke, "The orb, Kirven, what is it?"

Schram awaited the response as he had never, in all his travels, laid eyes on anything of this sort. Kirven glanced toward the globe and then back to Tomas. "It is a tracer globe. It seems someone is after one or all of us. We must split up for the globe will follow only that person it truly seeks."

"What happens if it catches them?" Tomas asked hesitantly; the question and tone at which it was asked catching both Schram and Kirven by surprise.

The canok stared at the man questionably before replying, "It depends on the globe and who sent it. Some can capture and hold who they seek, some can just extract desired information, while others simply kill."

Tomas fell back, nearly tripping over his own feet while a deepened expression of terror grew across his face. He knew the globe was after him. Schram knew it could just as easily been after Kirven or him. Each had their own powerful qualities. Kirven was strong with magic and Schram was the prince. Furthermore, they had not exactly entered the city inconspicuously. But no, Tomas knew the globe was meant for him, and when Schram turned to Kirven, it was obvious the canok felt the same.

Just then Tomas, seeing the globe growing near, screeched and ran toward the forest. Schram started after him but froze on Kirven's telepathic message, *"No, let him go."*

The globe did not even slow as it passed the two observers. It turned and proceeded down the path behind Tomas until both had disappeared in the woods beyond the city. Kirven began again, this time verbally, "We must go at once. Tracer globes also act as windows for whoever sends them. It is a sure bet they know we are here."

It was this final statement that made the two run even faster for neither of them knew who *they* were or what it would mean to *them* to know the two were there.

"Go to the cave," Schram shouted. Kirven was already heading there anyway but gave an accepting nod just the same.

Both collapsed on the cold, rock floor of the sewer that Schram played in as a boy. He called it his cave and frequently had gone there with the canok to talk, cry, or simply think. Kirven had never minded this dismal place because it took him away from the barrage of humans he sometimes found to be an annoyance. However, this time it was not humans from which he was hiding.

"What do you think we should do?" the canok asked, breaking the silence which had eclipsed the small chamber.

Schram thought this was an interesting question. Except when magic was concerned, he usually decided where their journeys took them, not because he was more intelligent, simply because Kirven had always just wanted to walk with him. Neither would ever claim to be the leader over the other. However, this situation was different. Magical forces were definitely involved. No goblin power they had ever crossed before could have created and controlled that orb, and what about Tomas? No, this situation was definitely grave.

Schram carried over three times Kirven's weight, and his well-developed strength in tune with his diligence with a sword had gotten them out of many tight situations, but he believed that no menial strength of his could ever fight the powers he felt they might now face.

He turned all possibilities over in his mind and then stated flatly, "We need help. We should return to Elvinott. Perhaps the elves have answers to what has been happening."

Kirven lifted one of his glistening white eyebrows at this notion. They had not returned to the place they first met in years. The elf land was indeed a place they could find allies, assuming it too had not fallen prey to the same fate as Toopek. There was a pause as Schram watched the canok toy with his idea. Then, Kirven rose to his feet adding, "Yes, Elvinott is the best place to begin. However, we will need many new supplies for it is not that long of a journey, but since the extended length of our last trip, we barely made it back as it was."

Schram was relieved to hear Kirven's favorable response, but his face remained grim as he had not thought about the requirements they would need and the fact that this town, his hometown, was no longer friendly. Feeling the exhaustion of the day's activities, he replied, "Let's rest now, and I'll sneak back to the shops tonight to get what we need."

Both ideas seemed satisfactory to Kirven who responded with a slight nod and proceeded to pace around the overly confined space of the cave to seek out a comfortable spot to lie. Finding no area to be any different from another, he enchanted a short spell, making the rock floor become soft beneath his feet. Rolling his body to its side, the ground seemed to move around him, conforming to his shape. Then, after a brief moment, his white eyes shut, and he was asleep.

It had been a long, trying day, and both the weary travelers needed rest. However, even as tired as he was, Schram found sleep extremely difficult. He repeatedly saw Tomas's expression, wondering what his old family friend had been keeping from them. He thought about the Tower of Council and his parent's castle, both protected with fortress strength yet seemingly destroyed at will. Then his mind fell to Elvinott, the land in which he lived the first five years of his life, his presence preventing a war and creating a treaty. This was definitely not the homecoming he was expecting.

Feeling Schram's restlessness, Kirven opened his eyes and slowly walked over placing his head across the young man's chest. In gentle tones, he said, "Do not trouble your mind, my friend, for now we only require rest. Tomorrow will mark the beginning to finding the answers we desire. *Ish mak.*"

They both drifted off into a peaceful sleep.

Their exhausted state and Kirven's enchantment caused the two to sleep completely through the night. Yet when morning came, they were brutally awakened by a piercing scream coming from somewhere outside the cave entrance. Schram leaped to his feet and ran over to the cleverly hidden opening. What he witnessed when he peered out into the street made him turn away in disgust. Five goblins were wildly tearing the flesh from the motionless body of a human woman. Two other goblins had hold of a second woman and were securely tying her down so they could join in the feast.

Kirven had almost as quickly reached the opening and stared wide-eyed at what was taking place before them. His stare became fixed on the girl who was flailing wildly trying to escape while she watched the goblins devour her companion. He bowed his head and sadly whispered, "Krirtie."

Schram immediately swung his head back to the street to take a closer look at those being terrorized. The dead girl was now totally unrecognizable as most of her limbs had been ripped from her body. One of the goblins seemed to be staring at the sewer entrance as he bit through solid bone. Schram's gaze swung to the other girl who was openly terrified and violently trying to break her capture's bonds. The goblin who had previously blocked his view had since moved to join the others, leaving Schram a clear picture of his childhood playmate. Without a word to Kirven, he leaped out of the cave with his sword drawn and at the ready. The canok, stunned by his sudden movement but realizing there would be no way to prevent his foolhardy attack, silently slipped through the entrance taking his place by the warrior's side.

Fortunately, the goblin's intense hunger made them oblivious to all around, and they were not alerted by Krirtie's second scream as she saw the two approaching. Schram knew they were outnumbered, and although surprise was on their side, there was a good chance this rescue attempt would be futile. However, he also knew that he would not be able to live with himself should he not try.

"Saktil nif samath Tarsi." And all around got pitch black.

The goblins stumbled back, scared, and disoriented. One bumped into Schram, and the prince drove his sword deep. Feeling the warm blood flow across his hand, he cut his blade upward letting the body slump to the ground. He could see no better than the goblins, but his advantage was that he knew from where the darkness originated. Although he could no longer tell exactly where Kirven was, he could hear the canok's growls as he viscously tore at one of the goblin's throats.

Then, as the spell began to slowly wear off and light began to creep back into the area, Schram adjusted quickly and moved into attack. The remaining goblins roared when they saw the situation. Already four were dead, and Kirven had just dropped a fifth, opening its insides onto the street. Schram never hesitated, grabbing the goblin closest to Krirtie by the throat and launching him into the remaining one, knocking both to the ground. In one motion, he ripped the ropes binding the still terrified woman and lifted her to her feet out of the way. After giving her a quick reassuring glance, he turned to face the two remaining goblins who had regained their footing and now stood before him, swords drawn.

"Drop your sword, and we won't kill you, human scum," spoke one of the goblins in the common tongue.

"Why don't you fat-bellied, slug-eating excuses for life come and make me," he replied back in the goblin's language.

Both their faces darkened. They charged at the much larger human, issuing various calls and hollers as they did so. Sweat slowly beaded down Schram's face as he watched the two beheaded corpses fall to the ground accompanying another scream from Krirtie.

Schram glanced over to Kirven who was happily heaving one of his victims into a nearby ditch. "Quickly," the canok said. "We must clean up this mess. Dump the bodies in with this one, and we will cover them, and then—" he stopped in midsentence when he realized his statements were falling on deaf ears. Kirven looked over to see that Schram had Krirtie in a deep and long lost embrace.

CHAPTER 2

The Road: Tigon

After the three cleaned up the alley as best they could, they slipped back down into the cave to try and sort out all that was happening. Schram had not seen Krirtie for longer than he could remember, and her present condition made his heart sink as she fought through the tears covering her face and the cracking in her voice.

"We didn't know what to do," she exclaimed. "They came into our city. Anyone who asked anything was killed. I have only been back for a couple of weeks, but nobody expected anything like this was about to happen." She broke into another fit of crying, and Schram gently placed her head against his chest trying to give any comfort he could. She pushed herself back as the need to speak of the horrors she had seen overwhelmed the pain she felt.

She continued, her tone carrying a lost, unfeeling notion which sent chills down his spine. "Many of the women were beaten and thrown into cages to be used as rewards for those goblins performing the best for their masters." She looked sadly into Schram's eyes. "The tower and castle are believed to be destroyed. Nobody knows the whereabouts of your mother and father. Neither has been seen since before the attack."

Schram now felt tears forming in his eyes. His head fell downward giving a quick, silent prayer for strength. Softly, he asked, "Since our return, Kirven and I have seen very few people on the streets. What brought you out that got you captured?"

She turned instantly pale. "My sister and I were coming to meet Tomas Sherblade to inform him that they captured our father when those goblins grabbed us. I would have been killed too if it was not for both of you, but my sister. Did you see what—" She nearly went into hysterics before collapsing back into the warrior's large arms.

"How did they capture Derik?" asked Kirven who had listened intently but remained quiet since returning to the cave.

"Not now!" interrupted Schram, glaring toward his friend. "She can talk more about her father later, when she is ready."

"We don't have later," he replied harshly. "We have had too many situations to go unnoticed long. We must move, getting out of the city within the next hour to be safe. Those goblins, although probably not high in their ranks, will be missed, and that will mean search parties."

"I would like to investigate my parent's castle before we—"

Kirven broke in firmly. "Out of the question! We must leave the city or risk being captured."

He frowned but knew the advice to be sound. "Kirven, I have traveled with you too long not to trust your judgment in such cases, but we still need supplies."

"I have all we would require for a short journey," stated Krirtie as she pushed herself up to sit on her own once again. "Elise and I had taken all we could to the edge of the woods last night. We were prepared to leave after we talked with—oh my gosh, Tomas. I forgot. We were to meet with him. He'll want to know you are both here. We must—"

"Tomas has been captured," Kirven blurted out causing Krirtie's cheeks to drop.

"We don't know that for sure," replied Schram. "We didn't see the globe capture him."

"The globe would not have lost him, and he could not have defeated it. Its power almost turned my magic against me."

Krirtie had a concerned and frightful expression growing across her face. She sat forward. "Was it a globe glowing with light and moving with incredible speed through the air?"

"Yes, do you know of it?" asked Schram, also noticing Kirven's ears arch upward as he spoke.

"One came into our house, ignoring everyone except my father. Right when he saw it, he ran. However, it acted quickly, and in only moments, there was a bright flash, and they both disappeared."

There was a long silence as Schram tried to work through all he had learned, and Krirtie fell to the ground again fighting off the tears and exhaustion she was feeling. They all knew that they should leave Toopek as soon as they could, but Schram preferred to sneak out at night. They had been lucky before, entering in the daylight, but to risk it again would be dangerous, especially with all that had occurred since their arrival. However, he also knew they faced as much or more danger if they stayed.

"If we can only make it to the forest," he broke in abruptly, "then we will have a good chance of escaping." He rose, motioning to the others to follow. "Come on, take us to your food Krirtie. We have a long journey to make, and we must move quickly. I believe it is the only way escape will be possible."

The seriousness in his voice created no comments in opposition, and the three, rather hastily, made their way out of the sewer. Kirven enchanted a simple spell, which erased the signs of their presence, but he knew that soon the bodies of the slaughtered goblins would be discovered, and a globe with their names on it could be close behind. Krirtie took one last sad gaze toward the remains of her sister and issued a short prayer in her honor, the last line echoing, "Vengeance will be mine."

Schram, seeing a look in her eye he had never seen before, removed a small pouch from within his armor. He sprinkled a bit of dust from inside the pouch across the remains of the bodies. A cold chill blew across them, and suddenly, the body of her sister began to fade and then vanish all together, and that of the goblins took on a different darker look and became swallowed into the ground. Nothing was said, but he could feel the appreciation when Krirtie placed her hand on his shoulder.

Kirven looked on with a questionable gaze and then curved it into a slight grin.

"Perhaps he has not forgotten everything," he whispered to himself before falling in beside the two.

The three did their best to slip down every back alley and side street, attempting to dissect the town unnoticed, but the sun now shown high in the sky, and although the beautiful late summer day brought happiness to the atmosphere, fear and anxiety raged deep within each of the travelers. They emerged from a narrow street only to dive back down it as a party of six heavily-armed goblins passed by its face. The leader looked down the alley, saw nothing, and motioned the group forward. Krirtie let out a sigh of relief and then froze when she realized that the pile of loose debris she had leaped into had just moved.

The girl held her body still as she reached calmly over to tap Schram on the shoulder and point to the pile of rubble beneath her. The warrior stood at the ready when Krirtie flung herself up, bringing what she could with her. There was only a faint grumbling from the drunken goblin as it rolled over, replacing a box across its face to block out the harsh late morning light. Schram relaxed, knowing that they could easily continue on without causing anymore disturbances or leaving anymore bodies in their wake. However, Krirtie had a different idea as she reached down, removed the goblin's dagger, and thrust it repeatedly into its body, not stopping until Schram forcibly restrained her.

Black goblin blood covered her hands and arms while the tears of sadness she had worn for the past few hours had been replaced with a stoic, cold expression of vengeance. She broke free of Schram's hold and removed some of the goblin armor, placing its sword and dagger at her side. Looking back to Schram, she said, "Now I will return the pain they have placed on my family, with steel forged with their own hands."

Schram was not sure how to handle this side of Krirtie he had never seen before. She had, in the past three days, been through more than anyone should have to face in a lifetime. He wished their time was not as limited as it was so he could take some time and help his friend when she was asking for it, but he knew that escape must be their first priority. If they could not, then they could never hope to regain control of the city and thus find true vengeance.

The three ran under the cover of various shadows before making one final dash for the tree line surrounding the city. Krirtie directed them through the trees. When they reached the well-hidden supplies, she broke the silence that had engulfed them since her display in the alley. Her voice was cold, and her statement direct. "Where are we going?"

"To Elvinott," Schram replied bluntly.

There was a pause before Krirtie smugly added, "Whose idea was that, Schram? Yours?"

Kirven, enjoying her displeasure, stated, "Oh, I assure you, Krirtie, Schram brought it up most eagerly."

She frowned. "Well then, tell me Schram, do you do it because it is the correct decision, or because of her?"

Schram's face hardened, and his eyes burned with fire. "We are going to Elvinott. If you do not wish to go, and that includes both of you, then let me bid you leave now, with all my wishes for a safe journey to be yours. We need help, and the elves may be our only hope."

Krirtie fell silent as Kirven drew a small crooked smile. None of the adventures he had been on with Schram had ever been quite so thrust upon them. He remembered back to times they traveled across nearly all of Troyf, looking for various treasures, but now it seemed they were looking for their own safety and the safety of the world they knew. *Could the time finally have come?* he thought. Looking back toward his friends, Kirven felt sorry that he had pursued the small confrontation between the two. He focused on Krirtie, no longer seeing the girl they had known several years before. Now, even through her hardships, she seemed more mature and confident but still somewhat innocent. He regretted pushing them into the fight he had so much enjoyed listening to, but he wondered what would happen when they reached Elvinott.

"If we reach Elvinott," he said under his breath.

Her long black hair cascaded helplessly down her shoulders while her trim but well-defined body carried her forward with a mystic agility. It seemed odd to Schram to be walking with Krirtie now. She was the first human friend he could ever remember having, and he had grown to think of her more as a sister than a girl, though he was certain her feelings had grown differently in return. However, when he looked at her now, he realized that she had developed into a beautiful and powerful woman.

As a child, Krirtie had always avoided most of the expected and common girl behavior, preferring to participate in the boys' activities. And although she did not have the strength to compete directly with Schram, she had always held her own rather well. She was also a deeply caring person, and by her lost expression now, Schram knew her thoughts were with her family. He wished that there was something he could do to comfort her, but her troubles were ones he knew she could only work through on her own. She was very strong, in body and mind, and in time, she would be at peace again.

"She will be all right," Kirven said softly, noticing his friend's deep concerns. "You know that she will."

"Yes, I do. It is just hard to see her like this when I can remember how happy she and her family were when we were growing up."

Her family, as well as Krirtie herself, had always treated him as an everyday boy, not the son of the king and queen. They never referred to him as Prince Schram of Toopek, a title he himself never used except in the company of his parents. Nor did they ever question his friendship and loyalty to Kirven, although to most people of Toopek, magic was unknown and unwanted. Canoks were infections they did not want invading their city, and if not for the fact that he walked with the prince, Kirven's welcome would have ended with his first step into town. But most of all, Krirtie's family never asked about the five years he spent with the elves as a baby.

Schram thought back to the time of his kidnapping and closed his eyes tightly. At only one month of age, he was taken from his parent's castle completely unnoticed. It was obvious that the elves were responsible for nobody else had the ability to sneak in and out of the heavily guarded castle without detection. However, this event that should have started a war, actually prevented one.

War between the elves and humans had been brewing for some time. The elves were unhappy about the widespread human villages that were appearing in and around their lands. Yet, when they peacefully approached some of these various colonies with their concerns, they were greeted with nothing but resentment. They had no power to stop or even slow the human expansion. The elves were torn. They attacked what they could and defended against the few minor invasions upon their land, but all this accomplished was to further the hostilities between the two factions. Excellent and proud fighters as the elves were, they were also intelligent. They realized that if war was raged, their numbers could not compete with that of the humans.

It was during these troubles that they learned of the birth of the new prince. Hoangis, the king of the elves, believed that with Prince Schram as the bargaining tool, he could turn the tables on the humans, making them an ally rather than an enemy. As Schram had thought about this many times in the past, the logic was ridiculous. The plan was a last-ditch effort by a desperate nation, and by some twist of fate, it worked. However, according to King Keith Starland and Queen Suzanne Starland, Schram's parents, it cost their son the first five years of his life. Though, when Schram thought of those years, he remembered living with people he took to be his family. The elves had treated him as if he was Hoangis's own son, with respect and love. The hardest day of his life was his fifth birthday, the day he returned to Toopek, a city he had never known. For five years, the leaders had sat at a bargaining table, drawing up a treaty to allow a peaceful resolution between the two warring parties, and Schram's return marked its completion. However, if not for the support from Kirven, his friend for his last two years with the elves, he could not have made the journey. Since that day, he could not remember a time when he did not know where Kirven was.

Schram looked down to his friend who panted softly as they trudged through the forest, hoping Kirven knew how much he still needed and relied on him. "Let's take a break for lunch," he broke in, his voice cracking slightly. "We started without breakfast and still have a long trek ahead of us."

The three travelers sat down in the small clearing, and Schram turned to face the girl who had been quiet most of the morning. "Are you all right?"

"I'll be fine, Schram," she replied softly. "Also, I am sorry about what I said earlier. You have always been honest with me, and I shouldn't get mad at you for that."

Gently, he placed his large rough fingers across the battered goblin shield she had laid across her knees. Taking her hand in his, he said, "I'm sorry too. I am the one who reacted poorly."

Kirven moved forward. "Well, as long as we are handing out apologies, I suppose I should throw mine to the bunch." He smiled and added, "But my real concern is whether we are actually going to eat during this break or just hold hands and smile?" He laughed slightly, hoping he had been successful in destroying the seriousness which he could see beginning to develop.

"Yes, we are," replied Schram proudly, knowing he had not actually answered Kirven's question.

The three ate lunch, exchanging jibes in good spirits and caught each other up on the paths each of their respective lives had followed since they had last seen each other. Soon after, they returned to the trail beginning their ascent into the mountains.

"We should hopefully come to Lawren by nightfall," Schram stated.

"But do not forget to be cautious, old friend," Kirven responded. "Those last two goblins acted much quicker than those in the past. We have begun to leave a blood trail behind us. If word continues to spread, the goblin search parties will begin looking for us in particular rather than just happening upon some weary travelers."

"Trust me, I know. That thought has been haunting me for the last hour. I am never confident when traveling in unfriendly country." He leaned closer to Kirven to speak in a lower tone. "I also am worried about Krirtie. She has been silent since lunch, and her pace continually fades, not to mention she insists on wearing goblin armor and weapons."

"Worry not, Schram, for she has much to sort out in her mind. She fought those last goblins with rage stemming from a violent vengeance for her family. She is strong and will always take care of herself."

"I suppose that you are right, but I still worry."

They reached the top of Mount Sawyer still about a mile shy of Lawren when the sun dipped behind the mountaintop. Schram, not pleased with the time they had made considering the nice weather and the recent, somewhat suspicious absence of goblin interference, turned to the others. "We must continue quickly. It is all downhill from here, and I don't want to be in these mountains after sundown if I can help it. I have already had an uncomfortable feeling of being watched for some time now."

Krirtie's eyes widened at this but still showed little expression of any sort, least of all fear. Kirven, occasionally dashing short distances into the tree line, also had felt eyes upon them but held his tongue for now. His inability to focus on the direction of the eavesdropper frustrated him, and his thoughts were tied up in this intriguing dilemma.

They proceeded down the west slope of the mountain when Schram stopped, motioning to Kirven to come forward. Krirtie, seeing the disturbed look on his face, drew her sword and took a position several meters behind them.

"What do you make of it?" Schram asked, pointing toward the ground.

A troubled look grew across the canok's face and was carried in his voice. "It is a tigon print."

"A tigon? I thought they were just creatures dreamed up in the fairy tales of elf-lore. My elf mother used to sing songs of the huge creatures of mythical strength but never implied that they were anything more than that, a myth."

Kirven still showed great distress. "No, they are quite real, but… this one is…well, wrong."

Schram now shared his added level of worry. "What do you mean, wrong?"

"Tigons are simple forest beasts, easily discovered and controlled through simple magic. Yet except for the sight of this print, I feel nothing." His voice now became even more concerned. "I should be able to feel its presence, even if it is no longer near. This worries me, Schram. This worries me gravely."

"Schram! Kirven!" Krirtie began in a voice hardly like her own. "I think you might want to come take a look at this."

The two moved quickly down the road to where Krirtie now was backing away from a commotion in some nearby trees with her sword drawn and eyes fixed as if watching a castle melt into a quake.

"Can goblin magic control a tigon?" Schram asked, drawing his sword.

"The goblins know no magic such as this, and even if they could, mine would still be able to overtake it. I am useless here. My powers are having no effect on the tigons or the weak-minded goblins. There is another force at work here, a much more powerful force than any lowly goblin could master."

As Schram looked on, he could not help but be taken by the awesome sight. Ahead of his small and seemingly inconspicuous party stood the two largest beasts he had ever seen. Their thick mane-encrusted heads alone were as big as a canok body and their four legs, which carried their massive striped bodies, looked as sturdy as the greatest of oaks. Schram, Kirven, and Krirtie might only have had a slight chance against one of the beasts, but two plus the goblins, he did not see how it was possible. Their quest to the elven village had already failed only a heartbeat after it had begun. A feeling of shame crept over him. He looked at the approaching sight and then back toward Krirtie. She was standing tall, sword raised, showing no fear. For her, this was to be her final battle for she was fighting her way to join her father and sister.

"Ist kat, Tam ols ilnes sleepin doth." Kirven's magic struck deep into Schram's head. He looked up, but nothing was changed except the movement of those approaching. The parade coming forward had stopped. The two tigons and the goblins were all looking around aimlessly, lost wonder on their faces, but what they were afraid of

was unclear. Kirven had said his magic could not penetrate their protection so how could he have put fear in their eyes?

"Quickly. We are invisible. Strike while you can for I cannot hold it." Kirven's voice became weaker with every word. Schram looked down to his friend and saw his four legs buckling underneath him. The shock of Krirtie's scream as she attacked woke him from his momentary daze. Then, Kirven's last statement before his body struck the ground bit into Schram's ears. "Hurry!"

With the fury of a thousand men, Schram charged. Krirtie had already dropped two goblins while the other three swung their swords blindly through the air. Schram, with every ounce of strength his broad human body could muster, plunged his sword deep within one of the tigon's bodies. The beast's front legs gave way to the pain as the other tigon thrashed its claws wildly through the air. Schram quickly removed his sword and again pushed it into the creature's body. Blood oozed from the now severely crippled animal, and it roared in pain. The trees even seemed to turn away as its last blood-curdled breath was spat upon the road.

The other beast had stopped frantically wailing its claws and entered a strange, piercing stare. It had lowered its head and appeared to be squinting, as if trying to focus over to where Schram was standing. The warrior looked over to Kirven to see his body lying motionless on the ground. He wanted to go to help him, but it was now apparent that they could be seen. Schram glanced to the two dead goblins and then over to where Krirtie was fighting two more. Looking back to the tigon, he saw only red fire burnt into its eyes.

Before he could move, the beast swept its front legs forward across Schram's chest, piercing his breastplate and digging its claws deep into his flesh. The blow sent pain surging through his body while he was tossed helplessly to the base of a nearby tree. He tried to struggle to his feet, but the tigon was already turning for a second strike. Then he heard a screech break through the air from Kirven's direction.

Schram looked over to see that one of the goblins had moved from Krirtie and attacked Kirven's already motionless body. The goblin had plunged his dagger into his belly causing the canok's white blood to seep across the road. Terror grew in his eyes, but he knew that he was powerless to help. He turned back toward the tigon surprised to see his approach had stopped. The beast simply stared at the human, bringing Schram's fear and adrenaline to previously unimaginable levels. The only motive he thought the tigon was employing was simply deciding which limb would taste better eaten first. Schram was locked somewhere between strength and terror with his eyes biting into the stare of the tigon. He could feel the heat of the beast's breath and smell its odor as if it were just waiting to take full control of its prey. Still however, he was not attacked. It seemed as if the tigon was fighting to obey conflicting orders. It wanted to attack, but for some reason, it could not. Schram felt this could be the opportunity he needed. His muscles stiffened, and he prepared his approach and final attack in his mind. He knelt slightly down to grab his footing just before he heard something.

"Don't worry, friend, he will not charge," echoed a deep voice from behind. "Quickly now, help your friends. I will handle the beast."

Too confused to look, Schram whirled his knife, striking the goblin still standing above Kirven in the back. Black blood gushed from the wound, and the goblin doubled over dead. He turned and ran to Krirtie in time to see her hack the last goblin's head from its body. Wounded and exhausted, she fell to her knees, landing with a small splash in a blackened pool of goblin blood. Opening his arms, Schram was just able to catch her as her body fell limp and unconscious. A rush of pain and fatigue swept his limbs, causing everything to begin spinning, leaving a cold dizziness to seduce his mind. He felt himself beginning to fall unconscious but fought to hold onto reality.

"Is she all right?" rang the same deep voice from before.

Schram, his memory of the past event returning, dropped Krirtie with a thump and whirled around to face his adversary.

"Relax, friend. I mean you no harm. I am Geoff."

Standing before Schram was an incredible sight. A man of human design but much too large to be human. He stood probably seven and a half feet tall and had hair like the mane of a tigon. His body was broad, even wider than that of Schram's, but his eyes seemed comforting and true. Beside him stood the huge tigon; its confusion and determination now absent being replaced with a softness of its own. Then, the sight which held Schram's eyes the longest was the body of Kirven placed at their feet.

Schram glanced down to where he had released Krirtie, and to answer Geoff's original question, he stated in a somewhat weak voice, "she will be fine. Her wounds are not deep. It is more exhaustion that inflicts her now." He lowered his sword but held it tight in his hand not replacing it to his side.

Geoff seemed pleased with her prognosis, but his tone did not lighten. "I am afraid that Kirven is not so lucky. His magic has left him because his body was not able to hold it. Until he is stronger, his magic will not rid him of his injuries."

Schram again raised his sword. "How do you know his name?"

Geoff smiled. "I have known Kirven for over five of your lifetimes. He helped me and my people protect ourselves against the dragons during the Oppression. He was only a pup then, but powerful was he with magic." He paused then added, "You must be Schram. Kirven introduced you to me when you were just a small boy in Elvinott. I am sure you were too young to remember. He said he felt something in you that he had never before felt in a human. Looking around, I see he may have been correct. Indeed you are a cunning warrior."

"A maneth. You're a maneth," Schram stated, now replacing his sword to his side.

"Yes, that would be an accurate deduction," he replied, amused at the human's tone as if he had solved the lost secret of the Ring of Ku.

Ignoring Geoff's comment and tone, Schram continued, "You are the Geoff that Kirven always talked about. The one who—" a sudden worry struck Schram as he remembered his friend. "What do we need to do for him? Will he recover?"

"Aye, friend," he returned. "It will take more than a rotten goblin knife to rip life from this stubborn magi, but don't tell him

I called him stubborn." Geoff offered a slightly twisted smile at the comment.

Schram's lips began to curl slightly as much from relief at the answer as the levity Geoff tried to impart. "But what about the tigon? What magic is this that puts him by your side?"

Even the creature seemed to understand and drew a large teeth-baring grin at this. Geoff scratched the tigon's head. "No magic, boy. Tigons are friends, harmless creatures of the woods. We are family. No magic could allow anyone or anything to attack their own family unwarranted. As for what magic put them in service for the goblins, I have no answer. Usually, a goblin is nothing more than a between-meals snack for a tigon." Again, he scratched the forehead of the beast, causing a growl of appreciation. "And not a very tasty one at that."

Just then Krirtie began moving as if she was waking from a restless night of sleep. Her eyes widened as she absorbed the sight before her. Grabbing a dagger, she arched her back to heave it at the two beasts standing above her.

"Wait, Krirtie. They are with us."

She paused, looked up to Schram, and fell back unconscious again. Schram only shook his head and smiled a pale smile.

"I am sorry about the other tigon. My attack was for protection."

"We understand," replied Geoff. "There is another force at work here. If not for the deep rooted kinship between maneth and tigon, my friend here would have given you and your friends the same fate. We must find what evil source is at work here. Many strange things have been occurring, this being but another one."

Schram nodded. After proper rites were given to the dead tigon and the goblins, Geoff and Schram built a fire and carefully bandaged Kirven and Krirtie's wounds. The two warriors talked absently until Krirtie began to stir and finally woke to greet the new company. The three ate and talked, Schram explaining the reason for their trip to Elvinott, and Geoff telling what he knew about the strange evil of late. There had been no movement from Kirven, and Schram was getting extremely worried. Always in the past, Kirven could use his magic to cure himself of superficial wounds, but these injuries were deep, and he was already weakened from the excessive use of his magic.

"What can we do for Kirven?" he asked, his worries evident in his face and tone.

Geoff, who had been the one confident voice on Kirven's recovery, now paused for what Schram thought was too long, giving a new aura of concern to the young warrior. Geoff started to speak, then stopped again to form his words correctly. "Kirven should have woken by now. His time without consciousness is too long for his wounds. I must take him with me."

Krirtie looked surprised, and Schram's immediate, seemingly unconscious reaction, was to reach for his sword. Never would he consider allowing someone he just met to take his friend of more than twenty years. Before he could speak, Krirtie interjected, "You mean that you won't come with us?"

"No, the maneth have their own issues at this time. I must see to their needs as well."

"Then we will accompany you," Schram insisted. "I will not leave my friend."

Geoff frowned. "No, you cannot. Your path lies along a different line than Kirven's right now. You know how important it is for you to reach Elvinott. Kirven will be along shortly thereafter. Time is of the essence. The sooner you arrive at Elvinott, the sooner they can prepare for the evil that is overtaking the land. You know this to be true. When you were a boy of only four years, Kirven was amazed at how you held your own in a world of elves. Now he, and possibly our world, needs you to repeat that action. Remain here tonight without fear. The tigon will alert you should danger approach. In the morning, head on to Lawren, and if you feel as such, stay there the day to recuperate. Then travel on to Elvinott. If you leave early, you can make it by just past midday. The weather should be in your favor. I will send word if Kirven cannot meet you there in which case you should continue to my camp. The elves will show you the way."

Schram's mind was torn in confusion. He could feel the sweat starting to pool above his brow. He was too old and too strong to be saddened by the thought of separating from his friend—as if leaving a part of himself behind. The emotion was odd to Schram, but he did recognize the advice to be sound, and he did trust Geoff, though he had only known him for hours. He knew what Kirven had taught him about maneths, and he had seen nothing and felt nothing that made him think Geoff was not as he appeared. That being said, he was a little shaken at the fact that Geoff had taken charge of their expedition so completely, explaining in detail what was going to be done without a discussion with him. In actuality though, he was happy to have the burden of leadership off his shoulders, even if only for a night. He was tired from the battle and rest was all that he desired. He nodded acceptance but still searched his mind for alternative solutions.

Chapter 3

Lawren: Selbee

Schram and Krirtie woke to the warmth of the morning sun pounding upon their faces. Schram opened his eyes and began to stretch before he leaped to his feet.

"Krirtie, quick!"

She rose like a cat, springing to her feet and drawing her goblin sword all in one motion. "What is it?" she screamed.

"They're gone. Kirven and Geoff are gone." He began searching the tree line with his eyes.

"I know," she responded softly while she relaxed her sword. "Geoff left with him last night after you fell asleep. He thought it would be easier and his concern for Kirven pushed him to get him aid as quickly as possible. Moving through the night was his best option."

There was a long silence before Schram turned back to face his friend.

"He was wrong." The big warrior squinted his eyes tightly. "He was wrong," he repeated softly.

Krirtie could see the pain in his face. She walked over to him only to be greeted with his shoulder as he turned away.

After a short pause, she added, "Come on. If Geoff was correct with his guidance, Lawren isn't far. We'll get some ale and relax for a while. In another day, we will be in Elvinott, and this whole ordeal will be behind us. The elves will know what to do. They will help us."

This statement seemed odd to Schram. Krirtie had never been to Elvinott and for that matter, never been around elves. But at this point, it didn't matter to him for he was about to do something he had not done for twenty-two years, something he could never remember doing. He was beginning a journey without Kirven at his side, and he felt alone.

They arrived in the outskirts of Lawren about midday and stopped before entering to absorb their view of the entire town. Schram glanced toward Krirtie who seemed to be captivated by what she saw.

"It is such a beautiful little city," she stated, noticing his gaze.

"It's hardly a city," he shot back. "A handful of permanent residents and enough crime to satisfy a country, let alone one small outbreak of shacks and taverns."

"There is no reason to be snappy, Schram. You must remember that with the exception of the training I did in Empor over the last two years, I have never been outside of Toopek."

Schram nodded an apology, knowing he should not take his current emotions out on her. He smiled and gave her arm a reassuring tug, causing both of them to laugh, though neither knew exactly why.

They walked through Lawren, and at the far side of town, they came to a small inn. After getting rooms, Schram decided to take her up on the idea for ales though he was certain there would be no point in trying to remind her that she agreed to pay. Coincidentally, adjacent to the inn was the Minok Café, and since it was a familiar place to him, Schram led the way inside. As they pushed through the swinging doors, a penetrating odor crossed their noses. Schram sucked in deep with a huge smile forming across his face while Krirtie looked away in disgust.

"What is that awful smell?" she exclaimed. "Never has such a rank smell struck my senses."

"Dwarven ale," he responded proudly. "Never has a better ale crossed my lips. I only dreamed they would still have it here."

Krirtie was pleased to see a smile back on Schram's face, but the thought of putting the source of that odor into her mouth turned her stomach. However, she did want something to drink, and since Schram was buying, she thought she would give it a try. She found a table, which in actuality was not difficult because, with the exception of one old man hidden in the shadows at a table in the corner and the somewhat voluptuous bartender Schram had spent entirely too much time talking to behind the bar, the tavern was empty. Schram returned with two large mugs of the brownest ale Krirtie had ever seen, and sure enough, the smell accompanied them. Schram grabbed his mug and doused a mouthful between his lips as though he was putting out a fire deep within his body. His face turned immediately blue while his taste buds violently adjusted to the newfound pleasure. With the release of one echoing belch, he smiled ear to ear and let out a relaxing, "*Ahh.*"

Krirtie, not so bold as to guzzle half her mugfull in one sitting, sipped hardly on it until finally she too found it to be a very tasty drink. The two sat innocently chatting, happy to have this moment of peace. Various travelers and residents passed in and out, all laughing and shouting and going about their respective businesses, paying no mind to the two alone at the table. They had just finished their third mug each and were about to leave with a whole new attitude about the trouble they were facing when Schram thought, *this town is completely at peace.* Quite pleased with how he was currently feeling he turned to his friend and said, "perhaps you were right, Krirtie. This is truly a beautiful city."

She smiled broadly as he rose to go take care of what they owed. However, the table jerked violently, nearly tossing their empty mugs to the ground, when he slammed back down onto the bench, fearful for what he saw currently entering the tavern.

"What is your deal?" she asked loudly, annoyed but still giggling as the ale started its cruise through her head.

Her back was to the door, and she had not seen the two goblins enter followed by the black canok wearing a strange white diamond patch on its fore brow. Schram's eyes were focused on the canok, and when Krirtie began to speak again, he quickly cut her off with a stare that spit tacks.

"Oh, quit being such a dolt." Her voice stammered and carried like she was in an auditorium.

"By all the gods, woman, shut up," he exclaimed in a hushed but powerful voice. This seemed to offend Krirtie, and she lowered her head.

But it was too late. The three new visitors had heard the commotion and looked over to inspect the situation. The canok seemed to be extra interested, almost as if it were probing into the two human minds. Schram tried to relax himself, but every time he glanced over, all he saw was the white diamond patch staring back at him. The goblins had inspected the entire tavern and said something to the canok that replied in gibberish. One of the goblins went outside as Krirtie looked up ready to go on a rampage for being spoken to so sternly. Glancing to see what had engulfed Schram's eyes, the very sobering situation came to her, and she held quiet.

However, as time seemed to pass extra slowly, her anxiety would not allow her to remain silent long. "Schram, Schram," she whispered. He swung his eyes back to her, color returning to his face as if being broken from a trance. "What is it doing here, and why does it look like Kirven?"

"I don't know," he replied. "Just try to look comfortable until I can find out what is going on. I am going to get us another mug of ale."

Schram rose and walked over to the bar, passing only a few feet from the remaining goblin and canok. After ordering the ales, he turned and realized the canok had jumped up on the adjacent stool and now faced him nearly eye to eye. Schram shot a glance over to Krirtie who still sat alone, but her terrified expression told that she had observed the movement.

"You do not like me, do you human?" the canok said in a raspy voice.

"I do not know you so therefore I hold no such judgments about you, friend."

"Ah, but I sense that you do know me whereas I am the one who does not know you." The canok paused and further looked over the human. "You are heavily armed as is your friend. But your armor is of royal workmanship. Your sword is not of a random traveler's make. It is of finely cut steel with the blood of a tigon left dried on the blade. No, you are not of Lawren. Then there is your friend." The canok looked toward Krirtie as she met his glance and looked away quickly. "She wears goblin armor with their sword at her side, but look closely, there is more goblin blood on the blade than there is steel. My companions are too stupid to notice, but I am not."

Again he broke for a moment to study the warrior. "Yet these trivial things are of no concern to me. What I want to know is why my magic has little effect on you." The canok fell silent and watched while Schram accepted all that had been said.

Schram remained stoic, but with that, he realized he knew not how to reply to the canok's statement. He thought immediately of Kirven and his magic. Even separated and injured, his friend was still protecting him, or at least protecting his mind from being invaded. Finally, he replied flatly, "I know only two things I can say to you, magic user," his voice gaining confidence as he spoke. "First, I know not of your kind or your questions put before me, and second, I believe that it is time for my companion and I to clean our weapons."

A smile came across the canok's face, and for a moment, Schram thought he looked just like Kirven, except for the color reversals. "Yes," the black said. "I suppose you should."

With that, Schram moved from the bar to return to the table, taking a seat next to Krirtie. Both his eyes and the canok's rarely turned from each other until the goblin who had left returned and joined the other goblin and the black. After a brief exchange between the three, all got quiet, creating an atmosphere as thick and still as an evening fog. And all that time, Schram could feel the canok's eyes still upon them.

"Almok, Ist macky tal," sprang a voice from the far side of the bar.

Who was that? he thought. The bar was empty unless someone had snuck in a back doorway. Then he remembered the old man that had been there when they had first arrived. *Was he still here?*

Upon hearing the words, the canok said something to the goblins and then proceeded over toward the corner table. Schram could not see the man other than the back of a black hood, which covered his face, but he could tell the two were talking. The man turned his head around and peered over toward Krirtie and Schram. A cold chill came over both of them equal to an open window in the dead of winter. However, the look and the chill were only temporary as the man turned back again to face the canok.

"Did you see his face?" whispered Krirtie. "It was…gone. All except for those two glowing eyes."

"Yes, I saw," Schram responded. "But his face was there. It was concealed beneath the shadow of his hood, and although hidden, there was something familiar about it."

A blank look appeared on Krirtie's face while she digested what he had just said. "Are you saying that you know him? I realize that you have traveled much more than I, but if I ever had crossed that evil thing's path, only one of us would have left alive for I would never wish to meet him twice." There was more fear in her voice than confidence. She had decided that she really just wanted to leave this bar and return to her room. The once festive atmosphere had grown cold and ominous. She looked at Schram for a response, but he just sat, sucking down his ale while he stared at the two at the far table.

Just then, the goblins, who had left when the old man had spoken returned, and with them came a sight Schram could not believe.

"A maneth," Krirtie whispered.

Accompanying the goblins was a maneth, as large as Geoff but with an older appearance. The mane around his head was frayed and messy, and a large scar showed distinctly above his eye. All Schram could think about was Kirven. What had he done letting Geoff take him?

"Let's leave now, Schram," exclaimed Krirtie as calmly as her excitement and anxiety would allow her to speak.

"No, we will remain. I must learn more about what evil is at work here." He glanced back toward the old man and saw the canok again returning his gaze. He even thought that the canok seemed pleased with their response to the new visitor. The goblins and maneth joined the two at the old man's table, and all sat talking among themselves, with the canok now and again peering over the group toward the two restless humans.

"You've been such nice patrons. Your drinks are on the house," rang a voice from behind causing both of them to jump.

Schram instinctively reached for his sword as he turned to stare into the person's innocent smile. "Oh, Susana, thank you very much. You have truly been a sight for sore and tired eyes today, and your service has been incredible." He flipped two gold coins in gratitude, and she scurried away as Schram's softened gaze admired her walk.

"*Ooh, Susana,*" repeated Krirtie in a sarcastic and overly flirty voice. "*You have truly been a sight for sore eyes.* Don't make me sick." She frowned and coughed while scooping up her mug and downing what was left.

Schram shot her a grin, which caused her face to redden even more. "I got us free drinks, didn't I?"

Her face softened, but it was apparent on Schram's face that his humor would be short-lived. "I have an idea that might get us out of here a little quicker," he stated, making Krirtie become instantly more attentive. It was obvious that she was now very uncomfortable and was quite ready to leave.

Schram rose and slowly made his way over to the bar, never once glancing at the group in the corner. Susana jumped happily over, her eyes gleaming to see him back to talk to her. "What brings you back?" she paused. "You know, I don't even know your name."

Smiling, he said, "I am Erik, and I came back to have a brief word with you, if that is all right?"

"Well, Erik, as long as it won't upset your friend too much," she glanced toward Krirtie, "I would be happy to spend more than the time required for a brief word with you."

A bigger grin came to Schram's face as he toyed with the bartender's proposal. "Perhaps later, but if you have been here as long as it appears, you probably know almost everyone in the town."

"You could say that," Susana replied, now leaning over the bar only inches from Schram's face. "Everybody, at one time or another, seems to stumble into the Minok. Hoangis used to come here almost every day. He is the leader of the elves you know."

Schram noticed that the girl seemed extremely proud and was trying to show how many important people she knew. "Really? Wow. I had no idea you would know so many prestigious individuals." He tried to keep his voice sounding amazed. "But I was wondering if you knew that giant man with the lion's mane or any of the people at the same table with him?"

She smiled, and he could tell that she knew who they were and was excited about telling him. She leaned closer and kissed him softly on the cheek. In a whispering voice, she said, "The big man is Selbee. He is a maneth. He used to come in a lot several years ago, but it has been only recently that he has returned. The canok is Almok. He has only been here with the old man, who I don't know, for the last three days. Almok was friendly the first day, but since then, he and the old man have spoken only between themselves or with the goblins and Selbee until you, that is. I saw you talking earlier, but I didn't understand a word."

Schram smiled and leaned over returning her soft kiss on her forehead. "You are truly beautiful, and I thank you very much. I will talk to you again, but for now, I must go." He turned and motioned to Krirtie to join him.

Susana, content with the encounter, nodded. "Do make sure that you return to the Minok for I will keep your table open."

Schram and Krirtie both glanced back with a grin and a frown respectively.

"Wait a minute," echoed a raspy voice from behind. "I am Almok, Schram, Prince of Toopek." Schram froze in his tracks. "I want you to know my name when we meet again."

Schram turned his body quickly around with fire burnt into his eyes. His words were going to be hard and direct, but he stopped and said nothing when he saw the situation.

"Schram, what is it?" Krirtie asked, her voice worried.

He looked around. The bar was unchanged. The group still sat in the shadowed corner while Susana had moved over to clean their table. "Nothing. I thought I heard something." He glanced back toward Almok. A smug smile had grown across his lips. Schram turned and walked out with Krirtie.

Their adjoining rooms overlooked the road, and they could see the front of the tavern clearly. Schram watched it for hours, observing everyone closely who wandered in or out of the swinging doors. Finally, one of the goblins emerged and seemed to be looking around cautiously. Then, after a moment, he continued down the road and into the nearby edge of the forest. To Schram's count, the ones remaining in the bar were Selbee, Almok, the old man, one goblin, and Susana. He smiled as he thought about the attractive bartender.

Not long after the goblin had disappeared, he returned, pulling a small covered cart. Schram could not see inside the small wagon, but he could tell there was something large inside. After resting the pulling forks securely on the ground, the goblin hurried back into the bar. As he was waiting to see who came out to claim the wagon, Schram noticed some movement in its covered end. A small pointed nose peaked out the back, and its eyes quickly surveyed the area. Krirtie had come over, and following his gaze, also saw the small creature.

"Do you think you can catch our small friend like you could when we were kids?" asked Schram.

"It's been awhile," she responded. "But I doubt that they have learned many new tricks." Without another word, Krirtie went over to her pallet where she was to sleep and took the fabric casing from the head cushion. "I'll be right back."

Schram saw her exit the inn and duck with quick silent steps, which would make an elf proud, into a shaded corner. There she waited to see what the small creature was intending to do. She had a good view of the cart and its contents, but her view of the tavern door had become obstructed. However, she still froze when she heard the hinges squeak and footfalls upon the wooden planks serving as a porch. She could hear the maneth and the two goblins arguing, but she could not make out the words.

Schram looked on but could not offer Krirtie any help. He again noticed the large scar above the maneth's eye and wondered what could have caused such a wound.

Finally, the group seemed to satisfy their differences, and Selbee went to the front of the wagon and bent over, taking the two forked handles under his broad arms. The small wagon rocked violently back, and the large maneth effortlessly pulled it forward toward the forest. The goblins, satisfied that Selbee was on his way for good, exchanged snide remarks accompanied with various gestures in the maneth's direction and then returned through the tavern doors. Moments later, Schram saw Krirtie scurrying silently after the cart, watching carefully for the rodent to make its escape.

Just as Selbee reached the tree line, Schram saw the small animal dive from the wagon and into a large outbreak of brush. *Krirtie will have no trouble catching that one*, he thought, musing to himself that the rat probably had a safe and secure feeling right about now. It was only minutes later when Krirtie burst through the door, holding up her bag, a violent commotion taking place within it.

"One large smelly thieving bandicoot, or as you like to call them, pig rat, at your disposal, Schram," she stated, her tone displaying her pleasure for her ability. "A real cute one too, but he is not happy about being here. Been yelling swear words the entire trip back. The innkeeper flashed me a questioning glance as I passed."

"Wat meen is?" the rat stammered, or what Schram took to mean, "What is the meaning of this?" Bandicoots have their own rather simple language, and all he knew about it he had learned from Krirtie. She had been fascinated with the small creatures as a child and used to catch them regularly. They are slick, shifty animals, and unless one knows how they act, catching them is nearly impossible. Krirtie had been around them long enough to pick up the majority of their language. They didn't have words for most things, but they would just throw in sounds to fill any gaps. Schram quickly realized after this first statement that he would let Krirtie do the talking.

"So uh call self rr wat, rat?" she asked.

The rat, taken back by the girl's proper use of his superior language, smiled broadly as he realized that he would have someone to talk to. "Fehr ss me," he added. "Name iers you?"

"Krirtie ss me," she motioned to Schram.

"Schram suh me," he replied, feeling stupid but trying to appear as if he followed.

"Schram ddss speak iitt no ss smart, aye?" Fehr said, grinning toward the girl.

She joined his smile. "No, Schram no smart. Cart ein do iitrt you what?"

Fehr's eyes widened as he became excited about being able to tell his story. "Dark night ss last," he began. Schram fell back with a sigh. Bandicoots were known for making a long story out of a trip to the bathroom. He could only imagine how this one was going to go. The rat glared up at Schram, frowning over the interruption, then excitedly began again, "Dark night ss last. Cart ittee open. Find wah nothing do ittee day…" One hour later, Fehr had finally gotten into the cart only to take a nap there. It was not his fault that he was uncomfortable, and he had to inspect what he was sleeping on. "Shiners," he continued. "Big shiner bag. Took some niine, yes. Me ddi keep. Me—"

"Them see," Krirtie interrupted before Fehr could go off on another tangent.

"Yes, show ew lovtttoo," he exclaimed. Then from one of the pouches hidden beneath Fehr's fur dropped several gold jewels and coins. "See, told ew shiners, aye."

"Yes, right ew rr you," she replied. The rat looked very happy to see her pleasure with him. "Helpful wah ew," she continued. "Food here. Take family, aye. Tell mm story."

Fehr became nearly crazed with excitement. The idea that he should go tell his friends and family about the wonderful adventure he had experienced sent chills through his body. Scurrying along frantically, he gathered all his trinkets back into his pouches and then turned to the door. "Krirtie, bye. Schram, bye. Meet ew er nice." And he was gone.

The commotion had brought Schram from his momentary sleep, and he rubbed his face as he focused on the girl before him. Krirtie smiled broadly. "I learned a long time ago that the best way to get rid of a pig rat is to remind them to tell someone else a story about an adventure." She giggled as she watched his little feet kicking up dust in the torch-lit street. "He sure was a cute one though."

"Cute wasn't exactly the word I would use," he stated in return, the anxiety clear in his voice. "What all did he say? I quit listening about a half hour through."

"Yes, your snores told us as much." She smiled and then continued, "Well, it seems that it was a dark night, and he had roamed around without finding any adventures. He fell asleep in a shrub and did not like it. Then—"

"Skip all that junk, I mean about the cart."

Giggling heartily over Schram's glare and only fueling his fury, Krirtie continued, "Oh, the cart, yes, I almost forgot. Fehr said it was a nice cart. However, it was not that well constructed. He said it was probably made by a dwarf that had had one too many mugs of ale."

Schram was about ready to explode while Krirtie did nothing except replay Fehr's story almost verbatim. Finally, he broke in with a voice that was most closely compared to a full shout. "If you do not tell me about what was in the cart, then you can sleep with the pig rats tonight. I can always see if Susana is not busy."

As planned, the last statement immediately stripped the smile from her face. "Fine, perhaps you would like to go out and catch Fehr again, this time by yourself. By this time his story will be twice as long. Maybe *you* can ask him what he saw in the cart."

There was a brief silence as the two looked coldly at each other. Then each of their faces began to lift and laughter ensued. "The thought of me catching and talking to a rat is not one that pleases me. I humbly apologize."

"I'm sorry too," she replied, giggling as she spoke as she pictured the sight of Schram awkwardly swinging a sack around as a mischievous rat taunted him with cackles. "He said there was a bag as big as a castle full of gold coins and trinkets in the wagon. He stole, no I mean borrowed, some of them and showed me."

"And stay out, you disgusting creatures!" interrupted some loud yelling from in the street.

Schram moved to the window and peered out. "Susana, having a bit of trouble?"

"No, nothing I can't handle, Erik, but thanks for asking." She seemed extremely pleased to be speaking with Schram again. "Goblins always get more annoying when one too many ales makes its way to their stomachs. It's funny, too many on a belly like that is obviously way too many."

Schram hollered back, "Boy, that sure is the truth. Say, can you help me a minute?"

She smiled. "Sure, what do you need?"

"I was wondering if the old man and the canok have already left?"

A strange look grew across Susana's face. "You know, silly, they left before you did. Don't you remember? Everyone is gone now. That is why I am locking up."

Schram fell back, beginning to second-guess his own recollection of the events of that day. "Oh yeah, that's right. I don't know what I was thinking."

"You want to come down and go for a short walk or something," she asked, not noticing the strange look left on Schram's face from the previous exchange.

"Sure, oomph." There was a sharp pain shooting through the bottom of Schram's back where Krirtie had lodged her fist. "Surely not. I really think I feel tired. Perhaps another night."

"Anytime. You know where I am." Susana bounced off as Schram turned to see the smug, satisfied grin on his friend's face.

"We do need sleep," Schram added. "We need strength to make the trip to Elvinott."

CHAPTER 4

KIRVEN: McCARD

Geoff was moving swiftly through the forest as if the sun was high in the sky and not the clouded over blackness of night, which hid both the moons from sight. The trees seemed to move their branches from the big maneth's path as he hurried through thicket after thicket. Kirven's legs dangled helplessly down Geoff's sides as his belly rested across the small of his neck. This was a comfortable position for Geoff to carry the injured canok, and he believed that it took the pressure off his wounds as well. Even bandaged as they were, one of the deep cuts made by the violent thrusts of the goblin dagger still spilled the canok's white blood freely. Kirven had lost much of his blood and had shown no signs of consciousness since the confrontation. Geoff was growing more concerned and knew that time was very important to the canok. Only the magical cures of the sorcerer Mi-Kevan could help Kirven now. He only hoped that he could reach him in time.

The night air chilled Geoff's bones with each step he took farther into the mountain forest, but he did not even notice the ice that was forming in his veins. He had removed part of his robe to use it to protect Kirven's defenseless body from the cold bite of the air, and although his body was still covered with his soft fur, the temperatures still fought to bring Geoff down. It was nearly dawn when the two finally made it to the maneth camp. Most of the camp had been up for hours, searching for Geoff who was supposed to have returned the night before. With all the odd occurrences taking place in their forests of late, even their greatest warrior was not above their concern.

A relieved look came over many of the maneths' faces as they saw Geoff bounding up the trail. However, this elation was short-lived when Geoff, in a cracking, frostbitten voice, hollered forward the only plea he knew could help. "Get the sorcerer! Maldor, run to Mi-Kevan's cave and tell him a grave situation has befallen us. Kirven has fallen prey to the evil work of the time, and only his magic can help now."

The younger maneth hesitated not a second before disappearing through the brush. The others within earshot rushed out to help Geoff and the legendary canok who had helped save their race so long ago. Many had not been alive during the Dragon Oppression when Kirven had used his abilities to ward off the dark magic the dragons were inflicting, but all had heard the tale of his heroic endeavors. The events nearly killed the canok, who was only a pup then, but Mi-Kevan was able to heal all his wounds and return Kirven's magic to him. Now the situation seemed to be repeating itself.

A special tent was almost immediately erected, and Kirven was laid upon a small pile of cloaks and blankets. A fire was built and warmth filled the small room. Kirven's body lay motionless, almost as if life had already been taken from it. Geoff knelt down next to his old friend while many of the elders who were also alive during the oppression entered to gaze upon their past time hero and friend. A deep sadness shown in their eyes as they viewed his lifeless body.

One knelt down beside Geoff and whispered, "Come, my old friend, you too require aid. The night has also not treated you with kindness."

"I will not leave him. Not yet."

Suddenly, a soft growing light appeared above Kirven's head causing both maneths to step back in shock. The light seemed to pulsate and grow brighter and brighter. A gentle humming began to accompany it growing in proportion with its size until—

"I hate it when you do that!" Maldor shouted as both he and the sorcerer appeared in the tent. "I would gladly have walked back, you spell-blowing idiot!"

A stern look crossed the magician's face as he glared at the young maneth. "Everyone except Geoff leave us now." He paused and then turning to Maldor, added, "and pray I don't move you myself.

Fortunately for you, I do not have the time or the energy to deal with you now."

The elders left the tent with Maldor mumbling under his breath as he followed. Mi-Kevan looked down at Kirven, sprinkled some dust on him and then turned to Geoff.

"Tell me everything that happened, skip no action, word, or event, no matter how insignificant you might believe it to be. Kirven's life may depend on it."

Although the maneth camp was within a good walking distance from the caves Mi-Kevan inhabited, Geoff had not seen him in several years, but he had not changed. He was human, at least in part and by looks, but at the age of greater than five hundred years there was more than just human there. His crisp white beard, which stretched to his belt, and his bright blue, red, and yellow robes had only grown longer and brighter respectively. Even during this great time of despair, he had to fight back the smile, which grew every time he laid eyes on the bizarre magician.

Geoff replayed the entire story to an ever-engrossed recipient. Mi-Kevan's eyes and ears twitched as he absorbed the events. Geoff was intrigued by the sorcerer's actions but did not know what they meant.

"And then I sent Maldor to find you," Geoff completed, his voice still somewhat hoarse and broken. There was a short pause as the tired maneth saw the magician's lips tighten between his beard and mustache. "Can you help him?" he asked hesitantly, almost as if he feared Mi-Kevan's answer.

The magician paused and looked back down at his old friend. He seemed to be having difficulty answering Geoff's question. Kirven had spent several years with the sorcerer following the Oppression, and both had profited greatly from the time. Geoff could not discern why now Mi-Kevan would hesitate to help him.

"Can you help him?" he repeated much more strong and direct this time.

Mi-Kevan glanced back up toward Geoff. His eyes spoke of an inner peace yet there was something deceptive about them. *Should*

I help him is a better question the magician thought to himself. However, his reply to Geoff was along a different path. "Yes, yes, I can. After all, the young pup would not hesitate to help me if the situation was reversed, would he?" He paused and sat back before adding, "Leave us now. We must be alone."

Geoff was shaken by the magician's comments, but there was nothing he could do on his own. No matter how much he was beginning to distrust the actions of Mi-Kevan and no matter how much he was against the use of magic to heal, in this situation, there was no other choice. Magic had brought Kirven down, and now it must also bring him back. Geoff did not understand Mi-Kevan's hesitation to help his old friend, but in actuality, there was very little he ever did understand about the magician. All he was certain of was that he did not want to leave the two alone.

He began to leave, turned as if to add something, then decided against it. The large maneth lifted the flap marking the door, but his anxiety was too strong. Turning back, he added, "If you need anything, I'll be right outside."

Hearing the concern in the maneth's voice, the sorcerer smiled up toward him.

"Relax, dear boy, Kirven has not left us yet." There was a short pause. "And tell that bumbling friend of yours that I am sending him on a trip when I am done here. I did not even have to read his thoughts to know what he was saying about me under his breath as he left."

Geoff smiled in return to this comment, but as he left the tent, all the fears he felt within him returned in force. However, he had little time to consider them further as his emergence from the tent sent a stir among all near, and a slew of questions were thrust upon the tired maneth. He raised his arms. "Hold your thoughts now, dear friends. We will have Lines tonight in which all our questions will be considered and answered, but for now, my thoughts are too troubled and confused to form accurate conclusions from all that has transpired. I ask for solitude until after the meal to tend to my injuries and calm my mind."

The depth and importance carried in the statements was clear to those around, and quickly, they respected his wishes and disbanded; several issuing reassuring pats on his shoulder as they passed. Geoff was exhausted, but he was certain that he would not be able to sleep. His body was so worn as he did not even take notice to the injuries he had referred to and found himself nearly collapsing outside the door slash in Kirven's tent. His head rocked back, and his eyes appeared to be staring directly into the brilliant sun, which now shown high in the sky. He thought about all the time he and Kirven had spent together. He remembered fighting, learning, and talking, each period having its own importance in their life. It had been over twenty years since he had last seen his friend, but that was only a short time to a maneth and canok, both of whom live lives which can span several centuries. However, these last twenty years had seemed long, and their reunion had proved to be far from pleasant. Geoff fell into a deep swamp of thought and perhaps did wink once or twice in sleep, but his mind would never let his body rest completely.

All were in their seats when Geoff entered and made his way to the head of the Batt Line. It was apparent from his glazed eyes and deepened face that he had not found true rest in the hours since his return. Furthermore, since there had been no word regarding Kirven, the added stress on not knowing pushed an inner war through his mind. Yet, all in the Line knew Geoff's judgment would be true and his mind clear when it came to their lives.

They sat in a large clearing. Two long rows of chairs behind two magnificently carved tables faced each other creating an isle between them at which the king alone sat at the head. In the two rows sat the top maneth officials and citizens with their importance to the nation ranked according to how close to the king they sat. Although Geoff was at the head of the Batt Line, short for Battle Line, he was still third in line to the king. Ahead of him were the first two of the Dimat Line, short for diplomats. They consisted of Alhize, Maldor's father, at the head, and next to him sat Selbee, one of the eldest in the village. Both good men in Geoff's opinion, but neither held the wisdom of King McCard, and Geoff feared that in the king's ill health of late, Alhize would soon be moved into the high position. Geoff had frequently been asked by the king to move to the Dimat Line, where he could take a seat only three down the line, but he had always refused. The Dimats worked to avoid all conflicts, and although Geoff had no love for war or fighting, he also knew that sometimes it was necessary. Furthermore, he was well respected, and without his strong voice for the Batt Line, the entire line would simply answer to the Dimat's leadership.

Geoff had made his way down the aisle, exchanging brief greetings to those around, and as quickly as he could, he took his seat at the head of the Batt Line. Once in his seat, he exchanged eye contact with those he had not greeted during his entrance, noticing that everyone except the king, who did not enter until later, and Selbee, who had missed many Lines lately, was present.

There were moments of idle conversation, and then the horns began to sound. All rose and became quiet as King McCard began to make his way down the aisle stopping to shake nearly everyone's hands or to speak over some last minute details. He stopped completely as he stood in front of Geoff. A sad but caring look grew across his face as he softly asked, "Has there been any word from Mi-Kevan, old friend?"

"No, no word as of yet," he replied as they held each other's hand tight without actually shaking.

"All of our thoughts are with—" the king paused as one of his fits of coughing came over him. Shortly he recovered and with a soft smile and tone completed, "Are with him for Kirven is in everyone's heart."

Geoff nodded, and the two broke hands as McCard made his way to the table. The king raised one hand to the group before him.

"We all know the tragedy that has befallen our dear friend and ally, Kirven. News of his ordeal spread rapidly following Geoff's return from the forest. However, I do not think it is appropriate for me, being only a leader over a group and not gifted in the unknowns of ministry, to lead us in a single prayer for our longtime companion. Therefore, I would like to ask each of us gathered here this evening to bow our heads and each give a silent prayer for what they feel in their hearts regarding Kirven and what he and our world may be facing."

There was a long silence as each maneth on the Line closed their eyes and issued what they alone were feeling. Geoff could feel the energy flowing from the entire Line. It had been a long time since the two usually opposing groups had generated so much positive force. Perhaps this would be the event that would again unite them into one nation. There had been so much pointless bickering over the past months that neither side was accomplishing anything. Now maybe the times were about to change. The question was whether the maneth population would be able to make and accept that change.

One by one, they finished their prayers and looked up to the king in appreciation.

"You may all be seated." There was a slight rustle as all the big maneth bodies tried to situate themselves in their chairs. Once things grew calm, McCard continued, "Since this is a special meeting to deal with the new problems at hand—," he broke off as another coughing fit overtook him.

"Are you all right, McCard?" Geoff asked, starting to get up.

The king rose his hand motioning Geoff to remain seated. "We will deal only with that business which pertains to it. If you have personal concerns regarding unrelated matters, please hold them for now, and bring them up during our regular Lines three suns from this present one."

Upon hearing this, many of the groups began shuffling away tablets that they would no longer need. Geoff had been watching the king since his first coughing fit and noticed that he always kept one hand pressed tightly against his right side. McCard seemed to be getting worse by the day. However, Geoff was certain that no matter how much his body seemed to be deteriorating, his mind remained clear and true. That in itself made him king.

Geoff rose. "Excuse me, McCard." He was the only one who called the king by his first name at the formal meetings, which depicted their unique and deep relationship, for it was strictly forbidden for all others. "May I inquire about the absence of Selbee?"

The king looked down, obviously upset about Selbee's empty chair before him. "He had business in Lawren. I believe it dealt with some poaching he believed to be occurring and that he had traced those responsible to Lawren. I had hoped that he would have returned by now for his input will be sorely missed, but evidently, his work is taking longer than was expected."

"Thank you, my king," Geoff replied as he retook his seat.

"Now, as I said before, we are all aware of the problems that have been occurring lately, and now we have the additional act that brought Kirven, one of the strongest doers of good ever to walk Troyf, down before us. It is apparent to me, now more than ever, that evil forces are moving across the land." Many of those on the Dimat Line shrugged at this last statement. Never before had McCard taken a definite stand on the issue. He had instead found a home somewhere near the middle. He always pushed being prepared for any enemy that should strike against them, but never actually acknowledged that there could really be a threat.

"I would like to hear from the Line, and do not hide your words for time could be the one option we do not have."

It was customary for the top three below the king to speak first. That would be Alhize, Selbee, and Geoff, but due to Selbee's absence, Alhize and Geoff alone would speak.

Alhize rose. "I do not hold with your talk of evil invaders, King McCard. Has anyone really seen the evil? Perhaps there have been a few more goblins in the forest mountains of late, but really, are they such a threat? I mean, they are nothing more than overweight drifters who will do anything for gold or drink. Geoff alone could take on one hundred, maybe two hundred, before he would even take a breath." Geoff ignored the gesture Alhize waved to him.

"As for Kirven, we are all saddened over his demise. Many of us gathered here served with the powerful canok many years ago, but let's remember, that was a long time ago. Kirven has aged as have we. And we all know that any entanglement with a tigon can bring the strongest down if they are not befriended with the forest creatures. I put this forth, we are in no danger. We should remain on our lands, living as we have for over two hundred years. If we should be attacked by some evil, then we shall defend ourselves properly, but I have seen nothing which dictates that we should go out to fight this alleged evil." Alhize took his seat to scattered cheers and approvals from many fellow Dimats.

"You are wrong, Father!" said a voice from the far end of the Batt Line. A hush fell over the assembly as all eyes shot in the opposite direction to see who had broken protocol and spoken out of turn. A deeply saddened and offended look grew across Alhize's face.

"You are out of turn, Maldor," stated King McCard in a polite yet stern tone. "Please return to your seat and allow Geoff to begin." Maldor looked down, the shame he felt for his interruption clear in his eyes, and he began to retake his seat.

"No, wait," interrupted Geoff. "Let the boy speak his mind. You asked us not to hide our words, and this is an open Line called under special circumstances. I see no reason I must speak first. Maldor, say what you will." Geoff smiled at the young maneth who had followed him as a child follows its hero since the first time the two had met.

Again a hush seduced the entire group as all eyes fell back on Maldor. "My father is wrong." His voice was weak and shaky. "He speaks of minor things and is ignoring what he knows to be true. Why have so many animals, our friends, fled to the mountains to the south?" His tone was growing in intensity and confidence with each word. "Why have we heard rumors that the elves have cut their trade with many human villages and possibly even Toopek? We know these things and many more like them to be true, but are we to believe that there is nothing wrong? There is evil afoot here, and we must meet with our allies and discuss what to do before more separation occurs. What if the elves decide to cut us off as well? It will start with trade and end with isolation. We must meet with those at Elvinott before it is too late." Maldor now appeared to be speaking more to his father than to the group. "Diplomacy is the answer most of the time, but there is also a need to act intelligently. Along with the elves, we rule the forest, but even together, we cannot mount the numbers to fight off a major opposing force. I am not saying to start a war because we don't even know who we would be fighting. Let's just not wait for them to attack us."

A long silence covered the assembly as everyone absorbed all they had just heard. Maldor had remained on his feet and began to feel uncomfortable as the stillness of the Line seemed to be closing in around him. He was about to speak an apology to his father when Geoff rose.

"You speak powerfully, my young friend, and you also speak the truth. Your words are my words. Let us not be ignorant in thinking we are strong enough to withstand any attack. All here know me well. I do not wish to fight anyone, but I can still remember. The Dragon Oppression was on us like fire to a dried oak. Our houses, our trees, our mountain..." There was a pause as he shut his eyes tightly causing his broad face to wrinkle. "Our lives all leveled. By what? An army of the fiercest dragons? Dragons and their goblin and troll workers together? No, it was not quite that many which attacked." Geoff glanced toward Alhize and watched as his face grew dark with sadness.

"Yes, yes. You remember too, don't you Alhize?" Geoff turned to face both Lines. "Five dragons. That's all, just five to level our land. We were not even a worry to them. The canoks and humans faced the brunt of their attacks." His voice took on a commanding tone. "Not again! Maldor is right. We must talk to our neighbors. I do not wish to be made a fool of again. The canoks are split now. They can no longer help us as they did in the past. When I found Kirven, he had been traveling with two humans, one of which was the Prince of Toopek. They told me of evil—evil much like that dealt out by the dragons so many years ago. His mother and father, the king and queen, are missing, and their castle destroyed. Toopek is now under the control of goblins and black canoks. The evil is spreading, and already it has at least one victory under its belt. The prince's name is Schram, and his companion is Krirtie. Together, they are going to Elvinott to speak to Hoangis, and I believe that we too should join in this conference."

Geoff took his seat as the stirring present normally during the Line was completely absent now. Many had shifted uncomfortably at the words regarding the takeover of Toopek, the largest and presumably most powerful of the human cities. Most of the elders knew of Prince Schram and the treaty between the elves and humans, but few if any had realized that Schram was the human traveling with Kirven. Geoff had put a substance to the evil. No longer was it some random goblin movements; they had attacked and taken over a well-defended city. A feat they could not have done alone.

"Those are dangerous words, Geoff," the king stated, breaking the seemingly endless patch of silence. "Indeed these are dangerous times. We must find out who controls the goblins and stop them no matter what the cost. In Selbee's absence, we will take a vote just between the three of us." He was now speaking primarily to Geoff and Alhize, "But I will act without it."

Alhize sat with his head lowered. "You do have my blessing, my king, for I too remember the dragons." He then turned to face Geoff as he spoke, "I lost much during that time as well." The sadness in his voice brought old memories of the Oppression to those who had lived it. Memories of those they had lost. Alhize turned to his son. "I wish to stress the need for extreme caution. It is dangerous to fight an unknown enemy, and we must be united in our actions." His voice had become soft, and Maldor could do nothing but bow his head as he remembered what his father had told him about the past.

"Very well then," stated McCard. "Geoff will lead a small expedition to Elvinott. You will leave at first light. Alhize, you will go to speak on my behalf as I do not feel well enough to make the journey." He nodded to the two lead maneths now standing before him. "Meet me in my tent, and we will discuss our plans."

Alhize gave an accepting nod as the king turned to Geoff.

"With all due respect, McCard, I cannot make this journey. I feel that I must stay until Kirven's fate is known for certain. He and I have been companions for too long to expect anything less of the other. I am certain he would remain if the situation were reversed. I feel there is another choice who would prove to be more effective than myself for this task you ask."

"I of course respect your decision, Geoff," replied McCard "but who would you choose to go in your place? By tradition, the Batt Line must be represented by one of top rank."

"I feel the best choice for this situation is to stray from tradition. Maldor is the one who I would choose most worthy." There was a commotion up and down the Line from both sides. Maldor was the third lowest ranking in the Batt Line. He had not even been seated on the Line for a year. His eyes widened, and he looked up in disbelief not sure if he had actually heard the statement correctly.

A smile slowly grew across the king's worn face. "Yes, perhaps it is time we stray from tradition." He turned toward the young maneth. "Well, lad, do you accept the said position?"

He rose. "I would—"

"I am adamantly opposed to this notion!" interrupted Alhize. "We have just described a situation which may well be the most serious one we have faced in two hundred years, and you wish a boy to be in a seat of near highest importance. I cannot—"

Now it was McCard's turn to interrupt, "You have no say in this Alhize. I respect your ideas, and they are duly noted, but Geoff has made his choice as is his right. Now it is Maldor's decision." Again, the king turned toward the far end of the Batt Line. "Well, Maldor?"

There was a long pause, and Maldor felt the weight of everyone's eyes upon him once again, but none were as heavy as his father's. He choked a small cough and replied in a voice hardly his own. "I do, your majesty. I do accept the position." Hearing the words, Alhize pressed his lips tightly together in clear disagreement.

"Very well then. Both you and your father shall meet me after meals. This concludes this Line. We have set the stage to accomplish much, and many of our decisions made today were not easily formulated. However, I expect total support for our choices across both Lines. We shall meet again when the group returns from Elvinott. All other business must wait until we have resolved our current, more serious problems. All agreed?"

The ceremonial roar rang out unanimously around the Line, and slowly the group disbanded their separate ways.

That night, Maldor spent the most restless sleep of his life. It was totally unheard of that a maneth of a mere fifty years be allowed to go on, let alone lead, an expedition of this magnitude. He wondered why Geoff had chosen him. The meeting with the king had taken many hours, and when it was finally finished, Maldor could not find him anywhere. There had still been no word from Mi-Kevan regarding Kirven, but Geoff was nowhere to be found. There were many questions Maldor wished to ask him, but he finally gave up hope and would try to find him in the morning. He was extremely tired.

However, now morning had come, and Geoff was still not around. Furthermore, Maldor had only been allowed to catch maybe one hour of total sleep as his nerves seemed to be working overtime. His mind was mostly sludge as he groggily stumbled into the meal tent to eat.

"Good morning, Father. It appears to be a fine day to travel," he stated, trying to sound confident under his exhausted stupor.

"Aye, my son," Alhize responded. "Did you sleep well?"

"That I did, Father. When will we be departing?" His abrupt change of subject made Alhize smile slightly.

"As soon as you eat and get down to the smith to be fitted into the king's armor," he returned, tearing half a loaf of bread off and handing it to his son.

Maldor's expression widened at this notion. Only top warriors and diplomats dressed in the king's armor. He assumed that he would be wearing his black training armor. "I will be wearing the king's armor? I had no idea. I thought—"

He stopped when he saw his father smiling as he spoke, "You won't be wearing anything if you don't run and get fitted."

"Yes, Father, I shall hurry."

"Son." Maldor turned to face his father who had stood up from the table. "You are making me very proud today. However, remember to trust in yourself. You are in charge now. I am just a diplomat. Come to me if you need advice, but you alone must make the decisions. Geoff and I talked at length last night about his decision, and once again, he proved to be wise beyond his warrior exterior. He has made a sound decision, and you will do him proud." The two looked at each other as they had never done so before and then fell into each other's arms. "I love you, son."

"And I love you, Father."

"Now, we must delay our leave no longer. Run and get your armor and join me at the forest break."

Maldor darted to the smith who already had his armor waiting. It was shiny silver with a golden star on the breastplate and a golden sword to match it swung at his side. The helmet was blue as the deepest of seas and fit snugly on the young maneth's head. His movements were much freer than in his training armor, and the weight was not as bad a hindrance. Even if he was not yet supposed to wear armor of this nature, he looked and felt as if it was right. Proudly he walked toward the group that was forming at the entrance to the forest. "Are we ready?"

"Yes, it appears you are," answered a voice from his side.

"Geoff, I had hoped I would see you before we departed. I have so many questions."

"You already know or will find all your answers on your own, my friend. Good luck, and may those of the forest and beyond guard your travels." Geoff shook Maldor's hand in a way the young maneth had never felt before. He was treating him as an equal, not like a young boy.

"Thank you, Geoff, and may they also look after you and Kirven as well." The two smiled appreciatively at each other and broke hands allowing Maldor to turn back to his small party and the surrounding group. "Come on, we must go at once." With a wave of his huge arm, the group of six guards and the two leaders made their way into the trees and out of sight with a trailing roar sounding in their wake.

One final whisper seemed to be echoing among the trees.

"May the gods be with you."

The next few hours went by slowly for Geoff. There had still been no word from the sorcerer, and no one dared disturb them for fear of breaking a spell in midstream causing possible harm to any involved. Thus, it was now a time for possibly the hardest of tasks for a maneth such as Geoff. It was a time of waiting. He laid his head back and thought about all that had been occurring. The two humans should have made it to Elvinott by now, and hopefully the maneth party would be there in another day, though he had the feeling their trip may meet trouble along the way. However, Geoff's mind was focused on the idea he had refused to speak openly about to anyone at this time, even King McCard. Disclosing what he believed too early would cause an unneeded panic among his people. They had to find out if the dragons were behind the evil. Those who remembered the dragon terror would not take lightly the possibility of their return, but if he were wrong, he would never be taken seriously at the Line again, thus ending any last grasp at a voice the Batt Line had. "Politics," he blurted out speaking to himself. "I must speak with McCard."

"Elves!" cried a voice from the center of camp interrupting Geoff's thought.

Geoff looked over to where the shout originated from and saw Randor, a young maneth Dimat pointing to the sky.

"Elves," he shouted again.

Soaring down out of the clouds were five flyer elves, with armor consistent of that of Elvinott. A group had already formed at the clearing by the time Geoff arrived. The elves landed and shook out their wings from the long flight. The lead elf, a beautiful female, approached Geoff as he drew near. "Greetings, Geoff, captain of the Batt Line," said her gentle but still powerful voice.

"Greetings to you, Stephanatilantilis, princess of the Royal Guard of Flyer Elves. What brings you to our village in such haste." Geoff's eyes showed intrigue but moreover were clouded with fear for what she was about to say. He was certain that it was not good news that brought the head of the elven guard to meet with them.

"I must apologize for arriving unannounced, but urgency outweighed all formalities. I must speak with King McCard. The situation is grave and not to be discussed in open chambers."

"I understand. I will—" Geoff was stopped in midsentence.

"Geoff, Geoff, come quick. It's the king."

Geoff looked over to see a young maneth, only twenty years in age, running toward him quickly. The boy ran up to him and whispered something in his ear.

Geoff's jaw nearly struck the ground at what he heard.

"By the gods of Troyf. Randor, show the princess's party to the feasting table. They look tired from their long flight." Turning to the princess, he said, "Stepha, would you be so kind as to accompany me to the king's private tent." She nodded, and the big maneth turned to the boy. "Young maneth, take me to what you saw."

The three walked down toward the king's tent; Geoff was waiting until he was certain the crowd was out of earshot before repeating what the boy had said. He leaned over to the princess.

"The king is dead."

CHAPTER 5

ELVINOTT

"Did you hear that?" Krirtie asked, looking back down the trail behind them.

"Yes, I did," replied Schram. "Someone has been following us for over an hour. I first noticed them about a mile outside of Lawren."

Krirtie stopped as she saw a bush move slightly and realized that there was no wind. She stepped closer to Schram and whispered, "Who is it? I did not notice anyone taking a particular interest in us as we left, and I was paying attention for just such an occurrence."

"I saw nothing as well." He pointed. "Continue walking, and keep talking to me as if I were still by your side. I am going to duck behind some cover and see who emerges." Schram drew his sword and after walking a bit with Krirtie, nonchalantly slid behind a large boulder that seemed to be the remnants of an old rockslide. Krirtie continued ahead, talking as if nothing were wrong, but still keeping one ear focused on what was going on behind her.

"*Aek!* Kill ee not! Friend ss me."

Schram's sword crashed down as Fehr leaped off to the side. Fehr screeched at the impact. "Agh! My tail. You stupid evil-driven minok." He was irate with pain and anger, and his words were flowing with perfect understanding. Schram fell back surprised at the little rodent's fury.

"What's going on?" hollered Krirtie, running back toward the two. "Schram, what have you done?"

"Tail iy Schram cut ugh. Mean ss he yes," answered Fehr's hurt and near-crying voice.

"You'll grow another one, you flee-ridden varmint," he shouted in return.

Krirtie's face was red with fire as she picked up the injured rat and cuddled him close.

"Schram, you are hurting his feelings. Haven't you done enough already? Now put that sword away before you hurt yourself."

Her words were cold and condescending and burned in the young warrior's ears. He reached over and snatched the rat from her arms and lifted him up by the skin between his ears holding him to the end of his sword. "Talk straight, and say why you are following us, or so help me I will cut off more than your tail!"

"Schram!" Krirtie raised her hand and slapped him across the face, but it did not even phase the big man.

"Talk, you bastard son of a lonely mud lizard." Schram's face stung from Krirtie's open-handed blow, but he actually was enjoying the name-calling.

"Mud lizard!" exclaimed Fehr. "I wouldn't call my worst enemy. I'll show you mud lizard!" The rat's paws were now flailing wildly as he tried to break Schram's hold.

"What is ever the matter? Can't the little lizard get away?" Laughter accompanied his sarcastic tone, and he launched the infuriated rat through the air, sending him tumbling down the trail. "See, I told you he could talk."

Krirtie's fist struck him hard this time. Schram stumbled back as the force of her weight crashed down on top of his surprised chest. She dropped her knees across his armor with a clank and stared fiercely into his face.

"If you ever pull another stunt like that one again, I will, with my own sword, cut off a piece of your body, and believe me, it won't be a tail, and it definitely won't grow back!" Fehr ran over and began biting at Schram's foot. "You sit down and behave," Krirtie stated, striking Fehr in the nose.

The rat plopped back with a thud. "Gee, what has got her so uptight?"

"I don't know," Schram replied, issuing the same hint of laughter in his voice even with Krirtie's full weight still upon him. "We were just having some fun."

She jumped to her feet screaming, "Schram, you—uh. Fehr, I want you to—*ah!*" She turned and marched forcibly up the path.

"Well, it looks like you really made her mad," said Fehr, still looking over toward the completely bewildered expression across Schram's face. "I guess I'll be going now."

"Wait a minute, rat. You still have not said what you were doing following us." Schram turned to holler up the road, "Krirtie, come back. I won't hurt him now. We may need food later."

Fehr glared at Schram, but even he knew Schram would never eat a bandicoot —way too salty. He came bouncing over, now totally back to his carefree self. "Oh yes, I almost forgot. I need you to come back and tell my family my story was true. They don't believe me, if you can believe that. They think that I am lying. They think I am not telling the truth. Imagine that, a fib from my mouth. A falsehood. A—"

"All right, I get the picture. Would you please just shut up!" His voice was agitated, rough, and very effective. Fehr quieted immediately. "Krirtie?"

"I am here," she stated, now standing behind him with the tip of her sword pressed to the small of his back. "You should be more observant. Someday, someone might not be so kind as to let you live."

"Ha ha, she got you again, *warrior*, and believe me, I use the title lightly. You should be glad she is on your side."

A smile slowly formed across Schram's face as he turned to greet his companion's sword tip. "Indeed I should be." He paused to allow time for Krirtie to relish in her achievement. After she and Fehr finished their fit of giggles and jeers, Schram set out to quiet them the easiest way he knew how. "Do you know what this rat wants us to do? The entire reason he was following us in the first place." Krirtie quieted to listen. "He wants us to return with him to Lawren so we can verify his story to his family who, if you can open your mind to believe this one, don't think he is telling the truth. Would you tell him how ridiculous that idea is?"

Krirtie, her expression still showing a little of the pleasure she had just experienced, turned to face the little creature. "No, Fehr, Schram is correct. We cannot return with you to Lawren right now." She paused. "But there is no reason you could not continue with us. We will be traveling back through Lawren in a few days. We can verify your story then."

"What!" hollered Schram. "Out of the—"

"Yes, good idea. I like it. Where are we headed? Is it far? Will there be other bandicoots living there?"

"Shut up!" He was now glaring at the excited animal and then back toward the girl. "There is no way this flea circus is coming with us."

"Sure there is for I have just decided."

"Well, I have just undecided."

"Oh, Schram, Prince of Toopek, why don't you just listen to yourself? For god's sake, loosen up." Her condescending tones drew a frown across his face like never before, yet she continued unhindered. "I'll carry him in my belt pouch so he won't hold us up. He is such a cute little guy, and I promise he won't make a sound. Also, I have to talk with him about his knowledge of language. It is truly amazing. Besides, you like him too. I can tell."

He stared at Krirtie and then down at Fehr's sad, pleading eyes. "We have wasted enough time as it is, but one peep from you, and my sword takes aim, understood?" He turned and started up the trail, not waiting for an answer to what everyone knew was an idle threat.

"There is no point in arguing anyway. You know that you always get your way, Krirtie. You always do." He stopped and faced his two now happy companions as Krirtie situated Fehr in her pack. "However, don't ever refer to me as Prince Schram of Toopek again."

"No problem, Prince," echoed Fehr's little voice.

Schram glared at the little rodent as he turned back up the path, their giggles just pushing him along faster, but even the warrior could not resist a small smile.

It was noon now, and they were deep into the elven forest and only a short distance from the outskirts of Elvinott. Not to Schram's surprise, they had run into little goblin entanglement as nothing with evil intentions could stray too far within the elves' magical forest boundaries. Schram imagined how pathetic they would appear when they finally did reach the Elf City. Two humans, one dressed in battered armor, which although it once glistened with the crest of Toopek royalty, now was dull and worn, the only symbol showing was the dried goblin blood etched into the metal. The other human walked tall, carrying her loose-fitting black, heavily dented goblin armor and sword as though it were given to her personally by the Gods. Then, if this sight wasn't bad enough, with them traveled not a powerful magic-wielding canok or an equally powerful maneth captain, but rather a thieving tail-less, flee-infested rodent. Yes, they were truly an impressive sight. Schram could only issue an exasperated sigh as he thought about their misfit companionship.

"Halt! Who travels unannounced through Elvinott forests?" echoed a voice from the trees ahead.

Krirtie froze in her tracks and drew her sword. Schram motioned her to relax and stepped forward. "Madeiris, is that you? It is I, Schramilis, greatest friend to the elves."

Suddenly, in front of them stood a broad-bodied human-looking figure but not human. His height was nearly that of Schram's, but his skin took on a shade of brownish green. His ears stood tall and pointed from the side of his head and twitched and turned as he talked, "Why have you come here, Schram, Prince of Toopek?" The elf's tone was cold and harsh, causing Schram to step back.

In all of his memory, Schram could not remember the elf prince referring to him by title. He was beginning to wonder what everyone's recent fascination with the comment meant. He stared back toward his old friend and responded speaking in elven, "Madeiritilantilis Malis, why do you speak as such? Am I not still the brother you once considered me?"

"Do you think us fools, Schramilis, human once of the elf world?" Madeiris drew his sword, and two more elves emerged from the trees and stood at his side. "How long did you think you could continue attacking us before we discovered who it was? Your people's actions have violated our treaty, and we now declare it to be null and void."

The other elves drew their weapons as well. "Let this day mark the end of peace between our two nations." The elves charged at the bewildered and confused humans with Madeiris centering on Schram and the other two attempting to control Krirtie.

Both humans reflexively drew their weapons, and Schram and Madeiris locked swords, allowing their faces to come inches from each other. "I know not of your talk of war," stated Schram, the muscles in his arms seemingly wanting to burst under the force of his mighty opponent.

"You lie!" shouted the elf as they pushed violently apart.

"Schram," cried Krirtie, her voice filled with fear.

Schram spun his eyes to witness an elven dagger being pressed to the throat of his companion. "Wait! Hold your swords, my friends. If I lie to you now, may my life end moments beyond my words."

The elves holding the disarmed girl looked to their leader for a command. Madeiris raised his hand to them and then gestured to Schram, speaking in elven, "You have your moment, but trust you I do not."

"I know not of what evil has befallen my first home of Elvinott," Schram began, never taking his eyes from Krirtie. "I only know what evil has befallen my parents' home of Toopek and what my companion and I have witnessed on our journey here, evil so great as to control a city and bring Kirven, perhaps the greatest canok on all of Troyf, into a dire condition. My companion over the last twenty-two years relies on the help of the maneth kingdom to live. We have come in peace under the guidelines of the treaty between our nations and desire only words with your great leader, if you will allow it." Schram lowered his sword and then threw it toward Madeiris's feet.

"And if I will not allow it?" he responded as he stepped forward, placing the tip of his sword to Schram's throat.

Schram swallowed hard and replied, "Then I ask only two things."

"Which are?" stated the elf, studying his face.

"First, let the girl go. She is of little concern to you." There was a pause as Schram glanced back toward Krirtie's sad face. Her head was held high, but there was an uncharacteristic look of fear in her eyes.

Madeiris joined Schram in his gaze toward Krirtie, but his opinion was grossly different, and his hard tone displayed little sympathy. "To me, she appears to be of great concern. A cunning warrior with much blood spilled across the blade of her sword, including some from the elves which now stand over her. However, if one were to look at her armor more closely, one would have to ask, for whom does this warrior fight. Is she pleased or angry that her goblin dagger did not present a fatal blow to my guard?" He turned back to Schram. "And the other thing?"

Schram reached inside his armor and pulled out a small bag and held it out past the blade of Madeiris's sword. "Second, I ask that you give this pouch to Stephanatilantilis, your sister and Princess of Elvinott and captain of the flyers."

A penetrating silence shrouded the forest. Madeiris stared deep into the eyes of his hostage, as if he were trying to enter his mind. Schram stood stoic, gazing back as hard and honestly as he could. Madeiris's face softened slightly. He stepped back and replaced his sword to his side.

"Release her," he commanded to the elves who remained holding a dagger at Krirtie's throat. "Keep your pouch, Schramilis, greatest friend to the elves, for today is not your day to die. I will take you to my father. The sky grows gray, and we all must talk."

"Thank you, my brother," replied Schram as he replaced his pouch and recovered his sword. The two embraced and held it tightly. "It has indeed been too long."

The three elves escorted Schram, Krirtie, and Fehr, who had gone unnoticed throughout the whole ordeal, into Elvinott. Krirtie, who was only slightly surprised by the appearance of the elves, marveled at the sight of their most beautiful city.

"A city carved out of the forest," she said in amazement as her eyes nearly popped from her head.

Complete buildings, houses, and shops were all carved into the trunks of the most magnificent oaks Krirtie had ever seen. Bridges and vines connected many of the trees on some of the uppermost branches. All the fixtures in the streets were delicately carved woodwork, with the utmost care and time going into the most intricate detail. However, it was the center of the elven village that held the most captivating sight. Schram watched as her eyes seemed to be drawn toward it as they walked closer and closer. He leaned near her. "It is truly beautiful, isn't it?"

"It is surely the most beautiful thing my eyes have ever seen."

Rising out of a spray of water was a wonderfully winged elf. Each of the long golden hairs appeared to have been individually carved. Her well-defined body seemed to move and come alive as the water from the fountain splashed across it. Her sword and shield glistened in the sunlight as her soft face depicted nothing but peace.

There was a long silence when they arrived in front of the fountain until Krirtie asked, "Is it true, can elves really fly?"

"Many can," Schram replied. "But also, many cannot. The reasons for this are not known."

"Don't they have any ideas?"

Schram smiled. "It is believed that Shirak, the elven god of flight, chooses those who are to be blessed with wings at birth. Those who are not chosen, fulfill their lives on the ground, becoming one with the animals and the trees of the forests. Those chosen can find an even higher self in the sky. This statue was carved for the princess of the royal guard and daughter to King Hoangis, Stephanatilantilis." His voice softened as her name crossed his lips.

"Is she the one?" Krirtie returned softly, hearing the passion in his voice. "Is she the one you have loved since the day I first knew you?"

Schram did not answer. He could hear nothing but his memories of Stepha and their last night together five years ago. He stared longingly at the beautiful figure wishing it could hold him like she did so long ago. He remembered the night they had sat together at the fountain, the moon's light reflecting off her golden hair illuminating the entire world. He had asked her to join, be his for that night and for all the nights to come. He could still see her eyes, her lips. He knew she was going to accept. Schram had embraced her as tight as he could before he placed the elven ring of joining made especially for her onto her shaking finger. *I cannot join with you, Schramilis, though my heart would wish nothing more. I will live for four of your lifetimes. I cannot face your loss years from now and have to live with it for an elven life. You are the only one I have ever and will ever love, but I cannot accept you.* She had run off crying, and those had become the last words he had heard her speak. Schram pulled the pouch he had shown Madeiris back out from his pack and reached inside. Among the many items, he pulled out the ring. Placing it in his palm, he squeezed it tight while a large tear formed in his eye.

"Schram?" whispered Krirtie from behind.

He jumped at the sound of a female voice, almost dropping his sack in the process. Quickly placing the ring carefully into its place and returning the pouch to his pack, Schram turned to face his companion. "Yes, Krirtie, what is it?"

"We did not realize that you had stopped. Are you all right?" Her voice was gentle and caring, a side the rough-lived human girl rarely let show. Schram returned her an affectionate nod, but she could see the sadness in his eyes. He had never spoken much about the girl who had hold of his heart, not even mentioning her name until now. Krirtie wondered what could have happened between the two of them to make him feel so much emotion now. "The others are waiting," she rather abruptly and uncomfortably said. "We should join them."

The two walked the rest of the way together in total silence. Slowly, Krirtie had noticed the color and sharp lines, which gave Schram his characteristically deep and tender face, return as his thoughts of Stepha faded, but his eyes still carried their sadness.

The more Schram came to his senses, the more he began to realize the peculiar behavior of the various elves in the city. Many had come out and stared at the two humans, but very few came up and greeted them. This was odd to Schram, especially since he recognized everyone and was certain that they recognized him as well. Many even clutched their swords or bows as the two passed. *What was going on?* he thought. *What grave evil could have put his first home against him?*

They walked to the foot of the greatest oak in the forest. Elven words were carved delicately into its base. Schram leaned over and whispered to Krirtie, "The Great Hall."

Madeiris was waiting at the foot of the stairs leading into the huge tree base.

"Elves of the trees and sky, these humans come as friends to discuss the evil which has invaded our land. For now, dispel that which has occurred and treat them as brothers. Accompanying me is Schramilis, Prince of Toopek and greatest friend to the elves. His companion is Krirtie, first warrior to the prince and newest friend to the elves." Krirtie smiled at her introduction though she had no idea what had been said other than her name. Many of the crowd began to relax, and there was even a smattering of cheers from certain areas, but neither lessened Schram's growing uneasiness. Behind nearly every elf's face was a stern look of distrust and hate. Something grave had happened.

"What about me?" echoed a quiet voice muffled from somewhere inside Krirtie's pouch.

Schram looked down at Fehr's tiny eyes poking out over the top of the pack. Both he and Krirtie had forgotten about their newest friend long ago, but it was the shock of his perfect elven speech, which caught Schram off guard.

Krirtie had heard nothing but a strange noise and lifted Fehr from her pouch into the air to check on him. The rat smiled. "I am Fehr." There was a pause. "One of the greatest bandicoots in all of Troyf." Another pause. "I have saved princesses. I am a slayer of dragons. I have—"

"Okay, enough already," interrupted Schram. "This is my other companion, which we happily had forgotten about. He has made getting into trouble an art form, so guard your purses well."

Soft laughter erupted from a handful of onlookers, and their fearful masks began to fade. An offended expression struck Fehr, but it was quickly replaced with a look of amazement as he observed the wondrous city they had entered. Krirtie still had no idea what had been taking place, but she did deduce that Fehr had a grip on the elven tongue and planned to plug him for information at her earliest convenience.

Madeiris smiled but chose to spend no more time outside the castle hall. He nodded to nearby elves, and together they pulled the two huge oak doors apart to allow entry into the hall. In a strong voice, he said, "We have much to discuss. We should begin at once."

If Krirtie and Fehr had thought they had seen beauty outside, they would be brought to near-death by the inside of the great castle. A majestic long hallway extended out from the doors and held magnificent artwork carved into its high-arching walls. The inside was lighted by fluorescing stones placed into the delicate wood, which emitted a soft light over the entire area. Krirtie openly gasped at the sight before her.

"Schramilis," said a voice full of love. "It has been a long time, my son. Welcome back to the home you will always have."

"Hoangis Tantalonas Madeirstephanalis, it has been too long, my second father." Schram's words brought tears to Hoangis as the two embraced. After a meaningful exchange in total silence, Schram pushed himself back and turned to Krirtie. "This is Krirtie Wayward, daughter of Derik Wayward, third signer of the treaty between our nations." The King and Madeiris looked at each other sternly upon hearing this introduction. "And with her travels Fehr, a bandicoot with an amazing grasp of language and who has helped us get information from, shall we say, some lucrative places."

Hoangis bid them both greetings and then nodded to his son. Speaking in common tongue so all could understand, he said, "Madeiris, please take Krirtie Wayward and Fehr to the dining hall and then show them to the guest rooms for they look famished."

"Of course, Father," he replied, bowing to the king and then escorting the two, to the dining area.

He turned and said, "Schram, let us retire to the hall to speak. I have many questions as, I am sure, you do as well."

The two entered the wondrous hall, and both took seats in grand wooden chairs next to a huge fire pit. The king sighed as he struck his flint block, and the wood in the pit erupted into flame. "So much has changed," he said sadly, almost becoming engrossed with the fire he had started. "What evil is it that knocks at our doorstep but is too cautious to enter?" He lifted his head to peer at Schram, but it was clear he expected no answer.

Schram studied the king and noticed that the years had begun to show on his face. The once tight, smooth curves of his cheeks had been replaced with creases and scars of a hard-fought life. His large round elven eyes had sunk deep into his head and spoke of worry and frustration. "Tell me, Hoangis, tell me what you know of this evil invading our land."

A long blank expression deadened Hoangis's stare on Schram. "No, my son, you must speak first. I know this will be difficult for you, but I must be brought to understand why the humans have broken our treaty and attacked the elves."

Schram's jaw dropped. He felt as if his body was falling helplessly down into a bottomless cavern. In a lost, pleading voice, he replied, "What humans? What humans have attacked you? From Drynak?"

The king leaned back, completely taken by Schram's unexpected response. "Know not you of these attacks, my son? Are you not here to explain what has happened?"

"I do not and am not."

Hoangis rose and motioned to Schram to join him. They walked in silence beside each other over to a large tablet. Carved into the top of the tablet in large elven letters read Treaty of Peace. Below it were three signatures, King Keith Starland, Prince Schram Starland, and King Hoangis Tantalonas Madeirstephanalis. Two columns, each with three signatures, were set underneath these. The left column contained the signatures of King Joseph of Drynak, the other large human city built on the Dry Sea of Nakton; Tomas Sherblade, the principal councilor to the king of Toopek who was instrumental in the writing of the treaty; and Derik Wayward, the commander-in-chief of the Toopekian defenses. The other column contained King Cowhanis's signature, the king of the small mountain-elf kingdom of Eltak, Prince Madeiritilantilis Malis, and Stephanatilantilis.

Schram gazed over the entire treaty that filled nearly five square feet of the huge wall pallet on which it rested. He looked back to the king who stood totally captivated by the document. "It is truly amazing that one small thing could have done so much good." Schram looked at Hoangis, hoping for a positive response.

The king, stoic and remorseful, turned to him. "For over sixty moons, we have noticed strange happenings in the forest, unexplainable and to our knowledge, unprovoked. The animals have been leaving their homes, being replaced by goblins, trolls, and any other scavenger that could adapt to the environment. We did not worry much in the beginning, thinking only that it was a signal for an early winter, but as time progressed, conditions in the forest grew steadily worse, and autumn passed very mild to Elvinott. However, we turned our focus to the gods as being the cause. We believed they were just pushing a natural progression of life, and only they understood the strange method they used. But no god would kill his own children to progress, not with the blades of goblins to wield their work."

The king's head fell down, and he closed his eyes tight. His words were coming extremely difficult for him now. Schram wanted to speak but did not know what to say. He began and then remained silent.

King Hoangis did not notice his dilemma and continued in the same lost tone.

"Three days back, I sent two parties out to investigate some noise that had been heard in the night. My daughter led four flyers while a larger party searched the grounds. The two groups, running into no difficulties, separated to cover more territory, but it was the ground party's cries that brought Stepha and her guard racing back. When she arrived at the source of the screams, all had been quieted. They had all been killed, many without even drawing their swords and bows. Stepha and the flyers had been flying with Shirak's silence and had approached the scene cautiously and unnoticed. This caution saved them. Above the lifeless bodies of the elven guard stood three hooded men, all appearing human, but it could not be determined from the black robes they wore covering their entire bodies. Two black canoks stood to the side with a handful of goblins thrusting their swords into the already passed elves.

Stepha drew on all her strength to remain frozen in the trees. Her eyes ached at what they saw, but she knew that any action would surely result in their death as well. When those on the ground were preparing to leave, one of the hooded men turned and gazed into the sun as if he had never seen it before. He removed his hood and let the warmth caress his face. Stepha stared long at the human before her for she recognized him from her childhood. He had aged much, as humans do, but she knew who he was." Hoangis pointed to the tablet. "Derik Wayward, third signer of the treaty and father to your companion."

Schram's heart stopped. Derik was a war man, yes, being commander in chief of the king's army, but he would never attack friends. Schram knew this, and if it had been anybody other than Stepha who had seen it, he would have discounted this report as false immediately. But Stepha held the same love for humans as Schram did for the elves. She would not have made the accusation if she were not sure. Schram's eyes fell back to the treaty, and his voice cracked as he spoke. "Then what happened?"

"The group assembled together, and the three robed men formed into a large glowing ball of light and with a flash, vanished. Fearing the canok's magical abilities, she and her party returned here to inform me what she had seen and to gather what was needed to aid passage to those lost." He did not refer to the elves by name as was customary to honor those who passed.

Tears began to form in Schram's eyes, and he squinted them tightly, trying to hide his weakness. He turned and looked back toward the fire, which still blazed in the pit. "I knew nothing of this betrayal." His voice was cut short as his dry throat would not allow words to pass.

"I know, my son. I could see that in your eyes when I first looked upon you again."

The king's words were gentle to Schram's burning ears giving him renewed strength. He took on a serious and strong tone as he began, "Hoangis, I too carry deeply distressing news which you must hear. What I will say may partially explain some of what has taken place, but mostly, it should throw only more questions into the air."

He replayed the entire story of Toopek, the castle, the tracer globes, and every other detail regarding the ordeal he and his companions had faced. Hoangis listened intently, almost expressionless, as he tried to make sense out of his tale and the strange pattern of evil infecting all of Troyf. Schram concluded his story speaking about Kirven and the maneths, but not mentioning the maneth Selbee at the bar in Lawren.

There was a long drawn-out pause as the king leaned back in the chair which both he and Schram had returned to. Finally, he began in a slow and saddened voice, "I will tell the elves what has happened to Toopek. They need to know that there is a powerful evil at work through the humans, but we still have much to do and discuss. Tomorrow we will meet with the elders here in the hall and determine what action should be taken. As elves, we will not sit by and let evil overtake us, but you knew that and that is why you are here. I believe now as I have from the first day I ever spoke a word to you and you answered, somehow there is elf blood hidden within you my son, but I know that is also not possible."

"I have often wished that there was," Schram added softly, his thoughts consumed with the vision of Stepha.

Seeming to read his thoughts, Hoangis smiled and continued. "There is one more thing you should know before you retire for the night. Following the disastrous events in the forest, I sent Stepha to lead a small party of the strongest flyers to meet with the maneths. She is to seek their aid if conditions with the humans were to worsen. She should already have arrived at their mountain village by now, and hopefully Kirven can spread the same knowledge that you have. We cannot have friends and allies turning against one another as I believe this infection wishes us to."

Schram nodded to the king, but his heart grew even more sore. Without Kirven, he had felt very alone, and as he talked with Hoangis, his desire to see Stepha had only intensified. Now he learned that even that comfort would be refused him. He thought about Kirven, hoping that he was still alive and that the maneths had not already been influenced by the evil. If all the maneths, not just Selbee, were working with the hooded humans, then Stepha was flying into a trap.

"Go rest your eyes now, Schram. I can see they ache to be quiet for a time." Again, the king spoke kindly, as a father to his son, "It is nice to have you back. You will always have a home here among the trees."

Schram smiled and bid him good night as they embraced once more. "Until tomorrow," he said. "Send word when you desire my presence."

Hoangis nodded and watched Schram as he left. Sadness crept over his face as he turned the day's events over in his mind before becoming completely entranced by the flames.

CHAPTER 6

The Past: The Present

"Dead!" exclaimed Stepha, trying also to keep her voice down. "What happened?"

"I do not know," Geoff replied. "We will know more when we arrive at his tent, but as you said, the situation is grave."

The two continued walking, being led by the young maneth who had discovered the king. Clouds had rolled in quickly over the mountains, and although it was still early in the day, the dark gloom brought a feeling of nighttime to the small village. The three stopped in front of King McCard's tent while Geoff lit the two torches marking his door and then turned to the boy. "Return to your home, young maneth, and tell nobody of what you have seen. I will make a formal announcement at the next meal should what you believe to have occurred be accurate." The boy shook his head that he understood and hustled off to his tent.

"You need not come in, Stepha, if you do not wish to."

"I have been witness to much death these past days, Geoff." Her voice was strong and hard. "I will come as you would for my king."

Geoff nodded appreciatively and lifted the mat as they both entered the tent. What met their eyes was distress beyond comprehension. The king sat in his enormous throne, facing the doorway. On his face, he wore a smile as wide as a mountain. In his chest, he wore a goblin dagger, thrust into his body several times, depicting the design of a star, the same shape that appeared on his armor. Geoff fell to his knees in remorse. He had assumed the gods had taken him by their own choosing, that the king's lifetime had run its course. Now he knew it had been a goblin dagger which had stripped McCard of breath.

He knelt down and removed the knife from the king's chest, the rich blue blood oozing from the wound as it was pulled. Stepha walked over and placed her hand upon his shoulder. "Goblins did this, but how?"

Geoff looked over at the girl, and although he was on his knees, she still was much shorter than the broad maneth. "No goblin-driven dagger took my king's life," he began, his deep voice quivering as he spoke. "The king knew his assailant. I am sure of it. I can see it in his eyes and feel it in the room. There is evil here, and this evil resides within the camp."

They both remained quiet as they tried to clean up the mess created from the skirmish and then took measure to clean the king's body. The two worked together well, and soon, they were prepared to leave and begin to talk of the problems they now faced.

"We must all speak. I have extremely disturbing news which Alhize and Selbee must also hear," began Stepha as she broke the almost monotonous silence which had filled the room for the past hour. "You must also tell them and the rest of the village what has happened to their king."

Geoff gazed toward the elf with a somewhat stunned expression. He had forgotten that she did not know about the party they had sent to Elvinott. He thought of young Maldor and hoped that they were all still safe. "Alhize has left with a group of guards in an attempt to reach Elvinott and seek consultation with your king and the humans. Selbee has been absent for days, and I fear that he too could be in danger as well."

The princess did not hear the last statement as she focused only on one word. "Humans? You said humans were meeting at Elvinott?"

Geoff tilted his head at the surprised, questioning fear carried in her voice. "Yes, humans. Two in particular, the Prince of Toopek and a warrior woman. They were traveling with Kirven until he was struck down and brought here."

"Schram is returning to Elvinott?" Her eyes now showed the same worry.

"Yes, Schram," Geoff replied. "I forgot you would know him as well. Great evil has befallen his homeland, and he seeks Hoangis's council and aid."

"We must stop him! Humans and their magic have attacked my people. He will be killed if he approaches." Her voice was growing irate with fear. She turned to leave. "I must speak with Kirven. Where is he?"

Geoff grabbed her arm firmly. "Kirven is not well. He has made no sound since his injury befell him. Mi-Kevan is with him now, and only he can determine when Kirven may be disturbed." He paused as his mind worked to carefully choose his next words. "If Schram was truly to be attacked by the elves, then it is too late for he should have arrived there already." Stepha's eyes grew dark, and tears began to fall. The stress of all that had occurred grew inside her to a level never previously experienced. Her mind was lost, and without warning, she succumbed to the pain and collapsed into the big maneth's arms. Time seemed to remain still for Stepha and Geoff as each knew that all they needed were these moments of no action.

Some unknown time later, without a word to each other, Stepha and Geoff left the king's tent and began walking back to where Stepha's guards had been resting. Although she still carried the pain she was feeling, she was the leader of the elven guard, and yielding to the sorrow and evil around her would be fatal to herself and those who relied on her strength. "I am all right," she stated to Geoff, though he had not inquired.

"I know," he returned with a gentle smile. "I have a proposition for you if you are ready."

"I am." She stopped and looked intriguingly toward the big maneth. "What is it you wish to propose?"

My guards should reach Elvinott early tomorrow morning as could you if you flew through the night. Leave now, and return to your homeland. Inform Alhize about what has happened to my king, and if the humans have not arrived, inform your people that these humans are friends for this much I am certain. Search for them if necessary on the roads to Lawren. It is imperative that we learn where the humans stand. Finally, if you would, leave two of your guards here. Many of my best warriors accompanied Alhize, and I do not like being shorthanded as these times grow dark."

Stepha, with a stern look now appearing across her face, replied, "Consider it as such, my friend." The two hugged again briefly. "What should we do next? Will you be coming to have council as well?"

"No, I cannot leave now, not with all that has taken place this day. Until Selbee or Alhize returns, I am the leader. In this time of evil and stress, this village will need guidance. I cannot forget my people." He paused shortly and then continued. "Tell your father that all will be prepared as it was many years ago. Also, ask your guards who will be remaining here to join me in my tent. I must learn of the human attacks on the elves. I find them very disturbing. And finally, tell everyone to pray for Kirven. If we are to get through this again, we will require his help and knowledge. I am sure of it. I am certain that it is no coincidence Kirven was attacked as such."

"I will do all that you ask, Geoff." Stepha smiled. "Tell Kirven when he wakes that I will find Schram. He'll know that I mean it."

Geoff nodded appreciatively as Stepha left to talk with her guards. "Good luck, Stepha. May Shirak fly with you once more."

Schram awoke to a pounding on his door. He stumbled to his feet, hollering for whomever it was to enter. The pale voice of a king's servant answered the call.

"Begging your pardon, Prince Schram, but there has been trouble this morn, and King Hoangis desires you and your companions' company to investigate."

"What kind of trouble?" Schram asked.

"I do not know, sir. Something happened in the forest. That is all I have been told." The servant looked to Schram, motioning a question of aid if he needed help with his armor.

"No, I will be fine," answered Schram. "I will get my companions and join the king in his chambers."

"No," the servant replied. "The king and an assembly of guards are grouping in the square as urgency is stressed."

"Fine, inform the king that we shall join him."

After the servant left, Schram reached for his armor; then, he stopped to look around his old room. It was exactly how he had left it the last time he had visited. He had always had this room, and

Hoangis had told him it would always be his. He glanced around, noticing all his old belongings he had used when he was a child. Then his eyes stopped on his elven armor, which was given to him on his sixteenth birthday by Hoangis himself, an honor bestowed only to family of the royal elven court, until Schram that is. Next to his armor sat the elven bow, which had been made especially to fit his larger body. No truer flight could ever be matched. He walked to the armor, which glistened even as it sat motionless. He gave a long sigh as he sat staring at it, almost as if he expected it to call out to him.

Minutes later, he left his room to meet Krirtie. The armor seemed to carry him as he walked. Slid over his back was his bow, and at his side, he carried his old Toopekian sword. Krirtie's eyes shined as she watched him approach.

"Your armor puts me to shame, Schram," she said while she ran her fingers over the breastplate. "This beat-up goblin gear looks dismal next to your shield and helmet alone."

Schram smiled. "I am sure that I could arrange to get you some new armor, not necessarily with the elven design though, if you desired."

"No," she returned proudly. "I wear this armor to avenge those who killed my father and sister." She turned and began to walk beside him as he made his way through the vast hallways to meet the king. "If I have to kill every goblin on Troyf, I will find out what happened to them. I swear it."

Schram looked solemn as his thoughts trailed back to his discussion the previous night. He knew Krirtie had to be told about the horrid sight Stepha had witnessed in the forest when all the elves were ruthlessly killed. However, he also knew that now was not the time. Too much was happening that he did not understand. In time, the moment would be right.

"And I'll help you do it," added a groggy voice from somewhere within Krirtie's pack.

Schram looked over and issued an annoyed greeting to the furry critter who he had all so pleasingly forgot existed. Fehr peered happily back. "Good morning. Schram. Hey, nice duds. Did I ever tell you about the time the king of the gnomes gave me royal armor for saving his daughter?" Schram's displeasure was evident in his uncaring shrug. His action brought a small but well-hidden smile from Krirtie. Fehr continued completely unconcerned with Schram's lack of enthusiasm for the discussion. "No? Well, it all started with this giant creature with two, no make that three, heads. You see, regardless of where I went, it could always keep me within…"

Luckily, they were just making it to the large doors leading out of the castle, which put Schram in the position he wanted to be in. "Hush up now, Fehr. The king is talking." Fehr frowned at the interruption but was growing bored already with the little attention he was receiving, so he dove back into the quiet of Krirtie's pouch.

"What's he saying?" Krirtie asked, hearing Hoangis but making no sense of the elven words he spoke.

"He is speaking of the fall of Toopek and the other evils, which have engulfed the land of late. Also, he says—" Schram paused and a look of disbelief grew across his face. "Oh no." His voice cracked, and his body tensed at what he heard.

"What? What has happened?"

Schram translated what he could as Hoangis relayed the story to those in the courtyard. "A scouting party this morning located a disturbance which had occurred in the forest and proceeded to investigate. A large group of goblins had ambushed a party of eight maneths and were fighting the party brutally. The elves sent arrows into the group and quickly turned the tides of the battle. The goblins still alive fled into the forests under pursuit of the elves. It is believed that most of the goblins have been killed. Of the maneth party, three lay dead while five are wounded, two severely. Among the dead is the first below the king."

Schram paused from his interpreting and turned to face the girl.

"We are to meet those who survived and escort them into Elvinott." He took Krirtie's hand. "Come on, we will walk with the king. I wish to be close to him when we meet the maneths, just in case there is trouble."

Before they walked out the castle to join the king, Krirtie leaned near Schram and whispered, "Did you tell King Hoangis about the maneth we saw in the bar with that awful hooded man?"

"No, I did not," he replied. "And for now, hold your tongue about it until I figure out what is going on." The statement seemed odd to Schram as he said it as the elves seemed to be the only ones he could trust.

Krirtie nodded in understanding, and they hurried through the huge doors marking the entrance to the castle and joined the king's side. Hoangis asked if they had been informed about the attack, and Schram explained that they had overheard his speech and that he had translated it for Krirtie. They followed a large group of guards and a cart to carry those injured. In the sky, Schram could see several flyers moving ahead to further guard the area. To himself, he wondered where Stepha was and if she was all right.

It was a relatively short walk to where the attack had taken place, and several elves had already cleared the area of any debris. The wounded maneths sat off to the side, and one in particular, who was only slightly wounded, paced back and forth with sword drawn. Schram's impression of the maneth was one in comparison to Geoff. He definitely carried the warrior build, but there was something lacking in his demeanor. *Experience maybe,* he thought.

As the company of elven guards approached, Maldor moved to intercept them. "Greetings, Hoangis, King of Elvinott. I regret that we must meet under these circumstances, but it appears that my mission to lead my father to Elvinott has failed."

"Greetings returned to you, Maldor of the maneth Batt Line. Know that all of our thoughts are with you and your loss. Your father was a good friend to all of the elves, and he will be sorely missed."

"Thank you, your majesty. He always spoke highly of the elves and the wisdom of their leader as well."

The King nodded to the young maneth who he knew was doing all within his ability to remain strong and respectful at this most desperate time. "Come, Maldor. Your guards will be cared for and brought to my city. Join my side as we return, and we will talk. There is much to discuss, and you appear weary from your travels."

Maldor placed his sword to his side and stepped into line next to the King's party. The group nodded respectively, and slowly they began their trek back. The King introduced Schram and Krirtie. Fehr had again fallen asleep in his pouch and went unnoticed. Their pace was slow, and for the first few moments, it went without any discussion. However, Hoangis broke the stifled air by beginning to freely repeat all that had occurred so Maldor would be brought up to speed. With the King's words, each felt the need to speak about what they had experienced. Schram again chose to withhold all he had seen regarding the maneth Selbee until he better understood the situation, but with only that exception, Maldor heard the entire story. The big maneth then replayed what had happened that had sent his party to Elvinott ending with the tragic and unimproved condition of Kirven.

Schram's heart sank at the news, and he longed to be beside his friend. He was not certain about the role that Selbee was playing in this game, but he had decided that he wanted to talk it over with Kirven before he spoke with anyone else. Furthermore, the existence of the white diamond–faced black canok, Almok, was possibly an even greater concern, and one which he knew only Kirven could aid understanding. As he walked forward in what had now once again become silence among those around, he realized that his next move was to head to the maneth village. He planned to leave that day as soon as it could be arranged.

However, all their plans were unknowingly about to change as they broke through the trees before Elvinott. Ahead of them was a wild commotion. Several elves were running through the square, hollering different commands and alerts. Schram's ears locked on one voice in particular.

"Stepha," an elven voice cried. "She is returning with the flyers."

His eyes strained forward to see if the story was actually true. He was greeted with the sight of a handful of flyers sailing gracefully down toward the fountain. At the lead was Stephanatilantilis, her long golden blonde hair dancing over her wings as she landed. Her appearance was exactly as it had been five years ago. She was truly the most beautiful creature in all of Troyf.

"That wondrous statue does not even begin to do her justice," broke in Krirtie's frail voice as she too watched the elf princess shake out her wings in the cool water with her two guards.

The King's party was still a good distance away, and a small crowd was growing around the flyer elves, so there was little chance that the elf could see them. Still, she seemed to be surveying the entire area with her beautiful elven eyes. Schram saw her lean and ask one of those nearby something, and the elf returned the question by pointing in the direction of the returning group. All seemed to become deathly quiet at that moment when their eyes met. They stared long and deeply at each other, seeming to have a complete conversation from an immeasurable distance. As they drew nearer, the trees in the surrounding forest could have spontaneously burst into flames and the sky could have dropped to the ground, but neither Schram nor Stepha would have noticed. As soon as they were remotely close enough to run to each other, they were already in each other's arms. It was a feeling so safe and comfortable that Schram felt as if all evil in the world would simply wither away beneath their passionate reunion.

Schram stared deep into the elf's eyes while he ran his fingers through her soft flowing hair. "I have missed you as I never would have believed possible, dearest Stephanatilantilis."

"And I you, Schramilis Starland," she returned softly, embracing him again with a kiss.

By now Hoangis had broken through the crowd and caught up to where his daughter and Schram stood. "Come on, children," he began, his voice understanding but still carrying the stress of the period. "We have much to discuss, beginning with why you have returned so quickly to Elvinott with two guards less than you left with." Schram and Stepha joined the king's side, and the small group continued toward the castle with a larger party filling in their steps behind them. Hoangis turned and bid a short message to those around, and then they filed inside.

There was much sadness in the moments to follow. Maldor, still dealing with the loss of his father, now was faced with the news of the murder of his king. Stepha further relayed that Kirven had shown no signs of improvement, and Mi-Kevan was still his only hope. Krirtie's heart sank as she watched each person deal with all the losses they were facing, and her thoughts went to her father and sister. Also, she saw the look in Schram's eyes as he gazed at Stepha. She knew it was a look he would never have when he looked toward her.

King Hoangis remained quiet as he took in each of their stories. Fehr also remained quiet though he tended to sleep through the more important conversations. Stepha concluded by recounting all of Geoff's final statements just as he had told them to her. Hoangis's eyes grew as big as two suns before closing with a biting completeness about them. His voice then cracked as it broke the heavy air. "Has it really come to this level again?"

"What is it, Father? What is it that Geoff wants or expects?" asked Madeiris, who had joined them shortly after their arrival.

"Many years ago," the king's eyes closed as he replayed what he could see clearly in his mind, "during the Dragon Oppression, the elves and the maneths united. Both groups realized they would be destroyed if they did not join forces. We were strong with magic, as all elves are, but it is a magic of the trees and animals. It was no match for that which the dragons possessed. We needed help or we all would have been destroyed.

"We turned to the maneths. They had strengths and various technologies, but even together, we proved ineffective. We did not know what to do. Distraught and lost, the elf king at this time returned to Elvinott and prepared the elves to flee to the forest. It was at that time when Kirven entered the maneth camp. Both the maneths and the elves knew of the rumors about how hard hit the canoks had been from the dragons, but neither of us were strong allies to the four-legged animals. Our paths never crossed, and all groups seemed satisfied with this situation. However, when Kirven entered their camp, he was more than just a shock to the maneths. Besides being bloodied and near-death, he was stone white in color except the black diamond patch on his head. Though they had

had contact with only a few canoks of late, the maneths knew of the delicate red coats, which they all wore, or at least had worn. It was Geoff's father, king of the maneths at this time, who had the insight to save the canok with magic. He called on Mi-Kevan then, as Geoff does now. When it was certain that Kirven would live, the king called for a Feast for All to be a ceremonial final supper for all the forest inhabitants as a united populous.

"It was during that dinner, a last ditch effort for survival, that Kirven spoke to us for the first time. He spoke only once, but it was understood by all. This was before the maneth had adopted the elven tongue. He spoke of a plan to destroy Draag Caverns, the dragon homeland. The canoks had been divided and could no longer do it alone. They could however hold off the dragon enchantment if we could get in and destroy their source of being.

"We did not know Kirven, yet something made us trust him. The plan was put into action, and by some miracle, it worked. We destroyed everything in those caverns. Many died, but we kept going. When we had leveled the entire caverns, we returned to the maneth lands. It was then that we realized that Kirven had acted alone to hold off the dragon enchantment. The canoks no longer were one nation, but rather a nation of scattered nomads. It was this action, which put the canok in the hands of death. It had only taken a short time for the sorcerer to help Kirven the first time for his wounds were physical and petty. However, this time, it took much longer."

The King's voice had grown solemn, almost as if he was possessed by the story he was recounting. "Mi-Kevan disappeared with the canok for seven days. Upon their return, it was clear that they had been to the Realm of Darkness, and it had taken all their combined strength to break free. Mi-Kevan remained only a short while, though I doubt he remembers anything about it. He was as dead as any living being has ever been. Kirven came before us and revealed that the dragons had fled. He did not know where they had gone or if they still lived, but at this point, nobody cared."

There was a long pause while everyone remained completely silent. Neither Stepha nor Madeiris had ever heard their father speak so passionately or in depth regarding the Oppression. Madeiris stepped forward and placed his hand on his father's shoulder.

"And now Geoff asks for the same Feast for All."

Hoangis nodded slightly. "And I fear that he is correct in making such a judgment."

The room grew uncomfortably quiet once again as each person went over in their mind all that was occurring. *Was it true?* Schram thought. *Was it true that the dragons had returned?* He rose and moved to stand beside his human friend.

"Krirtie and I will go to the maneth camp and join in this feast. We will also fight with the maneths and the elves to ward off this evil as they did so many years ago." His words were strong and penetrated the silence like a cold dagger penetrates flesh.

"I, of course, will return with my remaining guards to my village as well," stated Maldor as he too stood in front of the group.

Hoangis lifted himself up, and the strain he felt was carried through his tired bones.

"We shall all go, my friends. The time is indeed serious, and we must act fast and united. Madeiris and Stepha will join me and a large garrison of guards. We will all accompany you to the Feast." He paused his speech and regarded all those around him. "Now we rest for our leave will be before first light. Stepha, prepare your winged guards. They will be in dire need to scout possible ambushes. We all must reach the village safely."

The king's words ended as abruptly as they had begun, and he instantly seemed to fall into deep thought. Slowly the group left the hall, each going in their respective directions to prepare as best they could for the journey. Nobody knew what they might face or the extent of its danger, but all were certain that the fear was not unfounded.

Following her dispelling of commands to the flyer guard, Stepha was to meet Schram at the fountain as they had so many times in the past. The two sat together for an unknown length of time without ever speaking a word. Then they retired for the night, being together once more.

CHAPTER 7
The Feast

The journey the next day was relatively free of hardships. The large group made good time, and the few goblins they had run into had been spotted well ahead of time by the flyers, and an arrow pierced their bodies before any early warnings could be sent. Stepha had decided to rest her wings for the day and therefore was able to walk with Schram. The two had remained deep in conversation with each other, and for them, the long walk went quickly and as pleasantly as could be expected. Due to his involvement with Stepha, Schram had not noticed Krirtie become intensely interested in the stories and sideshow antics Maldor was producing for some of the younger elves. The actions originally were Hoangis's idea to help the maneth deal with his emotions and keep the elves' attitudes positive. However, as time had worn on, they had done much more than they were intended. With one arm, Maldor lifted a fallen oak from the path and then balanced it on his forehead, saying this gave great maneth warriors strength in their backs for long and dangerous missions. Those around sat staring in amazement, although they had no idea that Maldor's only mission before this one had been to gather fire pit wood and run errands for the elders. However, it was when he began telling stories that Krirtie became intrigued. He told about the time he traveled through time and space as the assistant to the great Sorcerer Mi-Kevan. He thought about what he had just said and suddenly found himself forcing his mouth shut. He wondered what would happen the next time he saw the wizard, especially if he had heard of Maldor's tales.

That night, the group camped in a large clearing and had gone far enough that they would make it to the maneth village when the sun was straight above the following day. Schram and Maldor both insisted on sharing with the elves in the night watch, but their limited vision did not compare to the elven sight at night, and their help was probably minimal. Schram, however, noticed something that night that he had been noticing more and more since the day in the bar in Lawren. He could feel things, visions of approaching animals or sounds. Only brief, but still there. He blinked his eyes and looked around suspiciously.

"You all right, little man?" rang Maldor's deep voice as he slapped the human on the back, almost knocking him over. "The night getting to you or something?"

"Maybe it is," he replied hesitantly. "I don't know. I just feel things, things I have never felt before."

"Maybe it is because you're talking to a seven-and-a-half-foot hairy beast rather than a short pointed-ear blonde with two soft wings, as you should be." Maldor smiled as he thought about himself as a beast.

"I wouldn't want to leave you alone here, Maldor. You might scare a wandering elf or something." Schram laughed a bit along with the maneth, but he could still see Maldor's pain. He placed his hand on his shoulder. "It is good to hear and feel laughter again. It has been long since I have felt much like it."

The two looked at each other, each understanding how the other felt. Soon, their watch replacements arrived, and Maldor and Schram rested for the night.

The next morning, the traveling proved easy. The weather was cool and clear, and the brilliant sun shone through a near cloudless sky. Their walk continued, and a good feeling began to grow within each one of the travelers. Combined with the well-accepted absence of goblin or troll entanglement, the journey proved to be a much-needed sedative.

They arrived at the maneth camp just before noon to a barrage of festivities and celebration. Schram was not prepared for such a reception, but he soon came to understand that this was not to be a sad situation. It was to be a time for a unified meeting of friends.

The preparations for the Feast for All were well in order with the huge tables and tents being erected around the Line. Flyer elves had flown ahead to inform Geoff of the approaching group, and they also passed the distressing news of the goblin attack on the maneth company resulting in the death of the maneth next in command and two maneth guards.

Horns sounded as the main party entered the village. Geoff gave an official greeting to Hoangis and then embraced his old friend. He then turned to Schram and Krirtie, smiling at the two humans. "I see that you two don't give up easily. When I heard Stepha's news, I feared the worst. I am pleased to find that worry was unwarranted." His voice became softened. "It is good to see you again, friends, but I am sorry to inform you that there is still no word from Kirven. Trust in the fact that you will be the first to know."

Schram and Krirtie nodded appreciatively as Geoff turned his gaze upon the woman held close to Schram's side. "Stepha, I thank Shirak your flight was safe. It is truly good to have you back in our village so soon, although the occasion was brought on by evil. It should definitely not be evil we dine with this night."

Stepha returned his smile. "The elves agree with your calling of the feast as we did many years ago when your father did the same. The times are indeed threatening, and only together can we fight the evil infecting our land."

Stepha's words were heard by many in the area, and they brought about a slew of cheers as the beautiful elf princess spoke about a united cause. Geoff stepped aside and bowed his head to the king's party as they entered.

"Guards, show King Hoangis to his tent." Geoff turned and opened his arms. "Madeiris, it has been too long."

"Yes, it has, dear friend," the elf prince returned. "With all the trouble of late, I feared you would not be free to meet with me at all before the feast. I am glad for this greeting. I have missed our talks." His voice was strong and true as he hugged his long-time friend. Geoff, though over one hundred years older than the prince, had taken a liking to the young elf when he had first seen the boy work with the animals. All elves have a magic with the forests, but Madeiris possessed a level he had never seen before. Geoff befriended the prince, and together they had embraced the land.

A strong voice broke in from the side, "I return with only the apologies for my failure, Geoff, actions for which I have no excuse." His voice cracked and became hard and distraught with each word.

Geoff turned. "Maldor, my friend, our thoughts are with you at this time of loss. Speak not of failing for you failed nothing. Your message got through to the elves as your responsibility dictated. You should feel proud of how bravely you acted. As I stand here as acting king of the maneths, I appoint you, Maldor, to take my seat at the head of the Batt Line."

Maldor bowed his head as is customary when receiving a higher commission. Geoff removed his sword and placed it above the young maneth's mane. "As I speak it, so let it be fulfilled." Maldor looked up at his boyhood hero and now king. "And know, Maldor, your father would be very proud."

Geoff replaced his sword as Maldor rose, his armor glistening under the high apex of the sun. "Let us show all of our guests the hospitality they deserve in preparation for the feast tonight." A roar sounded universally from the crowd and the rest of the elves filed into the camp. Geoff, Maldor, and Madeiris walked in together.

There were no formal guidelines for the Feast for All as it was a highly irregular event, performed only once in the history of Troyf. The normal Line was in place. However, at the end of the Line, there now rested a much larger table to make room for Hoangis, the elf prince and princess, and Schram. Krirtie was given a position second in the Batt Line next to the acting head, Maldor, a seat both seemed to appreciate. At the head of the Dimat Line was Alhize's seat, left empty in respect, and Selbee's seat also empty as he remained absent from the village. The rest of the Lines held their normal positions while all other maneth and elf citizens and guards took various seats at the tables completely surrounding the Line.

All were in their assigned positions, except Schram who had desired to stay by Kirven's tent a short while longer in case there was any change. He was set to enter the feast when Geoff made his walk between the Lines.

Cheers exploded through the dense surroundings as that time finally arrived. Geoff greeted most of his friends as he passed. He paused longer in front of Maldor and embraced him as the king had done to Geoff so many times in the past. Geoff turned and took his place between King Hoangis and the empty chair left for Prince Schram.

"Friends, neighbors, maneth, elf, and human alike." Fehr squirmed around violently on the table in front of Krirtie, obviously annoyed with not being mentioned as the representative for the bandicoot nation. "We are gathered here today, with the distinguished Fehr of the bandicoots." Geoff smiled at the small rodent who now stood tall on the table to receive a bellowing of applause and laughter. "We are gathered together today to join—"

He was cut off abruptly by a voice far down the Line. "I demand these proceedings halted. You have wrongly asserted your leadership ahead of mine without council and begun this feast when the situation has not dictated such an action."

"Selbee, you return." Geoff's voice was excited and positive. "Now truly the Feast for All will be complete. The true king can take his position at the head of the Line and lead us in the proceedings."

Cheers rang out from all areas of the onlookers as Selbee marched stoically down the aisle and then around beside Geoff. Krirtie looked up in horror as the memory of Lawren shot back to her mind. Her eyes searched the nearby grounds for Schram, but he was still at Kirven's side. Krirtie wanted to leave to get him, but there was no chance without drawing attention to her. In a silent panic, she froze in her seat. Her only option was to be prepared for whatever was about to occur.

Schram had heard the proceedings begin and decided that since he had been informed where everyone was to be sitting and he was one of the individuals at the head, then he should probably not be too late. He said a silent prayer for his dearest friend and then began to walk toward the feasting grounds.

Nobody had referred to Selbee by name at any time, not even Geoff who had only told Schram that the second seat remained empty due to the acting king's absence on business. Therefore, Schram assumed that the Selbee he knew from the bar was nobody of importance in the village, and thus keeping the occurrence to himself was warranted.

Schram heard the latest spot of cheers as he approached but could not tell what had occurred to bring such a powerful lift. It was truly a joyous occasion in the midst of all this evil to hear such positive strength bringing nations together. He finally reached the feast and began to make his way between the Lines when their eyes locked, like a saw cutting through wet pine. Schram froze on the maneth who wore the same deep scar above his eye that he had seen in Lawren.

"I give you, Selbee, who by rights will now take his place as king of the maneths." Geoff's voice was silenced as a dagger thudded in Selbee's chest.

A scream sounded from Krirtie as three maneth swords were immediately at Schram's throat. "The human has killed our king in cold blood. By law, he must die by the sword," shouted a maneth seated third in the Dimat Line as he pushed his sword against Schram's throat. Schram, standing tall, held strong and did not move.

"No!" Krirtie cried as she rose to her feet. "There are reasons for his actions."

It was apparent that her comment fell on deaf ears.

"Kill the human now!" shouted several in the crowd.

"He has killed our king. There is no pardon. He is no friend to the maneth."

King Hoangis turned to speak to Geoff but then held his breath.

Stepha whispered, "Father, can you not stop this?"

His voice was soft and saddened. "I cannot."

Geoff pounded his fist on the table to bring order to the commotion now bordering on a vigilante riot. "Order! I command order!" shouted Geoff.

After a smattering of continued shouts and jeers, the area began to calm. Krirtie screamed again as she saw blood begin to flow from Schram's neck as the maneth's sword was again pressed deep. Schram did not move.

Geoff raised his hands, and all eyes locked on the new king.

"Prince Schram of Toopek, humans have always been a friend to those within the forest. Your actions today jeopardize those relations. By our law, I hereby call for your execution in the name of Selbee, king of the maneth. May your God forgive you."

Schram held his ground, not even flinching his eyes from the king who just pronounced his sentence. One maneth lowered his sword from Schram's throat and moved to stand directly before him.

"Do I not have a chance to speak, King Geoff?" Schram asked, his voice strong although he had a deep anxiety growing within him. He could feel his legs begin to shake with each passing moment.

Geoff paused. "Your crime has forfeited your defense. Only a request from a top official can grant you speech. As none have spoken, your speech is forbidden."

Schram had not anticipated this response. He had not realized the significance of Selbee's death. Although Schram knew the truth about the now fallen maneth, all those around him held him as their leader. This murder was the highest crime.

The maneth guard before Schram raised his sword as those at his side held the human powerless to defend or even move. Sweat began to bead along Schram's brow, and he looked toward Krirtie. The woman had stood and began to draw her sword only to be constrained by Maldor, who also looked on in disbelief.

"Halt your sword, Meris. There will be no more killing today," the voice Schram knew so well echoed through the Lines.

"Kirven! You live." Geoff stared toward the canok as he approached.

"Kirven, we have always respected your words and knowledge, but this case is different. Even I cannot change what has occurred, and the law is clear. The sentence has been given and is just."

Meris began to draw his sword back when he felt it seem to gain incomparable weight. He fought to swing forward but gasped as the sword hit the ground. Kirven moved toward the group, his eyes rolling back to Geoff away from the now collapsed maneth guard.

"The boy shall be given a chance to speak. I have known him long, and his actions are always true. Look upon your fallen king. Does he not hold his dagger in his hand? Perhaps it would be the human lying dead now, and the swords to your king's throat. Would the sentence be so quickly carried? Two hundred years ago, a feast such as this was held to unite two different groups into one. Now, does it work to separate people as well?" Kirven paused in his speech and walked next to his young companion. "Any sword that breaks this human's flesh, does so to mine as well."

Meris had now regained his strength and raised his sword again. The young maneth guard motioned to Geoff and then drew his sword back.

"Wait, Meris," Geoff stated sternly. "Prince Schram will have his words." He turned his gaze to the human. "I trust you will use them well."

Schram let out all the air he had been holding for the past minute with a long sigh. Scratching Kirven lightly on his head as a gesture of friendship and drawing on the canok's strength, he recounted the entire story of the bar to the burning ears of those who listened. Several times shouts in disbelief echoed through the Lines, but all knew the details were too clear. Each bowed their head in shame with each passing sentence.

"I did not realize that he was the one next to the throne, or I would have spoken earlier. I would suspect that if you search his tent, you will discover the bag of jewels Fehr identified and possibly a goblin dagger like the one which killed your king."

The entire forest was still. It was as if the wind knew not to blow and the leaves knew not to wrestle. Geoff had taken a seat as the weight of what he heard seemed to weaken every fiber he had held to his entire life. He turned his eyes to Krirtie as if to ask if this were true. Without a word from the human woman, her expression confirmed. He shook his head but could not speak.

Maldor rose. "I will search the tent."

Meris broke in. "No, you side with the human. I will search it, and when I find nothing, his death must follow."

Geoff stood again. "Meris, your crime is that you have ruled out the possibility of truth to his tale. I do not wish to admit that the once second below the king could have turned evil, but he has not acted as a maneth elder should over the past moons. Many strange things have occurred, and I refuse now to declare guilt before I am certain. My worst fear and that which I now battle to hold back is that which may actually turn clear. The prince's story is true." There was a long pause and he added, "Meris, accompany Maldor to the tent. Report anything out of the ordinary. Miss not a stone for all our lives will be changed by your findings."

The two left immediately, and a strange commotion never before experienced on the Line seduced the entire atmosphere. There was little discussion, but it was clear there was great discomfort. All eyes locked on the two maneths as they broke back through the Line. Although the exact outcome still was not known, they both held deep expressions of lost sadness.

"What did you find?" Geoff asked.

Maldor stepped before the table of the king and emptied a large sack in front of him. Hundreds of gold coins spilled across the table, reflecting a brilliant light from the nearby torches. "I also found a small shovel fresh with dirt. Upon searching the nearby grounds, we found some broken soil in which these had been recently buried." He held up two goblin daggers identical to the one found thrust into the King's chest. "I believe that he planned on killing his way to leadership, and as king, who knows what direction was next."

Geoff's eyes fell to Meris. The maneth guard nodded. "Maldor speaks the truth."

The king's head fell down in silent prayer as did every maneth's. He rose and looked down to Schram. "It appears you have discovered that which our own eyes were resistant to admit. Evil in our own village. We are in debt to you for your aid, and I humbly apologize to you for the wrong we dealt you. We seem to be quick to believe deception in anyone but ourselves." He turned toward Kirven. "And thank you, my friend. Once again, you have helped us realize our ignorance. You are both welcome to our land once again as friends, as rightly you are called. Anything we have, we offer to you including this sack of gold, which rests before me."

Fehr began to smile as his eyes had grown to twice their normal size as he stared at the reflecting pile. Schram nodded in reply. "We desire nothing from you. I am here to join with the elves and maneths in a Feast for All to unite us as one. These are desperate times, and that gold will be used against that evil which brought it here. We will fight this spreading disease together as many did in the past, and we will win!"

A roar sounded from all who were present as everyone stood and pounded their feet, cups, daggers, and swords. Horns rang out, and the Feast for All began.

Geoff raised his arms. "Hear his words for they are spoken directly from my heart. This is a time to unite. The feast was to bring everyone together. We have found great evil among us, but together, we have discovered the truth. Together we are strong. United we are one. As friends, comrades, and family, we feast."

Food to satisfy every taste was carried in on large platters, and for a short time, everyone forgot about all that had occurred this night. There was laughter, shouts, and cheers the like of which had not been experienced in most of their lifetimes. Kirven and Schram sat next to each other and rejoiced in the presence of the other's company.

Suddenly, Geoff began pounding his large maneth club on the table to bring attention to the Line and the audience. The entire congregation grew quiet, and all eyes turned to the large ominous-looking figure above them. "Earlier today, in private chambers, those of us sitting before you now discussed the best action for us to take. Two hundred years ago, under Kirven's guidance, we marched our troops on the enemies' homeland and brought them to their knees. Today however, times are different. Besides the goblins and trolls who reside in every swamp, sewer, and tarpit on Troyf, we do not know who our enemy is. We do know that strong magic is being used to control the goblins, and that could mean that the dragons again have taken hold on Troyf and are seeking to set their rule across the land. Because of this, Prince Schram of Toopek has decided to lead a small group to the caverns of Draag to determine if the dragons are indeed behind this new evil. He will need a strong company to join him. I have recommended Maldor to stand by his side as warrior for the maneths." He turned to the maneth. "Do you accept, my friend?"

Maldor rose and bowed to King Geoff and Schram. Raising his sword, he replied strongly and simply, "I do."

Cheers again sounded throughout the Line, and Maldor walked to stand before the human prince.

"I too will accompany you," stated Krirtie, her eyes on her long-time friend.

"And I," stated Stepha. "My flight will be a great asset when approaching Draag." Hoangis's eyes hardened and turned on his daughter upon hearing this but then softened when he witnessed her determination.

"Don't forget me," echoed Fehr's tiny voice as he tried to sound tough and stoic but actually came across quite comedic.

Schram interrupted the laughter and cheers. "That will be all I will require unless you too will join us, old friend."

Kirven peered into Schram's face with the sorrowful smile he had been hiding since Schram's speech after killing Selbee. "I cannot join you this time, Schram. I have duties elsewhere."

"But your magic would be extremely valuable to our success," replied the human in a voice that clearly showed his surprise at the canok's unforeseen response.

"Require magic from me, my friend, you do not." He paused then added softly, "Do I what I must. It is required for my word has been given." Kirven left the table in silence and walked toward the forest.

Schram turned to the equally stunned Geoff. "My crew is thus complete." He bowed and followed the canok's steps.

Geoff raised his club. "The majority of us will not sit back and wait for word from Schram's party. I said that we do not know who our enemy is, but we do know where they have struck. Together with the elven force assembled by King Hoangis, we will march to the human city of Toopek and destroy the evil that has taken it hostage. In three days, the largest force ever compiled on Troyf will leave the mountains and fight for the good of one united kingdom."

Schram heard another round of loud cheers and hollers as he moved to sit beside his companion that had taught him so much throughout his entire life.

"Kirven, why must you leave me now?"

The canok turned and stared deep into Schram's eyes. He then turned his head without speaking and before them stood the ghost-like image of the black canok with the white-diamond spot, identical to Kirven in every way except the colors. "This canok, Almok, is my brother."

Schram, a fearful look growing across his face from the appearance of the strange canok, became even more stunned by his friend's words. "A black canok is your brother? I do not see how it could be so."

Kirven looked away, and the image vanished. His expression grew long, and his eyes narrowed. "It was years before the Dragon Oppression, and the dragons had just begun their plans. Their problems occurred with the canoks and the human magicians. Both had the powers to defend against the dragon's magic. One of the black dragons, Slayne, came up with the most evil of all plans. He took the form of a canok and attacked the greatest of the canok females, my mother. The rape was successful from the dragon's view as my mother was impregnated. A litter of four pups emerged, two were still born with canok bodies but containing dragon wings and heads. The other two you know: myself, a white canok with a black diamond spot, and Almok, the black canok with the white diamond spot. We were both immeasurable in the strength of our magic."

Schram shook his head in disbelief. "I never knew."

"You were not meant to know, until now that is." Kirven now stepped closer to the young man who was desperately trying to grasp all that was being said. "There is more, and it will be difficult for you to hear, but you must. On the day of our birth, Slayne returned to my mother in an attempt to steal those who lived. However, he did not expect the power hidden within her. She protected me from the black dragon's wrath, but even that was not enough. With Almok in his possession, the dragons had a newfound strength in black magic. They had the power of good from deep within Almok under the control of evil. Together, Slayne and Almok brought down the magic on the canoks, dividing the proud red coats."

Kirven's speech grew dark as his own words and memories entranced him. "At the time of the Oppression and the maneth-elf siege on Draag, I went against my brother in the most fearsome conflicting force of magic ever experienced on Troyf. For eight days, we incanted every attack we could muster combined with barriers of protection against the other's wrath. It was on the eighth day I was bested. I collapsed before my older brother's feet and knew with one more burst of his magic, I would forever sleep." Kirven fell completely silent.

Schram was lost in the tale and could not believe what he had heard. For all his life he never imagined any creature more powerful than his friend. His voice cracked slightly as he almost fearfully asked, "but you are here now?"

Kirven remained stoic. "I lifted my beaten, weakened head and peered at my brother and the black dragon, my father, standing at his side. My eyelids were heavy and vision blurred, but I recognized him. I remember his words as if he said them only moments ago. 'Kirven, my other powerful son, take your place with Almok at my side as it should be, as your destiny dictates it to be. Only the three of us together can lead the dragons to victory over the land.'"

"I will not, I replied. But they only laughed at my feeble words. I fought to regain my place, but their enchantment now was too strong for me to fight." Kirven fell silent as if he again felt the forces against him.

"But again, you are here now. You must have freed yourself. Please tell me how for I must know the truth."

He gently lifted his head to the human who appeared entranced by the epic. Kirven continued, "The dragons had already lost, Schram. The attack on Draag had been successful. Slayne and Almok were securing their future, and for that, they needed me."

He looked bewildered. "Their future? I don't understand."

"They knew that if the dragons were to ever hope to reign victorious over Troyf, they needed me by their side. As an enemy, I could be defeated, but the cost to them would be too great. As an ally, no power could stop us, or so they believed." Kirven stopped and gazed to the stars to soothe his mind. Softly he added, "A deal was made."

"What deal did you make with your brother that now would control your life?" asked Schram with a bit of understanding beginning to come to him.

His words seemed to find wounds hidden deep within his magical friend. Kirven stared at the human he had cared for like no other. "I must leave now for I cannot wait until morn." He turned to walk away.

"Kirven, wait," stated Schram hurriedly. "I still need your help and guidance."

There is so much you do not understand yet, but be sure that you will grow to know all, Kirven was speaking telepathically, but for what reason, Schram could not tell. *Because you are able to hear me, old friend,* he replied, answering Schram's thought. There was a pause before he continued. *Go to Draag as you have planned. However, you will not find what you seek there yet, but search the caverns well. Seek out Sabast, an old friend of mine. With him, I have left you a gift.* Kirven entered the trees outside camp.

Wait, Kirven, one more question. Schram was also speaking telepathically now, but he was not certain how. *How did you protect me from Almok's mind searching abilities when I was at the bar in Lawren since you were injured as such?*

Kirven appeared back through the trees with his white eyebrows lifted high. Speaking aloud and questioning, "Almok was unable to read your thoughts?"

"Yes, for a while. But when I left, he spoke my name to me in thought. Were you with me in the bar?"

Kirven looked at the boy. "With you I was twenty-two years ago as I am with you now and will always be. I am in your heart, Schram, lodged deep within the muscle that gives you life, but protect you at the tavern, I did not. Only a power greater than mine could fend off my brother."

"But what magic could be so powerful, and why was it protecting me? And why did it leave me open before I left?"

Kirven's eyes grew deep and saddened as he turned and moved before the human. "The magic did not go. It protected you then as it does now. You are the key Schram. The fate of Troyf lies in your actions."

"What do you mean, Kirven? I am but one human. What can I possibly do that you or others could not?"

"Soon you will understand everything." Kirven's voice trailed off.

"Wait, you still have not told me how Almok knew my name."

Kirven turned. "My brother did not learn your name from you. It was by the old man with him that recognized you." He acted as if he was about to say more, then altered his comment. "Now, I bid you my leave, my friend, but worry not, we will meet again." He entered the forest without looking back.

"Tell me," he shouted. *Tell me,* he added telepathically.

Your father, king of Toopek.

CHAPTER 8

The New Companions

The following morning held much anxiety, and little conversation seemed to take place. Geoff had called the travelers in for a formal breakfast party, but the atmosphere was much less than festive. The maneth cooks had prepared much food for their journey while the king had provided all other provisions that were required. Following the meal, each of the group returned to their tents to prepare themselves for their journey, except Maldor who had been so nervous all night that he had gotten ready several hours before dawn.

Schram worked hard all morning, trying to clear his head of his mixed feelings, but every time he was able to reassure himself and relax, that task proved impossible. Kirven's unexplained exit last night had brought many new questions from all those around, and Schram had definitely avoided answering them; mainly because he did not hold any answers. He just wanted to leave the maneth village and find the friend Kirven had spoken of. The journey to Draag was going to be a waste of time as far as their mission went. Kirven had told him he would not find the dragons there, but he had also told him, though not in so many words, that it was the dragons who were responsible for this onslaught of evil. Perhaps at Draag, he would not find dragons, but he could find a clue as to where they were.

"Are you ready, Schram?" asked Stepha, watching his troubled mind sift through its problems.

Schram had not spoken with her after the feast last night and very little this morning, and he found her voice soothing. He looked at her soft cascading hair, which danced about her shoulders and onto her wings. She was dressed in the flyer elven armor; its intricate pattern and green and brown color were identical to Schram's, though the flyers had a lighter cutting to be carried easier.

Schram stood and walked toward Stepha, taking her in his arms he said, "I love you, Stephanatilantilis, and whatever happens on this journey we are beginning, always remember this to be true."

She squeezed him tightly. "And I love you, Schramilis, but..." she began to say something else and then held her words as they held each other close, their bodies pressed together as one.

The four travelers and Fehr met at a small passage leading from the village. A large group had gathered to bid them farewell, and Geoff was saying a few words. When Stepha was not looking, Madeiris waved to Schram motioning him over.

"Greetings on this most dangerous but exciting day, Schram, my friend," he said.

"Greetings to you as well, Madeiris," Schram replied. "Or should it rather be farewell?"

Madeiris explored Schram's face as if trying to find a reason to bid him farewell and leave, but he had something else he had to say. "Many times Stepha has approached me asking why I did not kill you on the field as she had expected. I have answered her with riddles and excuses that my trust in you was greater than any other human I knew. However, I wanted you to know it was your second wish, and only that wish, which kept me from taking your life then." Schram's expression grew deep as he listened to Madeiris's words. "And I also want you to know that if you do meet with an untimely death, then I will fulfill that which you hold so high in your heart. You are the greatest human I have ever known, and it is that which makes you my friend and brother."

The two looked at each other and then embraced. "I will take care of your sister, Madeiris. On that, I stake my life."

"I am sure you will," he replied. "But remember to care for yourself as well, Schramilis."

They shook hands by wrapping their wrists around each other's in a tight bond and then nodded once to each other and parted with Schram returning to where his small crew was preparing to leave.

"May all the gods watch over your steps," stated Geoff to a slurry of cheers from the crowd. "We will be waiting for you in Toopek."

The group waved, and Maldor roared as they departed the scene, entering the woods surrounding the village. Their minds were set on the trek they had before them but also on what the elves and maneths had facing them in Toopek. There was very little for any of them to say as their journey began, but their minds worked like they never had before. Schram looked down and saw a canok track in the dirt and wondered if Kirven had gone the same way. Then he realized that it did not really matter for Kirven had his own path to follow, and it was a path which went separate from that of Schram's. Perhaps someday they would meet again as friends, or perhaps they would just meet.

⸻

They walked in silence for most of the early part of the morning. Maldor led, breaking a much clearer pathway with his sword and club as he went. Krirtie and Stepha, and of course Fehr, came next, walking side-by-side, occasionally speaking to one another in attempts to feel each other out. Schram brought up the rear, keeping an eye out for any stray goblins or trolls but really just consumed deep in thought. Since Kirven had left the previous night, Schram's mind had been an open wound for various attacking thoughts. No matter how much he worked to clear his head, the visions still broke through. He could see many things, none of which made sense. The past, the present, the future. Maybe one of them, maybe all of them. Their random order left Schram confused. He squinted his eyes as if that would close these visions off until with a thump and clang of his sword on a rock, he fell to the ground.

"Schram," rang Stepha's voice, "are you all right?"

Maldor came running back, sword held high, stopping in front of Schram and laughing as he spoke. "You must be careful, friend. Those malduck trees have roots like rabbits, always jumping out in front of you." He smiled as he reached out a hand to the bewildered human.

"I am fine," Schram said in an embarrassed voice, looking toward Stepha and Krirtie. Turning to Maldor, he stated proudly, "And yes, those roots are very dangerous. When we return, have someone remove this one in particular."

Now they both smiled, and the large maneth put his arm around the shorter human and said, "Come to the front with me. The branches grow thicker, and I am still not clear on our plans after Gnausanne, and—"

"*Shh!*" Schram interrupted raising his hand as all three turned to him with lost expressions. "Someone is coming at a rapid pace."

The three others looked at each other questionably. "I hear nothing," said Stepha, her elven ears twitching in the wind.

"Nor do I," replied Schram. "I feel it, or see it, or something. I cannot be sure, but somebody or something is coming."

Krirtie and Maldor now both had their swords drawn while Schram reached for his bow. Stepha, still looking questionably at him, took to the air. The three on the ground stood turning in circles as they all began to hear the rustle of branches of an approaching group. Stepha, her silent hover over the trees unnoticed, signaled the distance and direction of the party. Drawing an arrow, she let it fly and ducked into the trees.

A thump could be heard on the ground, and a slurry of goblin voices shouted as they watched their companion die. Just then a figure bounded out from the underbrush. Maldor moved in for the kill and then stopped and surveyed the disgusting figure.

Its body was reptilian, scales and gills shown clearly down its sides. It wore little armor, not that its hard skin would need any more protection, and its head sat flat upon its body with a snout protruding out much like a beak of a toucan. It walked on two legs, but all could tell it preferred a water environment. Not that it mattered because life was leaving its body quickly. Blood spewed from several areas of the creature's body, and his sword was more black with goblin blood than with the silver glow of the metal from which it was carved. The reptile man peered at the group, and terror came to his eyes. With a curdling strike of pain to his side, he doubled over and fell.

Sound erupted from the trees around them as four goblins emerged from the forest. Maldor and Schram plunged upon three of them as the fourth was left alone with Krirtie and the fallen reptile. The goblin charged at the helpless victim, and Krirtie moved and blocked his strike. The goblin turned and faced the human woman, and Krirtie swung wildly with her sword. The two fought ferociously each drawing the others blood until the goblin dropped to the ground dead, an elven arrow protruding through his neck.

"Thank you," Krirtie groaned, gripping her side and breathing heavily. "He was indeed a skilled swordsman for a goblin."

"As are you," Stepha replied, "for a human."

Krirtie believed Stepha sounded sarcastic but was in too much pain to care at this point. Schram and Maldor walked over, leaving the three beheaded goblins for the scavengers. They both looked down to Krirtie. "Are you all right?" asked Maldor, pushing in front of the stunned Schram.

"Yes, I am fine. I just need to catch my breath. Why don't you see to our visitor, the one the goblins were chasing," she replied, trying to show strength.

"Go," added Stepha. "I will bandage her wound." She turned to Krirtie. "Infection will come quick in the moist air of the mountains. Always make sure your injuries are properly dressed, or death may result just as certain as if the sword's cut had been true to its mark."

Her words burned in Krirtie's ears, and her condescending attitude putting Krirtie inferior to herself was really starting to enrage the human woman.

"I will care for my own injuries. Why don't you help them with the…the…" She paused, then added, "The thing over there."

Stepha smiled. "All right, but if you need help, just holler. I really do not mind helping you." She walked over to the two men who were standing helplessly over the creature.

"He won't let us near him," began Schram. "He just keeps repeating the same thing, and we have never heard anything like it before. Do you know what he says?"

"Abaluba zzywatic lyallitic fron…Abaluba zzywatic…"

She shook her head. "No, I have never heard words such as these."

"Perhaps Krirtie would know them," added Maldor.

"No, big man," stated Schram chuckling slightly. "Her vocabulary is limited to human and—" he paused. "Bandicoot." Turning toward Krirtie, he hollered, "Fehr, come quickly."

A tired face peered over toward them. "I am taking a nap right now. I'll tell you guys a story later—" He stopped in midsentence when his eyes fell on the fallen creature. "Hey, a gar. Wow, I haven't seen one of them since I took my family to Lake Ozak. What a wonderful trip that was. We spent the days lying in the sun and then scavenged through all the other traveler's stuff at night. In fact, I found this neat knife that also had a spoon, scissors, can opener, tooth pick—"

"How about if you tell us later and just come over here right now," interrupted Schram.

"Okay, but it is a wonderful story." Fehr hustled over to the group and examined the gar before them.

"What's he saying?" Maldor asked.

"Relax, fur ball, I was speaking gar since before you were born. I always took a fancy to different languages, so when I was just a young rat, I went to—"

"What does he say, Fehr!" Schram was growing agitated, and his tone displayed it.

"He doesn't want to die by goblin hands. Kill him now."

The three arched back, surprised by what the rat interpreted. "Tell him we can help him recover," the elf broke in.

"No good," said Fehr. "Gars are strange and believe only that Ankita, their god of life, can aid the dying. If you try to touch him, he will fight you with all the energy he has left or simply kill himself. However, suicide would condemn him to forever walk the dark halls of Dynrak, their hell as such."

"Don't glorify things, rodent," Maldor spoke sternly to Fehr but kept his eyes on the gar as he spoke. "Tell him we will give him what he desires, but we wish to know what happened. Why were the goblins chasing him?"

Schram looked up to the maneth, trying to determine if he was serious. Fehr relayed the message, and the gar looked hesitantly toward the group with much fear showing in his eyes. Maldor spoke again, this time more to Schram than to any of the others.

"He will not live much longer. A dying wish is one that should be held most important. We must honor that wish."

Stepha replied, "This is madness. We can save him. Schram, you must not let the situation dictate such an act."

The gar began to speak softly to Fehr. His words were choppy, and blood followed them from his mouth. He paused and cringed his side in pain, and Maldor's sword opened his chest with one quick thrust.

Stepha buried her head in Schram's chest as Maldor replaced his sword. "I am sorry," he said. "But honor in death is as important as honor in life."

Schram gripped Stepha tight as he stared at the reptile's body. "You were right in your actions, and if he could, the gar would thank you himself."

Fehr looked up sadly. "His name was Kalcall, and he did thank you."

Without another word, Schram pushed Stepha aside and moved over to stand above the still body of the gar. He spoke a few elven words and sprinkled some dust he carried within one of his pouches across the lifeless body. The group remained quiet and bowed their heads as the gar slowly vanished. Schram gave a deep sigh, then asked, "What else did he say?"

"It was difficult to follow. His thoughts were random, and he seemed somewhat lost. As near as I can tell, a large goblin force moved into the swamp where his people lived at the base of Lake Ozak and attempted to drive them out. It seemed they wanted to control the reservoir's feedback into the river. The gars fought hard but were scattered. He has been running for seven days, but every time he lost one goblin force, he walked into another one until meeting us."

Krirtie walked over and picked up Fehr. "Lake Ozak is where we are heading, isn't it?"

"Yes it is," Schram replied. "We are heading to Gnausanne though, which I believe is on the other side from the gar swamp, but this still is not a good sign. Hopefully the gnomes have remained protected from the goblin terror, otherwise Gnausanne may not be our best choice."

Maldor stepped forward. "I would imagine they have. The maneth have been trading with the gnomes for some time, and very little occurs at that lake of which they are not aware. They are a wicked bunch of little trolls when it comes to protecting their cheese and chocolates. I believe they are fine."

Schram shook his head, realizing their troubles were only growing. He looked to the concerned faces of the others and knew that they all must understand exactly what lay ahead. As far as he knew, he was the only one of the bunch who had ever traveled these forests by foot this late in the season, and what they didn't know was deathly important.

"Schram, what is it?" asked Stepha.

He motioned for all to listen, and it was clear he was every bit as serious as he could be.

"The area we are about to enter is perhaps the most dangerous on all of Troyf, not because of any evils possibly now present, which would only be an added danger. In the upcoming foothills, as we leave the mountains, the air will steadily grow cooler. There is a pocket before and up to the lake that never receives any of our sun's heat directly. What we have always known to be autumn is the coldest period here. We still have many days of traveling ahead, possibly more if we run into trouble, and I think we should all be prepared for the worst. It could be that we will arrive at the lake after it has frozen. In this event, chartering a boat across the huge reservoir would be of little use, and our voyage would be given a tremendous setback. The maneths have prepared us well provision-wise, but that does not necessarily help us deal with all the factors severe cold can add."

The group turned silent again, which was an occurrence which seemed to be becoming more and more frequent of late. Schram looked over his already faltering band and then began speaking in a lighter tone. "Let's continue awhile further and then stop to eat, that is, if your injury will permit immediate travel," he added turning to Krirtie. "I do not feel right eating over the ground, which claimed the fallen gar, and the goblin stench is affecting the entire area. Stepha, we must also prepare the goblins for passage."

"It is the elven thing to do," she replied sadly.

Krirtie interjected. "I am fine for traveling, Schram, and as for leaving this scene, the sooner the better."

"Fine, Maldor and I will take the front while you three follow and keep a close eye behind us. Another goblin party could come looking for this one and following our trail would be easy. And Fehr," Schram added looking at the little head peering from Krirtie's pouch, "you did well, thank you."

Fehr's eyes glowed as the two large men began hacking the branches from their path. Krirtie scratched his head slightly and smiled at their small friend who was proving to be quite an important companion, even in Schram's eyes.

The rest of the day went extremely slow. Rain began to fall shortly after they ate, and with a bite from winter's teeth, turned to large white flakes of snow. The maneth provisions had proved sufficient in preparing them for this event, but fighting the cold was one thing, trudging through a blanket of snow was another. They had left the mountains several hours ago, and on what were now essentially plains there was no protection from the fist of the winter wind. It did not take long for ice droplets to freeze on all their eyelids as the cold bite of the air made their eyes water.

Krirtie's pace had fallen severely, and Schram feared that her wounds were tightening on her. He wished Stepha could fly ahead and scout for a possible shelter for the night, but even if she could fly in this wind, the thin cells making up her wings would freeze immediately. Visibility was poor, and Schram and Maldor had lost all sense of direction with their eyes and traveled by wit alone. Stepha's frail voice called out to the two leaders when Krirtie fell face down in the snow.

Maldor turned and ran back to the now unconscious girl and lifted her into his broad arms. "We must find shelter, Schram," he stammered. "Frostbite creeps to her wounds quickly. This is the worst blizzard I have seen in my life. It is not meant for man or beast." He broke his speech trying to peer into the blowing snow. "If I am at all sure of our position, I believe to the west we will find some rocks and possibly a cave."

"I did not know that you were familiar with this track of land?"

Maldor shrugged slightly. "I'm not. I only think there might be chance of it, if I remember all I was taught as a young maneth."

"We will go west then. Can you carry her on your own?"

"Yes," Maldor replied, "but let our pace be as quick as possible."

"Come in close," Schram stated. "Walking as a group will help protect us from the wind." He peered around into the blowing snow, feeling as if someone was watching them.

"What's the matter, Schram?" asked Stepha.

"I don't know. Just a feeling I guess. Probably nothing but the cold creeping into my head."

They moved close together, all uncomfortable with Schram's new ability to feel and see things but learning to take it seriously. They walked for what seemed like hours with no stirring from Krirtie. Even the large maneth's joints began to ache as he slowly lifted his huge feet one over the other.

"There!" cried the elf, her elven sight fixed on a point to their left. "I see the rocks Maldor spoke of."

The others turned and stared into the wall of white. "I see nothing," began Schram through blistered lips. "Are you sure, Stepha? We would lose valuable time should it be simply a shadow."

"I could see no shadow in this wall of white," she replied firmly. She paused and then lightened her tone slightly. "I am sure."

"I know better than to doubt your sight," Schram replied, showing his apology clearly. "I trust yours over mine any day."

They turned in the new direction and gradually trudged their way through the stiff blanket of snow. Schram's eyes grew wide when the first sign of something solid registered in his mind. It was a large outbreak of rock and wood, some parts appearing natural while other parts were obviously built by someone *or something*, Schram thought to himself. He nearly collapsed when they finally drew within a close enough range to see the structure clearly. "Thank you Stepha," Schram's words carrying a much deeper thanks than just to Stepha. "If not for your sight, we would have walked right by it."

"What is it?" Stepha asked in return, obviously pleased at its appearance but hesitant about why it was there. With the landscape of the region, it was very apparent that it was not of natural origin.

"It appears to be an old mineshaft of some kind," stated the big maneth. "But that is unimportant because we have no other choice but to use it for shelter. We will die a cold death should we remain exposed."

Schram pushed away some snow and loose debris from the doorway. "Maldor is correct. We must use what luck and your sight has brought us."

With that, he kicked another board free and then slowly entered the shaft followed closely by Maldor carrying Krirtie in his arms and Stepha bringing up the rear. The mine was dark, and boards creaked underneath their feet, but being free of the wind's bite brought a certain security to the group. Schram dug through his cloaks provided by the maneths and found the flint he had stored in his pocket. Tearing a piece of cloth from under his armor and wrapping it around a loose board from the ground, Schram struck the flint, and the rag burst into flames illuminating the cavern. The walls glistened in an array of colors from the reflection of several different minerals and metal lodged within the rock.

Maldor appeared confused. "A dwarven mine? But how could we have gotten all the way over here? We must have gotten really turned around in the blowing snow and wind."

Schram stared back at his friend, sharing his feelings. Hesitantly, he shrugged and replied, "Regardless, we must go deeper into the mine and get away from the door. We will start a fire and try to take care of Krirtie, but we will have to remain here until this storm blows over and we can determine where we are. Stay alert, I still do not feel right about this place."

The three continued through the mine until they came to a large open chamber filled with several loose tools and small rail cars sitting on the beginnings of some tracks, which by all looks appeared to be for the collection of the minerals. Maldor started a fire and went to great effort to make Krirtie as comfortable as possible, redressing her wound in the process. "The frostbite did not get her. I think she will be fine."

"If she is, she owes her life to you," Stepha stated.

The maneth looked disturbed by her tone. "I did nothing for her that any one of us would not do for another."

Stepha looked down as she felt both Maldor's and Schram's eyes upon her. Schram turned to the maneth. "You did well, my friend. Come sit and eat for I am sure that you are hungrier than the rest of us. We will take turns watching for intruders and caring for Krirtie, but we walked through most of the night, and we are all tired. Stepha, you sleep first, then Maldor, and then me."

Each seemed reluctant at first to accept the fact that they could relax, and although the fire burned fairly brilliantly, the cavern was still quite cold. However, even with these things occurring, sleep came easy for each of them as they laid their head to rest. By afternoon the following day, all were wearing new attitudes and expressions, which only a solid night of rest and the stirring of their injured companion could bring.

"Where am I?" she asked softly, peering into the big maneth's gentle eyes.

"Hush now," he replied softly. "You are safe. Save your strength. A blizzard blows hard, and we will not be moving for some time."

"How did I—"

"*Shh*," Maldor interrupted. "When you're ready to eat, tell me, and I will help you. Until then, just rest." She closed her eyes and fell back to sleep.

Kirven walked slowly down the long corridor toward the two figures. A cold raspy voice greeted his upright ears. "We've been waiting for you, my brother."

"I know," Kirven replied.

"Have you come to honor our deal or betray us and meet your death?" asked Almok as he moved to stand before his counterpart.

"I have come to honor our deal as I said that I would many years ago."

The black canok's tone grew inquisitive. "But you are alone. Where is the one you were to bring to match us?"

"He was not ready," stated Kirven. "In time, he will come of his own will."

"Will you take your place by my side, my son?" the other figure now asked.

"I will, Father," returned Kirven.

"Then together, as father and sons, we shall call for the dragons to wake." His voice grew powerful. "Once again, we will be able to walk across Troyf being the rulers of the land as it was meant to be. Thank you, my sons. You have both done well. Call the dragon lords back to Draag for we have to inform them of the change in our plans."

Kirven, with his black diamond emanating power, peered at the black dragon, his father, as he took his position opposite Almok.

CHAPTER 9

The Dwarves

"How are you feeling?" Schram asked Krirtie as Maldor fed her some stew they had made.

"Much better," she replied. "I think most of my strength has returned, but I still don't remember all that happened."

"Well, to make a long story short—"

"Why would you want to do that?" echoed Fehr's voice from the fire as he played with some loose stones he had freed from the cavern wall.

Schram smiled and continued ignoring the interruption, "You nearly froze to death, as did we all, and Maldor carried you half the night until, by the luck of the gods—"

"And Stepha's keen eye," added the maneth.

"We came upon this abandoned dwarven mineral mine." Schram paused to let all this begin to sink in and then added, "It was truly incredible luck. There was plenty of dry wood to burn for fires, and it seems to be well ventilated to let fresh air in."

"How long have I been out?" she asked, examining the cavern as she spoke.

"You were unconscious for the most part of the first three days," stated Maldor. "But for the last two, you have been stirring and talking much. However, this is the best you have looked in some time."

She smiled at the big man, but a bewildered look appeared in her eyes. "Five days? It seems like only yesterday we were at the maneth village."

Just then Stepha appeared from one of the tunnels. "Schram, could you come here a minute?"

Schram immediately noticed she was deeply concerned about something, so he ventured over to her. When he was gone, Krirtie looked at Maldor. "Have they been together the entire time?"

A sad expression came to the maneth. "Yes, they have, my dear. I'm sorry. I know you love him."

She too showed of sadness, but a sparkle still twinkled in her eye. "My love for him is as a sister loves a brother. The pain in my eyes is with my family who I have lost."

Maldor gazed deep upon his new human friend. "I too have lost my family but have gained companions who give me hope that my family may again grow large." The two seemed to embrace each other with their eyes as their feelings of compassion relaxed both their bodies.

Schram had not noticed the business transpiring as he walked toward Stepha. His attention was directed toward the elf who had done everything in her power to assert authority over the group the past few days and only accomplished alienating herself from everyone, including Schram. "What is the problem, Stepha? Does the storm still blow?"

"No, that's not it. I mean, it could be. I don't know." She was lost, trying to explain.

"What is it? Just slow down." He put his arm around her, trying to calm her confusion. "You are not making sense."

She looked at him, flustered by his tone. "I mean, I never made it to the entrance. The tunnels have…" She paused. "They have changed."

A worried look appeared on his face. "Changed? How?"

"I mean, I went down the one we entered, and instead of making it to the entrance like we have the previous days to check the storm, I arrived back here."

"Dwarven enchantment. That's what I have been feeling. Kirven once spoke about it to me. It was to protect their mines when the dwarves were not around. Anyone could enter, but if they tried to leave, they would be lost in a maze. Come, this is truly a dangerous place, and we must tell the others before we become permanently trapped."

Schram relayed the story to the others who appeared distressed.. Maldor seemed particularly disturbed. "You mean we have to stay here until the dwarves decide to come back?" he asked.

"No," said Schram. "Every puzzle has a key. We just have to find the key."

"Well then, where do we start?" asked Krirtie struggling to her feet.

"Are you sure you can walk?"

"Yes, Schram," she said, annoyed with his question. "I will be fine."

"I'll stay near her just in case," added Maldor, smiling.

"Very well, if anyone has a choice on tunnels, make a suggestion now. Otherwise, we will head down this one." He pointed to their left.

The group looked questionably at each other and then had some silent agreement that gave Schram, and Stepha by his side, the authority to head into the shaft. The tunnel seemed to swallow up the light from the torches, but Stepha's sight led them along. Schram could see better in the dark than he used to be able to as well, but he discarded this new ability with the other strange things that were occurring within him. They walked for several hours, sometimes upward, sometimes downward, but never coming to a split or separation in the tunnels. Schram felt the enchantment strong and became more aware with every step that they would never find their way out if conditions stayed as they were.

The companion's pace slowed as their feet ached from walking on the hard ground. "This isn't the key you spoke of, is it?" the maneth asked as he took a seat on a large rock.

Schram turned to him. "No, that rock you're sitting on is one I recognize. We have passed it now three times."

"Aye, and many of the mineral configurations I have seen before as well," stated Stepha while she ran her hand along the smooth wall of the shaft.

"Maybe we will have to wait for the dwarves to come after all," Krirtie entered distressfully.

Schram replied, "No, we are missing something. Stepha, Maldor, did either of you take any of the mineral deposits from the wall of the mine?"

The two looked at each other hesitantly. "No."

"Then I don't understand what it could be." He paused then whispered, "Fehr." His voice grew louder. "Fehr, get out here, now!"

"What is it?" asked a yawning voice. "You know I am supposed to be in hibernation now."

"Just listen to me a minute, and I'll let you return to your ever-so-enjoyable-for-everyone sleep. Did you take any of the stones from the cavern wall?"

A hurt look came over the rat. "I don't steal, if that is what you are asking. If some of the glowing rocks accidentally fell into my pouch, well, so be it. I would return them when I discovered them."

"Why don't you check now and replace any you might find have made it into your possession," replied Schram, choosing his words carefully so as not to further offend the rodent.

Fehr briefly dug around in his pouch and in a matter of seconds produced three round shiny nuggets. "I don't know how these got here. It is a good thing you asked me to check for I would have hated to find them later."

Schram smiled at the little guy. "Why don't you just set them to the side?"

The rat dropped the stones nonchalantly into the corner and then dove back into Krirtie's pouch bored with the whole ordeal. "Schram, look, the tunnel. It divides up ahead." Stepha pointed down the shaft. About fifty feet ahead, a separate tunnel split from the first, and light could be seen coming from it.

"That was not there a moment ago. I am sure of it." Maldor rose and drew his sword.

"No," replied Schram, joining his side. "The dwarves' enchantment was to prevent anyone from leaving the mines with any of their minerals. When Fehr *acquired* the stones, he sealed us within the mine until he relented his claim to them."

"You mean that it is because of that thieving varmint we have walked until our feet bled while he sat in his comfy pouch asleep." Maldor's voice was becoming rough, and his face red under his mane. "I'll cut that little bugger's tail so far up—" he stopped his comment when he met Krirtie's glare.

"Can you people try to keep it down?" echoed Fehr's little voice. "I am trying to get some sleep. If I don't sleep, I will wake up in the most grumpiest of moods." He paused then added, "And, Schram, can we get out of this cavern? The moist air is giving me a cold." He then sneezed and ducked back into his pouch.

The group seemed shocked at his demanding attitude. "Well, you heard him," Schram said smiling. "Let's get out of here."

The group approached the new tunnel hesitantly and peered down its corridor not really knowing what they expected to see. It was simply an empty tunnel with light seeming to emanate from its walls. The sides were completely smooth all the way down to where they met the flat bottom, but they were of different rock. None of the minerals that were in the rest of the tunnels appeared to be present in this one. The group looked at each other in a silent question of whether they should enter or not when Schram turned and began to walk. Krirtie and the elf went next, followed by Maldor, still with sword drawn, bringing up the rear. "I think I am getting one of your funny feelings," the maneth stated, jumping at the sound of his own footsteps on the smooth surface of the tunnel floor.

"What do you mean?" asked the human. He tried to make his voice seem confident. "This is simply the way out. That is why we are moving steadily up. We have found that key."

Maldor looked at Schram's face, seeing the obvious worry, which did not appear in his voice. Trying to also put forth the same confidence, Maldor said, "Yes, I suppose you are—" He stopped in midsentence. "Schram, could you come back here a minute and take a look at this?"

The whole group froze and turned to see what had caught Maldor's attention. Schram walked back beside the big maneth, and shaking his head, stated, "It seems whatever magic opened this tunnel has closed it as well."

"It is solid rock," Maldor stated as he leaned his broad shoulder into the wall of rock that closed off the tunnel behind them. "It would take a hundred maneths to break through this surface."

"I doubt if even a thousand could dent this magical force," replied Schram now turning to face everyone's worried glances. "Come on, we only have one choice. It seems retreat is no longer an option. We have sprung this magical trap, so let's see who set it and why."

The four continued forward, Schram and Stepha both with their bows at the ready while Maldor and Krirtie held their swords. They walked for hours and hours until they all realized they had gone nowhere.

"It is as if the floor moves backward as we move forward. There is no way we could have needed to walk up this far. My legs feel as if they are about to fall from my body." The elf's voice seemed to be failing her with each word she spoke.

"I too am very tired," stated Maldor. "Are we condemned to forever walk this endless cavern, if we do not kill each other first? The monotonous shining hum from the walls will drive us mad in time. Maybe that little rug rat still has some of their stones."

Schram knelt next to his friend, shaking his head. "No, but their might be a similar answer. The magic would not let us leave the mine with any of the minerals, and perhaps it also will not let us farther if we pose any threat."

"What are you getting at?" asked Stepha.

"An idea that I am not extremely thrilled about testing." He motioned to the floor. "Throw down all your weapons. We must not possess any means to mount an attack."

"Uh, face the bandits unarmed?" exclaimed Maldor. "I do not think that is such a good idea."

"I think it will be the only way we will ever face them," Schram returned. "And remember, we are the invaders, the bandits as you call them."

Maldor frowned but reluctantly dropped all his weapons: a sword, two knives, a dagger, a small axe, and his magnificent maneth club topped off by his shield and a back-up batch of arrows he was holding for Stepha.

"Is that it?" asked Stepha as a smile of amazement grew between all their ears.

"Oh, I almost forgot." A goblin dagger fell from his leg armor. "I picked that off one of the goblins we met back with the gar. I thought Krirtie might want it," he added proudly.

All of the companions had piled their weapons up and were looking around for something like the first hidden tunnel to magically appear.

Maldor pushed his lips together tightly. "I told you it wasn't the weapons."

"I'm not so sure," stated Krirtie pointing down the corridor. "Look!"

Schram's eyes nearly popped from their sockets. Walking down the tunnel toward them was a small bearded man about three to four feet tall with a red hat and a long wooden pipe.

"What kind of dwarf is that?" asked Maldor. "You can see through him." He reached down to grab his sword without taking his eye from the approaching apparition. Not feeling anything, he glanced down. "Schram, our weapons have vanished."

Schram, ignoring Maldor's comment, walked toward the apparition. "Greetings, King." The others nearly fell over when he referred to it as king, but the disturbance did not slow his speech. "We come as friends."

The dwarf paused and objectively surveyed the motley crew standing before them. Then, with a puff on his pipe, he vanished before their eyes. Suddenly the tunnel they were in expanded outward into a large open hall, and at the front of the hall, stood fifteen dwarves all with their battle axes ready and motioning the group forward.

"I don't like this," the maneth stated.

"Relax, friend," replied Schram. "If they had wanted us dead, we would be as such."

The group, led and followed by half of the dwarven guard, walked down the hall, several times ducking to get beneath the low doorways. Maldor was over twice the size of most of the dwarves, and believed that if a fight did break out, he would be able to control most of those around them and possibly allow his friends the opportunity to escape. One of the dwarven guards seemed to realize what Maldor was thinking and thumped him in his back with the butt of his axe. Maldor turned and glanced at the little man and raised his hand to strike the inferior dwarf. Quickly, the others surrounded the maneth and had their axes ready to throw and surely kill Maldor before his hand could even move toward the dwarf's face.

"Maldor, halt!" exclaimed Schram when he turned at the commotion. The maneth looked back to him but did not seem willing to yield and show weakness. "If you wish to live," continued Schram, "lift your arms slowly and place them above your head. Any other movement, and you will never use your hands again."

He seemed torn between his pride and Schram's words. He stood like a magnificent statue over a small crowd of worshippers. It was strikingly apparent that the dwarves did not trust them at all, regardless of the fact that they were weaponless prisoners.

A battle-axe bit the maneth slightly in the small of his back, and reluctantly and slowly, Maldor gritted his teeth and carefully raised his hands above his head. The dwarves slowly moved from around him and replaced their battle-axes to their sides. The maneth's only thought was that he may have misjudged the small men leading him to who knows where, so he continued along quietly. Krirtie slowed so she could walk beside the big maneth, making both of them happier with the situation.

The walk ended in a large open chamber where, what appeared to be the lead guard approached Schram. "I am Jermys Ironshield. Our king, much against my advisement, has decided that you are to be welcomed to his presence. He has granted you his audience, but choose your actions and words carefully strangers, for his power is indeed great, and you can just as easily die here as you could have in the mine." The dwarf seemed to be forcing his superior authority upon them, which made Schram wonder what had been happening here that had caused such fear of any visitors. "Now you may enter, but remember, we will be near."

"Thank you, Jermys Ironshield of the dwarven guard. I am Schram, Prince of the human city of Toopek, and my friends and I stumbled upon your mine by accident during our mission of peace. It is gracious of you to receive us in these times of great evil."

Jermys looked stunned by Schram's response and bowed indignantly as they passed. The dwarf who had poked Maldor glared at the maneth as he entered and whispered something to Jermys after Maldor was through.

"Please come closer," said a voice from the far side of the huge chamber.

"I am Schram, prince of Toopek and greatest friend to the elves. With me is my companion from Toopek, Krirtie; Stephanatilantilis, princess of Elvinott and the flyer elves; and Maldor, captain of the maneth Batt Line."

The king bowed to each of them respectively but directed his eyes and words to the maneth. "You are Alhize's son, are you not, Maldor?" his voice was deep but crystal clear. Though he was sitting, Schram believed the king would only stand four feet and a handful of inches from the ground, and his long white beard ran a good chance of touching his feet.

"Yes, I am he," replied Maldor, surprised at the question addressed to him.

"Your father and I have been friends a long time, though I fear we have lost contact over the passing years." The king's voice saddened. "How is your father, young Maldor?"

Maldor's eyes softened, and his head fell. "I regret to be the bearer of such distress, but my father was fallen by the dagger of a goblin as he traveled to meet with the elves."

"I am truly sorry for bringing these memories back upon you. I did not know, and this news is as saddening as any of late." He gestured to Stepha. "And please forgive my speaking of his name. I do recognize those passed." Stepha bowed her head respectively. The king turned, stood up, and faced Schram with his hand out. "Please, Prince of Toopek, forgive our elaborate enchantments. This has become a troubling time for the dwarves, and we may sometimes be in the wrong with our actions. I am Krystof, king of the dwarven lands of Feldschlosschen."

"There is nothing that we must forgive, King Krystof," Schram stated. "These are desperate times for all and being careful is required if we want to reach an old age."

Krystof smiled. "An old age is one I saw many years ago. Come, let us have food together and speak of what has brought you into my humble kingdom."

The companions smiled at the thought of stopping and eating. None of them had realized while they were in the tunnels, but they had been walking all day and night was already upon them. The dwarves were very hospitable with their food, and soon everyone, including Maldor, whose seemingly bottomless appetite awed the dwarves, was sufficiently filled allowing all to retire to a separate large chamber with many wooden tables to talk.

The group told of the hardships that had fallen over the land and how they had come to be in one another's company. Then they spoke about the blizzard that had driven them blindly through the foothills only to end up lost and stumbling by chance upon the mine entrance. Then their trek through the tunnels, and only when they dropped their weapons did they meet the ghost dwarf and then the guards.

The king absorbed the entire story, changing expressions as each hardship and terror seemed to bring up memories of ones he too had faced. However, upon finishing their story, the companions watched a smile grow on Krystof's face. "You know," the king said, "it is kind of ironic that you made it through those tunnels to here. They were designed to catch those ever-annoying bandicoots and stray goblins or trolls who would venture into our mines taking many of our minerals. With magic, they usually walk themselves to death because they will never unload what they have taken. But if you don't take anything, no magic will act, and you will be free to leave. What mineral was it you four desired that sprung the trap when you tried to leave?"

The four looked at each other, all realizing at the same time that they had again forgotten about Fehr, even when they recapped their story to the king. Schram nodded to Krirtie, and slowly she reached into her pouch and pulled out their furry companion.

"It seems we have forgotten to mention our other companion on our journey," Schram stated.

The dwarves opened their eyes wide. "I'll kill it, Krystof," hollered Jermys.

Krirtie shoved the small chair backward and gripped the little rat tightly waking him from his sleep. "Hey, why you wake me?" said Fehr's little voice as he peered around the room. "Aye! Dwarves! What hell has brought me here? These little drunken bastards for some unknown reason have taken a completely unprovoked dislike to my kind."

The rat's words infuriated Jermys and the other dwarves, and they approached the girl holding the evil invader. "Hold your tracks," rang the king's voice. "These among us have traveled a great distance and faced hardships beyond that of our own. We will not take one of their friends from them because of our prejudices."

The dwarves angrily stammered back to their seats but never took their glaring eyes from the rodent infestation sitting in their council room. "I am sorry," added Krystof after he turned to face Krirtie and Fehr. "We are not accustomed to your kind coming as friends."

Fehr's eyes saddened. "The bandicoot are friends to all. I am very sorry if my kind has ever done you wrong."

All the dwarves, including the king, were stunned by Fehr's ability to speak in their ancient dwarven tongue with such fluency. "Aye, little one, it again appears that it is the dwarves who should be apologizing to you. We never attempted contact with you, thinking you only an unintelligent scavenger. Never had we dreamed that you could communicate, especially in our ancient language.."

"Feel sorry not," replied Fehr in his old choppy speech. "I am one of the few of my kind who took an interest in learning the languages of our neighbors. Most are limited to our own advanced language and would have ignored any of your communication attempts. If anything, it is both our faults for being closed off to the other." Fehr's words were lighthearted and free as he felt he was making new friends.

"Perhaps in the future, we will learn from each other," stated the king as another of his guards entered the chamber carrying all of the companion's weapons. The dwarf could barely be seen behind the massive arsenal of equipment he carried. Maldor's face brightened as he grabbed for his gear, a comfortable expression appearing in his eyes as if a part of his body had just been returned.

When each of them had taken their weapons back, it could be seen that the dwarf who had brought the weapons was the identical twin of Jermys. "I am Bretten Ironshield. I am pleased to meet all of you," said the dwarf, bowing as he took his seat next to his brother.

The king then began to speak, telling the companions of the evil that his kingdom had been facing these past months. Many times goblin forces had invaded their mines, attempting to gain entry into their kingdom, and every time, they had been driven out by force but also at great losses to the dwarves. The magic of the tunnels seemed to be useless against the goblins as if they were immune to its enchantment. However, from everything Schram had told them, it was clear that a stronger magic, possibly dragon magic, was protecting the goblins. Krystof said that they would concentrate on strengthening their enchantment and end these attacks.

"I cannot spare the men to help your friends in their attempt to retake Toopek. It would require passing through this treacherous winter, and with the cold season now moving into every area, the necessity, not to mention success rate, for such minimal aid would be low."

Schram thought about the maneths and elves. They should have reached Toopek by now. He looked toward Stepha who sat next to him and knew she too wondered what fate had met them when they arrived.

His thoughts were interrupted when Krystof broke in continuing his thought, "I will however send Jermys and Bretten with you. They are the best-skilled to guide you down the Ozaky. We have a secret tunnel under the river, which will take you to Antaag, the dwarven city that controls the southern mines. There you can find a ship capable of making the trip down the rapid currents of the river."

Schram stood and approached the king. "Thank you very much. Your help is greatly appreciated." Schram turned to the twin dwarves. "And that appreciation is carried on to you, my new friends."

The two dwarves nodded kindly, but Schram could tell this was no mission they had volunteered for. This was the king's choice, and out of respect for his leadership, they had accepted. Schram began to wonder if they would actually prove to be a help or a hindrance. He decided that he would have them lead the group through the tunnels, but if they wished to return to their home and fight beside their own, then that could become their accepted destiny.

Krystof motioned to the twins who looked at each other. Bretten spoke, "We are pleased with the chance to help you in your most dangerous quest. We give you our service as leaders through our country but recognize you as being in command and will respect your wishes as such dictates."

The two identical dwarves made a slightly humorous sight, but none of the group dared laugh for fear of making their obvious distress even worse. Krirtie rose. "Dear friends, as I stand now speaking freely, so you will learn to do. Yes, Schram has stepped forward to lead this journey to Draag, but he has often admitted misgivings and questioned his own judgments, looking to us for guidance. We respect his leadership, but our ideas, as well as yours, are held just as important."

Schram took a step toward Krirtie. "She speaks the truth. Please know that if either of you has any problem or fear of this mission, do not feel that you must join us. There will be no bad feelings, and no one will think you cowards. We are all friends, and we will honor your decisions as you have honored us with food and aid this night."

Jermys looked at his brother and smiled. "We are accompanying you of our own will. We know you to be great friends who we are learning to trust as you learn to trust us. Soon perhaps, we can all be called brothers." He paused and turned toward Krystof. "If you will be ready, and with the king's permission, we will leave at first light."

"We will be ready," spoke Maldor as he stood and lifted his sword in the air, creating a truly magnificent sight before the dwarves.

"Then let your travels be safe," stated Krystof. "Remember the times are filled with great evil, and many dangers may cross your path. Be strong, and guard each other well, and you shall remain safe and as one."

A resounding cheer broke across the chamber as the dwarves pounded the butts of their axes on the table, and Maldor gave his echoing roar, slamming the hilt of his sword down crushing the table beneath him, which only enticed the cheers further.

The king turned to Schram and taking his hand said, "May your god travel with you, my son."

Krystof stood over two feet below that of Schram, so when the human dropped to one knee, they were near eye level. "And may yours be with you in protecting your kingdom, Krystof. We will return with news of what we find, but I believe that it will be just as important for you to hold control of all your tunnels. Your intricate hidden pathways could prove to be valuable routes if this evil should develop into open war."

The king nodded understanding the importance of what Schram spoke. They separated hands, and Krystof turned to the still loud and excited group in front of him. "Sleep well tonight, friends, tomorrow is not far away, and with it comes another tiring journey."

CHAPTER 10

Toopek

"Feel the power surging within us, my sons. As more of my dragon lords approach the caverns, the stronger we are becoming. With you by our side, Kirven, I doubt there is any force that will ever oppose us, and calling for the return of the dragons will be little more than opening our mouths."

Kirven's eyes darkened as he listened to the words of his father. "Don't be overly confident, Father. There is still one who has the power to defeat us."

Slayne glared at his younger son. "It is you that is holding too much faith in your old friend, the imminent magician Schram. Almok spoke to me about this *powerful* wizard and his abilities from his previous encounter. Simple mind-blocking magic is no match for the three greatest sorcerers on all of Troyf." His eyes narrowed on the canok. "I trust your loyalties are clear in this matter."

"I will honor our agreement. You know that to be true." Kirven stared back calmly. "But we are but three of the four greatest magicians. Do not ever doubt that."

The dragon looked fierce as fire burned in his eyes. "If he were truly as powerful as you imply, he would have destroyed Almok when they first met and never allowed this joining to occur. Even now, I can barely feel his presence. He is not strong."

"No," replied Kirven. "No, he is not."

Blood gushed from the enlarged nose of the goblin guard as Geoff's final blow with his maneth club nearly separated its head from its body. "Those creatures are utterly disgusting, and they are staining my club with their awful black slop they use as blood."

"Perhaps you should consider using a more civilized weapon, barbarian," stated Madeiris, his eyes gleaming as he stood over the dead troll and goblin he had killed.

"What would you have me use? A bow? I could not hit the ground if I shot straight down. No, I think my club and sword serve me just fine."

The elf prince and maneth king both smiled as they turned and peered into the city. "It is nice being so close to the coast and not having to face the winter cold just yet," stated the elf. "I wonder how the others fared. They must be deep into winter at the elevation they are now hitting."

Geoff shook his head. "Aye, if the weather was not friendly, it would bite them hard. However, we have troubles of our own now despite the fair skies."

"Yes, old friend, that much is certain." He paused and looked across the area. "Are all your troops in position?"

"I believe so," Geoff replied, letting out a roar, which shook the window of the nearest building.

"What are you doing? Why don't you just walk down and tell them we are here!"

Several roars from all around the city echoed back in return. "Humans are stupid. They don't know what is in the forest, and the goblins don't care." He paused smiling. "And yes, the maneths are in position. Now, what do you see down there that might be of some help?"

Madeiris shrugged at his old friend. "Well, the castle has been destroyed, which is clear, but as for the rest, I find it very odd. There are goblins in the city, and two goblin guards are at the gates on all three sides, but their numbers are not strong enough to hold against the humans and definitely not us. I suppose it is possible the force attacking has evacuated, leaving only a sparse number of goblins to guard the city, but that would not make sense if they really wanted Toopek in the first place."

"Unless they already have gotten what they wanted from it," Geoff stated as he remembered what the flyer elf guard had told him regarding the *human* attacks on the elves.

"Aye, I see what you are saying. Then retaking the city should be no trouble."

"Unless whatever destroyed the castle still remains in protection. We will hold now and attack as the sun sets. My garrisons will go in while the flyers enter with air cover. We will use your ground troops to catch any of those trying to escape and as a possible cavalry if we need it. We don't want any word to get out yet about the battle, so guard the escape routes well. I don't expect much trouble, but that is usually when trouble seems to arise."

"Very well, I will inform my guards."

Madeiris hollered to an elf nearby and relayed the information to be passed. Word was spread around the lines, and as evening approached the forest, all seemed to die, and an ominous silence engulfed the land. Even the birds stopped their song in anticipation for what was about to occur. The goblins guarding the gate became noticeably disturbed at the situation, but besides looking around aimlessly, they did nothing. All the attack formations were in place, and with a deafening roar from Geoff, the forest erupted with life.

The flyer elves emitted blankets of arrows, each releasing a second before their first had impacted. The guards, which had been lucky enough to avoid the onslaught of elven arrows, were no match for the hundreds of maneths, which came thundering down from the tree line. The maneth troops barely had to slow as they flooded into Toopek, hacking any goblin or troll who did not cower and run. Those that did seek escape were cornered by the two approaching lines of troops and were quickly finished off as well.

The maneth guard stood in the center of town, looking around in disbelief. The flyer elves and Madeiris's ground troops swept the forest. Running into no escaping goblins, they quickly joined the group in the city center, not understanding what the explanation could be.

"What kind of battle was that?" asked Madeiris. "Nobody even came close to getting through your lines. The humans could not fight against them even now?"

"What humans?" replied Geoff, looking sadly around.

"Oh my, I didn't even realize."

Geoff hollered, "All troops, search the buildings. Any goblin remaining alive, keep that way and bring them to me. Any humans found, also bring to me, unharmed."

The troops broke up and began searching randomly through all the buildings. Several groups stumbled onto hiding goblins, but due to their resistance, they were killed in the process. As Geoff was giving up hope, Randor, a young maneth, yelled, "Geoff, I've found something."

Geoff, Madeiris, and several others ran over quickly and found Randor standing over two large wooden doors leading to what appeared to be some sort of cellar. The doors were chained and locked, and tapping could be heard inside. "What is it?" asked Geoff.

"I don't know," replied the young maneth guard. "I hollered and beat on the doors, but there was no reply, simply the continued beat of that sound resembling a sword striking steel."

"What do you suppose this is, Madeiris?"

"I cannot be certain. Possibly a storage or shelter of some kind," he replied. "Whatever is in there has been locked in from the outside, and by the sounds of it, for a long time."

"Everyone, back up," Geoff said as he raised his sword. With a clang, which pierced the ears of all around causing the elves to jerk in dismay, the thick lock split open. Geoff reached down and pulled the doors upward, releasing the trapped scents of death and waste. "Hello," he hollered in common. "Is anyone there?"

"Hello," answered a weak voice.

"We are here to help you," began Geoff. He stopped and stepped back as a large glowing orb suddenly appeared in the cellar and rose up before him.

It hovered above the group, observing the entire spectacle and then returned to face Geoff. "Who dares tread on dragon soil?" echoed a deep voice from within the globe, which pulsated with each word.

"I Geoff, King of the maneths, dare to return Toopek to the city of humans. Who are you who hides behind a ball of light?"

The glow seemed to grow for a moment, and then an energy charge shot from its center, striking Randor. Within a blink, both the charge and the maneth had vanished. "I hide from no being, maneth."

Geoff drew his sword and plunged it into the hovering object. "Then face me!"

As his sword contacted the globe, light exploded in all directions, blinding those who looked toward what they saw. Energy was flowing down the blade and was filling Geoff's body, causing him to shake violently. The seven-and-a-half-foot maneth was lifted from the ground as if he were a feather being pushed by a soft breeze. The elves had been able to adjust to the new light conditions and stood engrossed at the sight before them. Madeiris drew an arrow and released it toward the orb. It quickly veered its position, turning Geoff between it and the flight of the arrow. Deep within his flesh, the arrow set causing the maneth king to roar in pain. Another elf had taken aim, and Madeiris grabbed his bow, halting the action. Geoff had adjusted to the violent energy being sent through his body, but his maneth blue blood poured from his leg where the arrowhead struck. He gathered what strength he had left, and in one flowing motion, removed his maneth club from his back and dropped it into the globe. More light emitted from the impact, but the globe still held. He raised his club again, and with all his might, brought the blow downward. As contact was made, the globe vanished, releasing Geoff, dropping him twenty feet to the ground. When he landed flat, Madeiris's arrow was pushed farther through his leg, causing him to roar in agony and blood to flow profusely onto the ground.

Madeiris ran to where Geoff had landed and quickly removed his arrow, calling for some bandages. "I am sorry, Geoff. My flight was true, but the target was very fast."

Geoff squinted his eyes as the pain shot through his body. "Pay it no mind, elf, but perhaps you should consider a more civilized weapon." He motioned to his club.

Madeiris smiled as an elf ran up carrying many bandages. "Here are the wraps, Prince Madeiris. Also," he leaned closer and spoke softer, "humans have begun appearing from the cellar. It appears there could be hundreds crammed down there. Many carry dead and wounded. What would you have me do?"

Madeiris witnessed the sad appearance of the humans and then in a low voice said, "Have them go to wherever they can to care for their sick. Find out how many there are, and ask whoever leads them now to join me when his time is free. Also, keep it quiet. I do not want any panic started or Geoff to be bothered with this. He is too weak." The guard nodded and bounded off.

"Blasphemy!" exclaimed Geoff. "You pointy-eared idiot, elves are not the only ones in the forest with a keen sense of hearing. Now, if you'll bandage where *your* arrow went through, we can prepare to greet the human."

A blank look of surprise struck the elf prince's face as he gazed at the huge creature beneath him. "You never cease to amaze me, you old war maneth. Now, if you will quit being such a baby about it, maybe I will be able to finish bandaging it."

"Baby! You are lucky I don't take that bow and ring it around—"

"Your majesties?" said an elf from the side. "I am sorry to interrupt, but the human leader wishes to speak with you immediately."

Both the prince and king jumped as the elf approached, trying to look dignified and well-controlled. Their expressions dropped when they saw what greeted them. Dressed in mostly rags, stained and torn, a human male of about forty years approached with the aid of the elf guard and a walking cane. "I am Alan Grove, third lieutenant in the King's army of Toopek. I thank you for your help, Madeiris of Elvinott, and to you sir, who I apologize to for not recognizing."

"I am Geoff, King of the maneths, and our help was appreciatively given. However, we now have much to discuss, if you are able, Alan Grove. Is there any place we can go?"

"Yes," he replied, coughing violently and struggling to stay on his feet. "Follow me to the community center. There are tables and chairs there, or at least there used to be."

The group agreed on the idea and slowly attempted to make their way to the building the human had referred to, though their walk was very slow due to their condition. Madeiris, much to his own distress, helped the much-larger maneth along, and two elven guards practically carried Alan. Once in the room, all sat and let out a sigh of pleasure at the relief finding its way to their legs.

Geoff wasted no time with pleasantries as he still was not confident with the situation. "Are you the senior official left here?"

"I believe that I am," replied Alan's weak voice. "Our top six council members all disappeared by the magic of the orbs like the one that had you and was guarding us. Nobody knows the condition of the king and queen for it was over a week ago the castle was destroyed with no sign of either of them. Prince Schram never returned from his trip to the canok's homeland, and we fear he too has fallen. All other officials in the city were killed or fled to the woods when the first goblin attack hit. The city was stripped clean of anyone who resisted at all. Our entire city has been hacked down to a few thousand people all of whom are weak, wounded, and dying."

Geoff felt the human's pain as he spoke and wanted to say something that might ease his mind. "Let me begin by telling you that Prince Schram is well and is responsible for our presence here, but you will be told everything in good time. First, if you are able, I would like to know the events which put you and the others into the cellar and left only a few goblins to guard all of Toopek."

Alan drew in a deep breath and then began recapping the ordeal. "After the initial attack, very few problems existed considering the circumstances. We were an occupied city, but our people remaining alive were free to walk the streets and do what business they could. The remaining top officials including Tomas Sherblade, Derik Wayward"—Madeiris cringed at the human name responsible for the elves' deaths in the forest—"William Meyer, and others who you probably do not know by name held a secret council to decide what to do. The next day, all those attending the meeting were either killed, taken by those mysterious globes, or simply vanished." Alan paused as he bowed his head for those lost. "The following day, two hooded men appeared in the city. They knew their way around and were searching for something, or someone. We could not see their faces, but they looked human except for a large lump on their backsides, which was covered by the large drapes of their black robes. The magic they possessed was immeasurable. They wreaked havoc on the city, destroying the water pumps, horse and bongo stables and leveling everything in the harbor. We were completely cut off from the outside. Unless someone could escape on foot, there would be no way to get word to Empor."

Geoff and Madeiris looked at each other but did not speak. Alan saw their look, and after a moment to let everything settle, he continued unhindered.

"Then it happened." His eyes grew wide as he seemed to be witnessing again what he remembered. "The robed men moved to the center of the square and began looking toward the castle. Then those of us still around saw it. It was way in the distance, but gradually, it was drawing nearer—a small black dot, not anything identifiable, only a dot. It rose in the sky from behind what was left of the castle across the harbor. We could not make out what was happening, but a fear generated throughout everyone. The dot seemed to be slowly growing, almost as if it were flying in the air. As it drew within about half the bay's distance, all knew what approached. Our great grandparents had told their children and in turn word had been passed. None of us had ever seen one in real life, but we all knew a black dragon when we saw it."

Geoff glanced again toward Madeiris who sat as white as Kirven's coat. "Then we can be certain. Our worst fears have turned full circle, and the dragons have returned."

The elf turned. "And what have we sent our friends into at Draag?"

There was a long pause while each absorbed what had been said. Geoff arched his back, trying to take pressure off his leg. With a small, painful grunt, he shook his head in despair but knew he had to know the rest. He nodded to Alan to continue.

The human began to look confused and dismayed almost as if the dragon was still approaching as he spoke. Sweat dripped from his brow, and his gaze seemed to be fixed upon nothing. He cleared his throat and in a blank lost voice, began again. "The dragon was huge. It landed beside the robed men as smoke and black saliva dripped from its mouth. Its eyes were beet red streaks of fire etched into its jet-black armor-plated head with its nose shooting outward like a spear. It flapped out its huge wings, kicking up dust and debris to better the worst of our storms. The robed men seemed immune to the dragon's storm and stood strong, having some sort of conversation with the beast, but the words appeared as gibberish to all who were within earshot.

"This went on for a long time, or maybe it was short. I can't be sure. All I know is that the powers I was witnessing were like none I had ever seen before. But that wasn't all. Suddenly without warning, the conversation ceased. The robed men scanned the area and seemed to find pleasure in its desolate look. They chanted a strange foreign rhyme and then transformed into brilliant balls of fire similar to the one you fought." He pointed to Geoff. "The balls began to float and then moved south-westerly out over the sea before disappearing."

"What did the people do then?" asked Madeiris, not waiting for Alan to continue.

"What could we do?" he replied defensively. "The dragon looked around, and his thoughts seemed to command the goblin guard. The son of William Meyer, who had watched his father be taken by the globe, approached the beast invading our town. He asked the dragon from what hell it came and why it had attacked our city. In one breath, William's son lay as a pile of scorched bone. After that, the goblins gathered all of us up and stuffed us in the cellar where we all planned on dying. There were probably only about five hundred goblins and trolls left in the city at this time, but we were unarmed, hungry, and morally beaten. We could not defend ourselves against them, or anybody for that matter. After the cellar doors were shut, except for the presence of the globe, we have no knowledge of what happened. However, because of your contact with it, it is a good bet the dragons know you are here and we have escaped."

Geoff and Madeiris took in all the new information and then filled Alan in on where they all stood. "How many men can you gather that will fight and defend the city?" asked Geoff.

"I don't know, maybe three or four hundred, maybe more. Those that are left are by no means the strongest warriors, but they are loyal to the city. However, I do not wish to tell them they fight their former army commander as one of the black robed men."

"Then do not tell them," exclaimed Madeiris. "Those men who used to be your leaders have been permanently changed by the dragons as the canoks were two hundred years ago. They are no longer human, by any sense of the word. They now serve those who attacked you and will do anything in their power to crush what is left. I believe those taken by the globes will be responsible for the control over the dragon offensives, dragon lords so to speak."

His words struck Alan like salt on an open wound. "No, they must all know the truth," he replied flatly. "Humans may not fight like the elves or have the size and strength of your people, Geoff, but we are proud, and if we must destroy some of ourselves to destroy the product of the dragon's evil, then by god, we will do it."

"Madeiris!" shouted an elf as he burst through the door. "More humans are approaching from the south. Their numbers could reach a thousand."

"Are they robed?" asked the elf prince.

"No, they are in silver armor with two golden half-crescent emblems on the breastplate."

Alan interrupted. "Those are the troops from Empor, the human city, which separated from the kingdom because King Starland would not allow magic to be practiced in Toopek."

"Do they come in peace?" asked Geoff.

The elf guard turned to the maneth. "We do not know. Our flyers have made no contact but simply waited and watched in the trees."

Geoff rose, putting only a little weight on his leg. "Take two garrisons of maneth guard to the south wall, and arrange for all the flyers to be near. Alan, come with me. We need your help, or we could have a war among allies."

Geoff, Madeiris, and Alan all walked out to approach the oncoming army. When they were sighted, the humans drew swords and prepared to charge. "Wait," shouted Alan. "They stand with us."

The army commander rode past his troops and approached the three before them. "Who is it that speaks as friends?"

The still distraught human moved forward using his cane as he walked. "I am Alan Grove, third lieutenant in the King's Army of Toopek. With me is Geoff, King of the maneths, and Madeiris, Prince of Elvinott. Great hardship has befallen Toopek, and we welcome your assistance if that is what you bring."

"That is indeed what I, Prince Reynolds of Empor, do bring." The prince dismounted and approached the three. "Greetings to you all, though I am certain by this strange meeting that the times have grown grave."

"Greetings to you also, Prince Reynolds," responded Geoff in his deep tone as he stared at the human. "We do have much to discuss, so let us return to the city at once."

Geoff roared, and the forest around came to life. Coming from the trees, the branches, the sky, and the ground were elves and maneths as they appeared from their silent hiding.

"And I thought you a fool for approaching without guard," interjected Reynolds. "I see you were well protected. May my first impression be corrected."

The group turned in unison and escorted the Emporian army into the city.

The Emporian Prince stood before the group and tried to explain the situation, as he knew it, to the sad expressions and nods from those in the room. "We have had little contact with the Toopekian kingdom due to the prejudices each holds for the other. However, when about four to five hundred goblins broke through our city gates from the north and demolished our town, we feared our old home was probably hit harder. Leaving half our army there, we marched through the day and were to camp outside the city tonight. We were about to halt when we saw you approaching."

"Did the goblins stay and fight?" asked Geoff.

"No, that was the surprising thing," he replied. "They entered the city and left just as quickly. We killed about fifty and took about as many of our own wounded, losing only a handful."

"I don't understand," stated Madeiris. "What could their motive have been to leave Toopek in the first place and to make it so obvious with a futile attack at Empor?"

Geoff rose, now only half noticing his injury. "I believe that we are about to face a major offensive like one we have never faced before. Perhaps the actions thus far have been nothing more than attempts at confusing us or putting us against each other. Think, first the dragon lord showing himself to the elves to turn them against the humans, and now if we had not met the Emporian army outside the city, they might have attacked us tomorrow when they woke. We must always remain together in our actions. We now have a definite enemy to fight, which has the ability to use the humans to manipulate situations. These hooded men now wield a dark magic, and we must find some way to defeat them for I believe they assert control over the goblins, and it is the dragons who control them."

"We must get word to the dwarves at Feldschlosschen and Antaag and King Cowhanis of the mountain elves." Turning to Reynolds, he asked, "Have you had any contact with the king of Drynak?"

"King Joseph?" replied Reynolds questionably. "No, I have not heard from him in many years."

Geoff frowned. "We all must be united in this cause, or we have little chance of success. The actions of the dragons are different this time than in the past. Instead of flying straight at us and raking destruction across all of Troyf, they are destroying us from within, making goblins do most of their dirty work."

Reynolds interrupted. "Well, let's go to the dragon homeland, as it is fabled you did before, and meet them on our terms. Waiting for their attack on us would be foolhardy."

Geoff glared at the human. "You do not know of what you speak, Reynolds. You can't fight dragons on your terms. You must bend their terms to your benefit. Two hundred years ago, they required a base from which to work their magic, and in their absence with the canok's help, we destroyed that base. However, this time, I believe they are remaining at the base and sending others to fight their battles, but my question is, why have they suddenly retreated?"

The Emporian prince was furious with the tone the maneth had taken with him and rose exclaiming, "What would you have us do then, wait for the goblins and magic users to come in force?"

"No," replied Geoff calmly. "We should wait for our party to return from Draag with information about what is going on there and send word to all who can help about what is happening to gather more allies. Do you think this unwise, Prince?" his voice now growing condescending and sarcastic.

Reynolds stared at his opponent, and his expression finally calmed, dropping his red-face back to normal. "Your wisdom seems sound. I will inform my garrison to obey your command, and I will return to Empor to spread word of what we know. If King Joseph of Drynak lives, he will follow my lead. Will you send word to the canoks as well?"

Geoff was stunned by the question and thought a moment in consideration before responding with the only possible answer. "No, if the canok's wish to help us again, they will come to us on their own, but I don't expect it. The last two hundred years has hurt the canoks, not helped them."

With the accompanying nods from all about the table, the group of leaders gradually disbanded, each going their appropriate directions. Word of the dragons was spread across the land, although no one had seen but the one dragon, but that one was enough to bring back the memories of those who had fought them previously. Geoff, like most of the maneths and elves, did not sleep that night as the oppression of two hundred years past was relived in his thoughts and dreams. When they could finally clear their heads of the past, their thoughts were channeled toward their comrades, the two humans, Schram and Krirtie; Stepha, princess of the flyer elves; Maldor, captain of the Batt Line; and Fehr, the stray bandicoot looking for adventure. Geoff turned each of these friends over in his mind and prayed for their safety.

CHAPTER 11

Antaag: Arrested

Jermys and Bretten were indeed an amusing sight as they walked ahead of the companions. It was impossible to distinguish the twins from each other by the way they looked, walked, talked, and acted. The only difference was that Bretten seemed to follow his brother's lead more often than not, probably due to Jermys's high streak of temper he never felt the need to hide. The twins had been in three arguments since the journey to Antaag began, and each time, Bretten had pushed Jermys to his limit and then let him have his way.

Maldor and Schram had felt uncomfortable following too closely to the twins for fear of having to take sides. However, if the situation did arise where they became caught in the middle, they both agreed to take opposite sides so as not to favor one or the other of the dwarves. However, now they had fallen back far enough so they could muse at the two bickering brothers without worrying about being dragged into it with them.

"Look at how Jermys's little leg looks when he tries to kick Bretten in the backside." Maldor laughed in a quiet voice.

"I know. His legs are maybe one fifth of his entire body, and seeing them swing that high in the air defies all logic. It has to be causing him more pain than the kick is hitting Bretten." Schram was also laughing now.

Bretten took a second kick from Jermys as he yelled, "Come on you bearded, stubborn-headed rat lover. Say I'm right. You know that I am taller!"

Bretten turned to Jermys. "If there is anyone here who loves rats, it is the short, scraggly-bearded dwarf in front of me!"

Jermys shoved his twin as they again began an open fight this time drawing their battle-axes in the process. Maldor and Schram saw this but were too far back to stop them.

Jermys said, "To the mark, brother?"

Bretten replied, "So be it, to the mark."

They both raised their battle-axes as the rest of the companions came running toward them hollering for them to stop, but the dwarves were oblivious to their voices. Simultaneously, they let their axes fly, and both Stepha and Krirtie turned their eyes away in disbelief. The thump of the axe's impact echoed down the tunnel.

"Oh, nice throw, brother, right on the mark," shouted Bretten.

"Yours too. I can't believe the size of the nugget you cracked off, probably at least five pounds."

Schram and Maldor stopped running and just looked at the sight before them. The twins were comparing sizes of rocks their respective throws had freed from the cavern wall. Krirtie and Stepha had also realized what had happened and were walking forward to have a word with the dwarves.

"I think yours is bigger. You must have been right," stated Bretten admiring Jermys's rock.

"No, I think yours is—"

"You two better stop this bickering at once!" exclaimed Krirtie interrupting the two. "I thought you were trying to kill each other."

Everyone hushed at the force in the girl's tone, which even caused Maldor to take a step back. Bretten broke the silence with a deep and out-of-place laugh. "Kill each other? He is my brother. I could no more kill him than I could kill myself."

Stepha nodded slightly, knowing that dwarves, like elves, hold life at the highest level, and suicide would be an action neither could hold honorable. Bretten and Jermys both looked at each other and entered into a long, uncontrolled laugh. Their bodies were shaking so hard that they both fell over, rolling on the cavern floor. The others around again looked at the sight before them, and upon seeing the twins' pink faces and bouncing bellies, they also fell into a deep frenzy, everyone except Krirtie, that is. She became so infuriated that she drew her sword and shouted, "The next one to make a sound looses a limb."

Everyone heard the anger in her voice and saw it in her eyes and did their best to calm themselves. However, as Bretten struggled to stand up, he had to completely concentrate to keep his laughter from spilling across the corridor. He was successful as far as anyone heard, but his belly remained shaking violently under his breath. As he stood, his belt popped open under the strain, causing his short pants to fall to the ground, revealing his small dwarven buttocks. Upon seeing this, hysteria again broke out over the group including Krirtie who now dropped to a knee at the sight.

It took several moments for any in the group to regain their composure, but as soon as possible, they continued forward without comment. However, every once in a while, a muffled giggle would break through the silence, causing all to smile, all except Bretten, that is.

"Hey, Bretten," laughed Maldor from behind. "If you decide you do not like being a mining dwarf, perhaps you could find a different *career*."

The dwarf's grumbles answered the maneth as Schram added, "Yeah, but don't fall *behind* in your studies."

Bretten now was becoming livid. "Don't worry, brother," whispered Jermys. "I will not stand for this chatter." He turned sternly to the four behind, causing their faces to lose their smiles in preparation for the ear-lashing they were about to receive from the twin. However, when they saw his wide grin and the wink he made obvious, the good humor returned, and they eagerly awaited his comment. "Hey, come on, you guys, you are being very rude. How fair is it making Bretten the *butt* of all your jokes?"

That was all it took for Bretten. He turned toward his now hysterical brother, and with one quick swing of his battle-axe, snapped Jermys's belt, releasing his pants to his knees.

Again, laughter filled the corridor as the now red-faced twin openly fought with his brother. Schram and Maldor quickly recovered from their good humor, each grabbing one of the twins.

"Settle down, you two," flashed Schram. "This is how it all got started in the first place. We are sorry we made sport of you, Bretten, and we will not let it happen again." He paused and put the dwarf down, giving him time to cool off. Maldor too put the twin down, and both the brothers looked at each other with narrowed eyes. Schram saw the look and continued, "Now, let's forget this mess and get on to Antaag. I have no idea where we are or how much traveling we have left before we arrive, but I would like to get there today."

Bretten and Jermys exchanged enraged glances, but it was the diplomatic Bretten who stepped forward. "We are sorry, sir. Sometimes my brother's dwarven stubbornness gets the best of him." There was a brief silence before he added, "And I suppose that I carry that same stubbornness."

Jermys stepped forward and said, "Yes, his words are true." He paused then added, "and so you won't continue to wonder, we are about a mile from the tunnel under the river, which itself is another five miles across, then an additional two into Antaag."

Maldor sighed. "You mean we still have eight miles left?"

"I suppose you could say it like that," Jermys stated. "But my way was much more precise." He turned to Schram. "Now, if you guys can hold all the questions, we can be on our way."

Schram looked angered by the dwarf's unsaid message, blaming the four companions for the slow travel, but he said nothing in rebuttal. He assumed it would only hold things up more, and it had already taken too long.

The group split up again as they walked with Krirtie and Stepha in the rear but close enough to hear the two warriors exchanging battle stories and the twins arguing again about something held important to only them. The two females had become quite engrossed with each other, prying into each of the other's feelings. Inevitably, their talk and questioning changed from each other to Schram, and Stepha began to talk about their last night at the fountain.

"You mean that was the last time you saw him?" Krirtie asked.

"Yes, until I saw him again in Elvinott just over nine days ago." She looked toward the human woman. "Tell me about his life in Toopek. Were you his closest friend?"

Krirtie smiled as she remembered their life growing up. "Besides Kirven, I think that I was probably the only one Schram ever talked to. I was definitely the person he was closest with other than maybe his mother and Kirven. In fact, I only remember seeing him spend time with one other person, and that was a bushy-haired girl who I believe was from Empor because she was only in Toopek now and again. I only saw Schram with her two or three times, and they always seemed to be talking about things in the forest and beyond. I always assumed he was just humoring her or just pleased to have a new opinion on something. They definitely were not close because he did not even know her name when I asked it. Besides that, I was his only close friend." Her tone changed, and she put a question back in Stepha's hands. "Why did you leave him at the fountain?"

Stepha looked toward Krirtie. "Do you love Schram?"

The question froze the human woman, and a desire to be anywhere but where she was came to her. She choked on a few replies then said, "I thought that I did once, but when someone never returns your feelings, you can start to loose sight of what they really are." She smiled. "Don't get me wrong, I will always love Schram, but as you are asking, I do not."

"What about Maldor then?" the elf returned. "I have seen how he looks at you."

This question caught Krirtie even more off guard than the previous one. She began to blush. "I do not know what you are talking about."

Stepha smiled but did not feel like letting it drop. "Sure you do. When you were injured, he never left you side. Even now he repeatedly looks back to make sure you are still near." She pointed ahead, causing Maldor to swing his head back forward when he realized his gaze had been caught. "You see."

"Well," replied Krirtie still blushing, "even if such a relationship did exist, which I assure you it does not, there would be the same life span problem that you have faced with Schram. Maldor is young, only fifty or so. He will live over two hundred years whereas I will be lucky to see seventy. How could I pursue such a desperate situation?"

"There are more important things than age," replied Stepha in a saddened voice, which was directed more into the air than to Krirtie.

"That is ironic to hear from you, don't you think?"

There was no answer from the elf as she only peered absently up the tunnel. They were under the river now, and a musty odor was in the air as water slowly dripped in various places. It became an echoing beat which banged off the tunnel walls in the two's newfound silence as both became absorbed in their own thoughts.

Krirtie turned to the elf, knowing it was time to dissolve this subject of conversation, but refusing to let one more question, which would not leave her mind, go unasked. "Stepha?"

The elf seemed to jump from a trance, and after blinking her large green eyes, she turned to the girl. "Yes?"

Her voice was much softer than it had been, and she now sounded more like a mother speaking to a child rather than two individuals measuring each other up. Krirtie relaxed at this and continued in a much more confident tone. "What is the small pouch elves carry with them?"

Stunned by the question, Stepha stared blankly toward the woman. After a short pause, she answered in a flat but caring tone, as if she was speaking with utmost feeling but still on a very serious subject. "It holds the most pureness of being anywhere on Troyf. Elves have always had the power to aid in passage because of their love for life. By sprinkling a small bit of this dust across one that is passed, their sole is prepared to be accepted by whatever realm its life's actions dictates that it takes. It is truly a most beautiful thing when one is well accepted."

Krirtie shook her head. "I have always been consumed with the power and beauty that I have felt when the acceptance takes place around me, but that is not the pouch I am referring to. I mean the one that elves carry for personal reasons, at least I believe it is personal."

"Our life pouch? How do you know about such a thing?" She had become quite intrigued and had stopped walking as they spoke.

The change had made Krirtie slightly uncomfortable, but she still wanted an answer. "Well, when Schram first met your brother in the Elvinott forest, Madeiris looked as if he was going to kill him. They were speaking elven, so I could only go by their actions regarding what was occurring, and I was certain Schram was at death's door until he pulled out this pouch and mentioned what I later learned to be your name. Madeiris's entire face changed as he looked at Schram and this life pouch as you called it. I was just wondering what exactly it was." She broke off and then quickly added, "Do not feel that you have to answer if it is private."

Stepha smiled deeply and spoke mostly to herself, "I had no idea he carried one." The elf's eyes lifted and brightened on the girl beside her. "Very few humans know about such things because they cannot fully understand elves' appreciation for life. Every elf has a small pouch, which they always keep with them. In it are kept their most cherished possessions that are known only to the one who holds it. Upon an elf's death, it is their last wish to have their pouch passed to the one whom they love like no other. If there was not time for the elf to disclose to whom his pouch was to be given, it goes to the king who will inspect each pouch, and from the contents, determine who it was meant for. Never have I known a human to carry one, but perhaps with each day, I learn a little more about how much Schram is really different from those with whom he finds his heritage." The two began walking again. "I am not surprised my brother did not speak of this to me," she added in a much lighter tone. "It is a sacred thing. You should not disclose to Schram what we have talked about. It is private between him and who he holds his pouch for."

Krirtie smiled. "I will not speak of it again."

Stepha returned her smile but was thinking only about the human ahead of her. "Come on, we should catch up to the others. Our talk has dropped us back, and it seems that Maldor is growing anxious with you so far behind," a crooked smile crossing her face as she said it.

The small group continued trudging forward, and all bickering between them had subsided as they became tired and excited about nearing Antaag. They came to a spot in the tunnel that forked to the right and left. Jermys turned to the group. "Okay, you most glorious travelers, it's your turn. Which way should we go?"

Maldor leaped ahead, drawing his sword and using it to point. "This way. It slopes upward and shows no further signs of water."

The dwarves raised their eyes and cheeks. "How 'bout you, human? Is the big man right?"

"No," he replied, much to Maldor's disapproval.

"Ah, then we will go down the other corridor?" Bretten replied.

"No, that would not be the smartest of choices," Schram stated as he took a step toward the dwarves.

Bretten appeared stunned. "What are you saying then? We have to go back?"

The corner of Schram's lip twitched just a bit, and the others looked at him questionably. In one quick motion, he scooped the little dwarf off the ground and to the astonished wide-eyed group behind, heaved him into solid rock.

Bretten screamed as he sailed through the air, approaching the stone, and then he disappeared through the barrier. "We will go that way," stated Schram obviously pleased with his discovery but not having a clue how he knew.

"Very good, human, you continue to surprise me," Jermys said while he studied the man before him more closely.

"Are you guys coming or what?" came a disgusted voice through the wall.

One after the other, the group stepped through the hidden passageway in the wall and disappeared. From there, it proved to be only a short jog to Antaag.

༺༻

"It is an honor to make your acquaintance, King Kapmann. I am Prince Schram of Toopek, and these are my companions." Schram had referred to himself as prince more times in the last eight days than he had in the last eight years, but he felt the times deemed it necessary. After introducing his friends, not bothering to try to explain the sleeping rat, Schram described their mission and need for a ship to travel down the river.

The king was a taller dwarf, as were all those in the southern mines. However, with the exception of the height, both groups were similar in nearly every respect. He carried the same white beard and mustache, both of which were curly with the beard resting on the floor as he sat. The pipe he always seemed to be puffing on stretched about twelve inches downward and then curled another four inches back up, and small circles of smoke rose out in rings above his head. His voice was rugged and deep, but his tone remained soft and open.

"I will find you a ship and crew, but I fear you might meet with trouble. The blizzard, which recently passed through, dropped the temperature as well as a large amount of snow, and although the river will still be moving rapidly, I am afraid that the lake may be too frozen to cross. However, we will get you safely to Gnausanne if nothing else. From there, you can get horses to continue to Draag."

"Thank you, Kapmann. We appreciate your assistance," Schram replied, somewhat surprised at the king's abrupt response. He eyed his actions and got an uncomfortable feeling that the dwarven king was hiding something. "When will the ship be ready?"

"Be at the river in the morning. It will be there. If you are not sure about the way, the twins can show you." He pointed to the doors. "Now please, leave me. I have much to do this eve."

The stunned group was led to their sleeping quarters where they all plopped down, tired and withdrawn. Schram raised his head and looked to the twins. "How well do you know King Kapmann?"

Bretten jumped up. "We know he is good, but beyond that, our contact has been minimal. Krystof has always spoken of Kapmann as being a superb king and able to lead his people to mine an extraordinary amount of precious stones."

"I sensed that he was hiding something," Schram said. "And also that he had been expecting us. Did any of your people scout ahead and announce our plans to Kapmann?"

Jermys now also rose to stand beside his brother. "No, we are the first to bring any message across the river by the tunnel in some time. He could not have been expecting us by any of the Feldschlosschen dwarves' doings."

"I do not want to sound distrustful, but in these times of evil, I prefer to be safe." All nodded and listened to Schram intently as he spoke. "Bretten, do you think you could sneak down the river and see if any ship is being prepared?"

"Aye, it shan't be a problem," he replied, his tone depicting nothing but seriousness as he understood the impact of having this situation be not as it appeared.

"Krirtie, why don't you and Maldor look around with the idea of getting some food. Get into things, and see what you can find out, but don't be too obvious. If someone says something, just say whatever is necessary." The two nodded and then smiled toward each other.

"I will keep guard on the room while Stepha and Jermys take first rest. If we are all agreed, then let's go, and you guys all be careful. Something is not right here, but it may actually be nothing important. However, if there does turn out to be a problem, we might be forced to leave quickly tonight."

"Begging your pardon, Schram," interrupted Jermys. "But I think the King may speak to me, without all of you surrounding him. If he is up to something, which I really do not believe, I can find out." He locked eyes on the human showing his level of seriousness. Schram looked reluctant and motioned his concern forward. "Very well, but don't get your hopes up. I felt deception in his actions. If you have any trouble, and that goes for everybody, come back here immediately, and we will take action, together. If evil is afoot, it is probably out of the dwarves control or even knowledge, and that level of evil cannot be fought alone. Together, we are strong, always remember that."

The group disbanded, each going to their designated positions. Stepha approached Schram after the others had left and kissed him deeply.

"What was that for, Stepha?"

"Just because, Schramilis," she replied in elven and then moved off to find some much-needed sleep, leaving the human with a smile reaching ear to ear.

Schram paced the floor. It had been over two hours, and he had received no word from any of his companions, and the waiting was becoming unnerving. He walked to the door to listen for any commotion as Maldor burst in slamming the door into Schram launching him through the air with a thump.

"Sorry Schram, are you all right?" asked the big maneth, moving with Krirtie over to help. Stepha, awakened by the commotion, also jumped up to help.

"I am fine," exclaimed Schram. "Tell me, what did you learn that brought you back in such haste?"

"In actuality, not that much I'm afraid. We found the kitchen and rustled up some food." Krirtie opened a sack bearing a large amount of various food. "However, anyone we tried to talk to avoided all questions regarding the evil of late. We did learn, while we drank dwarven ale with a group of miners, that they had been working twice as many hours lately to raise what they harvested, but when it came time to record their final take, none of this extra work showed up."

Schram had become focused on the talk of ale and did not hear the last statement. "Wait, say that again. I don't understand."

Krirtie responded as an annoyed look came over her face. "The dwarves told us they had been working twice as hard, mining twice as much, but when it came time to add up the total take, there was no difference from what it was before."

"I understand what you say, but I don't know what it means."

Maldor now broke in. "Haven't the others returned?"

"No, I have not heard from either of the twins, and I am starting to worry," answered Schram, the strain showing in his voice. "Especially for Jermys."

Bretten then stepped through the door, peering back down the hallway to see if he was being followed. His battle-axe was gripped tightly in his hand, and his face was ghostly white. After he was confident the hallway was clear, he turned to the companions. "We have to get out of here, now!"

"What is it?" asked Maldor also drawing his sword.

"The river is crawling with D.D.s. A group noticed me and did not ask any questions. They simply attacked."

Krirtie spoke up. "What is a *deez*?"

Schram took her arm. "They are an old separation of dwarves, which have followed the dark path, usually called dark dwarves or D.D.s. They have become simple soldiers for hire. If you have enough money, they will do just about anything." He paused and appeared lost in thought. "However, I find this extremely peculiar. They also would have no love for dragons, and I don't believe they would take up arms with them, nor have I ever heard of them attacking dwarves in general, at least as far as I know. Bretten, you probably are more familiar with dark dwarves than I. What do you think?"

The dwarf frowned. "I would never have guessed that dark dwarves would move against half of what I have seen them do. At this point, I have learned to never underestimate them."

Stepha looked around and then moved beside the others. "Regardless, it is apparent that Kapmann will not have a ship for us tomorrow. We must locate Jermys and get out of here as soon as possible."

Bretten looked up surprised. "Jermys has not returned? But I passed the king's chambers on my way back and saw the king sitting on his throne, alone."

Schram drew his sword. "That settles it then. We will give him a short while longer to return and use the time to get the rest of us a quick bite of food. If he does not return on his own, then we will search for him under Bretten's guidance since he knows this city of tunnels better than the rest of us."

The group ate quietly and anxiously. They jumped at any sound, hoping it to be Jermys breaking into the room. As time passed and it became obvious the dwarf twin was not going to return, they gathered their things and prepared to leave. Bretten's worry for his twin was evident, but his actions showed only that he was to act as leader through Antaag. His battle-axe was ready at his side as they took the hallway. The companions followed closely behind, with

Maldor bringing up the rear, his sword returned to his side and the comfort of his club gripped tightly in his hand.

"Where do you think we should go to look?" Schram asked the dwarf.

"If he were taken as a prisoner, then he would be taken to the dungeons in the far wing." He paused as he thought about how to continue. His words were painful, but he pushed them out. "However, if he were taken there, it would not be to our benefit to try to rescue him, he would be dead already."

The dwarf's words were hard, and his expression stoic, and Schram could feel the pain within him. He placed his hand on Bretten's shoulder. "Not the dungeons. There must be another place."

Bretten looked up into Schram's reassuring face. "I pray you are right. I am learning to trust your feelings."

"So am I," replied the human. "Where else could he be if he was being held captive?"

"I assume it would be in one of the rooms near where we came into the city. They have many small quarters there where friendly travelers can stay as they pass through. I assumed we would be placed there and was surprised when our room was put this deep in the castle halls. Usually, these other rooms are simply normal rooms, but I have heard that they have been used as holding cells if the situation called for it."

"That must be it. We were put in the castle so they could keep an eye on us. Jermys must have found something out, and he was moved there." Schram became more enthused. "How far are they?"

"Well, since we left our room, we have been traveling right for them, mainly because they are near a place we can exit the mines. I believe that they are right around the corner."

Stepha stepped forward and whispered to Schram and Bretten, "If they did take Jermys hostage, would they not be keeping an eye on us?"

"Yes," began Schram. "They already know we have left our rooms, and they probably know about our small groups that did the investigating earlier. We will definitely meet with resistance."

Bretten lifted his axe. "There is a group coming behind us. I can hear the echo off the walls. They are still a distance back however."

Schram lifted his sword. "There is a group ahead of us as well."

"Halt!" hollered a voice from ahead. "You are all under arrest by the King's order."

Maldor whispered forward, "There are only ten of them. I will cause a distraction, and you make a break for it with the group."

"Easy, my friend. I think it will be Bretten's lead we follow."

The dwarf had frozen with his hand gripped tightly on his axe handle and his eyes fixed on the approaching dwarves.

"Silence your whispers, slime," rang the lead dwarf.

In one quick motion, Bretten flung his battle-axe, opening the leader's chest like a book. With that, Schram and Maldor lunged forward, blocking the guard's axes with their armor and swords. The dwarven guard scattered as the two much larger warriors came bounding in with their swords flying. Those getting around Schram and Maldor were quickly taken by Krirtie or Stepha. The confrontation lasted only a few moments, and when it was over, every dwarf, including Bretten, was on the ground.

"Schram, come quick," the elf yelled, her voice piercing Schram's ears.

"Get your hands off me, elf. I am fine." Bretten was fighting to get away from Stepha and back on his feet. "Bloody lucky throw from the bastard."

"What happened?" asked Schram as he approached.

"What does it look like! I got shanghaied in the leg by a wandering throw," exclaimed the dwarf.

"It appears he took the blunt end of an axe in the leg," replied Stepha. "It will bruise, but he will live."

Maldor smiled at the fallen twin and reached his hand, which was actually the size of Bretten's entire head, down to help the dwarf to his feet. "Nice mark on the leader, little guy. Your brother would be proud."

The dwarf rose to his feet and gingerly put weight down as he said, "Let's find Jermys quickly. These guards were looking for us.

The ones behind are drawing more near, and whatever power directs them, there will be more coming. In larger numbers, we will not be able to defeat them."

"Hey, Bretten, is that your overexcited, belly-aching voice out there blabbing away?" shouted a voice from behind a door from ahead.

"Jermys?" shouted the twin.

"Who else? You ignorant, woolly-bearded rock eater," the voice returned. "Now come, and open this door before I die of boredom in here."

"Ignorant; woolly-bearded!"

A crack was heard as Krirtie slapped the offended little dwarf across the face, shutting him up. "Maldor," she exclaimed. "Break the door down."

All the other companions froze as Krirtie and Maldor approached the door. With one kick, the hinges buckled, and the door exploded from the walls.

"It is about time. I was—"

A second crack echoed through the hall when Krirtie's hand crossed the other twin's face in a bittersweet reunion. "Now let's get out of here. Bretten, lead the way."

The dwarf grumbled as he passed and, joined by his twin, they led the group to a tunnel which they followed away from the city. They met with only one area of resistance, and it ended as quickly as the first. They ran toward some nearby trees which marked the forest outside Antaag and plunged into the bushy outgrowths. Without a comment from anyone, they continued well into the woods at a pace to make the swiftest creature proud. Bretten and Jermys used their axes while Schram and Maldor broke through with sword and dagger.

"Did you learn anything from the king before you were arrested?" Schram asked Jermys.

"I did not even get to see him," the dwarf replied. "I got to the doorway to his throne room, and somebody slugged me from behind. Next thing I know, I heard fighting outside a locked door and then the voice of my brother."

Schram relayed what Bretten had witnessed at the river to the dismay of the other twin. The group sat in the black of night mystified about what they should do.

"We need to put more distance between us and Antaag," stated Maldor. "We still do not know exactly what is going on there or to what lengths they will go to capture us again."

Schram rose from where he sat against a large oak. "You are right, my friend. We will travel down the river a distance and then rest for the night. Hopefully, sometime tomorrow we will find a way to cross the river to get to Gnausanne. If not, we will have to travel either on around the lake by foot or head south and seek the help from the mountain elves."

Stepha now rose. "The wind and snow has stopped, and the temperature has risen slightly. I could probably fly ahead now on my own and seek out the elves."

"No," replied Schram. "Out of the question. Storms can roll in here in the blink of an eye, and I won't gamble your life on the weather. You know what could happen if you got caught in a storm." His voice now softened as he realized his reaction had been for many reasons other than the ones he was stating, and he did not want his feelings to appear as the driving force for his decisions. "Besides, I don't want us separating again unless it's absolutely necessary. We could all reach the mountain elves in an extra day by walking so not that much time would be saved. For now, we will all stay along the river."

Bretten stepped forward. "I am sorry, Schram, but I must leave." His twin's jaw dropped, and he started to say something, but Bretten raised his hand to silence him and continued in a strong tone. "I must return to Feldschlosschen and inform King Krystof about what we discovered in Antaag."

Schram's, as well as Jermys's, eyes softened, but it was the human who asked, "How will you get back across the river? You know the tunnel will be watched."

"I will make it," replied the dwarf flatly. "Jermys knows I must go. He understands, don't you, brother?"

"Yes I do, but there is no reason I should not be the one who goes."

"Ah, but there is. You are more familiar with this side of the river. I could lead them farther without problem, but you are the best choice. You know this as well as I do."

The discussion seemed to have its own conclusion as all parties accepted the reasoning behind the actions and understood why the dwarf must return home.

Maldor broke the silence. "I understand, my friend. Until we meet again."

"Until we meet again," replied Bretten.

"Take care, Bretten," stated Schram. "We will miss your company."

Krirtie and Stepha both nodded to the twin and gave him a soft little hug as his brother approached to stand beside his twin. "Guard yourself well, you stubborn dwarf. I will miss you, my brother."

"And take care of this band of misfits, as well as yourself." The two hugged, and then Bretten glanced toward the group. "Keep this bull-headed maverick in line. He can't even talk to a king without almost getting us killed." With that, he smiled and darted into the trees.

Jermys turned to the companions who all wore sympathetic expressions. "I have the worst feeling that I won't see that bloody dwarf again," he whispered as he tossed his battle-axe into a nearby tree. Schram said nothing, but the feeling had occurred to him as well, although something was different about it.

CHAPTER 12

Den-Hrube: The Dark Dwarf Captain

The group traveled hard the next day, seemingly refreshed after a sound night's sleep. They had taken turns keeping watch, and with the exception of a passing rabbit or other forest dweller, their night had been free of interruption. Schram felt uncomfortable about the lack of pursuit and wondered why Kapmann had not sent any. He knew the king had to know what direction they took when they ran, and if Kapmann really wanted them as captives, there would have been guards after them. *Why had none come?* He thought to himself. Schram did not want to over think what was happening, but he had a bad feeling about King Kapmann, a feeling that would not leave him.

Late in the morning, they stopped for a brief lunch and then trudged on, making it to where the Ozaky River fed into Lake Ozak's reservoir before nightfall. The water level was low, and large chunks of ice could be seen across its surface, but it still appeared passable by boat as freely moving water showed through the icy patches. A cold wind blew off the lake and bit the companions as they sat leaning their backs against the side of the riverbed exposed due to the low water level.

"This ground cut out by the river makes a comfortable chair," grumbled Maldor as he fell back against the side and kicked his huge maneth legs forward. "I could fall asleep right here, right now, if not for the hatred pushed forward from my empty stomach."

"Relax, big man, we'll get some food in just a while," Schram replied, smiling. "I want to find us a less accessible shelter for the night first. I am sure somewhere along here we will find a cave of some sorts. I was hoping the lake would either be flowing with smooth water or solid ice so we could simply raft or walk across respectively. As it is, we can do neither. It would take a much larger boat than we could build to make it through those ice patches."

Jermys added, "Bretten told me about the boats he saw at Antaag with the D.D.s. He said they were huge. I'll bet they would go through that ice like it wasn't even there."

Schram glanced at the small twin and could see the worry in his expression as he thought about his brother. "I don't know what role the dark dwarves are playing in this game, but I have a funny feeling we will know by the end of our journey. If we can't get across this river here, we will have to travel through the heart of dark dwarf-claimed territory. If this should end up the case, I have a funny feeling that we would not be considered invited guests."

Jermys smiled at that. He knew his dark cousins never had guests unless it was a financial benefit to do so, and even then, the alleged guests rarely left alive.

All had grown somewhat calm and silent until Stepha broke out in a hushed voice, "You were saying you wanted to know what the D.D.s were doing. It looks like we might be about ready to find out."

She pointed up the river toward a large vessel slowly floating down with the current. Many of the dark dwarves could be seen on the deck with their bald heads and beardless faces being a dead giveaway to their identification. "That's one of the boats Bretten told me about," whispered Jermys. "It's loaded full of precious stones from the Antaagian mines. See the short plump bald dwarf at the helm. That is Den-Hrube. He is one of the few D.D.s Bretten and I have had run-ins with before. He's a real prize. He would cut his own mother's throat if he thought he could make a profit by it. However, he is also one of the few dark ones that holds respect for all dwarves. He won't attack another dwarf kingdom unless provoked, but in the same respect, it doesn't take much to provoke him."

The companions hustled over to some cover near the water's edge where they could hide from the ship's sight but still observe its actions. As it approached the mouth of the river, the ship lowered its sails to slow as it met the ice. A crash rang out as the first contact was made, and a dwarven crewman fell overboard as the ship lunged sideways. Suddenly, another dwarf fell, and the deck of the ship went into chaos.

"We're under attack!" hollered the helm's man as he violently turned the wheel to swing the port bow forward to face the attackers and, as was the case, the companions.

"Attack?" questioned Maldor. "From where?"

The group peered back into the forest beyond the dry riverbed and saw the same motionless trees as before. Stepha pointed. "There, did you see that movement? It looks like…more dark dwarves?"

"Why would they attack their own? And why was this attack so short?" Maldor put forward.

"It doesn't matter," returned Schram. "We are sitting ducks out here between the two. I am certain that those in the forest have seen us. For our own safety, we have to find a time to move."

Suddenly, the trees exploded as dark dwarves rushed from the trees, releasing arrows toward the boat. Those on board answered with their own display of arrows and catapults, but they too were outnumbered. The sky was so full of fire that it seemed one could walk across the flow of arrows.

The onslaught of attacking dwarves seemed unconcerned by the small group between them and the water. Their attacks were centered on overtaking the boat. The companions took arms and fought to hold against those dwarves who engaged, but slowly, they were being pushed back to the water's edge. Many of the dark dwarves carried small rafts to be used to attack and board the larger ship, and Schram motioned to the group, pointing to one small band carrying a raft. The others understood without comment, and in moments, the offensive was in motion. From first impact, the fighting was fierce. The dwarves were caught by surprise, but with their numbers, they quickly recovered. Twice Schram was dropped to the ground only to have one of his friends kill the attacker from behind. All members of the group were injured and bloody, but with Maldor's final sweeping sword and club, the dark dwarves released control over the raft and began to be pushed back. Schram saw other dwarves taking notice to the side battle and turn to aid their comrades. He hollered to Jermys and Stepha, and while the others fended off the barrage of arrows, the elf and dwarf loaded the raft into the water. Maldor fought off several dwarves on his own, giving everyone time to board the rickety vessel. When Stepha's arrow lodged deep in the last attacker's chest, the maneth turned and leaped with a violent force and deep grunt into the raft.

Several shields were placed to protect against the flight of arrows, and the group began to evaluate what the situation was. The battle on the ship had grown even more bloody, and because they had had to run upstream to recover the raft, the companions now were drifting straight into the heat of the fight. Maldor dropped his shield and began trying to row to avoid what he could foresee ahead. However, his piercing roar echoed over the water as an arrow bit into his thigh. Krirtie shifted next to the maneth and used her shield to protect both of them while Stepha and Schram answered the attack with arrows of their own in both directions, toward the boat and the shore. Jermys moved quickly around the little boat, swinging his axe at those who had been thrown into the water or were swimming from the shore to attack. Schram saw the dwarves on the ship being quickly overtaken by those of the forest, and he feared that if control changed hands too quickly, then the attack could turn and would then be centered on the five of them.

"Starboard, Maldor, starboard!" hollered Schram trying to compete with the noise from the battle. "Get to the other side of the ship. It will shield us from those on the land."

The big maneth dug the oars deep as his blue blood oozed from several places on his rough body. Slowly the boat turned perpendicular to the current and made its way to the far side of the dark dwarves' ship. Still many attacked the companions' small raft from the sides, but Jermys hacked violently with his axe, sometimes hitting the attacker aside while other times he opened their bald skulls to the river. Stepha could now center her arrows directly toward the larger boat, and soon, bleeding and dead dwarves were collapsing overboard.

The battle had definitely favored those dwarves attacking from the forest, and as they launched the hacked and bloodied body of the former captain overboard, they took charge and control of the ship. Luckily, they remained unconcerned regarding the small raft except the return of mild bow-fire, and soon, the larger ship was being maneuvered straight toward the near bank, beaching it on the side. Ropes immediately reached the sandy ground, and as Maldor pushed their little craft away, the companions could see the precious cargo of stones quickly being off-loaded.

"Schram," hollered Jermys, pointing over the side. "Their captain lives."

The human peered in the direction and saw one of the dark dwarves from the ship flailing slightly in the water. "Maldor, can you slow us down a bit?"

"I will try," he replied, but the pain he was feeling slurred his words.

The boat gradually began to fight the rapidly moving water, and with the dwarf and elf holding one hand, Schram reached out and grabbed the now unconscious body bobbing in the water. With one mighty pull, he heaved the dwarf into their boat, causing the tiny raft to rock down and then return level.

"Okay, Maldor, if you are able, get us out of here, then get us to the other side."

"I will try, Schram."

With that statement, Schram glanced at the maneth for the first time since they entered the boat. He was shocked by the amount of blood that flowed from both of the maneth's arms and the sight of the arrow still protruding from his leg. "Hold your stroke, Maldor. I will take over."

"I am fine," he blurted out weakly as his body began to hunch over.

"Krirtie, help me move him to where he can lie down. I will guide the boat." Schram moved beside the big man whose mane even began showing signs of blood as his helmet was knocked from his head. Together, he and Krirtie helped Maldor situate himself along the floor of the raft, and Stepha began working on his arrow wound.

Schram then took control of the oars, and Krirtie moved to inspect Maldor's upper injuries, much to the big maneth's displeasure.

Twice Schram heard Krirtie or Stepha say, "This won't hurt a bit," followed by the piercing roar of a maneth in pain. He was extremely glad that he had only sustained minor cuts as he looked at Jermys, realizing that the dwarf, although appearing obviously seasick already, felt the same way.

Since the switching of positions, Jermys had stood like a pirate guarding treasure over the unconscious body of the one he knew as Den-Hrube. The pathetic-looking creature had not even flinched a muscle, but the little dwarf stood with his bloodstained battle-axe at the ready.

Schram's stroke was not as deep as Maldor's had been, but the strong human had little difficulty navigating the river's current and pushing them across the several mile stretch to the other side. Schram had glanced back a couple of times to make sure the D.D.s had not decided to follow. To his pleasure, they seemed completely engrossed with their newfound treasure. By the time the group finally reached the northern shore, the sun had dropped until a brilliant crimson burst had filled the sky. The weary travelers beached their vessel and helped the wounded to the embankment.

"There is a small cave up ahead," shouted Jermys, glad to be off the water. "I will start a fire and get Maldor situated."

"Fine," replied Schram. "How is the…dwarf?"

Jermys glared at the human. "I am not skilled as such, but by my best estimation, if his wounds don't kill him, the cold bite of the water surely will."

"Get him in front of the fire as well," said Schram, obviously upset by Jermys' poor prognosis. "We need that ogre to talk."

Stepha and Krirtie helped the dwarf lug the two over to the fire while Schram scouted the area for any signs of possible visitors. Then he returned, grabbing more firewood in the process.

"How is everyone?" he asked, entering the crude excuse for a cave that Jermys had discovered.

"We are all fine," responded Krirtie. "Maldor didn't look too well, but as soon as we gave the big baby some food, he grumbled in pleasure and fell right to sleep. He will probably be sore and cranky in the morning, but he will live." She completed her thought with a silent prayer and smiled at the peaceful bulk of weapons beside her.

"How about our fine captain?" Schram asked, turning to Jermys who still stood suspiciously over the dark dwarf.

"He does not move," the dwarf replied. "But I have seen these crafty bastards play dead for hours only to leap up when you're not expecting it. I say we kill him outright now. That way we are sure."

"I don't think he'll live," entered Stepha somewhat surprised by Jermys' acceptance of death, something not part of dwarves' normal makeup. "But we won't bring about his death either!" She glared toward the dwarf who took no notice to the response.

"Stepha is correct," returned Schram. "We need that dwarf to tell us what was with that ship." He looked toward Jermys. "You keep first watch. If he or anything else stirs, wake me immediately. Otherwise, I will see you in three hours to switch. Now, let the rest of us eat and try to get some sleep. We have had a long day."

The group slept the night without a stir from their captive or anything else for that matter. In the morning came the question of what to do. Maldor had woken, and although he felt as if he had died and was now walking the world in the afterlife, he said he would be able to travel. It was only a half day's travel to Gnausanne, the fabulous gnome city where the companions hoped to get horses to facilitate their journey to Draag, but transporting the unconscious dwarven body of Den-Hrube would greatly hamper their time.

"I say we chop the bloody bastard's head off," exclaimed Jermys. "Then our problems would be solved."

As Maldor nodded in approval, Stepha shot the pair a piercing frown. Schram rose and threw another log on their dwindling fire. "No, we will give him until noon. If he still does not wake, then we will leave him to live or die. Let it be his decision."

"I heartily disagree," stated Jermys firmly. "This vile creature tried to kill us, and letting him live will only give him another opportunity."

"I agree with the dwarf," added Maldor despairingly.

Schram looked down, seemingly unsure for a moment as his friends questioned his decisions, and then he returned confident once again. "You both are forgetting that we do not even know if this vile creature is even our enemy. After all, it was his own people that put him in this condition in the first place."

The dwarf glared. "Let me assure you, human, he is our enemy. Scum like this has no friends. His actions, as well as those he led, are to serve only their needs. He just did the one thing dark dwarves swear to never do, he trusted his own people, and they betrayed him."

"Does that mean that the dwarves of Antaag have joined forces with the dark dwarves? Are they too now our enemy?"

Schram's words shot like a dagger. "I trust your words are in good faith and not meant to strike me a blow." Jermys stared long at the human standing hard and tall before him. "It would be a shame to take to arms against one I call a friend."

A silence filled the small cave as the two locked eyes, neither flinching a muscle as they gazed fixedly and intently upon the other.

"Ah, perhaps there is some hope for you yet, Jermys of Feldschlosschen," echoed a weak, grating voice from the side. "A mining dwarf who combats his leader. Truly an intriguing situation."

In a wink, Jermys had drawn his axe and wheeled around, placing it at their captive's throat. With the same speed and agility, Schram had moved, and his sword tip rested against the dark dwarf's chest, right above his heart. Both were stunned at the other's quickness, but this surprise was absent from their expressions.

"Ha ha ha ha," rang the deep rustic laugh of Den-Hrube as a small amount of blood trickled from his lips. "I should not have spoken for indeed a good fight it would have made."

"I told you this sewer rat was playing dead. Next time you will not be so quick to rule my opinion out. Let me cut one of his legs off to teach him a lesson."

Maldor, Krirtie, and Stepha were quiet, completely caught by surprise by the whole affair. The wounded dwarf again filled the small cave with his laughter. "Go ahead, Jermys, give it your best swing. You know I will not help your pitiful band. Your group is as good as dead already."

Jermys looked infuriated as he raised his axe. "So be it, you traitor to everything but yourself."

He began his swing, causing Den-Hrube's eyes to grow wide with adrenaline. Krirtie and Stepha turned away while Maldor bowed his head. The blade of the axe pushed inches from the dark dwarf's curled black nose before Schram intercepted it, locking it in his grips. "No! Not yet!"

"What's the matter, human? Don't you have the stomach for a little blood?" Den-Hrube had turned his eyes upon Schram. "Or maybe you just talk a good game, and when push comes to shove, you are more yellow than your exterior appears." Turning back to Jermys, he added, "What kind of bastards have you surrounded yourself with now? You are nothing but a—"

His chatter was cut off as Schram's fist struck across Den-Hrube's face with such a force as to bring Schram to his knees and spray a stream of coagulated dwarven blood across the arch of the cave. Schram stood back up and wiped the blood from his knuckles. "I wish to know about your ship and your dealings with King Kapmann at Antaag."

The dark dwarf spit a ball of blood at the warrior above him. "And I thought Kapmann was a fool—"

Jermys lodged his boot deep between their captive's legs and added, "I don't think that was the answer he was looking for, Hrube. You might want to restate your reply."

"And who are you that I should help?" His voice now broke often as more blood was garbled in his throat. "A dwarf and human who would fight to the death, two women who look as battered and beaten as a tigon's breakfast, and a maneth who looks as if he was fathered by an ogre. No, I would sooner be a rat's dinner than a group of nomads informant."

Maldor's body twitched as the dwarf had spoken of him. He drew his sword and slowly approached the crumbled figure before him. Den-Hrube issued a grimacing smile. "Yes, you pathetic ogre, come and join the party."

Maldor stood above the beaten figure and then glanced toward Schram. The human made no attempt forward and even stepped closer to Jermys. Maldor reached down and grabbed a fistful of the dark dwarf's skin. Lifting the creature above his head, he filled the room with a deep growling declaration uncommon for even his rough exterior. "Then let your last wish be answered."

With his free hand, he held his sword vertically below Den-Hrube's throat, causing the dwarf's eyes to display their first sign of an emotion similar to fear. With one twist of the maneth's hand, Maldor released the body, letting it fall the length of his sword. As Den-Hrube's head struck the hilt, Maldor thrust his arm upward, severing the dwarf's head from his body. "But I don't think a rat would have you!"

Not a word was spoken while the group gathered their belongings to head toward Gnausanne. They each had thoughts obscured with the sight of Maldor's action against the dwarf, but Schram and Jermys also were consumed by their behavior toward each other. Both wished forgiveness, but neither was able to ask for it. The weary travelers had already had a full day of excitement, but they all knew that they had a mission, which could not wait for better times. The fact was that better times might not ever be coming, at least without their help. Without a word, they headed toward the city of gnomes.

The tension in the days' walk seemed to grow with each wordless step they took. They would jump and draw weapons at any sound, even one made by themselves. Then came the embarrassing smile and the replacement of weapons before returning to their passage.

Finally, they sighted the gnome city on the horizon, and the group seemed to relax. Their shortest journey yet had taken years in their minds. The silence had never been broken, and although Schram did not know what he was going to say, he did know that something had to be done.

He began slowly, grabbing for any word that would come. "I am sorry, friends, and especially to you, Jermys. I acted irresponsibly, following my anger and not my head. The dwarf looked down and then started to speak but Schram raised his hand, silencing him. "No, please let me finish. Den-Hrube's final minutes were dark and bitter, but also necessary. Each of us saw a side of ourselves we rarely let out, but it is important to remember that side exists. It keeps us in balance with who and what we are and what we are trying to accomplish. When Den-Hrube spoke his last statement, there was nothing more I wanted than to see his pathetic body stripped of all life. However, when it was all over, my anger with him was not satisfied. That is what I am capable of feeling, and it scares me." He stopped and saw that the entire group appeared to be feeling the same.

"I too am sorry and ashamed," stated Jermys. "We are all friends, and as the times grow worse, should only be drawn closer and stronger."

"Well said," replied Krirtie, grabbing Stepha's arm and walking closer to the others. "We are five, plus Fehr," she added smiling, "who are becoming one. From this point forward, let's remain safe with that knowledge and know that our new friends will always be with us."

The group smiled at each other and formed one large circle linking their arms, giving each a newfound peace and power. The pace following that break was much quicker and lighter as idle chatter filled much of the final distance. Still, a slight tension from the morning's activities floated amid their minds, but it had been successfully pushed aside by the ever-growing bonds between each of them.

They arrived in Gnausanne well into the afternoon and were very pleased to see that it appeared the evil of late had not touched this small city. Perhaps there was nothing redeeming about it, and it was well-known that the gnomes would offer no resistance to any force. It just wasn't in their makeup. After grabbing a bite to eat and getting a room, the travelers decided to indulge in some of the extraordinary specialties the city had to offer. However, each discovered they could take only so much wine, cheese, and chocolate before they felt tired and sick, so they soon retired for a restful night of sleep. In the morning, they decided they would nose around for information and try to find some horses or cervues to continue to Draag.

CHAPTER 13

Gar Swamp

"These gnomes are so nice," stated Krirtie. "I can't believe that they are cousins to those awful trolls we've run into."

Maldor smiled. "Aye, the maneth have traded with them much over the years for the exotic food they possess. Besides their kindness, they are also trusting and honest but by no means ignorant. It would indeed be a sorrowful merchant who sought to cheat a gnome."

"I hope the others are finding out more than we are about our needs. With the exception of seeing that group of trolls in the bar, this entire city seems unconscious to the threat of the dragons." Krirtie looked around. "I see no evidence of anything out of the ordinary here, not that I would know what ordinary around here would be," she added with a smile and soft laugh.

"You have a beautiful laugh," the maneth said softly as he stared into the human woman's eyes. "I believe you could bring sunshine to the grayest of skies."

Krirtie blushed as she hugged the huge man before her. "You are the special one, Maldor." She was about to say more, then stopped and just enjoyed the way he felt pressed against her body. "Come on." She separated but remained gripping his large hand tightly, her fingers barely able to reach around his. "We should find the others and see if they have gotten the horses."

Maldor returned with a squeeze of his hand, and the two headed back to the inn. As they approached, they heard the exaggerated hollers of a dwarf fighting to control a bongo on which he rode. The reddish-brown antelope stood about four feet high at the shoulder and had vertical white stripes and spirally twisted horns that flailed wildly as the violently kicking Jermys was tossed frantically into an adjacent water trough emitting a large splash.

The soaking dwarf rose, steaming from the cool bath, which came nearly up to his belt as he stood. Reaching for his battle-axe, the infuriated dwarf shouted, "this beast is breakfast!"

"Hold it," shouted Schram running toward the trough, laughing harder with each step. The drenched dwarf stood with pride as his beard soaked up water like a sponge. "That bongo cost too much to have your foul temper settled with one swing." His laugh drew a condescending snicker as his tone changed. "It all deals with how you approach the animal." Schram also had never been on the back of a bongo, but he had spent many days on the back of a horse and was certain there would be little difference. Grabbing the reigns of the largest antelope-like creature, he swung one foot over and rested on the animal's back. "There, you see, nothing to it."

"I did that, you stupid barbarian. Try and make those beasts move somewhere. Then, you'll see the light."

"At least it won't be the water I see," he stated, further taunting the dwarf. Jermys had climbed out of the trough but had not lowered his axe or began drying himself off. He only stared into Schram's smiling face. The human shook his head in disbelief. "Really, Jermys, it's no big deal." With that, he issued a short sidekick to the creature.

The bongo leaped with a fury unfounded, kicking its hind legs over twice its height in the air and then bounding back with a front kick to match it. One savage turn and twist later and Schram was flailing wildly through the air, finding a final resting spot at Jermys's feet. Without delay, the dwarf dumped what was left of the entire trough across the human's face and body. "Now that is something to laugh at!" the dwarf exclaimed.

They both stared at the animals with hatred while those around laughed heartily at the sight. A soft, caring voice greeted Schram's ear next as Stepha drew beside him. "Dear boys, you should never kick a bongo. They take it as a sign of aggression. They don't like aggression." The elf walked up to one of the antelopes and placed her hand between its horns, scratching it gently. With a slight nod, the bongo knelt on its legs so the elf could climb on its back. With a soft note from her almost-magical voice, the antelope bounded forward as gracefully as a bird in flight.

"Everyone is a show-off," grunted Jermys. "Imagine her calling me a boy. I am 175, no, I mean 150 years older than that girl, and she calls me a boy. She is lucky I don't…"

His voice trailed off when Schram, still sitting, put his arm around the dwarf's shoulder and said, "I know, my friend. Believe me, I know."

"You look as bad as I have ever seen you, Schram," stated Krirtie smirking slightly as she spoke. "And keep in mind, I have seen you look pretty bad."

"Thanks," he replied, scraping the mud off his armor while climbing to his feet. "You are always one to have a kind word for a humiliated soul."

The four stood together, exchanging grins as Stepha slowly made her way back down the road toward them. Maldor had been looking slightly uncomfortable since first seeing the bongos even with his newfound pleasure of Krirtie's touch. He spoke in a questioning voice, "Pardon me for asking, Schram, but there is five of us, not counting Fehr, and I only see four bongos, not that I would be able to ride one anyway as I am sure I outweigh them by twofold."

He smiled at the troubled maneth. "Yes, we thought of that. We believed that you would probably break the animal's back should you try to ride for too long, so we pursued an alternate idea."

"An alternate idea?" he asked inquisitively.

"Yes, it was mostly Jermys's expert bargaining, but the farmer we dealt with threw in an extra animal, free of charge I might add, that should do well for you."

"Free of charge?" returned Maldor as his eyes narrowed, and he released Krirtie's hand. "Where is this extra animal?"

Jermys could barely keep still as the anticipation grew within him. Schram fought to keep his expression straight. "Well actually, the gnomes at the outskirts of town would not let us bring it into the city, so we left it tied to a large oak. But don't worry. It is on our way out so we can pick it up on the way, and there is no chance anyone would ever try and steal it because…well, just because."

"But I would give it a more than fair chance of pulling the tree down to escape. After all, the trunk was only about two feet at the base," Jermys laughed out loud as he spoke.

Maldor began to show his growing displeasure, and his tone displayed his concern. "Am I to then guess that it is not a horse you have for me?"

"A horse?" repeated Schram. "No, it is not a horse." Now everyone started to smile even though they did not know what was going on. "Don't worry, big man. We have much to discuss before we leave. If you're really lucky, night will come quickly, and we won't head out until tomorrow." Schram motioned to Stepha to join them inside when she returned from her still-graceful gallop through town.

She answered with a wave of her own, and as the bongo leaped forward, the rest of the group went back into the inn, Maldor mumbling under his breath with each step. Once Stepha joined them at the table, ales were ordered all around and the group, relaxed for the first time in a long while, sat and joked about the morning's activities.

Finally, they began to idly fall off into singular smiles, and Schram's face grew serious and saddened. "I think it would be wiser to stay another night here and enjoy what relaxing moments we can because our journey from here becomes much more hazardous. Stepha was able to find out that large goblin forces have been seen marching through the forests toward the Gar Swamp. Even with the warm front, which seems to have entered the lake country, it does not appear that it will be sufficient to raise the temperatures enough to make boat travel through the icy waters possible, so we must go by land. The freedom from cold will be our blessing however because according to what Stepha learned, the number of goblins and trolls could rival two thousand."

A somber look struck the group while Schram continued. "The one good note in this is that due to the large number and their direction, we can assume that the maneths and elves were successful in their attempt to retake Toopek, and these are the goblins fleeing that attack."

"Then perhaps they have learned what happened to my father," stated Krirtie slamming a goblin dagger into the wooden table.

Maldor looked up to Schram, and both men bowed their heads, asking for forgiveness for what they knew one of them had to say. Breaking the brief period of silence, which had left Krirtie wondering what was going on, Schram slowly formulated his words. "I also feel it is time that we all are brought to know all that has happened thus far."

Krirtie looked up from where she had been staring at her dagger and gazed fearfully at Schram and then toward Maldor. "What? What do you know?" she asked sternly.

"You never questioned why the elves attacked us when we approached," Schram began. "For this, I was glad. However, there was a reason, and I think it is time you learned it." He swallowed hard, and he fought to find the right words. Krirtie's face grew cold as she seemed to fear what was to come from her friend's mouth. "Several days before we arrived in Elvinott, there was an attack where—"

"Wait a minute," interrupted Maldor. "I will be the one to tell her." Not waiting for an objection, the maneth stood and took Krirtie's arm, leading her outside.

All was quiet at the table. Each of the companions knew what this knowledge could bring upon someone. The silence seemed to be contagious to the other tables as well, and only when a shattering scream broke through the door, did anyone move, and then it was to only bow their heads again.

Stepha rose and walked toward Schram who was totally oblivious to her movement. He jumped when she placed her delicate hand on his shoulder and gently kissed his cheek. "I am truly sorry, Schram, but she had to be told. You know that as well as anyone. I am going to return to my room but ask that you join me when you are ready. I do not wish to be alone this night." After issuing another soft kiss, she walked to the stairs and then disappeared.

"I too will retire," said Jermys watching Schram's gaze. "Tell Krirtie my thoughts are with her."

Schram nodded to the small dwarf as he left the table. His world once again grew quiet. He poured the rest of his ale down his throat and slammed his empty mug down, shattering it across the solid wood of the tabletop. Schram looked around, quickly realizing what he had done and prepared to apologize to any who questioned it, but none did.

The short gnome tending the bar walked over and quickly brushed the broken glass aside, replacing it with a full mug of ale. "Here," he said in an understanding voice. "This one is on the house."

Schram nodded appreciatively. Krirtie and Maldor then reentered the inn, and following a quick hug, the maneth turned and went up the stairs to his room, only winking to Schram as he passed.

Krirtie slowly approached the table, and Schram saw the redness around her eyes depicting recent tears. She sat beside her human friend of nearly twenty years and without a word fell into his arms as the tears again began to flow. "I'm sorry," was all Schram could mumble as he too fought to ward off the feelings of sadness he was feeling for her loss and the possibility that his parents had been destined for the same fate.

She pushed herself up and wiped her eyes as she softly spoke, "There is nothing for you to be sorry about. Maldor helped me understand your motives for not telling me, and indeed, they were honorable. I will be all right." She placed her hand to Schram's cheek. "I have my old best friend in you and many new friends as well. I would be foolish not to lean on that wall when I need support."

Schram stared into his companion's eyes. "You are truly an incredible woman. I am beginning to understand just how intelligent Maldor is."

She smiled back to him as she removed her goblin sword and armor, placing it next to the dagger still lodged in the table. "I don't think I want to wear this armor anymore. If possible, may we purchase some before we leave tomorrow?"

"Sure," he replied. "It may not be easy to find a proper fit, but you're about the same size as a big gnome, so we should be able to find you something."

She smiled toward him and without another word returned to her room. Schram remained alone at the table, consumed in his own thoughts. As he finished his last ale, he rose, and tossing a few gold coins on top of the pile of goblin armor, he retired to Stepha's room.

―――

The next morning was by no means a joyous one. However, as the companions mounted their bongos, it became apparent that there was going to be some humor in this day's journey. They bid farewell to the few gnomes who had helped them, and the three rode slowly down the street followed by Maldor on foot and Jermys wildly being tossed about.

As they reached the outskirts of the city, a loud gulp rose from deep within Maldor's throat when his eyes fell upon his stag. Tied to a huge oak tree was an enormous cervu. This elk-like creature stood seven feet at the shoulder, and its antlers went another five higher. However, it was not the animal's size or its magnificent antlers that shook Maldor, but the foam that oozed between its lips as it struggled to free itself from the rope holding it to the tree. It noticed the group approaching and did not try to hide its violent temper, beginning to kick wildly as the group drew closer.

"Suddenly, my bongo doesn't seem so bad," came Jermys's little voice.

Maldor looked up to Schram, almost pleading with him to find another answer but knowing that there was not one forthcoming. He hesitantly approached the big animal, trying to make eye contact to calm it, drawing on all he knew from his maneth ways to befriend the creatures of the forest. As he drew nearer, the cervu quit kicking and became amazingly passive, making even Stepha become impressed. Maldor stroked the elk's coat and turned back to his friends who had also moved closer. "It will be all right. We have reached an understanding."

With a whack, the maneth hit the ground, and a sharp pain erupted down his back where the animal's antlers had struck. "What is that understanding?" hollered Jermys laughing. "He's the boss?"

Maldor grunted and jumped back up to face the large animal before him, which also seemed to be smiling. Without a word to it, he leaped on the elk's back, and releasing it from the tree, they plunged into the trees with unbelievable speed and agility. "Come on, dwarf. Catch me if you can."

With that, the group of riders at the edge of the forest leaped forward and entered the trees down the path left from Maldor's passage.

They made excellent time behind the maneth's lead as it was barely approaching midday, and they had already entered the soft marshy grounds marking the edge of the gar swamp. Various grunts and moans could be heard from the dwarf as he fought to control the wild beast on which he rode. They had been free of incidence but had however passed many slain gars and goblins alike. Within the last five hundred yards alone, they had seen at least ten bodies hacked into oblivion.

Maldor halted his huge stag and bounded down to the ground, giving the cervu time to rest. The others soon caught up with the maneth, and seeing him on the ground with his sword drawn, they quickly did the same and joined him. "What is it?" asked Schram following Maldor's stare.

He quickly realized how his standing with his sword drawn and raised must appear to the others, and the maneth dropped it to his side. "I am sorry to have alarmed you. I have been riding with my sword at the ready since we passed the first gar. I guess I forgot that I was holding it as such. I am only wishing to rest my stag. He has been having a slight bit of difficulty fighting through the spongy ground, and I think that it will be better to walk them through the swamp. We will want them fresh when we reach the plains."

"Oh, walk them," sounded a tired and beaten dwarven voice from behind the others. "I was just beginning to get this beast under control."

"You look a little worse for the wear, Jermys. I've been waiting for you to join me at the lead." Maldor's deep voice carried a small spite of humor.

The dwarf dropped from his antelope and replied, "I felt my presence would be more importantly fulfilled guarding our rear flank."

The maneth smiled and nodded, allowing Jermys to keep what pride he still had. Schram looked about the area questionably, and then satisfied that they were in no immediate danger, he replaced his bow to his back. With that, Stepha followed suit, and Krirtie slid the shiny curved scimitar sword that they had purchased from a bushy haired peddler before they left into its scabbard. Maldor remained with his sword hilt in hand as did Jermys with his axe, though his was directed toward the bongo.

Schram finally said, "We will grab a quick lunch and rest our mounts as Maldor has suggested. Then we will continue on foot through the swamp unless walking becomes too difficult whereas we will then ride across the deep spots."

The companions nodded in approval, and Maldor began passing around different amounts of the dried foods he carried. The warmth that had been felt in Gnausanne had left the swamp, and the group also used this opportunity to better weather themselves against the cold. They all had briefly inspected some of the gar bodies that they had passed and knew that their death had occurred many days earlier. Stepha had aided passage to each of them as she rode but this level of pointless death was hard for the elf.

Krirtie noticed an extra deep sadness occurring in Stepha's eyes, and since she had learned how deeply elves value life, she assumed this was the origin of her pain. However, she also noticed the same mourning in Schram's face as he sat silently beside the elf with his arm on her shoulder. She remembered what she had overheard King Hoangis tell Schram when they were speaking alone after the feast. Laughingly he had said, *Like I said before, somehow some elf blood flows within your veins.* As Krirtie looked at her human friend, she believed it to be true.

The companions traveled at a much-slower pace now as they trudged through the slop of the swamp. The blackened water came up to Jermys's neck in many places, and Schram moved closer to the dwarf just in case he hit a low spot. Krirtie removed Fehr from her pouch as he frequently was submerged below the water level. The rat never stirred at these movements as he had entered deep into his hibernation.

The group stopped abruptly as Maldor flashed a warning with his sword. Schram moved ahead to view what the maneth saw. "Look," said Maldor pointing. "There are some more goblins and another glowing globe."

"How many do you estimate altogether?" asked Schram as Krirtie, Stepha, and Jermys joined the two up front.

"I would say one hundred, maybe two," returned the maneth. "And I only see two of those floating light balls."

Stepha's face froze on one of the balls. "Those look like the balls the hooded human turned into when I saw them before."

That statement knocked Krirtie a blow as she thought about her father and what she had learned the night before. Everyone was silent as they watched the migrating group ahead of them. Finally, Schram whispered, "We will lie low here until they pass. Keep a sharp eye out, but if we are discovered, we are as good as dead. They have too many goblins with them, not to mention the magicians. Indeed we must remain quiet and still."

The companions stood motionless for several hours as the seemingly endless band of goblins pushed its way through the swamp. Twice Maldor's mount flustered about, and twice he had quickly urged it to calm. The second time, the animal had taken longer to relax, and Schram feared that if it stirred again, it might become necessary to kill the elk rather than risk being detected.

Gradually however, the troops in front of them thinned and then diminished altogether. Several small bands still followed, but for the most part, the danger had passed. Schram signaled to the others to come closer. In a whispering voice he said, "We are going to turn more northwest and try to get around that mass of travelers. I estimate there were probably five or six hundred of them, and they are stretched over several miles. I am also amazed that they are controlled so well as to never break formation. Whatever leads them has definitely got a firm control on their feeble minds. Anyway, I think they will remain heading southwesterly and attempt to clear the swamp and reach the river tonight. We, on the other hand, can work through to the plains of Nakton and, then hopefully, tomorrow hit the foothills of Draag."

The group nodded to the plan, and they slowly boosted their stags ahead, breaking the cramps that had grown in their joints. The pleasure of moving again, even through such a sad and desolate place as the swamp, gave the group a hidden comfort. They only met with two stray bands of four and three goblins respectively, and none of them would be able to relay any message to those ahead as they sank into the black mud of the swamp.

They rode for another hour across the long flat rolling hills of the plains of Nakton as the sun began to dip beneath the horizon. There were no caves of any sort on the plains, but the weary travelers stopped beneath one of the few clumps of trees they found dotting the landscape. Beside it was a small hot spring, which they found even more enjoyable than the comfort of the tree cover. After starting a small fire and getting a good warm meal, the companions retired, taking their normal order for watch.

CHAPTER 14

BOREWORM: THE SEPARATION

The next morning, Maldor rose with a soft roar to greet the newfound warmth that was attacking the land. The temperature had been rising steadily the last two days, and with the exception of the cold they experienced while in the swamp, traveling was becoming much more pleasant. However, all knew how quickly that could change, and a blizzard like the one they faced near the Feldschlosschen mines could blanket the unprotected plains. Therefore, the warmer weather was truly a blessing from the gods in Schram's eyes as the bright light caused him to stir from his night's rest. All the companions now were up and about making ready to greet another day of travel, except for Krirtie, that is, who remained motionless by the fire. Maldor moved and lightly stroked her long black hair to wake her from her sleep but then paused and just smiled at her, deciding to let her rest as much as possible.

Stepha and Schram prepared a light breakfast while Jermys and Maldor took to readying the animals for today's ride. While the food was being completed, Schram sent Stepha over to wake Krirtie. He almost dropped the meal into the fire when the elf screamed and began shaking the woman to wake her.

The elf's yell brought everyone running but none faster than the large maneth, who nearly knocked over his cervu to get by it. "What is it?" he exclaimed as he approached the two knelt over the human woman.

"I don't know," returned Schram. "She appears to be unconscious."

"What's that?" asked the maneth, reaching his huge hand down to a point on Krirtie's arm and pinching a large white worm between his fingers.

"Don't, Maldor!" hollered Stepha. "Release it immediately."

The stunned maneth released the worm, and both he and Schram arched their heads back as they watched it slide back into a hole it had chewed through entering Krirtie's body. "Why didn't you let me pull it out? If it is what has made her sick, I could have gotten it out of her body."

Stepha replied flatly, "It is what has made her sick, but you could not have gotten it out of her body, not without taking her whole arm off with it."

"What is it?" asked Schram, still staring at the half-inch hole left from the entry point of the worm.

"It is a boreworm," the elf replied. "They enter through the skin anywhere on the body and make their own pathway toward the heart. If they reach it, death will come in a matter of seconds. However, their movement through the body is slow because they frequently have to return to the surface to dispose of the wastes from their digestion. But if you try to pull them out when they surface as you suggested, they stretch out their long back tentacles and grip with amazing strength to any muscle or bone they can cling to. Pulling them out when they are attached as such would remove whatever they were attached to as well. To do so would have killed her."

"Then how do we help her? We can't just watch her die." The maneth was stumbling over his words.

"There is only one way that I know of," she answered hesitantly. "But it is by no means full proof. Furthermore, I am not even sure we can find what we need."

"What is it?" stated Schram. "We must do anything we can to help. Krirtie is as important as any of us, and if there is even a slight chance, we will risk it."

The elf nodded and rose. "Jermys, use your axe to cut off a tree branch and bore a hole into it. The branch needs to be at least an inch in diameter with the hole all the way through. However, the bigger the width, the better. And hurry!" The dwarf disappeared without question, and Stepha turned to the maneth. "Maldor, go to the springs and begin pulling the plants out from alongside the water's edge. Inspect the roots until you find a small gray-brown worm crawling through them. This is the most important part so look hard. If we do not find this worm, there will be no hope of helping her."

Maldor nodded. "I will find this worm. I guarantee it."

Now Stepha turned to Schram. "Dump the food you have cooked because we need the pot. Boil some water, and put one of those fig leaves you always have with lunch in it. When the leaf is good and hot, place it over the entry hole in her arm. This will help blood flow and cause the worm to return to the entry point to clean away his passage. Then keep the water boiling because I will need it for the herbs I will be gathering, and know that if she is to live, we must act quickly."

As Schram went to work following the elf's instructions, Stepha disappeared from their camp, giving Jermys a nod of approval as he returned carrying eight differently sized wood chips each maintaining a respective hole.

Maldor was the last to return, and he cringed as he peered at the ghostly white skin of the human he had begun to care so much for. "This is the only one I could find," he said, holding out his hand to the elf who was busy over the fire. In it could be seen a small, inch-long gray-brown worm, which was dancing furiously, trying to find some soft ground in which to dig into but finding no such surface on the maneth's palm.

"It is smaller than I would have hoped for, but should still do," replied Stepha removing her potion from over the fire.

"That smells really sweet. What is it?" asked Schram as he leaned toward the pot.

The elf turned to the human. "Basically, it's poison with a lot of sugarcane in it so the worm will eat it."

"How are you going to get the boreworm to eat that potion?" asked the dwarf questionably.

"I am not," replied Stepha. "It would not do any good just to kill the worm while it was still inside her body. The boreworm's skin secretes a toxin that leaves the victim unconscious. If we kill the worm inside her body, the toxin will remain, and she will not wake. We must poison the worm Maldor recovered, and then let it crawl down the hole left by the boreworm and die. The boreworm will in turn have to eat our poisoned worm to clear his passage again and then return to the surface to dispose of the waste. In doing so, it too will become poisoned and hopefully become weakened enough to be removed when it surfaces. If it does not come straight to the surface, it could die within her body thus sentencing her to death as well."

"Can't its tentacles still grab the bone when it is poisoned? If we try to remove it, won't we still risk harming Krirtie?" The maneth showed a deep concern, which grew the same across all their faces.

Stepha appeared saddened. "Yes, but the poison renders the worm much weaker in its ability to hold firmly to the tissues. Also, we will use the wood Jermys brought to extend the hole out farther from her body to bring the boreworm a greater distance out from the skin to make its deposits. Undoubtedly, we will take some of her arm with it, but hopefully, it will only be some surface tissue. Depending on when the worm entered, it should not be too big in size yet."

They all looked worriedly around, but they knew it was their only chance. Stepha moved beside the big maneth. "Maldor, since you are the strongest, you will be the one to grab the worm when it appears at the wood's surface. You must pull with all your might and not worry about either breaking the worm or harming Krirtie. This is the only way to remove it."

The maneth nodded, but fear still showed distinctly in his eyes. Stepha saw this clearly and continued trying not to hide any truths about the situation. "And finally, I must caution everyone. This is not a safe procedure or a surefire one. Many things could go wrong, and even if we do successfully remove it from her body, it will then be her body that must still save her from the remaining toxin. I have seen some never wake from their unconscious sleep." Her voice grew incredibly dismal as she spoke to the group. "Now, let us waste no more time. Maldor, place the worm in the pan of herbs and then bring the whole thing over to me by Krirtie."

Maldor did as he was instructed, and as he arrived at Krirtie's feet, he bowed his head to say a silent prayer. Stepha took the now slow-moving worm from the pot and edged it into the hole left by the attacking parasite. The poisoned worm slowly slid down the passage and disappeared inside Krirtie's body. Stepha took one of the wood pieces Jermys had brought back and placed it over the hole and motioned for Maldor to sit beside her. "Now we wait," she stated softly. "If it takes over fifteen minutes, we must assume that the procedure did not work and respect Krirtie's right to die as she would prefer to die, as the gar we met in the mountains many days back. Though I did not say so at the time, the choice was true and correct. Dignity in death is as important as dignity in life."

The group grew deathly quiet as Stepha's last statement brought the possibility of Krirtie's death before each of them. All eyes focused on the hole in the small piece of wood, and with the passing of each minute, the tension inside each of them began to mount. The silence became almost overwhelming. Each knew in their heart that it had been twice the time Stepha had stated, but they just couldn't bring themselves to give up.

Stepha's eyes began to tear as she started to pull the wood away. Maldor reached his hand quickly down. "Five minutes more. That is all I ask. Then we will honor her death." His words were choppy and lost in his sea of sorrow, but he fought to keep his composure as he stared at the wood. He seemed to be pleading with everything within him to see that invader appear at the face of the hole, but nothing came.

More time passed, and Schram knelt down to feel Krirtie's heart. "Her beat is weak. She will not live much longer."

Tears too were flowing from his eyes as he spoke. Maldor saw his pain and knew how deeply everyone felt for the human woman. "Very well," said the maneth softly. "Stepha is right. Her right to pass with honor is required for us to fulfill." He paused as he too fought off the onslaught of despair. "I act on this matter for the bravest woman I have ever known." Maldor removed the goblin dagger he had picked up for Krirtie many days before when they fought off the goblins chasing the gar. He closed his eyes in one final prayer as the others also bowed their heads.

"Wait!" exclaimed Stepha. "The worm. I see it!" She quickly moved to replace the wood.

The startled maneth dropped the dagger, striking it against Schram's boot. Moving back over beside the elf, Maldor peered into the hole in the wood and saw the faint, slow movement of something within it. Stepha pressed the wood into Krirtie's skin, trying to draw the worm farther from the girl's body.

The worm's head slowly picked its way through the wood extension, and red blood from its victim could be seen around its mouth and tiny fangs. When it reached a point about a half inch passed the surface, Maldor grabbed the parasite and pulled with his mighty maneth force. The elastic body of the boreworm stretched like a rubber band, and it reached nearly three feet in length under Maldor's pull, but the big maneth would not relent. Finally, with a snap and burst of blood from Krirtie's torn flesh, Maldor, the worm, and the block of wood all released from the girl and were flung to the ground. The worm relaxed back to its now normal five-inch length, and Jermys wasted no time recovering it from where Maldor had let it fly and quickly tossed it into the fire, causing a strange orange smoke and powerful odor. The maneth in turn jumped back to his feet and was in an instant back at Krirtie's side where Schram and Stepha had already begun flushing and bandaging the wound left by the intruder.

Maldor gazed at what little color was left in the human woman's pale face. A ghostly white vision lay before him motionless, almost appearing as if death already had a firm hold on her. "Will she live?" he said hesitantly, but not really wanting to know the answer.

"It is out of our hands now," returned Stepha softly. "Her body must now fight on its own. You should know though, any chance she has is due to you. Once again, you should feel proud for what you have done for her."

Maldor only shrugged at the elf's comments as he pulled a blanket up over the still body beside him. The others looked at the maneth, and all knew he would not leave Krirtie's side until she was well or dead, regardless of how long it took to decide. Schram motioned to Stepha and Jermys to leave them alone, and the group followed him back over to the springs. Schram wiped the recent tears from his cheeks, then began to speak softly but firmly, "Krirtie cannot be moved until her fate is decided. In whichever case, Maldor too will not leave. However, I wish to reach Draag as soon as possible to see if that large band of goblins was heading there. As this is the case, I will go on ahead and investigate as dictated by our original plan. If I am not back in three days, I want you four to turn northwesterly and head to Drynak under the assumption that our fears were correct and the dragons have returned and are being led from the caverns. You must also assume that I have been captured or killed, and it will be your responsibility to get word back to Geoff and Hoangis."

The two looked at their leader, and Stepha made it apparent that she was against this new plan. She said in a stern voice, "I do not think we should split up, as is how you felt not all too long ago. We will be able to determine if Draag was the goblin's destination whether we arrive there tomorrow or in a week. They were not hiding their footsteps as if they could have in numbers such as those they were traveling in." Her voice turned sarcastic. "I think the danger Krirtie has been faced with has eaten at you as well, and you do not wish to have anyone else's life on your shoulders." She paused and then continued when Jermys gave a slight nod. "We did not join this mission as guards for a human expedition to Draag. No, we are all warriors fighting our way together for a common goal. Don't split us up just as we near our mark. Going in alone would be suicidal, but you know that and don't expect to return." She looked away, feeling more tears and knowing she had said too much.

"She is right," added Jermys without all the emotion that was carried in Stepha's voice. "But I also realize the importance of speed in this endeavor. Our journey has already taken much longer than was originally planned, even since I joined the group and before that you lost over a week due to the blizzard and the mines. We may not see weather as good as this for several more months, and thus I think Schram should set out today and gain the advantage given us by Keabda himself. However"—his voice now gained in strength and emotion—"I do not feel you should go alone. I should accompany you."

Schram and Stepha both began to object, but Jermys cut them off. "Please hear me out first. Schram, you should not go alone that is for certain. Neither Maldor nor Krirtie, or the rat for that matter, can join you for obvious reasons nor can they be left alone without someone to help them in case trouble arises, and Krirtie must be moved. Stepha, your elven sight, accuracy with a bow, and ability to fly would prove vital on this open plain whereas my lonesome battle-axe would be of little use in seeing the prospects of an early ambush. However, when riding with Schram and entering the mountainous regions surrounding Draag caverns, my dwarven mine-sight and confidence in such areas could prove useful. So you see, logically, I am the only choice."

The dwarf smiled and then moved back to where he had placed his armor. Schram turned to Stepha who remained facing away as tears again streamed from her large green eyes. Neither of them wanted it to be so, but they both knew that the dwarf's words were wise and accurate. "Dearest Stephanatilantilis, know that you are the one I love more than any other ever in my life. I pledge my forever love to you now as I did five years ago."

She fell between his broad shoulders, and all she could say was, "I love you too, Schramilis of Elvinott."

He pushed her slightly away as Jermys approached leading the bongos toward them. "In three days, if you have received no word from us, then head for Drynak." He pulled a small Toopekian crest from his side pouch. "Give this to King Joseph of Drynak, and he will help you in any way that he can. Have him send a message to Geoff and your brother regarding all that has happened. Then, when Krirtie is able, you three head toward Draag or Toopek, whichever you and Joseph decide is the best choice." He looked over to Jermys who was already fighting to calm his mount and then gazed back to Stepha. "I love you."

They broke hands, and tears again burst from her eyes as she followed his walk to his bongo. With a quick jump and pat on the animal's back, they were off across the plain. "Take care and protect yourself well, Schramilis," she said softly to herself. "And I love you too." She wiped her eyes and gently dipped her hands into the bubbling water to clear her face. She knew she had to return to Maldor's side, but she feared the worst. It would take all her strength to make herself go back, but she had to remember their cause. Together is the only way they would survive.

She pushed herself to her feet and slowly made her way back to where Maldor sat with Krirtie. She briefly glanced back to watch the last sight of her two companions disappear in the distance before asking, "is there any change?"

The maneth did not raise his head, and his voice showed nothing but worry. "Her heart beats slightly stronger, but there has been no signs of consciousness."

"That is still a very good sign," she replied, trying to sound positive among all the misery.

"Where are the others?"

"They have headed to Draag to investigate the caverns and the possibility that the goblins we passed were headed there."

The maneth rose as if he was going to follow them immediately but stopped when Stepha placed her hand on his shoulder. "Wait, Maldor, you must watch over Krirtie. When she is well, we will join them. Until then, our primary concern must lie with her."

It was apparent in his frown that the big maneth was not pleased with the separation of their party, but he also realized the importance of helping Krirtie. He returned to his position next to the human and lightly stroked her hair as Stepha began preparing both of them some food.

The elf spent most of the remainder of the day off alone, supposedly standing watch but actually lost in her thoughts about the human who had escaped her so long ago only to be taken from her once more. She nearly jumped from her armor when Maldor silently appeared behind her. "There is some food inside. Why don't you get something to eat and try to get some rest? I will take watch for a while and periodically look back in on Krirtie. However, she has shown no indication of waking and will more than likely sleep through the night," his voice cracked on his last words.

Stepha put her arm around the huge maneth whose mane had become tangled and frayed. She rubbed his back as she spoke, "She will be all right. Your love for her is too strong to let her leave us now."

The maneth turned, somewhat stunned by the elf's comment, but saw she was looking straight into the night sky and speaking as much to herself as she was to him. He smiled at the princess and then ushered her to the fire to get some rest. *Perhaps she could find some peace in a dream*, he thought as he returned to the silence of the night.

The two rode hard across the plains, only stopping once to allow the stags a break and for water. Jermys had quit fighting his mount and accepted the fact that the bongo was in charge as they rode, and this greatly increased the time they made and the comfort in the dwarf's buttocks.

There had been little talk between the two for much of the trip and especially now that the mountains marking the region of Draag Caverns could be seen in the distance. Schram broke the silence as he gazed toward the ominous horizon. "There are three places I know of on Troyf that I have never had a desire to visit, and Draag Caverns tops the list."

The dwarf looked ahead and then back toward his companion. "Might I ask what the other two places are?"

Schram stopped his bongo. "The Realm of Darkness and the South Sea Peninsula."

Jermys gulped as he thought about the area known to be the heart of the afterlife, and conversely, the region near the South Sea that is controlled totally by dark dwarves and any other nomad scum who could live there. "And Draag Caverns is worse than these?" His comment carried more than just the touch of disbelief. It plainly showed that the dwarf had no idea about what lay ahead.

Schram just looked ahead as if engrossed with what he was about to enter and not noticing the dwarf's concern. "Come on, let's get into the foothills. I don't like sitting out here like birds on the water. You never know who might be watching the pond."

The dwarf peered toward the upcoming tree line and unhooked the helve of his axe just to satisfy his consciousness. They rode at a quick pace through the foothills and nearly were thrown from their stags as the animals came to an abrupt halt. Both companions urged their mounts forward, but the bongos would have nothing to do with it.

"They sense something," stated Schram. "We must continue on foot and be cautious."

"Aye," responded the dwarf who patted his bongo on its neck, almost showing a bit of affection and sadness at their split. The antelope bounced its head several times in response and then, before darting back into the wood, poked Jermys in the back with its twisted horns. The dwarf grunted and then smiled as he watched the animal leap through the brush. "As bad as an elf, always needing the last word."

Schram nodded understanding and even chuckled a bit as he began to peer through the trees just ahead of where the stags had stopped. With a thump, Jermys was on his back with the human's hand pressed tightly over his mouth. Raising his finger, Schram motioned to the dwarf to not make a sound. Suddenly, the sounds of footsteps on the ground and tree branches being hacked aside broke the silence.

Jermys quickly understood and regained his feet before joining Schram at the edge of the trees. His eyes widened at the sight before them. "It seems they were headed to Draag as you thought," he whispered. "Now we can return and tell them what we have seen."

"No," Schram replied. "We must see where they are all going and why. I still have seen no dragons, and in a situation as grave as this, we must be sure."

"I was afraid you were going to say that." He paused and again turned to observe the goblins' behavior. "What are we to do then?"

"I don't know yet," Schram quickly added, expecting the question. "For now, we guard our backs and wait."

The two sat on guard as they watched the goblin activity. Hours went by, and night was beginning to fall across the region. They had not eaten since their small breakfast before splitting with their friends, and now both were starting to show and feel the signs of hunger.

They sat in long periods of extended silence with neither of them even wishing to speak about what was happening. Each became lost in their own thoughts about where they were and what they were doing. Everything had seemed to move so fast that their choices had to be made quick and decisively. There was no time to think about whether it was the correct decision or not; they just had to do it and make the best of what happened. Now however, they were forced to do nothing but evaluate what had brought them here. Schram could think about nothing except how his group of companions was now cut down to only two, and in the back of his mind, he feared that the evil forces they were approaching had a hand in that split.

Without any apparent notice to the ominous situation, Jermys turned to Schram and broke the monotonous chain of silence. "That is really completely amazing."

"What?" replied Schram, surprised by the dwarf's sudden words.

"Well, considering that this is probably the same group of goblins we passed earlier, we must assume then that these caverns are simply enormous."

"Why do you say that?" he replied, his tone showing some interest.

"Because they have been slowly filing into the cavern entrance to the west, and there are only maybe fifty left to enter. If those caverns can hold the over two thousand goblins that we saw not to mention those already inside, on their way, or entering somewhere else, then they must be justifiably huge."

"Aye, I see what you mean." Schram looked at the dwarf who seemed stunned by the human's sudden interest in the action at the cavern entrance. "I assume they will leave a squadron to guard the front. Tomorrow, once we dispose of these guards, we will join the party inside."

The dwarf shrugged his shoulders and in a sarcastic, condescending voice said, "you mean you want to break into the caverns and snoop around, then after you have found out what you want to know, simply leave and tell the others?"

"Yes," replied Schram smiling.

Jermys only grumbled under his breath as he went back to his watch. The only thing Schram could make out was, "Stupid human barbarian."

CHAPTER 15

DRAAG

As the next day's sun rose breaking its light across the trees, Schram woke to a much-surprising and interesting site. Jermys pointed down toward the cave marking the entrance where the two had seen all the goblins enter and where they expected to see several goblin guards remaining outside. However, on this new crisp and refreshing day, the entire mountainside was calm and free of movement. The wind even seemed to be dormant. The trees made no sounds, and their branches sat still as they pierced through the chill air of the dawn.

"Why do you suppose there are no guards?" asked the dwarf seeing his counterpart's strange stare. "Are they waiting inside, do you think?"

"I doubt it," Schram replied flatly while stretching his arms. "Goblins prefer to show that they have control of a place and not wait in the shadows for an ambush. I think, more than likely, they feel Draag is safe from any invader and don't deem guards necessary." He paused and turned toward the dwarf. "Or they know we are here and are simply inviting us in."

His words grew quite solemn although their intention was to be light and humorous. Schram saw the concern in Jermys's eyes and softened his tone. "If you do not feel comfortable with entering the caverns, I want you to know I understand and will bear no hard feelings. There is a very good chance we will both not come out the same as we go in, or come out at all."

Jermys shook his head in disgust at the accusation of withdrawing while Schram continued. "May Keabda be with us as we travel." He raised his axe. "After all, I did not spend all last night sharpening this blade only to wait while you had all the fun."

Schram approached the dwarf and knelt down beside him to share his view of the entrance. "Did anything out of the ordinary happen as you watched last night?"

Jermys shrugged. "The rest of the goblins filed in, and about an hour ago, nearly two hundred trolls arrived and meandered in as well."

"Trolls?" he replied questionably. "Whoever or whatever is controlling the goblins must also be organizing the trolls now as well. Before we have seen only isolated numbers of trolls, but now our enemy might have doubled in size and strength."

"Trolls are no threat in a war. They are the lowest form of life on all of Troyf, even below the bandicoot." The dwarf laughed slightly as he thought about Fehr. "I almost went down there last night and killed them all single-handedly out of boredom."

Schram said nothing, in fact he gave the impression he had not even heard the dwarf's words. He only stared mesmerized by the cave. He turned to the little man beside him, and without speaking, he asked if he was ready.

The dwarf answered the question with a nod of his head, and the two climbed through the brush and began descending toward the entrance.

Schram led, with his sword drawn, followed closely by the axe-raised arm of the dwarf who took small steps through the nearby trees to ensure they were not being observed. They reached the entrance to the cavern, and Schram halted, peering as far into it as he could, trying to gain some hint to the mysteries these caverns held. The tunnel was much like a dwarven mine as it twisted its way into the mountainside. Torches rested along the walls as their flames danced, slightly illuminating the passageway. Jermys seemed a bit taken back by the superior workmanship that went into building these tunnels though he would never admit it. The two looked at each other one more time as if each was giving the other, and themselves, one more chance to back out of this plan. As nothing was said, Schram rounded the corner and entered the caverns of Draag.

They traveled slowly down the corridor, not beginning to know what they would find or should expect to find. No footprints from the goblins or trolls could be seen on the ground as the floor of the cavern was hard shiny rock, which resembled polished marble. The walls however were rough and jagged but still appeared to consist of the same gray-white stone.

They walked for several hours, coming to many different forks and small rooms, but never seeing any signs that anyone had been there in a long, long while. "Do you suppose these tunnels are enchanted like our dwarven mines?" asked Jermys as the two stopped to rest in front of a pair of tunnels running perpendicular to each other. "Could we simply be walking in circles?"

Schram shook his head. "No, I don't think so. I don't feel any enchantment here, and I do know the caverns to be incredibly expansive. We must keep searching."

The dwarf frowned slightly while he watched the human fidget over their situation. He knew his thoughts were not on their immediate problems but rather were focused on something completely apart. "I mean no distrust, Schram, but I have the distinct impression you have some knowledge about which I do not. We originally were going to just investigate outside Draag and see if there really was dragon activity. Now we are inside wandering the caverns and searching for something, and I believe that you know what that something is."

The human stared at his friend who was returning his gaze with suspicion. With a deep breath, he answered, "I am sorry for being so illusive with my behavior, but the truth is I don't know what it is I am looking for exactly. To tell you what I do know would only lead you to believe me more a fool than you already do."

The dwarf held his tight stare. "For starters, if I thought you a fool, I would not be with you now. There is something wrong here. To prove my point, I can only ask one question. Where are all the goblins and trolls we saw? In even the most plausible explanation that I can draw up in my mind, there should at least be some sign that they were here. For some reason, whoever or whatever is behind this entire situation has made it so nobody from the outside would suspect anything out of the ordinary. If we had not seen those huge parties enter, we would be led to believe that this place is deserted. That fact in itself tells me that no fool has brought us here, but if you leave me in the dark regarding why you changed our plans, then we are both fools."

"Me for not telling you and you for going along with it," completed Schram.

Jermys smiled. "Exactly."

The human scratched his head and slowly slid his sword back into its scabbard. "You make perfect sense, friend, but what I am about to say will not necessarily aid your understanding. I am looking for Sabast."

Again his face fell into a strange wallow of suspicion. "Who in all of Sakton's castle is Sabast?"

"I don't know."

"How did I know you were going to say that?"

"I don't know that either."

Jermys frowned. "What do you know?"

Schram looked away, becoming lost in his thoughts. "He is, or was, a friend of my old counterpart, Kirven. I was told he had a gift for me that was vital to our cause. However, I don't have any idea what that gift is or where we can find him, so I guess we are back to square one."

"This Sabast, he lives in Draag?"

"I think so, but again, I don't know. I myself only heard his name for the first time less than twenty-five moons ago." Schram paused and added, "It is one thing to have to find Sabast, but I have no knowledge of who or what he even is. As long as I traveled with my friend, never did I hear him speak his name."

Jermys paused for a long time, holding the corridor in a strange silence. He was just about to add another question about their new goal but, instead, held his tongue. He realized by Schram's face he had nothing more to add, and further questions would only draw more stress about their mission. He drove his tone lighter. "Well, the sooner we find Sabast, the sooner we can get out of here."

"If we can find our way out of here."

"I will get us out," replied the dwarf. "If there is one thing dwarves can do, it is find their way through tunnels. We have a sense about us you know."

Schram smiled. "Okay, how 'bout using that sense to pick a direction to go now?"

"No, we can find our way out after we are already in," added the dwarf now turning it into a chuckle. "You must be the one who gets us lost."

"Getting lost in tunnels?" he replied. He pointed to a new corridor. "Humans seem to be able to handle that part of it without problem. We have a sense about it you know."

They both smiled and were becoming less and less anxious with each step they took. They continued wandering through the vast maze of tunnels, never arriving at anything other than empty rock cavern after empty rock cavern. Occasionally, they would happen upon a piece of rotten wood or other loose debris but never any sign of recent activity. The caverns seemed to be free of all life except their own, and an eerie feeling was returning to each of them. The torches along the walls had begun to become fewer in number as they moved deeper into the maze, and Schram grabbed one to carry with them to ensure they always had light. However, again he noticed that his eyesight seemed to be growing in its night vision ability, and the necessity for light was more for Jermys's use although it acted to comfort him as well. It was during these thoughts that the peculiarity of the torches' existence at all finally struck Schram. However, even more peculiar than that was the fact that as the torches got fewer in number, and everything physically should mean it was to get darker, the more light seemed to be emitted. What it all meant only added to his frustrations.

They continued through a long corridor that was growing steadily wider in size as they approached what looked to be a much-larger and well-lit room. The two kept to the shadows as best they could, but light from ahead made it seem like midday, and hiding became less and less possible. Schram had discarded his torch hours earlier as it had become apparent that it was not needed although he found it hard to let go. As they breached the chamber's entrance, both their eyes widened at what they saw.

It was a large dome-shaped room with a ceiling almost beyond sight at its apex. Its walls were completely smooth and well-polished as light seemed to grow in intensity as it bounced off them. Their eyes followed it upward until they met a tiny doorway at the top, which let the sunlight find its way inside. The room was perfectly symmetrical with identical doorways 180 degrees from each other. However, one difference was present. Placed into the rock directly 90 degrees to the left of where they had entered was a shiny large mirror surrounded in delicate gold trim. The mirror was perfectly clear, not a scratch or crack in its delicate oval shape.

"We are in the center of the mountain," stated Jermys, still with his eyes and head fixed upward. "That opening could only be at the top of the peak we saw as we approached."

"I agree, but what is its purpose? Nothing that spectacular was created just to let light or air in." Schram had answered the question with his eyes focused on the strange mirror. He moved closer to it and replaced his sword when he arrived at its face. "And what is the purpose of the mirr—" he stopped as he was completely taken back by the crystal clear reflection he saw before him. He reached out and touched it, shaking his head in amazement. He again put his hand forward and rubbed his finger across the delicate and smooth glass. Turning back to his friend, he said, "My dirty finger doesn't even leave a smudge." But the dwarf greeted him with nothing more than a blank stare full of confusion. Schram instantly grew concerned. "What is it?"

His voice was slightly shaken. "I was not watching you directly, but I swear for an instant you vanished. When I glanced back however, you were there again."

Schram's expression held the same confusion. "That's odd because for just a moment I felt we were in incredible danger as I noticed the presence of strong enchantment. However, I was so intrigued with this mirror that as soon as it passed, I had forgotten about it. If you had not said that, I probably would never have remembered." He paused as he thought about what had happened. He shrugged and tried to lighten the talk. "Perhaps, we are just letting our long travels into unknown lands get the best of us." However, it was clear in the dwarf's eyes that he did not agree.

As the two looked at each other, each wondering what they should say or where they should turn to now, they both were alerted to the sound of quick-moving footsteps approaching from the corridor behind where they had entered. Without speaking another word, the two quickly ran through the other large doorway and disappeared down an identical corridor. They ran hard for several minutes, then stopped to listen for the pursuit.

"That mirror must have been some kind of alarm, and you must have triggered it when you touched it," said the panting voice of the dwarf.

"Maybe, but I don't think we are being followed," returned Schram.

The dwarf hushed and placed one of his extended ears to the floor. "You are correct. There is no one after us, nor do I hear anyone in the entire cavern." He swung his eyes back to the human who was staring back in the direction they had ran. "What is going on in here?"

"Let's backtrack and see what we find." He began to draw his sword but then decided against it and left it in its scabbard. Jermys saw the movement but did not feel the need to remain lax, and he drew his axe before taking his first step behind his friend.

They walked back down the huge corridor, which again grew more lighted as they approached the circular mirror room. When they arrived at the room, it was again empty.

"If that mirror was not there, I would be confused about which way we were going."

The dwarf said nothing in return as once again he was caught up in the strange craftsmanship of the tower. Finally, he replied, "Where did they go? They were only a matter of steps short of this room when we fled, and there is no other way out." Replacing his axe to his side, the dwarf went to inspect the mirror he hadn't had a chance to previously.

The immediate thought regarding the whereabouts of those they had heard did not strike Schram as odd until Jermys mentioned that there was no way they could have gone another direction. Schram glanced at Jermys and then turned to follow the other wall, looking for anything that could be a hidden passage. "If they didn't simply turn back, I don't know where they could have gone."

Jermys ignored the comment as he said, "You are right. It is impossible to put a mark on the glass." He turned and quickly redrew his axe as he yelled, "Schram, where are you?"

Schram was surprised that the dwarf had made no comment after his last statement and wondered what had so caught his interest as to ignore him. He too drew his sword when he realized he was alone. "Jermys, where are you?" When no answer came, he ran around, checking every point of the room but finding no trace of his friend. He paused and replaced his sword as a sickening aloneness began to haunt him. He knew the dwarf must have triggered some secret passageway, which only he had found. If it was possible to return, Jermys would have already reappeared. He thought about all his possible options and then realized he must still fulfill his mission. He had to find Sabast, no matter what the cost. Perhaps with his help, he could find Jermys, but without the dwarf by his side while he searched, Schram knew his success would take a giant leap backward. He gave the room one more complete search, looking for anything that could simulate a secret tunnel or path, and the only possibility he came up with surrounded the peculiar mirror. He inspected every inch of the frame and glass surface but to no avail; he found no passage and no dwarf. He repeated the actions he had taken when he too felt the evil and Jermys had said he thought he had vanished, but nothing. He was still in the room and still alone.

He issued a long sigh and then turned down the tunnel they had fled to when they had heard the others approaching. To himself he thought, *My only action is to go forward. First, I broke up our group. Now I have separated from Jermys. What more trouble can I bring?"*

"Schram, where are you?" the dwarf called again. When no answer came, he ran around, aimlessly checking every point of the room but finding no trace of his friend. He paused and gripped his axe tightly as he wondered what he should do. He looked back up at the clouds blowing across the tower opening and then shoved his axe back to his side. "I must find this Sabast," he said out loud although there was no one around to hear. With a bound displaying no hesitation or fear, he disappeared down the corridor they had ran to when the others approached.

He walked through the long winding tunnels for the remainder of the day, and when he came to a crack in the jagged edge of the wall, he slipped between sides using it as a secure place to rest. Being in the caverns, he had no way of determining what exact time it was, but he imagined that it was probably near the middle of nightfall by the depth of pain carried in his limbs. However, before he allowed himself to drift off to sleep, he thought about Schram and wondered where he was and if he was all right. The dwarf also worried for Krirtie and if she had been able to pull free of her dire fight against death. He was not familiar with the sickness that could be brought on by the effects of a boreworm, but with all he had seen on the plains, he was certain she had been placed in grave danger. Then, right as his small body began to fully relax, Jermys's thoughts fell to his brother, and he believed he could almost feel Bretten returning his thoughts with a message of safety for himself and Feldschlosschen.

Schram had been walking for hours. He had come to many large rooms since he left the circular mirror room, but none of the them showed any promise of holding any answers. The floor of the cavern he was now in had grown much softer, and water splashed beneath his feet with each step he took, but he pressed on. In the distance, he could hear the sounds of falls or rapids, but he could not tell exactly from which direction they came. He continued down the passage where the water seemed to be deepest and with more motion. As he came to a huge open cavern with long stalactites hanging from the ceiling, the water level was at his waist.

He peered around the large chamber and saw a natural rock ledge above the water level, running the circumference of the room. He began to move toward the side but stopped when his eyes became fixed on a strange swirling pushing the water against its natural current. Suddenly, erupting through the water's surface was a loud roar which echoed hard off the cavern walls. Accompanying the sound was the large snapping fangs of the slime-covered creature which had issued it. Its neck and head were all that raised from the water, but those alone dwarfed the human before it. Its skin was brown and scaly but did not appear to be as thick as some of the large creatures he had crossed in his life. He had drawn his sword at the first sound and now raised it before the beast. Again, the creature roared, reaching its long, jagged teeth towards the human.

The attack was easily defended, and it was then that Schram realized this creature had no limbs of any kind. He rushed toward the serpent's neck, thrusting his sword beneath its flesh while holding its jagged teeth at bay with his shield. Green blood began to fill the area, and Schram twisted his blade, tearing at the creature's insides and felt its life beginning to drain from it. However, just as he believed the fight was about to end, he felt a long slimy appendage gripping his throat from behind. The beast's tail tightened firmly and ripped the human downward, causing him to lose hold of his sword leaving it protruding from the serpent's neck. A large splash erupted when Schram's back struck the water, and his body was pulled under. Frantically, he dug his fingers into the creature's tail, trying to loosen its fatal grip about his neck. The fact that he was underwater was of no concern to the human since the tight flex of the muscle around his throat prevented any water from entering his lungs, and the need for air was blocked whether above or below the water's surface. He fought violently, trying to break its hold if even for a minute to gain the surface and another burst of air, but his attempts seemed futile. He felt his eyes rolling back into his head and his senses beginning to fail. With only seconds of life left within him, he remembered his dagger.

He held one hand, pulling against the serpent's tail while the other reached for his pouch and dagger. He swung the small weapon wildly around, flailing more toward areas around his head and neck than to anything he saw or felt. When resistance was met, he thrust through with everything he had left. The temperature of the water warmed as the creature's blood again flowed throughout it. Schram surfaced, coughing roughly while he discarded the piece of tail that had become embedded to his throat. He was still dazed and confused, but his adrenaline caused him to find the necessary strength to block the repeated snapping jaw attacks from the equally injured and panicked creature. It swung a final lunge toward the dazed human. Schram gathered all remaining energy within him and reached his arm out to recover his still deeply lodged sword. In one continuous motion, he removed it from within the serpent's body and swung it parallel to the water's surface. His blade bit back as he forced it through the creature, causing its head to separate. A small swirling was still seen several minutes later as the spastic muscles of its body jolted in their final flex before finally coming to a permanent rest. Schram half-walked, half-floated over toward the side, and with a slight push, he edged himself onto the ledge, his long deep breaths trying to draw every bit of air from the cavern.

He had no idea exactly how long he remained motionless against the rock wall but was certain it had been several hours. He leaned over and carefully scooped a handful of water to his mouth, half expecting another creature to hook his arm and pull him to a defenseless death. He almost wished for such an event as his exhausted body collapsed once more. Again, he seemed to stare blindly about the room for several minutes until gradually his thought began to return to his command. He pushed himself to his feet, issuing a small quiver in pain as he moved. As he looked around the room, he was amazed at the extreme beauty it held. The water, which had been murky brown in the previous tunnels, here although it was mixed with his and the serpent's blood, was now a shiny blue with bubbles dancing throughout it. The small pool formed in the room was lively and full of motion as a fifteen-foot waterfall splashed down from a higher level. Schram followed the ledge and found that it encircled the entire room, and a separate exit passageway could be seen on the far side. Still, he felt tired, and the temperature in this room was more comfortable than in the previous tunnels. He decided that this would be a good place to rest since he was sure that the hour was growing late. However, he didn't feel secure sleeping on the ledge, and as he looked around, did not see any protected places to rest.

Disgusted with the idea of walking farther, Schram grabbed his sword and dagger, which he had tossed aside after the battle, and after dipping his hand in for one more splash of water, he began to make his way around the chamber. The ledge passed right in front of the water's path as it plunged downward from the falls, and it looked as if hundreds of years of constant bombardment had worn its way through, separating the ledge from the cavern's side as the water splashed between. Schram reached his hand into the falls and was amazed at its warmth. As he prepared to leave, he looked up and examined the area where the falls originated. From this angle he could see another ledge, much smaller but big enough to hold a sleeping human. Schram glanced around and saw several stones that he could use as steps. In a few moments, he was scaling the side of the cavern in an attempt to reach a safe haven for the night. He was at the top and only needed to swing himself over the side to be securely on the little ledge. He reached over and grabbed hold of a huge rock projecting from the base. He began to add pressure to the rock and pull himself free of the stones when the rock he had hold of exploded under the force, and his body was thrown into chaotic swings. His momentum carried him sideways, and the water of the falls was pushing his body off the rocks where he now rested. He reached through the water but could find only slimy projections, which his tired hands and arms could not grip. With one last effort, Schram was pushed free of the ledge and tumbled down with the water, landing with a thump on the rock base.

"Who dares enter my nest uninvited!" sounded a deep, violent voice.

Schram, dazed from the fall but still alert, leaped to his feet only to turn and face the tumbling water. He swung his head and quickly realized that he no longer was in the room he had previously been in. He had fallen through the falls and landed inside a hidden cavern. However, more important than where he had arrived was what now rested before him. He drew his sword to face that which had spoken the cold statement. Schram's skin turned white as snow, and sweat formed in every crevice in his body sending a dull chill down his spine. He raised his sword, gripping the hilt so tightly that his knuckles looked as if they were about to burst. He stood as tall as the awesome sight before him would allow, but still he appeared as an ant before a mountain. However, this mountain had two eyes and a whipping tail, and the breath it breathed was alive with fire. He stood humbly in front of a huge dragon who in turn stared back with unrelenting hatred.

"I am Schram," he stated, but his voice was distorted and more weak than expected. He swallowed hard reaching to find any hidden strength.

"And who is Schram?" roared the dragon as fire again bellowed in his speech, pushing a wall of heat across the human.

He raised his shield more and fought to stay conscious as his mind became clouded with fear. "I am Prince Schram of the human city of Toopek. I have come in search of one called Sabast and have intruded on your domain only by accident. I ask for your forgiveness for the interruption, and I shall be on my way."

The dragon lifted its vast wings to become the most threatening sight the human had ever witnessed. He wanted to drop everything and run, but he knew that if the dragon did not want him to escape, he would not. The beast took a step forward, and his breath nearly burned Schram's flesh through his armor. "I know not of one called Sabast nor do I believe that to meet him is your true business here. I give you one more chance to speak the truth, human of Toopek."

The dragon's words brought with them a deep and intended fear to Schram. His eyes whitened, and he had no idea what he could say. His body began to sweat not only from the tense confrontation but the shear heat being issued from the dragon's breath. His mind grew dizzy, and all his thoughts became random and lost, and he now was struggling only to keep conscious rather than from any concerted effort to talk. More beads of burning flame seemed to trickle down his brow, and he felt his mind beginning to slide. Yet suddenly and for no apparent reason, something within him calmed the stress he was experiencing. All laws and reasoning vanished, and he concentrated on only one statement. He did not know why he had to say it; he only knew that he had to say it. In a voice, which echoed a far cry from that he had used previously, he stated, "Kirven sent me."

The dragon's eyes narrowed as it focused on the human. Sweat now covered Schram's face, stinging his eyes as the salt ran through, but his mind had become more and more clear. The dragon remained locked down on him, surveying him throughout. Its eyes were blood-red against the green scales of his body, and its sinister, grimacing smile gave no indication of its next action. Without removing his gaze, the dragon snarled, "What has Kirven sent you to do?"

Schram had already been praising his life to God and Shirak and did not expect the response. The surprise that he would live to speak another word showed clearly on his face and gave him confidence that he might still be able to free himself from this situation. He replaced his sword, knowing it would do little good, and even took a step forward to land only feet from the beast's lowered head. The dragon tilted its head slightly caught by the action. Schram's lips pressed tight together, and then his tone showed nothing but the utmost seriousness when he spoke, "He sent me to find Sabast in the caverns of Draag and retrieve a gift which was left with him for me. If you do not know of this Sabast, then I will leave you in peace as I stated before. However, if you do know of him, then I will do everything within my power to gain that information from you for it was my friend's last wish before we parted, and for me, that in itself is most important."

Schram stepped back, and although his words were strong, he still carried fear about him. The dragon smiled slightly and roared so loud as to shake rocks loose from the walls and send the human tumbling backward. Now Schram really accepted the fact that he was about to die. "Come here," sounded his massive voice.

Schram climbed to his feet and walked to where the dragon had lowered his head. The two were now face to face, only inches apart, the rotten dragon breath choking the human. The dragon lifted his head. "Perhaps Kirven was correct in seeing something within you. As I probe your mind, I do feel a hidden strength waiting to be tested."

Schram followed the dragon's head. "Sabast? You are Sabast." He paused, then added, "But you are a dragon."

"Yes," replied the creature. "Come with me to my den, Schram of Toopek."

He followed the dragon back through a short passage and arrived in a large open chamber piled full with gold, weapons, and many other lost artifacts from many years past. "This is amazing," he stated as he became engrossed in the room.

"Consider it many years of lonely wandering to retain some small material worth," replied the dragon softly. "This is what you came for, boy. Kirven left it for me to guard, saying he would send someone worthy to recover it when the time was such that it demanded it."

Schram looked toward a small box the dragon held before him and suddenly felt a strong magic growing about the room. He reached out and opened the box, causing a strange golden shimmer to explode across his face. Inside the case sat only one item, though staring at it filled Schram with emotion. Resting on the silk-covered bottom was a small dull copper-colored ring. He picked it up and stared over it carefully and then forced his eyes back toward Sabast. He let out a gentle sigh when their eyes met as the strength required to pull away from the ring was strangely enormous. Softly, he asked, "Do you know of this ring?"

The dragon ignored the question and continued with his own discussion. "Kirven said nothing to the fact that you would be a human." His voice showed little confidence that Kirven had made a wise choice. "I cannot believe he would not have told me. Furthermore, he said that a dwarf would accompany you. Did he stretch the truth in that as well, trying to give you more support in my eyes?"

This comment allowed Schram to forget his confusion regarding the ring and concentrate on the new words he had just heard. *How had Kirven known about Jermys and what was all this about?* "How do you know about the dwarf?" Schram was pleased that he had asked the question if for no other reason than to try to establish some level of reasoning he could understand.

The dragon looked angered. "I already told you that Kirven stated that a dwarf would accompany the one who returned to claim the ring. Why he believed as such is of no concern to me, but why the dwarf is not here now is. I will ask only once more, where is the dwarf?"

Schram was stunned by his unfeeling and unrelenting response. He took a step to the side to try and help him relax, but a strange uneasiness was growing within him. He did not want to give away any chance Jermys might still have to escape if this was not as it was suppose to be. However he knew he had to say something. "Why is it so important that you find the whereabouts of this dwarf whom you do not even know really exists or not?"

Sabast's eyes began to grow dark and cold. Fire began to trickle from his nostrils in beads of molten liquid. The startled and slightly fearful human took a step back before the surprisingly gentleness in the dragon's tone issued a little calm to the growing tension. "I made a promise long ago, and a gift I have for the dwarf as well."

Schram remained concerned, but something in Sabast's actions made him feel unthreatened by the dragon. He answered, "We were separated in the caverns. I do not know where he is."

Sabast rolled his eyes back into his head, and he became lost in deep thought. Then, like paint was thrust upon them, they returned to their eerie red color. "He sleeps near the cavern entrance. You will therefore have to take his gift to him." The dragon removed another box from the pile, which appeared exactly like the first one only slightly larger. After chanting some magical words, he handed the chest to Schram. "Only the dwarf may open it."

Schram grabbed the chest, and right as his fingers touched it, it shrunk down to the size of a small coin. Astonished but staying in control, he placed it in his pouch. "You still have not answered my question. Can you tell me about the ring?"

The dragon laughed, which left the human even more confused. After a short pause, which allowed time for Sabast to regain his sinister smile, the dragon lowered his head and peered hard toward Schram. "How much do you know about *the deal*?"

The question struck Schram hard, returning his memories from the last time he had spoken to Kirven. They had talked about the deal the canok had made with his father, the black dragon. However, Kirven had not said what the deal was in particular, only that it was created after the dragons had failed in their oppression and Kirven had been bested by his brother. Schram relayed this to the dragon who listened intently, then grew sad.

"Kirven spared you the truth because he wanted you to be free of hatred for him," the dragon began. "But I must tell you everything for you to understand." Sabast curled up his huge body to better fit inside the nest he had made for himself and then drew a deep breath, which gave Schram the impression that it was to be a long night. He stepped closer and sat down right beside the huge creature, sliding the ring on his finger as he moved. A sudden surge of power rocked the young man and then seemed to settle within him, giving him a newfound feeling of strength.

Sabast mused at Schram's expression and then continued, "There was no dragon oppression two hundred years ago, or at least not how it has been told." Schram appeared stunned by the statement, but Sabast gave the distinct impression that his tale was not to be interrupted so the human remained silent, though he was feeling a strange sensation growing throughout his body. "There was one black dragon, Slayne, with an evil plan, and unfortunately, he had about fifteen other dragons who would follow him. It was because of these fifteen that his plan could have gotten this far. Slayne used his magic to severely weaken and destroy all the other dragons. He was indeed powerful, but he also had surprise on his side. They did not expect the attack from him, and that is why he was able to succeed. However, even so, his attack on the other dragons left him weak and reckless. He was no longer able to efficiently deal with the other races across Troyf, which were also strong with magic, specifically the canoks and a few more advanced human populations. It was then that he used his allied dragons to attack the humans, and since they were also caught by surprise, there was little resistance. However, his plan for the canoks had already been put to the test as he now had a son by his side and had divided the rest to fight among themselves. There was only one threat left to his great plan, and that threat was his other son, Kirven, the twin. Kirven could feel what his brother felt, and he knew that the attacks were only from a few dragons although the humans believed they were fighting an entire race. Kirven believed that if he could keep Slayne and Almok busy while others set out to destroy Draag, then perhaps those trapped dragons could be freed and, in essence, tip the scales against Slayne. During this time, Slayne's allies flew wildly across the land, attacking anywhere they saw life, which further made it seem as though it was a huge dragon offensive and not fifteen puppets from one evil puppet master. Kirven faced off against the two in what was probably the bloodiest conflict ever experienced. However, Kirven was bested, but he still refused to take his place by his father's side. Because of this, the deal was made." There was a short pause, and the dragon tilted his head slightly, and his tone changed to almost a monotone. "Kirven pledged his obedience if he could be freed until the eggs hatched."

The entire tale left Schram drained, but the last comment was completely out of sequence. "The eggs?"

Sabast faltered growing more saddened as he replayed the ancient story. "Slayne had not only stripped the dragons of all their life abilities, but he had stolen all of their eggs as well. He knew that the dragons would never attack the other races unprovoked, but he could make their young hatchlings do so if they believed that the others were responsible for their parents' extinction. Slayne could then see the fulfillment of his plan as he would rise to become emperor over the kingdom."

Schram leaned forward. "I still don't understand. What part did Kirven play in this?"

"Don't you follow?" roared Sabast. "The Dragon Oppression that began two hundred and thirty years ago with the rape of Kirven's mother will in less than a year, as the eggs begin to hatch, finally come to a close. The dragon young will be taught to kill everything in the country or force its obedience, unless you can stop Slayne."

Schram's eyes grew wide, and the dragon snarled at the now humbling boy. "What can I do? I am but one human, not strong with magic, even when possessing an enchanted ring."

The dragon roared again. "Kirven gave his life to search for the one who had a chance to harness the power of the Ku Ring, and he believed, though I struggle at this time to know why, you to be that one. Now go, for we have talked too long, and you must meet your friends and tell them what is about to happen and prove my impressions about you wrong. However, don't tell them that you are the chosen one to fight the black dragon. Only tell them to prepare for the attack of the hatchlings. They will be young and possible to defend against if your weapons are correct. Also do not tell them why you must go to Black Isle and seek the help of Taiju, the Wizard of the Ring."

Schram froze when he heard his next destination but did feel his comprehension was such to question it. "I understand, but tell me, could the dragon parents still be saved and brought to our aid?"

"No," Sabast stated softly with deep emotion flowing from him. "Most are dead, and those that live are too weak and insane to remember clearly what has occurred. With Kirven and Almok both by his side, Slayne now will be strong enough to control all the young dragons and make them willing servants before his rule.

He grows more powerful with each passing day, so do not be hasty in your actions. You are the key which can unlock this tragedy. Be true in your effort."

Schram bowed his head then asked. "One more question, Sabast. Why were you spared from Slayne's wrath so long ago?"

The huge dragon twitched in discomfort as the question seemed to strike even worse memories. "I was young, then, very young." His tone was lost and confused but his ideas clear. "I was one of the dragons that followed him in his quest, thinking he was the greatest dragon to have ever lived. He was the guide to return life to the way it was meant to be for dragons, at least what he convinced me life was suppose to be. We attacked a maneth camp, and by some accident, I was caught under one of my companion's fierce attacks. I was so injured that I made easy prey for the maneths. The other dragons just looked down at me in disgrace and left me for dead at the hands of those we had attacked without cause. I was prepared to die." His voice fell off. "I deserved to die."

Schram lowered his head in sadness, feeling the dragon's pain. "Tell me, Sabast. I must know."

"Kirven approached my near lifeless body, and without question used his magic to save me. He gave me life once again. He then hid me here, and I swore loyalty to defeating Slayne and his evil plans. It was then he gave me the two gifts and a message. The two gifts have been given, and the message was told to you as well. Seek out Taiju, he is the only one who can help you now."

CHAPTER 16

KIRVEN'S RETURN

A yawn stretched Jermys' mouth causing him to fully wake to face his dire position. Spending the night in the cramped crevice for protection had done little for his comfort much less his attitude. The small dwarf grumbled in despair as much from his morning tightness as from his rumbling stomach.

"Damn human," he stated to himself. "He would be carrying all the food when we got separated." He stumbled around slightly and then worked his way through the tight spacing of rock to end up back in the cavern tunnel. I guess it will be up to me to find him now, he thought to himself as he began to walk back down the corridor. I am hungry enough to eat a rat. He chuckled when he thought about Fehr's expression if he had heard that. With a sigh, he decided that the only way to satisfy his hunger would be to find some food somewhere in this maze and he was off in the same direction he had ended in the night before.

His pace picked up slightly as he felt he was nearing a new and unexplored tunnel which was much better lit as he could see bright light from several hundred meters back. As he approached the light, a worried expression suddenly grew across his face. He began hurrying toward the cavern opening and froze when he arrived at its mouth. His jaw dropped and the dwarf became momentarily paralyzed as he was lost in his thoughts.

"How could I have gotten turned around and wound up back at the entrance?" he hollered as he peered into the late morning sun. "I am a dwarf, and it is impossible for me to lose my way in tunnels. I know I went the right way."

Bellowing laughter echoed from a raspy voice from beside him. "It looks like we don't have to hunt for breakfast after all," continued the voice in the broken goblin tongue.

Jermys blinked back to his senses and turned to face the group that had previously gone unnoticed due to his confusion. Without pause, he removed his battle axe and flung it striking the lead goblin that had spoken right between the eyes dropping him to the ground. Without hesitating a moment more, the dwarf ducked a swinging goblin sword and dove back into the cavern.

The fear-driven dwarf ran with lightning speed only to be followed by the dying laughter of the goblins at the entrance. He turned a corner attempting to slip into a different set of tunnels and ran hard into the fat belly of another goblin whose own laughter was interrupted only by the force knocking him and the colliding dwarf to the ground. Within seconds there were three goblin daggers at Jermys' throat and the dwarf removed his hand from the knife at his side and raised it into the air. More laughter filled the corridor while the dwarf slowly pushed himself to his feet mumbling under his breath.

The goblins led him out to the cavern entrance where the group of eight poked and taunted the dwarf for their amusement. Jermys had been cut several times as the swords and daggers of the goblins broke through the gaps in his armor tearing at the dwarf's flesh. The dwarf had fallen to his knees but refused to drop his head before his captors. One of the goblins removed his sword and held it as if he were going to swing level and behead the bloodied dwarf. Jermys stared at the approaching goblin as those around backed off to let their leader have all the room needed to deliver his deathly blow. However, as the goblin neared his victim, he suddenly stopped and stood at attention with his eyes moving to a fixed location beyond the dwarf. Jermys turned in time to see a hovering ball of light burst into flame to be replaced by a tall, hooded figure wearing all black. The creature looked and moved like a shadow, and the only facial features which could be clearly determined by the dwarf were the two white glowing eyes within the hood. Jermys did not understand how something could appear so dark in the bright sun of the morning, but the effortless motion that glided it across the ground displayed the presence of very little true life. The figure approached the group and without a word or the appearance of any excessive use of energy, the being stood before the lead goblin and with a simple touch of its finger to the goblin's forehead, sent the creature writhing away in pain. He fell to the ground in rolling convulsions and then became utterly silent. Jermys' eyes grew as large as saucers while he watched the goblin's bitter and excruciating death and the fear generated caused all in the area to fall back with a shutter. The being turned around and faced each of the other goblins but inflicted only a silent message of obedience.

Then its ominous eyes covered the small dwarf drawing any color out of his skin leaving Jermys a pale white. The being raised its hand and outstretched one finger leaving it pointed inches from the dwarf's heart. Jermys' chest burst with pain as he felt as if a knife had split him in two. His heartbeat grew loud, bouncing through the air like the pounding of a hammer on stone. The goblins nearby covered their ears as the beat crashed through their bodies dropping several of them to their knees. Then with a twist of his hand, the hooded figure silenced Jermys' heart. The dwarf felt the pain in his chest disappear and a lightness came to his body. He dropped to the ground and rested himself allowing death to take him calmly, and the figure controlling his life watched without feeling. Just as the last breath was pushed between his lips, Jermys cried in pain as the being before him again lifted his finger and brought the pound of the dwarf's heart back to life. Two of the goblins fell over dead and black blood boiled from their ears. The other five now were all on the ground, powerless to defend against the penetrating beat. Jermys screamed as the creature's cold fingers gripped his arms sending a paralyzing chill through his veins. The creature moved his face inches from the dwarf's whose numbness was reaching all areas of his body now.

"What is your business here, dwarf of Feldschlosschen?" echoed a deep voice that Jermys believed had to be the voice of death itself.

The terrified dwarf could not form words as his mouth simply uttered an array of various noises. The impatient creature released the dwarf sending his paralyzed body to the ground with a deadening thud. The hooded figure turned and paced a couple of steps away from the decrepit dwarf and Jermys could see what was hidden beneath the creature's robe causing the bulge in its back: The black and green scales of a tail of a lizard. The creature quickly turned to again face the dwarf whose feelings were beginning to return to his body. As Jermys sat up, he realized he was positioned right next to the goblin he had originally killed with his axe, but he only noticed this for a moment as the dark figure took a step forward and removed its hood. The glowing eyes that were present at first, changed to the soft blue eyes of a middle-aged human male, with the other facial features to match. His brown, curly hair danced about the delicate skin making up his cheeks and face. The human knelt before the dwarf and in a soft, sympathetic voice said, "relax friend dwarf, let not my previous appearance frighten you. I have been put under an enchantment by the evil dragons and only with the strength I gained from you was I able to break it." The human reached out and took Jermys' hand sending a surge of confidence and security through him. "Now tell me, what trouble has brought you to this awful place?" His voice was caring and completely uncharacteristic of the previous viscous creature that had confronted him only moments ago.

Jermys smiled and moved closer to the being gripping its hand tighter as he nearly leaned on its shoulder. In a silent, whispering voice Jermys said, "I came here for you, kind soul."

"Whatever do you mean?" replied the soft speaking human.

The dwarf sat up and holding his secured look, reached over and recovered his axe from the dead goblin's forehead and flung it at the human's head. "I came here for you!" he yelled.

Without a motion, the human took the blade of the axe directly between the eyes. As it struck however, it as well as the dead goblin body, disappeared. Jermys' face grew pale and he could only stare fearfully back at the dark figure's soft eyes. The human motioned to the side, and the dwarf hesitantly turned his gaze to his left. His eyes widened as they fell on the actual body of the dead goblin still with the axe protruding outward spilling his black blood over the ground. Jermys returned his stare upon the being before him whose face had again taken on the glowing, shadowed look of death itself.

The creature sent a bolt of energy from its finger which dropped the dwarf back to his knees. Jermys was frozen as it approached him ready to bring a sea of pain and what the dwarf hoped would be a quick death. The outstretched finger grew near, and Jermys could feel a cold sensation spreading throughout his body. The dwarf struggled to get back to his feet, but the power engulfing him was too strong and kept his body planted. Just as the being's finger was about to touch Jermys' forehead, a series of thumps broke the silence that had blanketed the area followed by a crash of unexplainable magnitude. Jermys noticed the five remaining goblins falling to the ground with elven arrows piercing their bodies. The creature before him now was Maldor who was swinging his maneth club wildly at the hooded man beneath him. Arrows from nearby trees erupted into the fallen creature's body, but they seemed to have little effect. The dazed human swept out its tail and whipped at the maneth striking him across the chest and sending him to crash into the rock wall supporting the entrance. The onslaught of arrows continued and the man seemed to become confused. With a burst of brilliant light, he formed into a floating globe and then disappeared as quickly as a bubble reaching its end.

Jermys fell down lost and completely dazed by the whole ordeal as Krirtie and Stepha rushed down from the trees. The elf ran to the dwarf and immediately gave him water and some small pieces of bread to chew. Maldor climbed to his feet just in time to catch the flailing arms of Krirtie's worried embrace. "That sucker packs a punch!" stated the equally dazed maneth staggering over toward the elf and dwarf. "We should leave quickly before he returns."

"No, that is not necessary," stated Stepha, still trying to help Jermys regain his senses. "Schram told me that when they vanish like that, he believes it takes all their energy and not to fear for a sudden return."

Maldor made an offended face as he immediately wondered how Schram had known this but then turned his attention to the dwarf who was struggling to stand up. "What the…how did? I mean, why…" Jermys' voice was choppy and mixed.

"Take it easy," replied Krirtie. "You are talking like Fehr."

The dwarf's eyes showed that he now was back in control and displayed a strong dislike for the human's statement. "Why, I had everything under complete control until you guys broke in and fouled everything up." He paused and slowly a smile grew across his face. "But thanks, your solution proved to be adequate as well." He paused then added with a smile, "Krirtie, you are well!"

"Aye," she replied in her best Dwarven accent, also smiling.

The group shared the moment, and Maldor helped the small dwarf to his feet brushing him off in the process. The maneth waited until he was certain that Jermys had his bearings before he asked the question that was truly on his mind. "Where is Schram?"

The question was quick and abrupt but it was one which brought all attention to the dwarf. Stepha was perhaps the most interested and listened intently for the response. Jermys sighed deeply and it was clear just in his first words that even he did not understand all that had happened. He retold the story in the most simple but complete method he could ending on the creature/human he had fought outside the cavern entrance.

"We must go back and find him," broke in Stepha. "He could be in great danger. What if he meets up with one of the dragon men?" Her tone at this point was strange and it became apparent that something about the creature he had faced bothered Stepha even deeper than what was obvious. "What if in his search for this Sabast, who we don't even know exists for certain, he runs into something which is beyond even his expectations? Remember, this is Draag we are talking about."

Maldor rose his hand as if to silence the elf so he could speak. "We will find Schram as well as the one he seeks, that much is certain. Now dwarf, you lead, and I will take the rear."

Wasting no time, Jermys recovered his axe from the fallen goblin and made his way back into the caverns, still trying to completely regain his senses. The rest of the travelers fell in to their respective positions except Maldor and Stepha who quickly gathered up the goblin bodies and disposed of them in some nearby brush with the elf aiding passage before sliding in behind.

"The travel to the mirror room I told you about should be fairly easy unless we happen upon some stray goblins or trolls, so we should make it there by early evening."

The evaluation was passed back through the group ending with Maldor who growled in response swinging his club to stay loose. After a long pause, Jermys added, "you still haven't told me what you guys are doing here. Schram said that you would head towards Drynak when Krirtie…" he paused as the memory of Krirtie's injury struck him. "Krirtie!" he exclaimed, "you are well?" He repeated it again as if he did not remember his first exchange.

The girl smiled at the dwarf who had stopped with outstretched arms for a hug. "Yes Jermys, thanks to you and the others I pulled through the ordeal with little more than minor pains and aches."

The two embraced tightly before the dwarf said, "it's Maldor and Stepha who did most of it. They deserve most of the thanks." Jermys stopped talking a moment as he saw Krirtie and Maldor exchange glances which told of a new-found and rising love. He smiled and then repeated his previous question. "I thought you were going to Drynak."

Stepha stepped up and in a humored, but still forceful tone, stated, "we changed our minds."

That answer seemed good enough for Jermys as he took Stepha's hand and with a small smirk from the corner of his lips, they continued at a quick pace down the corridor.

Jermys was accurate in his estimation of the time they would arrive at the mirror room, and as they entered, the rest of the group became as captivated as Schram had been the first time he embraced its beauty. He again told them how Schram had all of the sudden disappeared from the wall opposite the mirror so they began searching there for any signs of a hidden passage. After several minutes however, they looked at each other and without words told that it was a hopeless endeavor. Maldor was the first to speak as the elf went over to investigate the mirror up close. "Perhaps we should try that corridor," he said pointing to the cavern opening in the opposite direction of their entrance. "If Schram did find a passage, it is likely that his magic sprung it and we would die an old death before finding it on our own."

Stepha frowned, but it was the dwarf who spoke up adamantly. "That is the one I went down that ended up back at the cavern entrance where I met you. I am not incompetent and I never get lost in tunnels. It is a physical impossibility. There is another way through this maze!"

"Then if you have a better idea regarding our choice of directions, I will openly greet it with cheer!"

His sarcastic tone was drowned out by Stepha's strikingly concerned pitch. "Someone is coming!" She motioned towards the dark corridor Maldor had wanted to investigate. "We must have set off some sort of alarm."

The group froze and then all darted to the other cavern making as little noise as possible. They crouched silently in the doorway all with weapons drawn as the approaching footfalls slowly grew in intensity. "It sounds like only one or two," whispered Maldor. "Yet, it also sounds as if they are stepping lightly to avoid detection. They must be planning to surprise us."

"I hear nothing," stated Krirtie, "but if it is only a few, we shouldn't have a problem with them."

"Unless it is another one of those human/dragon bastards," added Jermys. "That other one was bad enough, but two more?"

The group remained silent. They could all make out the hidden movements of something in the shadows just beyond the rooms light. The figure's large eyes sat like ominous lanterns piercing the blackness until it recognized that the room was empty. A sword tip broke the light's plane first followed by the large warrior figure.

"Schram!" hollered Stepha who was almost into his arms before the others could even move. "You're safe! Thank Shirak you are safe."

The reuniting of the companions was brief but still held enough pleasure for all of them to lift their spirits clearing the atmosphere as a whole. They all exchanged stories which left both Schram and Jermys regarding the other with questionable glances when it came to their separation. All was quiet however when Schram dug into his pocket and gave Jermys the tiny chest left to Sabast's safe keep by Kirven many years before. The dwarf looked hesitantly toward the box before reaching to take it from the human's hands. When it was totally in his possession, the tiny chest grew in size until it was about equal in size to that of the dwarf. Jermys fell back in surprise but slowly recovered and reached forward to release the latch swinging the door open. A brilliant light erupted from within the chest blinding all except Schram, Krirtie, and the dwarf. Jermys knelt down and removed the object inside the case and in an instant the case and the blinding light disappeared.

In his hands rested the Hatchet of Claude, the legendary dwarven hero who with only one small axe at his side slew all the evil beasts of the mineral mines enabling the dwarves to flourish. His blade was said to be of a magical cut which would split the most fearsome armor plating. Jermys stood staring at the illuminating weapon in a lost expression of disbelief. He looked toward Schram with a pleading cry of appreciation though no words could be formed. Finally, his broken speech won over and his words lit the air with excitement. "This hatchet has been lost for centuries. . .more lifetimes than I could ever begin to measure. Its return by your hand will etch the dwarves in debt to you forever."

Schram smiled. "Let it be the symbol that reseals the broken bonds between neighboring dwarven factions. We need all to defend the land from the evil about to strike."

He had chosen his words carefully and told his companions only what Sabast had instructed him to say, but Stepha could see that he was hiding something, and also that he was changing. She went to him as the others huddled around the dwarf and his fabulous gift, but she did not have a chance to speak as Schram raised his hands to get attention. "We must leave Draag now. Stepha, do you think you can lift us out of here?"

The elf was caught completely by surprise and only nodded approval as an answer. With that, she moved over and put Jermys and Krirtie under her arms and with a quick flap of the muscles in her wings, lifted them up with ease. The voyage took quite long as the mountain was much higher than even the eyesight held it to be, and those down below waited anxiously for their turn to be rid of the awful caverns. Maldor went next and then Stepha returned for Schram.

She landed in front of him and without speaking, surveyed the human she loved so dearly. After a short moment, she asked, "What else happened, Schramilis?"

The human looked at her and a sadness came to his eyes. "I cannot say other than this ring has some power which I can feel but have not begun to understand. I feel as if something is loose in my body and my actions may fall prey to its commands if I can't gain control of it myself." He held the hand with the ring on it out to the elf.

She studied the pattern of a smaller ring surrounded by a barrage of weapons including the shape of a strange bow with a bent sword along its string both etched deep into the unique, dull metal. Her eyes spoke of nothing but confusion and her growing anxiety filled her with dismay. Her voice was not strong when she gripped his hand tightly turning both their knuckles pale white. "Take the ring off. At least until you better understand its powers and can do with it what Kirven intended for you to do." She paused while she quickly wiped a tear from her eye. "I see changes in you, and they are changes which scare me. Not simply difference in your abilities and behaviors, but physical ones as well. I can't directly put my finger on it, but you are beginning to appear different." She burst into tears and fell into his arms.

Schram too was caught with emotion and his apparent reality of the situation swooped upon him. He appeared lost as he fought against a sudden burst of pain. He clenched his fist and pushed the girl back. "The ring will not come off. I have tried from the moment

I put it on. I don't believe it will ever leave my finger. I will either take control of it or it will of me, but we will not separate."

The two just looked at each other and fell back into each other's arms. Still in the embrace, Stepha spread her wings and gently they began their ascent. They arrived through the huge opening in the ceiling of the long tower with a sigh from everyone around and realized they were atop a huge mountain well above the tree line. The air was quite thin and the temperature much cooler than it had been at the base of the cavern. The sky was gray, and although there were only patches of snow left on the mountain top, it looked as if it could be blanketed in less than an hour. Schram noticed everyone's gaze upon him, and while he and Stepha added extra clothing, he motioned to the group to begin the long descent. "I don't know if this will be as easy a journey as if we had stayed in the tunnels, but I am just glad to be free from those awful caverns." His words were followed by confirming nods and grunts from the other companions as they slowly began their trek downward behind his lead.

They had traveled for nearly an hour and were deep in the trees now but still had only covered about a quarter of the mountain's descent. The temperature had continued dropping and snow had begun to fall lightly in small swirling flakes although little of it could break through the thick tree cover. Even the brisk wind proved to be well disrupted causing the companions little grief from the cold. They had come to a tiny break in the thicket and although Schram did not want to waste too much time hanging around the mountains of Draag, he thought it would be better to stop now for a bite of food while they still could. Besides with everything else that was happening, darkness was beginning to show its inevitable occurrence and that usually meant more danger in its wake.

He cleared off the snow from a large fallen oak trunk and all sat down with varying degrees of sounds erupting from each of their mouths as their tired legs were given rest. Schram was the first to speak after all were passed their rations of food. "I don't see the point to travel too far into the night, especially if another blizzard could be brewing in those clouds to the south. I think we should find shelter within the next hour. However, it will have to be somewhere well-protected and easy to defend for I don't have to tell you how dangerous these grounds really are."

The group all nodded agreement, most without even breaking between their constant bites. They sat quiet for many long moments only speaking idle comments which obviously served no purpose other than to break the monotonous silence that was making all of them uncomfortable. Schram rose and began gathering his belongings causing everyone to get to their feet.

Again they began walking, but before they could get out of the clearing, a deep raspy voice sounded behind them. "Ah, leaving so soon, Prince Schram of Toopek?"

The party simultaneously wheeled around drawing each of their preferred weapons in the process to face that who had gone unnoticed. However, what they greeted nearly brought them to their knees. In front of the five warriors stood one huge, dark dragon with two canoks standing on each side. Schram's eyes showed terror as he looked upon his old friend Kirven and recognized the voice of his bastard twin Almok. All the words Sabast had spoken now seemed to be true; Kirven had taken his place by his father and brother to lead the charge of evil across the land and the eminent placement of the black dragon, Slayne, as Emperor over all of Troyf. Schram fought hard to overcome his fears, but seeing his closest friend standing before him as the heart of his enemy was proving too difficult to handle. Slowly, he stepped forward breathing deeply in an attempt to calm his nerves. In the strongest voice he could muster, he stated, "yes Almok, brother to the great Kirven and son to Slayne, Lord of the Dragon Oppression, we have decided to leave the Land of Draag."

The black dragon laughed as he heard the human's words. "This is the one who will defeat me. I feel nothing but a reckless child with little control over a wild ambition. He is of no concern to me. You have evidently been ill in your choosing my son." Again the dragon bellowed laughter this time accompanied by Almok. The rest of the group stood frozen, each holding their weapons in defense but not certain if they could use them against such ominous opponents. Slayne then surveyed the group until his eyes widened with intrigue on two things. His first comment directed toward Krirtie. "Ah, the Sword of Ku, an ally but still of little concern but," his stare then hardened on the dwarf with a bite which caused all to step back one pace. "Where did you get the hatchet, dwarf?"

Jermys fought through the fear as best he could and even took a step forward to now stand beside Schram. "I got it as a gift from..."

Schram rose his hand silencing the dwarf in mid-sentence. "Where he got it is of no concern to one so powerful as you." His tone denoted sarcasm causing the dragon's eyes to narrow on the human. Schram continued without even the slightest inflection carried in his speech. "Yet, I feel worry and fear growing within you now that was not there a moment ago. What is it that causes such distress in you from those who you could allegedly destroy so easily?"

Slayne pushed his lips together tightly as Schram's words struck him deeper than any sword could hope to reach. He arched his neck and sucked in a deep breath. At once all the companions raised their shields as the adrenaline flowing hot through their veins made this a reflex rather than a physical action. Schram stepped forward in an attempt to block as much of the wall of fire from his companions as he could raising his shield higher when he heard the dragon roar the exhale of broiler temperature heat. The ring on his shield hand throbbed, but that was the only pain he felt. Schram peered around his cover and saw a magical barrier emitting from his shield forming a protective bubble around the entire group. The dragon's flames danced harmlessly off its sides and were quickly extinguished.

Everyone in the area was completely taken back, but none were more surprised than Schram who wore a crooked smile as he lowered his arm removing the magical barrier. He stared at the dragon and then towards Kirven who gave no indication of understanding what had happened but simply showed the same frown which mimicked Almok's. All was silent in the forest causing a eerie stillness throughout the clearing. Finally, Kirven arched his head downward and spoke to Slayne in the random, mixed gibberish common to canok's speech.

The black dragon smiled and said loudly, "I believe you are correct my son." Then he turned back to face the small group who remained stunned staring back. "Kirven seems to think you have no idea what just happened and it was simply a fluke or an outside force at work. Whatever the case, it will be of little aid against the brunt of the three most powerful wizards on Troyf."

With that, the two canoks moved closer to Slayne and all seemed to be concentrating on the others. With a flash of light, two giant beasts appeared on both sides of Schram and bolts of energy shot from the dragon's eyes directly towards the human. Maldor leaped in front of the two girls and met one of the serpent creatures head on. Krirtie soon joined him as Stepha sent arrows in the direction of the creature Jermys was violently engaging. Schram again raised his ring and shield feeling the intense power of the dragon upon him.

Maldor's sword was having little effect on the thick scales of the serpent, and he threw down his weapon and attacked with his body. The creature lunged and the two crashed together like a rock slide meeting its base. The maneth's arms bulged and his muscles exploded beneath his armor while each fought to better the other's strength. The maneth had a firm grip around the serpent's snake-like neck, but the creature was still able to flail its body wildly shaking Maldor violently through the air but not freeing itself from the maneth's hold. Krirtie moved closer and with one downward swing, sent the curved edge of her scimitar deep into the creature's body causing it to shriek in pain. The serpent's free tail swung rapidly around and sent the human woman sailing into the base of a large oak. Maldor froze on Krirtie and this gave the creature the chance to break the maneth's grip. With one quick twist, Maldor too laid on the ground. The serpent wasted no time as it dug its teeth deep into the maneth's flesh and then used this grip to hurl him in the direction of the girl.

Jermys' small reach was having little effect on the beast before them, but the little man continued swinging wildly accompanied by Stepha's barrage of arrows. The serpent attacked ferociously, but could not get close enough when facing the brunt of the dwarf's magical hatchet which cut through its thick scales as if it were cutting air. After taking another elven arrow harmlessly off its chest area, the serpent moved from the dwarf and attacked the elf. Stepha immediately leaped into the air, but the beast caught her foot in its mouth. The dwarf turned and hurried to attack from behind falling into the cleverly set trap. The serpent allowed Jermys to move in close pretending not to notice the dwarf's planned offensive. With a quick flick of his tail, the dwarf was cleared from the area releasing his hatchet and falling unconscious to the ground.

Schram could see and feel all that was occurring around him but was powerless to help as he faced the brunt of the magical and powerful attack. His shield was absorbing the energy being shot into him, but it felt as if he were holding up a falling boulder. He didn't know how long he could last as the strength behind the energy charge did not seem to be weakening. Already he was on his knees and knew his friends were about to be attacked again, and they were not able to mount any defense. He felt the strength in his arms begin to fail.

He concentrated all his mind on his defense, centering both on his physical and his mental abilities, but to no avail. The incredible dragon magic slowly was engrossing his body. Slayne's eyes were growing in anticipation of what he felt occurring. Drool even began falling in balls of fire between his rows of jagged teeth. The canoks were still in control over the serpents but it was clear that they too saw that the end was near. Schram chanced a glance toward Kirven but saw nothing but opaque dragon fire burnt into his eyes. The human felt his arms beginning to fail and only at that time did he really understand how desperate his ignorant idea had been. Moments before the final wave of hell was pushed across him, Schram heard a faint calling from a far away and a mostly unrecognizable voice. He concentrated on the words but could gain nothing from their meaning. As he thought, his ring began to pull on his hand drawing his mind further into the spell. In a strange voice totally unlike his own he repeated as strongly as he could, "*aln jon fri dschungel.*"

Slayne's eyes narrowed and became hard while the two canoks stared questionably at the clearing now void of everything except the two bloodied bodies of the serpent creatures. "Perhaps I have underestimated the strength of the boy."

Neither canok spoke in return. The three turned from the clearing and moved slowly on an ominous trek back into Draag.

All was motionless across the clean, hard plain depicting the boundaries of the Dry Sea of Nakton. Five small figures did not disturb the peaceful serenity that had existed for several days as the weather had remained unseasonably calm and warm. Schram was the first to move although his strength was almost nonexistent. He could only twitch his body slightly, but his consciousness enabled him to wake the others with speech. Krirtie rose her head in a dazed look of confusion. She leaned over and gently woke Maldor as Stepha too began to stir.

"What happened?" the human girl whispered softly as she left Maldor's side in an attempt to help Schram.

"I will be fine," he responded weakly, pushing her hand away. "I am just tired from the use of magic. See to the dwarf. He is truly injured."

Krirtie and Stepha both moved to help Jermys who remained unconscious with his magical hatchet at his side but still on the ground. Krirtie turned back to Schram. "He does not move and blood spills from a wound aside his head."

"Replace the hatchet to his belt. Perhaps its enchantment will help restore the dwarf's strength."

Stepha grabbed the hatchet and placed it to Jermys' sleeve causing an expression of peace to fall across his face. She turned to Schram. "What happened?"

"I don't know. I felt something, or heard something, but that was it. It was something from a dream or a vision."

"Did someone help you?" asked Maldor.

"I don't know. I heard words, or I knew words, or they were told to me. However it occurred, we are hear, and Slayne, Almok, and my old friend are not."

There was little more talk after that exchange. Schram was deep in thought and meditation trying to determine the source of what occurred. Jermys had appeared calmed once the Hatchet was returned to his side and in time his eyes blinked, and he rose before the pleasant looks of his companions who were busy building a camp and fire. "Either I am dead and have gone to the hell of blind miners or somehow, we escaped. I am not sure which I would prefer the case to be."

"Ah shut up, dwarf!" rang Fehr's little voice who had been forced to wake during their magical voyage.

Jermys glared and added, "it must be hell."

Stepha smiled. "I will tell you all that we know, but it may not answer your questions. After which, you must rest. Your injuries are indeed grave, and you need some time to heal completely."

She filled the dwarf in on the occurrences in the forest, and then, as the others slept, joined Schram on his watch. His cheeks rose when his eyes caught her shadow approaching and the two fell immediately into a deep kiss and embrace. "When will you be leaving?" she asked.

"How did you know?" he replied softly, surprised by her question and knowledge about things even he was not certain of.

The elf held her smile and shook her head slightly while she took the powerful man's hand in hers. "The black dragon said you would be the one chosen to defeat him. I don't understand it, but I think it has something to do with that ring and the talk you had with the one called Sabast. I assume you are going to be leaving to search for the knowledge you need to control this magic which has befallen upon you."

Her words fell off as tears began to form in her eyes. Schram squeezed her hands tightly, and he could feel something in the ring surge with power. Softly he spoke. "Once again, your insight serves you well. I must go, for you are correct that I seek the answers to the mysteries within this ring." The two stared longingly towards each other as they both fought to stay in control of their emotions. "I love you Stephanatilantilis, and I always will. However, I must go, and it must be tonight. When I am to rejoin you, I cannot say for I do not know."

The tears she had been holding back now began streaming down her cheeks. Her golden hair danced in the wind about her wings and even in all her sadness, Schram could do nothing but see her beauty. She collapsed in his broad arms and the fragile elf let her well-constructed guard down allowing her emotions to escape upon the human she loved more than any other. She seemed to die in his safe embrace for hours only to be brought back to life when he pushed her back. In the most caring voice she had ever heard from his lips, he said, "I must go now."

She gripped his hand. "Will you tell the others?"

"No," he replied softly. "You know as well as I do that they would not let me go alone."

She shook her head gently and in a soft tone which caused the human to turn back to meet her caring gaze, she asked, "Schram, I would like to go with you. We would not have to inform the others. I could help you. You know that I could."

His worried stare turned to a small curled smile. "I know you could, but this is something I must face alone. Don't worry Stepha, we will be together again." As he said it, he thought of Kirven's last words to him upon leaving the maneth village and now finally understood the tone he had used when he had spoken them. He thought about his old friend and bowed his head in sadness.

His eyes rose as the elf spoke. "For five years I have carried this." She reached her hand out and opened it to Schram. "I finally know that there will never be anyone but you who I could rightly give it to, if there is room on your hand for another ring and you would accept it."

Schram's eyes nearly fell from him as he stared at the elven ring of joining which nearly matched the one he had offered to her so many years past. Without taking the ring or speaking, Schram reached inside his pack and dug into his life pouch removing that very ring from so long ago. He extended his hand and spoke softly in return. "I can accept only that which you could accept from me."

Together they reached out their free hands and took each other's ring, and on the Dry Sea of Nakton, they joined as two becoming one. The passion and love that was exchanged in that moment went beyond anything either of them had ever felt before. They both knew that no distance would ever separate them, and as one, they would always be together. After the silent exchange and the endless flow of emotion, Schram disappeared into the night.

CHAPTER 17

Taiju

Schram awoke in an unfamiliar room with the most serious pounding rocking his head. The pain seeped through his skull as if his head was exploding. He glanced around his cell-like room and realized he had no recollection of where he was or how he had come to be there. The cell was roughly six foot by twelve foot and contained only a small cot and a single door at the far side away from the bed. Light came from a large candle set on the center of the rock floor in front of the door. He sat on the edge of his cot and gripped his head trying to stop the throbbing so he might have a chance to remember what had happened. The last thing he knew, he was leaving Stepha on the Dry Sea of Nakton and had walked several hours. After that, his mind was blank.

Remembering Stepha, he looked down at his hand which contained the Ring of Joining she had given him. Seeing it, his eyes moved and saw the ring on the adjacent finger, The Ku Ring. However, it now looked different. It was no longer the dull, greenish brown copper ring with an almost indistinguishable pattern. Now it was shiny and well-polished, and the design carved into it was as clear as if it had been created only minutes before. A long curved sword circled the base of the ring with a delicately worked bow etched into its blade. Connecting the hilt of the sword to the blade tip was a large golden hammer and a small axe. The arrangement of the four weapons together formed into a separate loop of their own across the face of the ring's surface.

Schram's head again shot with a violent eruption of pain, and he bent down, placing his head between his knees and covering his back with his arms. It was then he realized he was without his armor and weapons. A worried feeling crept up the human's spine as he tried to piece together anything he could in his choppy mind. He lifted his head and then leaned back against the wall. Softly he spoke several words, and with a quick pulse running from his ring finger throughout his body, the pain in his head subsided. He jumped up, almost afraid of what he had done on command and not understanding it. *How could he have worked magic through the ring?* he thought. He didn't even know how he had gotten to where he was, much less, what the ring and its magic were all about.

With a sudden pop and cracking, the huge bolts and hinges on the large wooden door began to turn and the door slowly swung open, crashing against the inside wall when it was fully ajar. A cool burst of air rushed in and replaced the dry musty scent that had gone unnoticed previously. By the sounds made by the joints in the door when it opened and the tomb-like smell which had been in his small room, Schram imagined that it had been a long time since it had been opened and therefore a long time that he had been held there. He slowly calmed himself and then walked out into the dark hallway, recovering the candle as he passed. The candle put out an amazing amount of light, and he saw that his room had been at the end of a great corridor. Like his room, the corridor had no windows and the only entrance or exit seemed to be a large door near the end of the hall. There also were no pictures or artwork of any kind, but rather a long empty stone corridor whose smooth, plain surfaces were broken only by the sight of the huge wooden doors of the cell and the supposed exit.

Schram continued towards the door without a bit of nervousness despite the uncomfortable situation. There was something familiar about the hall, and he felt that there was nothing to fear there. Suddenly however, the air before him began to swirl and seemed to take on a dark hue and shape. Schram froze and watched intently over all that was occurring in the hallway but was still unsure regarding what he should be feeling. The belief that there was nothing to fear quickly disappeared when the shape growing ahead of him formed into an ominous black dragon and the deep bellowing laugh familiar to Schram's ears echoed through the hall.

The dragon's eyes beat the human back as drools of flame struck the ground beneath him. He wanted to be strong and fight Slayne once again as he had before, but he still had no conscious knowledge of the power he now possessed. He peered at the dragon taking a step backwards when he saw the beast fill his belly with air knowing that within moments the entire hall would explode in flame. Slayne arched his neck releasing the wall of fire as Schram fell to his knees and raised his hands in protection as a reflex. He could feel the heat and pain as his flesh began to burn off the bone and then there was nothing.

Schram awoke in an unfamiliar room with the most serious pounding rocking through his head. The pain seeped through his skull as if his head was exploding. He glanced around his cell-like room and realized he had no recollection of where he was or how he had come to be there. The cell was roughly six foot by twelve foot and contained only a small cot and a single door at the far side away from the bed. Light came from a large candle set on the center of the rock floor in front of the door. He sat on the edge of his cot and gripped his head trying to stop the throbbing so he might have a chance to remember what had happened. The last thing he knew, he was leaving Stepha at the Dry Sea of Nakton and had walked for several hours. After that, his mind was a blank, although there was something familiar about this room but he could not place it.

Remembering Stepha, he looked down at his hand that contained the Ring of Joining she had given him. Seeing it, his eyes moved to see the ring on his adjacent finger, the Ku Ring. However, now it looked different. It was no longer the dull, greenish brown copper ring with an almost indistinguishable pattern. Now it was shiny and well-polished, and the design carved into it was as clear as if it had been created only minutes before. A long curved sword circled the base of the ring with a delicately worked bow etched into its blade. Connecting the hilt of the sword to the blade tip was a large golden hammer and a small axe. The arrangement of the four weapons together formed into a ring of their own across the Ku Ring's surface.

Schram's head again shot with a violent eruption of pain, and he bent down placing his head between his knees and covering his back with his arms. It was then that he realized he was without his armor and weapons. A worried feeling crept down the human's spine while he tried to piece together anything he could in his mind. He lifted his head and then leaned back against the wall. Softly he spoke several words, and with a quick pulse running from his ring finger throughout his body, the pain in his head subsided. He sat up gently with a lost expression glowing from his wide eyes giving the impression of a student who had finally discovered how all the preliminary lessons he had been taught could now be used to solve the whole problem. He again peered at the ring on his finger and his smile faded knowing that he still had little idea on how to harvest the power contained within it.

With a sudden pop and cracking, the huge bolts and hinges on the large wooden door began to turn and the door slowly swung open, crashing against the inside wall when it was fully ajar. A cool burst of air rushed in and replaced the dry musty scent which had gone unnoticed before the clean air came in. By the sounds made by the joints in the door when it opened and the tomb-like smell which had been in his small room, Schram imagined that it had been a long time since it had been opened and therefore a long time that he had been held there. He slowly calmed himself and then walked out into the dark hallway, recovering his candle as he passed. The candle put out an amazing amount of light, and he saw that his room had been at the end of a great corridor. Like his room, the corridor had no windows and the only entrance or exit seemed to be a large door near the end of the hall. There also were no pictures or artwork of any kind, but rather a long empty stone corridor whose smooth, plain surfaces were broken only by the sight of the huge wooden doors of the cell and the supposed exit.

Schram continued towards the door without a bit of nervousness despite the uncomfortable situation. There was something familiar about the hall, and he felt that there was nothing to fear there. Suddenly however, the air around him began to swirl and seemed to take on a dark hue and shape. Schram froze and watched intently all that was occurring in the hallway but was still unsure exactly what he should be feeling. The belief that there was nothing to fear quickly disappeared when the shape growing ahead of him formed into an ominous black dragon and the deep bellowing laugh familiar to Schram's ears echoed through the hall. The dragon's eyes beat the human back as drools of flame struck the ground beneath Slayne's mouth. Schram wanted to be strong and fight the black beast once again as he had before but the revelation about the power he now possessed which he had felt back in his cell had been stripped away from him by the surprise of seeing his enemy before him. Fear shot through his body as his mind became a scrambled mixture of inconsistencies. He peered at the dragon taking a step backwards when he saw the huge creature fill his belly with air knowing that within moments the entire hall would explode in flame. As Slayne arched his neck preparing to release the wall of flame, Schram remembered something from deep within the boundaries of his mind. He softly chanted some words just as he saw the dragon shoot his hot death across the room. Schram felt the heat burning his flesh but his thoughts remained clear and distinct as his enchantment relaxed his body and mind. Slowly he raised his arm to bring the face of the Ku Ring to the brunt of the flames. Then, there was nothing.

 Schram's tired body gently forced his head upward until his senses again began to function revealing sharp pains in both his knees. He rose to his feet knowing that he must have fallen to his knees from exhaustion, though he had no recollection of where he was or what had made him so tired. It was pitch black and although his eyes seemed as if they should be able to focus naturally on something, he could not make them do it. He felt down his arm trying to find his hand bearing the Ring of Ku, but before reaching it he realized that he was now without his armor and weapons. He rubbed his thumb across his ring and without thinking, he recited a single word that caused his ring to explode in a fire of light. He saw he was in a long, blank corridor that was completely empty including walls that were bare of everything except where two exits broke their plane. One doorway stood directly behind him and when Schram approached it, he got the distinct feeling from somewhere within him that it was wrong to head back. He turned to again face the long corridor and began to slowly walk down its path.

He continued walking but his steps seemed more hesitant as he neared the huge wooden door resting on large, rusty hinges at the end of the hall. As he drew within about ten feet, the door exploded with nearly immeasurable deadening cracks sending piercing screeches and whines as it slowly swung open.

He passed through the doorway and the light from his ring revealed a huge open chamber with many sparkling jewels and statues and a magical fountain of a snake of some kind coiled above a small pool. Beyond the fountain there was a peculiar wall of darkness that seemed to swallow the light emitted from his ring. The void was completely opaque, and Schram could not feel a thing within it. He glanced around the room and then slowly approached the huge fountain. A crash sounded behind him as the large wooden door he had passed though suddenly slammed shut and then magically vanished being replaced by a magnificently carved wooden creature appearing to have a white feathered head and two large wings. He stared briefly at the new carving and then turned his attention back towards the fountain. The winged creature was fascinating but he was more captivated by the creature on the fountain. He could not remember why this snake-like figure on it seemed so familiar. He studied it more and more and slowly his mind began to form it into a different shape as if breaking a spell which protected its identity. As he stared longer, it became clear that it was not truly a snake, but it was something much more primitive or simple. It appeared like something almost swamp-like or parasitic. The widest part of its body was at its head while it gradually tapered down into a much skinnier and pointed tail. It had two large eyes which stuck out on two tentacle-like projections above its toothless mouth. As the water ran down its body, it gave the creature's skin a slimy appearance.

"Come closer young Schram," issued a soft but ominous voice from within the void.

Schram shot up. The voice, like everything else he had experienced, was familiar, but he could not place from where. He dropped his arms to his side and repeating his previous word, the ring's light vanished. The void, which had been in front of him, now crept up and engulfed the entire room. However, as it did so, Schram learned that he could still see, just as if the room was still lighted. It began as shapes and outlines, but as his eyes adjusted, he could see with night sight that would make an elf jealous. He peered through where the darkness had been and saw more of the same style of room with similar artwork as well. Along the far wall were several other magnificent wood carvings of tigons, canoks, dragons, and the like. He surveyed the entire wall and then stopped at a large pool that had a huge brown head sticking up from it. Two eyes rested high above it and blinked several times as the human approached. "Good," the creature said. "You have adapted well to your vision. You are accepting your gifts."

Schram's pace was slow while he tried to comprehend exactly why he knew this creature and felt no fear in its presence. To his memory, he had never seen it before. To his knowledge, he knew that they had been together a long time. "Who are you?" he asked when he drew near.

"Might I ask the same question to you?" the creature returned in the same voice that registered somewhere within Schram's mind.

He paused a long while as indecision nearly caused the human to fall to his knees. He knew what he remembered but suddenly his mind was a blank. He began to speak, then stopped, then with a burst of relief he completed his thought. "You know me, oh great one. I am Schram, Prince of the human city of Toopek."

The creature recognized his relief at the sudden revelation but added, "what if I say you have not told me all of who you are?"

Schram looked puzzled, first with the fact that he had subconsciously addressed this creature as 'great one` and then the fact that the question itself made him doubt his own identity. "Do you say I am not Schram?" he said hesitantly.

"No, that did not I say." There was a long silence while they stood locked in some sort of riddle of words. The creature then closed its eyes as if it were reaching inside itself to draw some hidden power. Suddenly, there was a burst of light between them which began to spread out into a long oval circle of glass. With a second burst, a silver backing appeared, and the large mirror hovered in front of Schram. "Now, I ask you again, are you Schram, Prince of Toopek?"

Schram looked into the glass trying to understand what he saw. He was still the human son of the King and Queen of Toopek, but he was also something more. His hair was long and straight, reaching the center of his back, and its color was jet black, not the dusty deep brown it had been. It was pulled back and tied by a band revealing his tall pointed ears which twitched as he looked. His skin was that of a human with just a light touch of the brownish-green tint common to elves. With the sight of his new found physical changes came a flood of knowledge from deep within his mind. Schram reached out his hand and passed it over the mirror sending it into oblivion. Again staring at the creature he called great one, he spoke, "I am Schram, Prince of Toopek, but I now live in harmony with the legendary Lord of the Elves, The Great Ku, who has come to once again work his magic through me. That who gave the elves their power of being, now gives me the hand at which to understand the power." He paused and looked at the creature before him. "And you are Taiju, Lord of all who seek the power of a magic hand. You are that who has been taught by the gods, and he who now teaches me. You are my master."

Taiju smiled as the young magician before him came to know himself. "I am not your master nor am I one who has been taught by the gods. I am a tool in the process of the knowledge of that which is not natural to being. You have much power inside you. It is good to see you have the knowledge to discover it." He paused as he looked over the boy, "but if you didn't, you would never have survived the training and the joining of two minds to work as one. You spent more time leaving the cell than I would have even imagined possible. Learn much you did in those steps, repeat them many times as well, each giving you new knowledge."

"Master Taiju, will I ever remember the training?"

"In time you will know all," his voice was soft and calming. "It would be too much for your body to handle now, but as you grow, you will come to understand what energy flows from within you, and what it took for you to find it."

Schram shook his head as he tried to absorb what the creature said then followed with his next thought still speaking much like a student to his teacher. "How long have I been here?"

Taiju grew solemn. "For thirteen months you have fought to learn the secrets locked within yourself and the ring you now wear." Schram's eyes grew wide as the creature continued. "It took you four months to simply make it into that previous hallway from the room before. The ring's power is great but it cannot be rushed or for that matter even taught. You had to learn how to harvest its power, and learn how to live with it. You have faced death more times and with more reality than any being ever should. Yet, in the end, a harmony was reached, and the capacity of such a joining has never been experienced before. You are as much elf now as human, and as much human as elf, and you will justly live your life span as such." He paused and then anticipating the next question asked, "what do you feel about what you have missed this past year?"

Schram's face grew lost and he closed his eyes. "I feel much fighting and bloodshed. The young dragons have begun their attacks and the war is raged on three main fronts, Elvinott, Toopek, and Feldschlosschen. All three are holding but no offensives can be mounted. It will only be a matter of time before they all give in to the dragon armies."

Taiju looked a bit surprised. "Your insight is leveled beyond that of my own. Indeed your strength grows more each day." He switched tones as he slid more into his pool to wet his drying rubbery skin. "What would you do if you were to leave now to help the effort?"

There was a long silence as Schram searched his inner feelings for the answer. Finally he said, "I would return to Toopek and be an active force behind its defense."

Taiju frowned. "While Elvinott and the dwarves fall in defeat? You must find a new way to defend these attacks for each day more dragon young enter the fighting where only a handful have been killed since it began four months ago. With each offensive, the goblins and trolls are able to move closer to each of the respective kingdoms. What is the only answer? Where can you be most effective?"

The student was now being pushed hard to find the hidden knowledge within his mind. Schram's half-elven eyes grew wide with excitement as a door within him suddenly was thrust open and its contents spilled widely past his lips. "The staff of Anbari. I have the ability to control its power."

The revelation was soothing and his mind relaxed deeply as the words struck his ears. Taiju closed his eyes and suddenly the room and everything around Schram dissolved. A burst of brilliant light exploded around him like a storm breaking the shore of a still dawn until slowly the environment melted into a new form. He stood in a small clearing of a forest made up primarily of tall oaks and maples. He smiled broadly for what he believed to be the first time in as long as he could remember. The realization of knowing where he was and why he was there sent a shiver of confidence through him like none he had felt before. He recognized the familiar forests surrounding the city he had spent the majority of his life and with a quick leap forward, he began a descent towards his friends.

His armor had been returned to him as well as his weapons although for some reason he felt that he would not need them. Yet, their presence was still quite reassuring. As he got within about half a mile from the city gates, his elven ears sensed that he was being watched. Within the next five minutes, the eaves droppers were no longer hiding their presence, and the noise in the trees and bushes, though well disguised, was clear to Schram and spoke of maneths and humans. Suddenly, five feet in front of him, stood a huge, heavily armored maneth. He spoke no words but just studied the man/elf before him. His eyes narrowed and his recognition was slow, but in a soft, questioning voice, Geoff said, "Schram?"

The human smiled at his old friend's confusion and happily replied, "a maneth, you're a maneth."

Geoff grinned as he remembered the words Schram had first spoken to him what seemed like so long ago when they had first been brought together. "By all the gods, I don't know what has happened to you, but I know this must be a slight light amidst all the darkness. I have a million questions but," there was a short pause while the two embraced tightly with Geoff's big arms almost squeezing all the air out of the large human, "I imagine there will be time and there are several people who would be mighty interested in seeing you."

Schram's smile broadened as he thought about his old companions. Several visions of them had been returning to him since he began his walk, but none as clear as the one of his beloved Stepha. He only hoped she would not fear all that had changed inside, and outside, about his character. He passed his finger across their ring of joining and a warmth grew throughout every limb. As they reached the city walls, Schram could feel the elf's presence. His feeling was so strong that his body began to ache as he yearned to see and hold her again. He didn't even notice all the destruction as he entered the battered town. There had been much commotion as word had spread of the stranger in the woods, and Schram looked ahead through the people to see a large, young familiar maneth returning his gaze and then running into one of the fortified buildings still standing. Within moments, he reappeared from the building with two females close behind, one human and one elf. All were smiling and running towards the approaching party, but Schram could only see one. Her hair was golden blonde, and her large green eyes were already pools of tears as she lifted her wings out to let them catch the wind and increase her foot speed. Schram pushed himself by Geoff and fell into her arms. Krirtie was not far behind the elf as she too joined in the embrace. Maldor hit the group like a tidal wave and soon all were on the ground rolling in one giant and excited hug.

The atmosphere in the town was much lighter that night as, although he looked slightly different, all rejoiced in the return of their Prince. Spring seemed to have arrived early this year and much of the usual snow as well as the cold temperatures were absent. Schram spent most of the day talking with his old friends about what he knew about his ordeal and learning what he had missed with the war. Stepha told him about Jermys' decision to return to Feldschlosschen with the Hatchet of Claude, especially when he learned that his brother, Bretten, had never returned from Antaag. "However," Stepha continued, "as he had hoped, the recovery of the Hatchet reunited the two dwarven kingdoms and under the unified symbol of Claude, they now stand together to defend their nation. Yet, as of the last message we received, there had still been no word about Bretten and the Antaag King swears no betrayal in this matter."

"What about your father, Hoangis, and the elves?"

Her face grew sad. "The elves have been hit hard by the dragon attacks. Madeiris returned to Elvinott immediately to tell father what we had discovered at Draag. I remained here with a single squadron of flyers to help protect Toopek from the air attacks of the dragons and to wait for your return." She leaned over and kissed him again as the others around smiled. "However, my father sends word that the magical enchantment of their forest is weakening and the goblin and troll armies are slowly moving closer and in large numbers. Also, on a couple of occasions small bands of dark dwarves have been seen among the goblins. If they become organized against us, the dark forces numbers would greatly outnumber us."

Schram appeared lost but remained stoic. He knew this was no time to mix words so his statement was direct and abrupt. "We must go to Elvinott. I seek..."

He was cut off by a small voice from behind him. "Hey, is it true? Has that blind, nit-wit human returned?" He stopped as Schram turned to face the small rat. "My gosh, would you look at those ears!"

Everyone laughed and Schram scooped Fehr up issuing a large grin of his own in the process. "Well, I suppose it is nice to see you again too."

All continued laughing while Fehr's excited speech followed suit. "Oh boy, it is so nice to see you. I have so many stories to tell. I'll bet you do too judging by your long black hair and those goofy ears."

Stepha appeared offended by the last comment and thumped the rat lightly on the head. "You are too late Fehr. We already told Schram all that has happened thus ruining your fun. Now be quiet and let him finish, and just so you know, I think his ears are simply delicious looking."

That made the young human magician blush while Fehr only turned to the smiling elf and sarcastically added, "You would! After all, they are as big as yours."

Schram regained his color and stood up before his friends. "As I was saying, I must return to Elvinott and speak with Hoangis. I would very much like my old friends to accompany me, but I realize because of the time period, it may not be possible. You all know of the current situation of Toopek better than I. If you cannot be spared here, then I understand completely. The protection of our cities must come first. As I was told, Geoff and Alan Grove have been leading the war effort with aid from Prince Reynolds of Empor. I, as Prince of the City, will relinquish all rule to those three which will make any of those who might resent a maneth and a third lieutenant leading them fall in line as well. We have come to a pivotal point in the war, and what we do from here on out may have a grave impact on our future. Trust your feelings and weigh your choices carefully, and most of all, know that it is my greatest happiness to be with all of you again. You were, and will always be, my most cherished friends." He stopped his speech and put his hand across Stepha's allowing the backs of their Rings of Joining to rest against the other. "And some of you have become much more." She returned a smile toward him and both could feel the love again flow between their touch. "I must go now and speak to Geoff and Alan. I will be at the adjacent inn having a bite to eat when you have reached your respective decisions."

Schram moved to leave but stopped when the elf grabbed his arm. "Schram, I require no time to weigh my options. I will be beside you as I have been my whole life."

Schram stopped and embraced the elf once again. Maldor and Krirtie looked at each other and smiled, but it was the human who spoke. "We too would join you without question."

"Does that we include me?" sounded Fehr's soft but distinctive voice.

"Yes, unfortunately it does," stated Schram now bearing a large smile. Turning to speak toward everyone, he added, "I had hoped you would all want to come. This time we will need each other even more than in the past. It is a mission nobody can assume will be free of danger and therefore goes beyond life-threatening. However, we are all as one."

A crash sounded as Maldor slammed the hilt of his club downward shattering the table in front of them. "I have waited for this day that the war may take a positive turn. We will follow you as always, Schram." He roared an echoing blast upon finishing his statement.

"Very well," broke in the human. "You must all prepare those who you lead to expect your absence, for we will leave tomorrow." All nodded in confirmation. "Then if you have no other plans, meet me at the inn for dinner and drink. It will be refreshing to be among friends."

Stepha smiled as she remembered the troubled human who had left her over a year ago to resolve his inner conflicts. He seemed to have come to terms with the forces of the ring, she thought, but what do these changes mean? The desire to speak with her father was strong with her as well ever since she had sent a message to him regarding the Ring Schram had been given and his immediate, worried but still illusive, reply. There were many questions she had which she did not wish to ask Schram, but since her father obviously knew something, perhaps he could shed some light on them. For now however, nothing mattered, for she was about to spend a reunion night with the man, and elf, she loved as no other.

CHAPTER 18

ELVINOTT FALLS

"Trouble, your majesty!" shouted a panting voice of an elf messenger who had run with the news. "Our scouts have seen huge rebel goblin and troll forces mounting along our borders. They have made no movements into the forest, but the flyers can feel the little enchantment left in the wood fading. It is believed that the attackers will no longer fall prey to its sleep inducing magic."

The sadness and worry that had filled Hoangis' eyes for so long now came to a boil as he reached deep into his mind to find the lost answer. Softly he asked, "how many?"

The guard was caught by his King's lost voice, and he too began to feel great despair. "The scouts say numbers could reach into the several thousands."

There was a long period of silence as Hoangis paced the floor staring blankly into the air. "Is there anything else?" he finally broke in. "Has there been any word from my daughter?"

"No your majesty, and we are not even sure if the messenger made it through with the last parchment you sent."

The king frowned and then let his emotions calm. A soothing expression grew across his face before he fought through his next decision. "Pull all our troops back toward the south front. We are going to flee Elvinott."

"Retreat Lord? No! I am sure I speak for all when I say we would rather reach our end here."

Hoangis' eyes burned on the elf. "Do not let the evil time cause you to forget that which you have lived by your entire life. Do not speak of death again." His voice bit through the guard and he lowered his head in shame. Hoangis did not pursue the feelings as his thoughts turned back to the previous discussion. "We have no other choice now than that which I have stated. To stay and fight against these numbers would only serve to end as you have described it. We would not only lose our city, but our being as well. We will punch a hole through their south lines. They should not be expecting an attack and therefore will be caught by surprise. Then we'll head to Feldschlosschen and join forces to aid the dwarves in holding their mines."

He paused and looked around the large room making up his Great Conference Hall. Glancing over to the wall which bore the Treaty of Peace between the elves and the humans, Hoangis spoke softly and only to himself. "Schramilis, where are you now?"

The companions peered through the trees at the sight before them. None spoke at first but only looked at the apparent impenetrable wall of goblins camped near the Elvinott borders. Maldor broke the silence with a soft whisper. "The numbers seem to extend completely around the woods. Elvinott is in for a major offensive. Even if we could get back to gather Toopekian troops, they would arrive back here only in time to pick up what was left."

All was silent again as nobody responded to the maneth's comments though it was apparent from the flat expressions that all had heard. Schram stared blindly ahead concentrating on devising any plan to reach his first home. He turned to Stepha. "Do you know any secret paths that I may not be aware of?"

The elf shook her head. "No, you took us by every secret trail I knew, and all were as bad as this one."

"Then there is no other choice. Fehr, it will be up to you."

The rat jumped up, completely taken by surprise. "How can I get you out of a mess this time, big guy?"

Schram ignored the rat's light mood and continued with his previous thought. "I don't know that even you can get through this goblin wall, but I think you have a much better chance than any of us. You must take this document to Hoangis, nobody else, and tell him of our position. Then hopefully he can help us."

Fehr took the scroll which had magically appeared in Schram's hand and stuffed it into his pouch. Without a word or a lost moment, the worry-free little creature darted through the bushes and vanished. The rest of the group followed him with their eyes as best they could and were all equally amazed at their friend's ability to move so silently at times even passing within arms reach of several trolls and goblins but still going completely undetected. Krirtie only smiled as she watched, knowing Fehr would have no trouble outsmarting those foolhardy creatures even if he were noticed. Just seeing a bandicoot was hard enough, but catching one, those goblins didn't have a chance.

"Even if Fehr does make it," Stepha began, "whose to say that my father would help us break into the city only to face this imminent and most overwhelming force. Even with me being one of those trying to enter, I doubt he would risk any other lives for such a useless gesture."

Schram turned to the elf who had begun to show signs of tears as she thought of her homeland and family. Putting his arm around her, Schram said, "my parchment spoke nothing of you or anyone else here. As far as your father will know, I am the only one trying to reach him, and I trust he will stop at no ends to help me enter."

The rest of the group was stunned by their leader's comment, but none more than Stepha. She ducked from under his hold and circled to face him directly. In a stern voice which Maldor feared would be loud enough to alert the goblins to their presence, Stepha said, "Schramilis, I would appreciate you telling me exactly what is going on, and this time do not leave anything out. You can start with why you need to see my father, why he has acted so oddly since I described your ring to him, and why now you say he will risk anything to bring you to him."

He looked at the beautiful elf and then, noticing Maldor's worried gaze from the corner of his eye, glanced toward the goblin armies which were still plopped on the ground like large sacks of potatoes. They were totally oblivious to everything except satisfying their own digestive desires and following them with plenty of drink. His face relaxed and he turned back to face Stepha who had become white with anger. He spoke more softly. "All I can say now is that your father is as interested in me as I am in him. It was his great, great grandfather who, with his immeasurable ability with magic, first created the Ring I now wear and all the weapons it controls. It is that same person I have allowed to be a part of me, and now your father must judge who controls who in this joining."

Her face gained no color. She dropped her head softly speaking the name she had been sworn never to voice again. "Ku, it is Ku who you are fighting."

"No my love, it is Ku who I have become a part of."

Stepha walked away without another word while Maldor and Krirtie could only guess at the lost confusion on both her and Schram's face. The maneth knelt down beside the human woman and said, "Who the hell is Ku?"

Krirtie only could shrug showing she had no answers.

"All are in position, your majesty. One squadron has been left on each front to give the appearance that nothing is being planned. They will fall in behind as we attack to guard to the rear. The flyers are ready to begin on your order and the main ground force will follow their lead. All of our elves are ready..."

"Hoangis! Hoangis!" shouted a voice across the road. "I have found one who brings a message from Toopek."

The king's ears jumped at this and he shoved the guard aside and headed to meet the approaching elf. He could see the guard carrying something but could not tell what it was. However, as they reached each other, Hoangis recognized the body of the old visitor to his kingdom. The guard carrying the motionless figure spoke in between breaths. "We found him dragging himself along the ground with this dagger lodged in his belly. By the look of the blood trail, he had been traveling as such for hours. He spoke perfect elven but all he said before falling unconscious is that he had to speak to you and that he had never seen such a lucky goblin."

The king placed his long, wrinkled fingers over the bloodied body of Fehr. Slowly, his eyes opened. "Hoangis, is that you?" pushed his small voice. "I bring word from Schram."

The King again raised his hand over the rat's body and magically the bleeding stopped. In a soft voice, uncustomary of late, Hoangis asked, "what is this message you bring?"

Fehr felt a surge of strength growing through his body and now tried to even stand in the elf's arms as he spoke. "I do not know sir. Schram gave me this parchment." He removed the scroll from his pouch and pushed it toward the King, "But as much as I tried to open it, I couldn't break the seal." He paused then added, "I hope you know I only wanted to open it so in the event I lost it I could still succeed in getting the most urgent word to you."

The king smiled briefly. "I know Fehr. You did well, but now try and rest." He motioned to the guard holding the rat to take him to the southern lines and see that he was cared for. He told the other guard to send word to the people to be prepared and then to meet him back by the fountain. When he was alone, the king spoke a few words and the seal broke and released the scroll. He read Schram's message slowly, trying to learn exactly what had happened since they last spoke over a year ago.

Dear Hoangis, my father and great, great grandson, I am at your western boundaries and must warn you of a goblin force of immeasurable numbers mounting here. I strongly desire your council as I am sure you do mine. I wait for your sign, Schramilis.

Hoangis looked up to the sky and closed his eyes in a silent prayer. Time seemed to fall deathly still and if not for an inquisitive voice from behind, he may have remained locked in deep thought for eternity. "Father, are you well?"

The presence of his son's voice proved soothing even though it was quite a startling break. He placed the parchment in a pocket of his robe and turned to his son. "Yes Madeiris, I am well. What brings you here?"

"A guard says he was to meet you here but was too busy with the troops to leave. I told him I would come."

Hoangis smiled slightly. "Good, I was only going to have him send for you anyway. We have much to discuss."

Madeiris grew solemn and he replaced the bow he had been carrying all day. In a heavy and stern voice, he stated, "there is a rumor among the elves, one which until this moment I refused to believe. Yet, as I look within your eyes, I see that this rumor may indeed be true. Do you really intend to lead the elves out of Elvinott?"

"No my son," replied the king. "You must lead them. I will remain here to guard certain sacred tablets that can never be removed from this forest. If they were to fall into the wrong hands, the only result would be destruction throughout the whole land."

Madeiris became infuriated. "I will not allow you to remain alone father. You would have no chance against the force which will soon after our departure collapse on the city."

The king frowned. "It was not a request, Madeiris. Though I am your father, I am first your king, and you will follow my rule." He stopped and his voice softened. "Fear not for me my son, you will face a far greater danger than I."

The elf-prince bowed his head and then embraced his father. "I will honor your decisions as I have never before believed you to act outside that which is correct and good. However, I wish you to know that I will also return to reclaim our lands in your name and return you to your proper place as King of Elvinott."

"I know you will, my son," stated Hoangis breaking the hug but still keeping his hands on Madeiris' shoulders. "However, I am not certain that my proper place is how you have described it. Tell your sister that I love her and that you have both made me proud your entire lives."

Madeiris wore a brief but solid frown as he heard the strange words stemming on a final goodbye. The two elves stared at each other and exchanged something no words could ever properly identify. Then, with a nod, Hoangis added, "Now go, for the elves require your leadership like never before."

With that, the two parted, but each knew they would always be together. The king returned to the Great Hall and struck a fire in the pit. With a crash louder than a powerful thunderbolt, Hoangis could hear the first attacks of his people doing what had never occurred before, fleeing their homeland. He closed his eyes once more as if that would protect him from the horror he heard, but knowing that no simple action could block the agony his elven ears allowed him to hear. He only prayed that their surprise attack would be successful and the elves could escape.

The sounds of battle in the distance brought Maldor and Schram to their feet. Stepha and Krirtie returned from their positioned watch and all the companions peered ahead towards the goblin camp. If Schram felt surprised, the confusion with the goblins was leveling on hysteria. They were running and jumping with fights even breaking out among themselves as they all tried to grab weapons to prepare for the attack which the other fronts were facing. As they eventually quieted and the confusion was put to rest with the commanding shouts of those in charge, the army formed long battle lines and prepared to charge. With the bellowing holler from the leader, the goblins plunged across the imaginary line marking the boundary of the elven forest and began descending the woods. A few goblins immediately fell prey to the last remnants of the elven enchantment and their bodies were pulled into a deep endless sleep, while others seemed to become lost and confused only partially affected by the magic. However, the majority of the force surged forward only slowed by the interference created by their own lost comrades.

The companions looked on in disbelief, not really knowing what was happening or why, but all sure that it was not for the good. Schram stood and motioned for the others to follow and the four entered the now empty clearing where the goblins had recently camped. Although there were a few goblins remaining, they were only alive for moments. The group looked around hesitantly but soon noticed all remaining had entered the attack and now this side of the forest was free of all goblin and troll existence.

"Come on," Schram began firmly, "we will move swiftly in the goblin's shadow. Our help could prove important. I am not sure what Hoangis is up to, but he definitely cannot face the brunt of this attack for long."

The group exchanged worried looks as Schram stepped forward into the forest each wondering exactly how much help five barbarians would be against a battalion of soldiers with only one idea in mind, to kill anything that resisted them.

They passed several bodies held by the elven forest magic and quickly killed those lost and wandering aimlessly in circles. However, there were few bodies of attackers brought down with arrows and those that were seen showed of inaccurate placement or otherwise a long distant shot. Also, there were no signs of any dead or injured elves, which, although pleasing, left a deep wonder free to build within the group. Schram was concerned with the fact that it was obvious the goblins had faced no real resistance when they attacked and that Elvinott may already be under alien control. His step quickened only to be matched by that of the others as they too tossed over the strange situation.

Schram made a quick motion to Stepha and quickly she was in the air. She burst up through the trees and silently moved ahead quickly catching the rear flank of the attackers. They were now within site of the main city and were being shown no resistance from magic or elven forces. Very few battle sounds could be heard in the distance and the concern Stepha had felt had grown to intense fear within the flyer elf. She moved forward and was slowly nearing the attacking armies when she felt a sharp pain in her foot. She spun through the air and dove just in time to avoid the piercing fire of a blue dragon's breath. She crashed into the upper branches of the trees as another burst of heat exploded the tree into flame. The dragon roared and several of the rear goblins turned to see what was happening and then ran panicked away completely unconcerned with the flyer elf only seeking to avoid being caught in the dragon's fury themselves.

Stepha had lost all control of her flight and was now bouncing through the trees as fire erupted around her. She struck the ground and the force knocked what little air she had left in her out from her body. Still the adrenaline flowing through her veins lifted her quickly to her feet and she sped back towards the others releasing an arrow in the direction of the blue. Surprisingly, it struck with extreme accuracy piercing the young beast deep in its throat causing a screech of such intensity the forest and ground shook.

The dragon landed and folding up its huge wings, lunged after the girl. Stepha ran with extreme speed through the thick tree-lined forest, and because flight was impossible in such cover, the dragon lumbered along not far behind. She glanced back and seeing no sign of immediate pursuit, grabbed another arrow from her pack and knocked it into her bow. Silently she waited and heard nothing. The pain she had previously been able to ignore now throbbed in her legs and she believed a bone could be broken. Tears began to stream across her cheeks but not from any pain or sadness, simply because she thought she was going to collapse.

She leaned against the foot of a large oak using its trunk as support when a raspy voice appeared behind her. "What were you doing approaching Elvinott alone from behind, elf?"

Stepha turned and launched her arrow in one motion, but this time the dragon merely let it dissolve in a magical field he had created. Terror grew in the elf's eyes as the beast only smiled and took a step forward. Sucking in a deep breath, flame exploded from its mouth and completely engulfed the helpless girl. The tree she stood against burst into flames. However, Stepha stood still, untouched by the dragon's fury. His eyes grew dark, but even as he began to draw another breath, all the fires he had previously ignited quickly and unnaturally extinguished. He tilted his head in inquiry and spoke to the nearly unconscious elf. "What magic is this, elf? Speak and I may spare your life."

He ended his statement with another scream as Krirtie thrust her scimitar deep beneath his scaly flesh. The curved edge of the sword bit through the beast's neck and slid down near its belly as if it was cutting through air. She withdrew the sword and prepared for another thrust as the dragon's reflex lifted its wing and sent her to the ground hard, racking her head at the base of a nearby tree. The blue turned its head and looked down at the fallen human with a grimace of pain and hate.

Maldor leaped between the two raising his shield as he positioned himself to protect the fallen woman from the fire bolt which resounded from deep within the dragon's belly. The flames encompassed the two and even reached out burning the dragon's own wing in its whipping heat, however, just as before, the fire dissipated with little to no harm. The dragon roared causing its blue blood to pour even more profusely onto the ground.

"What's the matter? Not confident with your powers?" stated Schram standing tall before the blue dragon.

"You are the cause of this. I sense great magic by your hand," answered the dragon turning to better face the magician before him.

Schram nodded. "And I sense little magic at yours, dragon."

The blue frowned. Maldor and Krirtie rose and moved nearer to Schram. "I am Robdon, Great Blue of the Dragon Realm. I act by the hand of Slayne, the greatest dragon in the kingdom and sole survivor of the human and elven attacks upon my parents and all the great dragons of old Draag."

Schram again showed no expression but only nodded. "And I am Prince Schram of the human city of Toopek. I am a friend to all on Troyf including the dragons, but to let you leave now would only allow you to kill others as you would have killed this elf. You are too brainwashed to ever accept the truth about the past, young dragon, and I am extremely sorry that a life as precious and long as yours must now be cut so short."

Robdon narrowed his eyes and appeared like an overpowering force dwarfing the human before him. His voice was cold and a deep sense of fear was carried within its sounds. "I know of you Schram of Toopek. My master has told us many stories about the human leader responsible for most of the unprovoked oppression. I am privileged that it will by my hand at which you die."

Light exploded from the dragon's eyes in the form of two bolts of energy. The force carried with them knocked Maldor and Krirtie several feet causing the maneth to grip his chest fearing it might explode. Schram stood stoic, simply reaching his two hands up to intercept the flow of power. As the two met, the energy began to swirl and dance between the human's fingers. The dragon continued his assault but it quickly became apparent that his actions would be of little concern to those before him. Schram continued controlling the fiery attack forming it into a magical, much larger, ball of his own.

After several moments, Robdon halted his attack and only stared in disbelief back towards the ball of his own magic now looking back upon him. Softly, the dragon spoke. "It appears you are indeed powerful, human, but if you kill me, it will only show that my master was right. You are our enemy."

Schram knelt down in front of the dragon and replied with heartfelt honesty. "I am not your enemy. I wish that if you must die, that you know at least that. I only pray that I can convince all the other young dragons of that same fact before it becomes too late. Slayne has condemned many of the dragons to death by commanding their attack upon us, and hopefully someday he will go where you are about to go. Then, let you find your revenge upon him as you learn the truth."

The dragon lowered his eyes. "As I said, if you kill me now, then you are the enemy."

"No Robdon, for I will not raise any of my magic against you. If your magic was strong enough to kill me, then let it be turned to you. If this is the case, then it is your time to die."

Schram removed his hand from the ball of magic he had harnessed from the large blue dragon and released it back towards the creature. Instantly the massive scales and armor making up the dragon's skin burst into a sheet of flame. Painful screeches and screams echoed from the beast causing all in the area to look away. As the magic slowly won over the dragon's blue body, silence again seduced the forest.

Without a word, Schram walked over to Stepha and placed his hand on her forehead. Her body was soothed and her strength slowly returned. "I can do nothing for the pain in your legs, but rest assured that there are no broken bones." He turned to the others who remained engrossed by the sight of the dragon's body dissolving into the ground. "We must continue to Elvinott. It is only a short distance and I feel something drastic may have occurred."

Schram stood and moved over to where now only a few scorched remains of the great beast were left burning on the forest floor. As quickly as the fire had engulfed the dragon it seemed as if the forest had engulfed the fire. Stepha moved beside him and spread dust across the last of the dragon remains. Schram nodded understanding and motioned to the others that they should delay no longer.

The talk between them was nothing more than idle chatter and very little of it was directed towards Schram, though most of it was based on the magician. Stepha occasionally stepped up to talk to their leader but every time returned to walk with the others saying nothing. They passed relatively few bodies and only when they arrived at the Elvinott City border did they come across a dead elf.

The streets were empty, and Stepha began to cry as she looked around her desolate and destroyed home. It looked as if a wave of death had passed through and simply wiped out everything in its path. The ground showed of much recent activity and all of the tracks seemed to disappear to the south. The group stopped when they arrived at the fountain, which now stood only as a broken notch in a lost city. The statue of the Princess lay in several pieces across the square and the absence of all noise was a sensation that could drive even the sanest man or elf to the brink of madness.

Schram's expression seemed as lost as the city when he turned and spoke his first words since they had left the clearing where they had fought the blue dragon. "Never in my life have I felt the pain I feel at this moment."

Stepha fell into his arms and began to cry while all around simply bowed their heads. Maldor walked toward the forest line and watched for any returning goblins, trolls, or even elves, but nothing within eyesight or earshot seemed to have life. He shortly returned to where the others stood trying to make some sort of sense out of the horrific situation.

There had been silence since his leave and his weak, crackling voice added little to calm their spirits. "It appears they fled to the south, possibly to seek refuge with the dwarves. If they were able to break through the lines, they should have been able to make it there safely. Those at Feldschlosschen would have a strong force to give support."

Krirtie added sadly, "but it doesn't make sense. Why didn't any of the goblins stay here to hold the city?"

"They did not want Elvinott," replied Schram. "They wanted every elf dead. There is nothing to protect this wood now. Its magic is drained from it and now Elvinott is simply a region of forest, no different from anywhere else on Troyf." He paused suddenly when he felt something strange burning inside him. "I must go to the Great Hall. I will be back shortly."

The others looked at each other questionably, and Stepha joined Schram's side as he took his first step towards her father's castle. He glared toward the elf with a look she had never seen in him before. Immediately she stopped and Schram continued alone.

The castle was littered with goblin and troll bodies as they had tried to lute it of its riches. Schram walked slowly down the long corridor having his childhood memories attack him with each step he took. More bodies lay outside the doorway of the Hall and when he peered inside, perhaps a dozen more could be seen spread across the floor. A fire burned low in the pit and the slumped body of an elf could be seen staring blankly into its dying flame. The elf's head rocked up as he heard the approach of another visitor. The aged face of Hoangis greeted Schram like the cold chill of an open doorway in winter.

"My King, you are alive."

Hoangis only grimaced and, ignoring the greeting replied, "is it true my son, have you become one with Ku?"

"Yes father, it is true."

"When I gave the ring to Kirven, I never dreamed it would be you he would choose to seek its power." Hoangis coughed causing blood to protrude slightly between his lips. "I tried to control its power many years ago, and it nearly killed me."

"I know Hoangis. I remember the time."

The king seemed to become confused and lost. Schram knew that with each moment that passed he was falling further and further into the greater being. His voice was frail and full of regret. "The elves have fled their home, and all of our defenses are lost."

"Hoangis, I know of the tragedy befallen our people, but now is our time to act, and I need your help. You must tell me where I can find the Staff of Anbari."

His eyes grew wide. "Yes, yes, the Staff of Anbari. Use it as it was used two hundred years ago."

"Where can I find it father?"

The elf's confusion seemed to clear and his voice grew less tied to the despair surrounding the loss of his kingdom. Again he coughed causing him to have to force his reply, "the map room."

Schram was surprised by the condition of the king and knew without his help, Hoangis would never make it to the map room on his own. They pushed slowly through the hall towards a large chamber that Schram had only been allowed to enter one time before, when he was going to return to Toopek for the first time in his life. Hoangis used this room which contained a giant floor map of all of Troyf to show Schram how all the different races on Troyf all fit so closely together. Sad memories consumed the human as he lifted the huge latch and effortlessly threw the large oak doors ajar.

When they entered the room, Schram's ring began to hum a soft murmur. "What is it?" he asked. "What makes it sound as such in this room?"

The king dropped to his knees and it was clear that his body was nearing its final breath. "Schram, before you hear this, you must swear to honor my last request."

He looked at Hoangis and thought to say something strong not allowing the king to lose hope, but both knew it was his time. "Yes father and king, I will honor you as you would honor me."

Hoangis pulled three pouches out of his robes and handed them to him. "Those are for Madeiris, Stepha, and yourself. I know it is customary to have only one, but I could not where you three were concerned. I also know you are not my true son, but you have always been as important to me as if you had been." Schram nodded appreciation and a giant lump began to form in his throat. Hoangis continued, "and will you swear that when I do pass, you will deposit my body into the fountain rather than aiding my passage with the dust from the sacred past?"

"The fountain?" Schram replied surprised.

"Please do not question, for I must be sure."

"I will honor you, my father."

Even in this most desperate time, the king formed a soft smile bringing a new peace to his eyes as if he had just accomplished something great. In a slightly stronger tone, he stated, "now quickly, go to the map and place your hand bearing the Ring of Ku over the Elvinott forest. This is the room in which it was created and it will grow with power the closer it gets to its origin."

Schram walked across the huge floor map stopping above Elvinott as the hum had become an almost ear-piercing scream. He placed his hand across the city and an immediate and uncomfortable silence struck the room. Light began to travel from his hand to different positions on the map. The shape of a hatchet appeared where Feldschlosschen was while a sword and bow lighted up in Elvinott itself. A hammer shone in the base of the Canyon of Icly and a long rod could be seen in the South Sea.

"There!" cried Hoangis. "There are the Weapons of the Ring. Each possesses its own power and each is a deadly force, especially with the wielder of the Ring by their side. The staff you desire is there." He pointed to the South Sea.

Schram removed his hand from the map and walked down to the Sea. "But where in the sea? At the bottom?"

When there was no answer, fear filled his mind and he swung to stare back at Hoangis. Without approaching, he knew the king was dead. A tear came to his eye, then another. Silently, he wept allowing all his memories of his elven father to flood his mind. With his pain, the Ring again began to hum and a soft soothing addressed him from within his body. He looked at the golden and copper color of the seemingly ordinary ring and his mind and body became completely relaxed. He saw the ring on his adjacent finger and thought about the king's daughter whom he loved so much.

He really had no idea how long he stood there. Time seemed to stand still as his emotions flowed through his soul. He woke from his thoughts and drew a deep and long breath. Schram lifted his head and took his first step towards the king's body. His thoughts of love and admiration were consuming his being as he leaned down and scooped the small elf into his large arms and began his slow and solemn walk to the fountain.

The others ran to greet him as he drew within eyesight, but all stopped in their tracks when they realized the situation. Only Stepha continued forward while the others bowed their heads. "I am sorry," Schram began, "But he gave his life to save his kingdom. I wish you had been able to be with him."

Schram's words went unheard by the elf who could only fall to the ground in tears. "Why did it have to be now?" she screamed.

"I have to honor his last wish, Stepha. Will you join me?"

She rose to her feet and the two walked toward the fountain, Stepha completely unaware about what was to take place. Krirtie and Maldor stood aside and bowed their heads to honor the Elven King, while Schram stood above the wall of the fountain. "May your passage be smooth and well protected, as your life should make you deserve."

Lightly, he placed the body into the water. All stepped back and none of them knew exactly why this was taking place. Even Stepha, who stared blankly toward Schram as he fulfilled her father's dying wish, would not dishonor this action with an argument or even a question.

Suddenly, a faint light began to grow within the water gradually growing in intensity. With a small explosion came a swirling red stream of water which shot upward above the fountain carrying the king's body into a magical red cloud. The bright red light echoed a sweet song as its brilliance blinded those who watched. The cloud hovered for only seconds before it dove down and began rushing through the entire city. As it passed each shattered, broken, or totally destroyed structure, a magical metamorphosis occurred. Everything began to grow and change in its wake.

Maldor blinked as the cloud passed a small, beaten-down elven house carved into a small oak and when he opened his eyes, the house was restored to its previous beauty and charm. Everything was being restored exactly as it had been before the attack. The luster and shine of all the delicate wood work and tree carvings was again apparent each time the cloud moved passed a new area. It beat a path through the entire city bringing new life to where none remained. Then it seemed to center its force on the fountain. There it began the most marvelous restoration ever conceived. The many bits of wood chips and fragments making up the once beautiful figure were lifted high into the air above the fountain. The group watched in disbelief while the spinning pool of wood gently rested in its place at the center of the fountain. The original beauty and workmanship was present to every last cut and groove. However, even more magnificent was the incredible shine now emanating from the statue. It was not the shine of well-sanded and stained wood, but rather the brilliance of polished silver. The figure's hair was a spectacular gold with the same gold making up the bow she held out in her hands.

Maldor jumped first but not from the sight. He, as well as everybody else, had just seen the movement of a large party of goblins back-tracking into the city. "They're returning," he stated abruptly.

Even with this new sense of urgency, all seemed powerless to even lift their weapons. The strange cloud absorbed all their energy and fears and again consumed their attention. Suddenly, the cloud moved from the statue and appeared to look over its work as a critic would investigate a painting. After an approving pause, the cloud shot through the air and expanded into a huge red, obscure vapor that covered the entire forest of Elvinott. Schram heard a whispered *thank you* the moment before the cloud exploded into a showering rain covering the entire surroundings.

As the mist struck the maneth's face, he was awakened from his encapsulating trance and quickly drew arms to face the attackers. However, he slowly lowered his sword when he witnessed the large group of goblins now sleeping peacefully in their tracks. All attention was turned back towards the statue but nobody seemed able to speak. Suddenly, the remaining cloud released a short down pouring of rain and was instantly replaced by the brightest sun seen in over one hundred years. The light reflected against the gold and silver carvings making up the curves of the statue's body with a brilliance never before witnessed by those who still stared blankly upon it.

Schram turned to the others but spoke only to Stepha. "Go on, it is meant for you."

The elf princess looked at Schram and then back at the statue and with a questioning expression, lightly lifted herself in the air and landed on the platform adjacent to the statue. In a slow and hesitant motion, she removed the bow that the silver statue held outward. A faint rumbling could be heard through the water and steam rose around Stepha and her self-appearing statue creating an ominous appearance of two identical bodies. However, as quickly as the red cloud had vanished, so did the vapor and standing at the fountain's center was the elf princess, holding the exquisite golden bow. Next to her was the powerful figure of the leader of the flyer elves, her silver arms raised in victory and the gentle flow of water cascading down her golden hair.

"Our home is once again protected," she stated proudly.

"That it is," added Schram reaching out his hand. "Your father was completely drained after this last feat of magic, but Elvinott and its forest have been returned to their original beauty and strength. The enchantment of the wood, which was slowly reduced by the dragon magic, has been replenished and it is emanating a power that even exceeds that which was present before. Elvinott will remain secure for the rest of existence."

Stepha flew back to Schram's side and spoke strongly but still showed the tears falling from her large eyes. "My father, where is he now?"

"He is in the forest. He is in your heart. He is everywhere a drop of rain fell, and there he will remain forever. It is his spirit that now binds Elvinott and protects it. It is his strength that created this most magnificent city." Schram reached into one of his pouches and pulled out the small sack Hoangis had given him for Stepha. In a soft voice, he said, "your father had another last wish. He asked that I give this to you."

Her eyes began to profusely lose their tears now as she took the life pouch from his hand. Without speaking, she walked into the nearby trees to be alone. Schram also felt he wanted peace and quiet as he looked into his pouch so he too left the city center and found some shade under a nearby tree. Maldor and Krirtie looked blankly at each other but realized that this was personal and something restricted to only their two friends. The two did not by any means mind. It had again proven to be a rather tiring day and having a chance to relax together was a satisfying fulfillment of their true desires.

Schram slowly opened the pouch, having no idea what it may contain inside. His eyes were filled with wonder as he began to empty the contents onto the ground. The bag contained only two items, a diamond-shaped rock and a small parchment rolled up with a magical seal. Schram looked at the rock getting a faint sense of enchantment from it but not knowing its source or purpose. He slipped the rock into his pocket and then quickly spoke the necessary words to break the seal revealing the king's message. It read simply, the joining is granted with all the blessings possible from a king and father. Schram smiled as he thought about his beloved Stepha. He had completely forgotten that their joining had never been made official since they had performed their own ceremony in private on the Dry Sea of Nakton. A peace flooded over the human as his elven ears twitched and he closed his eyes to sleep.

Minutes later a faint kiss woke him accompanied by the soft eyes of his elven love peering down at him. In her hand she held an identical parchment which had been left in her life pouch. She fell into Schram's arms and without speaking, both found their deepest feelings moving to the other.

CHAPTER 19

Feldschlosschen, Again?

Several hours passed before Stepha and Schram returned to greet the others who sat talking at the fountain wall. They were deep in conversation and did not hear the two approach. Schram drew his dagger and placed it to the center of Maldor's back. Krirtie looked up and saw her childhood friend but said nothing to spoil the fun. In the raspiest, goblin voice Schram could muster, he bellowed, "oh, so it's a no good, pig slime maneth that is the cause of my companion's seemingly wakeless sleep at the forest line."

Maldor froze and looked hard at Krirtie. In one rapid, violent motion, he threw Krirtie clear and spun to face the goblin with fire burned into his eyes. He nearly slugged Schram when his laughter caught his ears. He blushed slightly as he tried to remain mad and not join in the fun that was at his expense. Schram dropped his dagger and embraced the big man. "It sure is good to be among my friends again. However, it sure would be nice if they were better warriors and not let unknowns easily sneak up on them from behind."

Maldor only grunted, but eventually he too found humor in the situation, especially when Krirtie began protesting about being shoved aside like she was unable to take care of herself. With the moods of the companions all at new levels between them, they each took comfortable seats on the ground and relaxed finding new and unrealized confidence and pleasure in the company of their friends and the security of the now protected forest. Finally Stepha changed the light conversation to one of the importance at hand. "Where to now Schram?"

Instantly all expressions changed to stoic ones being directed toward their leader. Schram's smile too grew long and in a tired voice, he replied, "I prefer to get a safe night of rest in the belly of Elvinott. We will be able to find good, pure sleep here free from any fear of nightly ambush and such. If we leave by first light, we will be able to make it to Feldschlosschen by nightfall."

"Feldschlosschen?" rang Maldor, "why do you want to go there?"

"I have one last duty to perform for Stepha's father," he paused and put his arm around the elf. "If the elves did escape, which I feel they did, then they have joined the dwarves there and," Schram paused, "Feldschlosschen is on the way to the South Sea."

The expected stir erupted from the companions including Stepha pushing away the grip of Schram and standing to express her thoughts. "Schram," she began, "while you were with my father, we all talked a bit about certain things." Maldor and Krirtie looked hesitantly at Schram who returned with an intrigued gaze and then glanced back to Stepha. "We do not mean any disrespect and though I can only speak assuredly for myself, I believe we all would follow you anywhere." The others gave confirming nods as the elf continued, "but going all the way to the South Sea cannot be any whim you have dreamed up. We just feel that you have been keeping things from us, things we feel we should know."

Schram smiled and rose to stand beside his beloved elf, now officially his wife, as humans would call it but much more than a simple spouse to elves. Taking her hand in his, he turned and faced the others. His voice was confident and reassuring, giving a positive sense to his words. "My dear friends, I am sorry that I have seemed illusive, to say the least. However, until now, I did not know where each step would be taking us. I had to speak to Hoangis and use his wisdom to guide our passage. Furthermore, I believe that if each of you reaches deep into your mind, you will each come up with the answer that could turn this war to our favor." He turned to Maldor. "Where are the battles being fought?"

The maneth looked surprised at being put on the spot, but with his familiarity with all that had taken place, the answer came easily. "There are three main fronts: the humans and maneths at Toopek, the elves in Elvinott, and the dwarves at Feldschlosschen and Antaag. Now however, only two fronts remain as it appears the elves have joined forces with the dwarves."

"Correct." He paused and turned to Krirtie. "And Krirtie, how do you think the numbers of each opposing group fairs?"

"Well," she replied, "if Toopek has been any indication, as long as the dragons remain in small numbers, the sides seem to be about even. But also remember that there are hundreds of goblin and troll parties spread through the small human villages scattered across the mountains and forests, like we saw when we passed through Lawren."

"You too are correct," stated Schram to the happy face of his companion. "So Stepha, we know that with every day that passes, another dragon is made ready for battle, and the human-dragon magicians which lead them are preparing to join the attacking forces. What can we do to defend ourselves?"

The elf looked questionably back to the teacher who seemed to be pushing them to find the answer on their own. She shrugged her shoulders causing her wings to flap slightly and answered, "I don't know. It seems Slayne's plan to wipe out the elves failed but he was successful in changing a wide-spread, three-front war, into a much narrower two-front attack. Also, as I am sure he has realized the reinstatement of the magic to our forest, he will put double guard on preventing the elves return here. For the past year, it had been our main defense and now that it is even stronger than before, he won't let us return to hide within its boundaries." She stopped and peered at him without another answer. Shaking her head, she added, "but as for what to do now, we need another force to turn the tables. Otherwise, it appears we are just delaying the inevitable."

"Exactly," shouted Schram catching the entire group by surprise. "Now who would this other force be?"

The three appeared completely puzzled and all aimlessly searched the vast caverns of their minds only to draw blank expressions and giving only silence in reply. Schram moved a couple of steps to better face the entire group and in a much calmer tone said, "imagine that this has all been one war lasting for over two hundred years. Dragons live for an immeasurable length of time and only see a regeneration and new hatching every three to four hundred years. Slayne knew this and at the start of this great war attacked the one group who he felt could bring about the end to his plan of dragon domination."

"The canoks," interrupted Stepha. "You want the canoks to help."

Schram gave a crooked smile and nod as both Maldor and Krirtie shook their heads realizing they too should have realized the answer. Krirtie now broke in, "I forgot that you are one of the few humans, or any creature for that matter, that knows where the canoks reside now. Wow, the South Sea, I would never had guessed."

He shook his head giving a negative response that again made them all become confused. "We do not go to the South Sea to find the canok homeland. It would take more than talk from me to get them to join in this war. They are a depressed and somewhat disgraced race. The dragons split the canoks in half, and even if we did go to meet with the white reign and ask for assistance, they would have their hands full just dealing with the blacks that would see it as whites trying to gain power. Kirven could possibly gain their support, as he is the most respected of all the whites, but because I am human, although they treat me as if I was canok, my request is not enough for them to risk what little they have left. Which is even more the reason we must go to the South Sea. Kirven will probably realize my intention and possibly even be able to convince the whites to attack us. If that happens, we will be in dire trouble, for the combined power of the whites is immense."

"But why would Kirven do that?" interrupted Krirtie. "Although he is fulfilling a deal or something, I don't think he could ever harm you, regardless of who he claims allegiance to."

"Claims allegiance with," stated Schram, "and Kirven is as honorable as any creature on Troyf. I do not fault him for that as shouldn't any of you. He made a deal to save the land, and now he is honoring that bargain. Kirven will do anything in his power to stop us, as we must do to stop him. This war will only be our victory when Almok, Slayne," there was a long pause before he continued roughly, "and Kirven are all dead."

A silence hit the small group as the reality of Schram's speech struck their ears. In a morbid, hushed voice, Maldor asked, "then why do we now head to the South Sea?"

The mood lightened slightly. Everyone had become engrossed with Schram's talk about Kirven and had forgotten the original purpose for the conversation. Just when the sun took its first dip behind the tops of the trees surrounding the city, they all turned toward their leader for insight. Schram replied, "Over two-hundred years ago, Slayne used the magic in the Staff of Anbari to divide the canoks into what they are known to be today. Anbari was the black sorcerer of the South Sea and with your father's aid," he motioned to Stepha, "I was able to locate where the Staff now resides. It appears that in gratitude, Slayne returned it to the burial site of the former sorcerer, the bottom of the Black Pool in the center of the South Sea. If I can recover the staff and gain control of its magic, perhaps I can then reverse the damage inflicted by the dragon's black magic. If I can return the pride and respect due the canok race, then possibly they will aid us. I feel it is the only way."

"There are a lot of ifs in your statements Schram, but your reasoning appears sound." Maldor rose. "Tomorrow we leave for Feldschlosschen and the next day, through the mountains to the South Sea."

His strong words seemed to drive the others and soon all were on their feet apparently ready to face whatever obstacle they came to. Yet, in the back of each of their minds was the seed of truth that each knew that this was far from a realistic plan and its failure would be much easier to come by than its success.

Their pace the next day was faster than any of them would have believed possible. The solid night's rest they had been blessed with signified the first time since they had ever began traveling together that they had slept without at least one on watch. The safety and enchantment of the surrounding forest gave a reassuring comfort and peace to the weary travelers and they were rewarded with a wakeless night of uninterrupted and pleasant dreams.

It was near sundown now, and although they had passed many goblin, troll, and elf bodies, the enthusiasm was still high as they grew closer to the dwarven mine city. Schram and Stepha were quieter than the other two as they took careful measure to prepare each of the elves' bodies they crossed to begin their passage to the greater life. Each life pouch was carefully stored to pass the honor of the departed to the one he loved. Their day was much more solemn than Maldor's and Krirtie's, but as dwarven bodies began appearing as well and the group came to a large clearing where it appeared a fierce battle had taken place, all began to again feel the pain and loss common during war.

They were roughly a mile or so from Feldschlosschen and by the looks of the dead, the elves and dwarves had been victorious, for the most part. It seemed as if a large band of trolls had blocked the elves escape route and an ensuing battle had taken place. Since the majority of troll bodies were slashed down their backs, it also appeared that a counter force of dwarves had attacked from the rear to clear a pathway through the lines. The scorched ground depicted of dragon involvement and one red beast lay beaten and bloodied to the side of the field. Its body was brutally slashed and nearly fifty arrows were lodged in its rotting flesh. Its insides spilled onto the ground and the smell of death was strong as it bit at the companions' noses. The elves believed that the foul odor was the gods way of showing displeasure at the ill treatment of the dead. Schram approached the dragon's body and waved some dust across its length. The odor gradually dispersed and the dragon body disappeared seemingly into the ground.

"He was accepted," Schram stated softly bowing his head. "He was acting by the command of one he took to be honorable. He was only acting as any of us would act should the circumstances have placed us as such."

There was no verbal reply to his comment only the soft nods of each who watched the sadness of the time really begin to unfold before their eyes. The remaining dead were offered the same aid in passage until the clearing was filled with a new expression. It no longer spoke of death and destruction, but now appeared as a white light of hope somewhere in the future. It was elation in the time of sadness with a memory of the past so strong as to never allow those who passed through it to forget. It was an ominous place that Schram knew he would never forget.

Each of the companions now carried mixed emotions, but the fact that they were so near Feldschlosschen gave them the necessary strength to drive forward. Furthermore, both Schram and Stepha now believed that the elves had made it to join the dwarves, and this alone settled their hearts more than being assured of their own safety could have. However, their pace came to an abrupt halt when they arrived just short of one of the outermost mine entrances.

"Didn't we leave this party yesterday?" stated Maldor looking at the goblin and troll parties standing between them and the mines.

Schram frowned. "I assumed we would meet some resistance, but trying to force our way through two-hundred would be futile."

"What do you think we should do?" asked Krirtie now drawing her brilliant sword to be equal to the other's warlike poses.

"I don't know. We could hold up here but whose to say whether this group would ever leave and each day we remained we would risk being discovered. If we head south-easterly we will come to a second entrance but my guess is that all are equally guarded. If we could only get word to the dwarves and elves that we are here." Schram broke off and each fell into their own deep and silent thought.

"Perhaps I can help," entered a soft female voice from behind them.

Each of the companions simultaneously whirled around to face the person who had arrived completely unnoticed. Maldor was closest and had the girl by the throat before any other words or actions could be uttered.

"Who are you?" he stated in a harsh but still quite hushed tone.

"Put your weapons away. If I had wanted to harm you, I would have alerted the guards."

All were quite taken by her abrupt and forceful response but none could argue with her reasoning. Schram nodded and turned his lips slightly upward while replacing his sword. The others followed suit except Maldor who only released the girl keeping the hilt of his sword firm in hand.

"Who are you?" asked Schram, "and where did you come from?" He spoke softly and seemed to be unusually captivated by the woman's homely beauty, studying the curves in her face trying to discover what he found so familiar.

The girl walked toward the human in a bouncy, girlish step letting her curly brown hair flop about her shoulders. Stepha, turning slightly red, moved a step closer to Schram nearly standing directly between him and the mysterious girl. "Schram, who I am is not important, but if you want to get into the mines, I suggest you move on my signal."

Schram began to speak. His concern over the woman who he could not recall seeing before but had just called him by name was clear in his tone. "Wait, just a minute Serana."

"And just how do you intend to do anything that could help us in this tight situation?" interrupted Maldor in a distinctly disbelieving tone.

Schram frowned but was interested in the answer so did not redirect his previous thought. Serana giggled slightly at the maneth's stale stare and poked him sharply in the stomach causing him to expel a belly full of air. "Just watch," she replied.

Before anyone could stop her, she bounded through the trees toward the goblin camp. "Hey you sap-bellied swamp walkers from the black of a serpent's intestine," Schram's eyebrows rose as he listened to the sweet little girl's taunting hollers, "why don't you come and get me, unless your bodies are too fat to squeeze through the trees." With that, the girl bounded to the side drawing a parallel line between the goblin armies and the companions.

The infuriated faces of the goblins stood dormant only a moment as the heart of the camp took to the forest after the girl. Several of the attackers even passed only a few feet from where the small group hid, but in their fury, they rushed by totally oblivious to anything but the memory of the taunting girl.

"Not bad for a wench," stated Maldor, "but where she will run to is beyond me. That direction has only limited tree cover before she's on the open eastern plains. Shouldn't we go after her?"

Schram shook his head. "No, I don't think we should worry about Serana, or whatever her name is. I think she'll be just fine." He turned back to the mine entrance. "Now, there are only eight guards left and they are only concerned with the chase. Do you think we can take them?"

By the time he had finished his statement, Stepha had already dropped two and was drawing on a third as Maldor and Krirtie attacked by hand. Schram quickly joined the skirmish and before any warning was even thought to be sounded, the last goblin fell to the ground dead.

The group hurried into the cavern and put as much distance between them and the mine entrance as they could. They could hear the goblin hollers echoing down the corridor as the returning army found the bloodied remains of their comrades, but no pursuit into the mine was forthcoming. Schram felt a magical presence similar to that of the Elvinott forest, and anyone entering seeking harm or having an opposing evil intention was severely dealt with usually resulting in a sentence to aimlessly walk the dwarven caverns until greeted with a long and depressed death.

They walked down a long descending corridor and came to a branch point where they had a choice between three different directions. Maldor was the first to speak. "All right magician, which way?"

Schram turned and without speaking stepped through the solid rock making up the cavern wall to his left. The others simply looked at each other questionably while they waited for some sign that they could follow. "Are you guys coming or what?"

Stepha stepped forward followed by Krirtie, and together both of them hesitantly outstretched one of their legs, and feeling no resistance as it passed through the wall, they slowly pushed their whole body through. Maldor now stood alone in the shaft and an eeriness began to creep to his body. Quickly, he jolted over to the wall and with a loud painful thump, crashed hard against it. Schram could be heard laughing hysterically followed by the fwack of a hand silencing him upon contact. Maldor rested on the ground in front of the wall with a deep red color churning in his face and the hairs of his mane standing on end. He froze when the delicate hand of Krirtie appeared out of the rock and gently grabbing the maneth's hand, pulled him through the secret doorway.

Maldor was greeted by a red-faced Schram who looked very apologetic since the outline of Krirtie's hand could still be seen clearly across his cheeks, and beside him stood Stepha and approximately ten dwarven guards. Maldor's eyes froze on the one he recognized as the dwarf he had threatened on his first visit to Feldschlosschen before they met the king. This dwarf wore a smile ear to ear and the maneth realized all had been present for Schram's cruel trick. However, he was still simply happy to be safe with the dwarves for he was confident each would get their own in return.

His thoughts were interrupted when the familiar dwarf approached him with an outstretched hand reaching way up above his head to greet the maneth. "I remember you Maldor as I can see in your eyes that you do I. I am Roepkee. It seems in our first meeting we got off on the wrong foot due to mistrust and disbelief. I wish to make sure all those feeling are extinguished. Please except my apologies and know that we are pleased to have you as visitors once again." He turned to the group, "all of you."

Maldor took his hand and in a humbled, crooked smile, bid him the same greetings and apologies. The dwarves led the group through the secret tunnel and explained all that had taken place for the past few months leading up to the elves' move to join them in the mines. The story ended as they reached the king's chambers where King Krystof, Madeiris, and Jermys all had a joyous reunion with the travelers.

After the exchange of pleasantries and Schram's inevitable explanation of his return and the changes in him that had occurred, Jermys took the floor before his old friends. "When I returned to Feldschlosschen, the city was in chaos. There had been repeated goblin attacks and it was believed that even Antaag had fallen as many of the origins of the attacks seemed to be coming from their mines. When I told the king about Kapmann's deceit and that the southern dwarves had allied with the dark dwarves, all trouble came to a head. King Krystof was prepared to wage war against Kapmann until I showed him the Hatchet." Jermys rested his hand on the small glowing axe by his side. "When Krystof saw it, his eyes nearly popped from his head." Both he and the king chuckled slightly and blew thick puffs of smoke from their mouths in the process.

Jermys nodded toward Krystof with a soft smile and then continued with his tale in a tone depicting of a new-found knowledge held deep within him. "Well, word spread like fire to a dried oak and by some quirk of fate, Kapmann himself came over to bid offerings to us for the safe return of the legendary Hatchet of Claude. It was during these conferences that all distrust was lost and everyone's actions explained. The leader of a rebel band of dark dwarves led by one Den-Hrube had approached Kapmann. It seemed goblin armies were constantly bombarding these dwarves and they desired precious stones with which to forge new weapons. Den-Hrube did not wish to wage open war for the necessary metals against his own kind, no matter how distant the relationship was, so he made a deal. In exchange for the stones, he agreed to leave a garrison of troops who would be loyal to the Antaagian King and help protect and hold the Ozaky River. It was these troops which betrayed Den-Hrube and attacked his ship. Kapmann only wanted to hold us overnight until the ship was gone to avoid any possible trouble. When he heard we were wandering around, he got scared and thought we might send a false message of his betrayal back to Krystof. That was why he came over here himself. However," his voice grew saddened, "the question of my brother still remains unanswered. Kapmann swears he heard nothing regarding any of us after our escape until word about the Hatchet reached him months later."

The entire group grew silent as the dwarf finished his story and Schram searched his feelings but could gain no insight toward Bretten's whereabouts as he could with other things. Suddenly, a puzzled look crossed his face. "Do either of you know where the Dark Dwarves were living when they faced these goblin attacks which spurred the need for your precious stones and minerals?"

The two dwarves looked surprised by the question but held no restraint in the response. "Sure," began Jermys, "Kapmann said they had mentioned being attacked at the canyon base. That could only mean Icly. Do you think it is important?"

Schram's lips pushed together causing his cheeks to wrinkle. He shrugged his shoulders. "I don't know. It just seems odd that the goblins would center an attack on the dark dwarves. After all, they would prove helpful to the dragon's cause with their continued attacks on human and elf populations. I don't understand their strategy."

The king became quite intrigued. "Do you think they could have been deceiving Kapmann in wanting the stones only to get inside Antaag?"

Schram shook his head again. "No, judging from the brutality of the betrayal we witnessed on the river, I doubt the dark dwarves were deceiving anyone. But I just can't figure out what the dragons want in that canyon, except. . ." His face lifted as he remembered what happened in the map room at Elvinott. He rubbed his finger and then continued in a different tone noticed only by Stepha. "Except for a few medicinal shrubs and clean water, that canyon has little to offer."

All nodded in agreement except Stepha who only studied her husband. She then stepped forward, "how many elves made it to safety?"

Madeiris smiled. "Nearly all. We lost only a few during some isolated encounters, the worst of which involved a fierce attack by a red dragon. Luckily the dwarves showed up as a welcome cavalry and Jermys' magic axe was able to slay the beast with ease. However, our father remained in Elvinott. We have heard no word from him or anyone outside of the mines, and by the looks now growing across your eyes, I fear for what we do not know."

Both Schram and Stepha bowed their heads and the human placed his hand on the elf prince's shoulder while he slowly replayed the ordeal they had faced. He ended with the exchange of all the life pouches they had collected on their trip to honor those who lost their lives in the struggle. Madeiris was now the king and it was his duty to see to the pouches proper placement. Schram then continued to describe their plans to travel to the South Sea, not going into the utmost detail but delivering a clear picture none the less. It was finally agreed that they would stay the night in Feldschlosschen while messengers would be sent to Antaag to expect their arrival in the morning. From there, they would be able to follow some of the extended and now abandoned southern-most mines which would carry them through much of the forest before the mountains. All were satisfied with the plans, and following a rather cheerful dinner and further exchanging of stories, all retired except Schram and Madeiris.

"Madeiris, there is one more thing you must know before we part tomorrow," began Schram, catching the elf slightly lost in his own thought about all he had heard.

"What is it, old friend?"

Though his voice was strong, Schram could hear the hidden burdens he now felt. He replied softly, "I must perform one more act in honor of your father." Schram reached into his pocket and pulled out the third life pouch he had been given by the elf king. "Your father asked that I give this to you when we were alone, so as I complete his last request, so do you become king."

The room was devoid of noise as Madeiris took the pouch, a large tear forming in his eye. When the elf held the sack totally in his possession, the pouch vanished and was replaced by a brilliant bright light. Schram, startled by the occurrence, stumbled back, but quickly regained his composure when he felt the safe, caring presence of the former elven king. The light rose slightly and encased Madeiris' head erasing the tear and giving the elf the most calming appearance of peace Schram had ever witnessed. The lighted cloud remained only moments, but as it began to dissipate, Schram too became completely relaxed. The two stared blankly at each other for several minutes and then almost simultaneously blinked and awoke from their calming trance.

Madeiris was the first to speak. "Thank you Schram, from both my father and me. You have given us one last moment together which means more than you could ever truly comprehend. Let me also extend my pleasure as well at the joining of you with my sister, however, let me also extend the words of my father. You are as much an elf as any in Elvinott, but remember your heritage. You are human too, and as time dictates, you could very easily be placed in the same position which I have been placed in, to assert yourself as leader over your people. Never forget Toopek Schram, all of Troyf may depend on it."

He opened his arms and the two embraced tightly. The elf pushed himself back and his wrinkled face clearly described the strong emotions he was feeling. His voice cracked slightly when he continued. "Your joining with Stepha is perhaps the most important thing to ever occur between the elves and humans, even outweighing the Treaty marking your leave as a child. It was built out of love. It broke down every barrier that was thrust before it and made a human into an elf and an elf into a human."

There was a long pause. They both stood locked in a stare which left them wandering through Hoangis' last words. Finally, Madeiris motioned to his friend. "Come Schram, you have a busy day tomorrow, and my sister would not be pleased if I kept you too long from her side."

Schram nodded and fell in behind, both making their way to their rooms for the night.

CHAPTER 20

Southern Mines: Bretten's Trail

It was before dawn when Stepha and Schram joined Maldor and Krirtie at the entrance to the tunnel beneath the Ozaky. There were mixed emotions on their faces as each remembered the last time they had traveled this path. King Krystof and Madeiris had come to see them off, but to everyone's surprise, Jermys had not returned to bid them farewell.

The group waited several minutes exchanging more pleasantries with the King and checking to make sure all of their equipment was in order before Schram finally motioned that they must leave. Just as they took their first steps, a dwarf's voice could be heard hollering down the corridor behind them. "Quit it, you vile creature or I'll have you made into goblin feed!"

"Ah shut up! You short, bearded, bush-whacking dwarf. You're too small and powerless to hurt anyone, or anything!"

The companions could see two fiery-red eyes bouncing up and down as the infuriated dwarf ran towards them. "Wait!" he shouted. "I'm coming."

"Ahoy," returned Schram. "We hoped you would be coming to see us off."

The dwarf was panting as he arrived holding a large sack that jumped and tossed like it was filled with popping corns. Fighting to gain his breath, Jermys began, "when we told you we had not seen him, the truth was, we did not know to be looking for the varmint. I went in to the elven barracks last night after dinner and found the little rascal taunting a group of guards who were keeping him locked up. It seems they had gotten wind of our general dislike for the thieves so they had been keeping him hidden. Despite some slight wounds which seem to be healing nicely, he seems fine, though he is a might bit mad at this method of travel."

"You bet your dwarven butt I'm mad!" shouted a stern rodent cackle from inside the bag.

With a laugh, Jermys said, "well, unfortunately for all of us, may I present Fehr, the most annoying bandicoot alive today."

A small cloud of dust was kicked up when the rat's body struck the floor with a thud. Krirtie was quick to grab the little guy in a loving hug followed by the exchange of kisses on each others' cheeks, though Fehr's was more of a sloppy lick. "I'm so happy that you are all right," stated the girl as she squeezed him tight.

"She speaks for all of us," added Schram. "You did exceptionally well this time, as always." He paused and added, "and think about the story it will make." He smiled at the rodent who returned his gaze with a smirk that displayed how proud he was feeling.

Krirtie shifted Fehr about her body and placed him into her side pouch. Turning to the others, she happily stated, "now we can go."

"Wait just one minute," broke in Jermys. "With the king's permission, I would like to join you. With the elves here to help defend, there is hardly any reason I must stay. How much help could one dwarf really be, even if that dwarf is me. And besides, they need someone to lead them through the mines."

The companions smiled as they all knew it would be no trouble finding their way across the river mine especially with all the activity taking place within it as troops moved between the two cities daily. However, all looked toward Krystof to see if he would allow the venture. Jermys was correct in saying one dwarf would not make that much of a difference, but considering that it was this dwarf which carried the Hatchet of Claude by his side and had been single handily responsible for the death of the dragon in their fight only a few days ago, this was still a big request. The king peered at the dwarf before him and then in a stiff tone said, "yes, I believe you are correct in giving your aid as a guide to these travelers, for without you, it is obvious that they could not find their way." Krystof winked one eye then added, "and may all of your gods be with you on your journey. Be careful my friends."

The group had arrived at the fork in the tunnel where the hidden passage led into Antaag when Schram spoke. "Jermys, where does that corridor lead to," he asked pointing to the opposite wall which appeared to the others to be solid rock.

The dwarf squinted. "Oh, I forgot all about it. It leads to the southern-most mines which have long since been abandoned. Nobody uses it anymore and most probably don't even remember it exists."

"How far south does it go and does it have an exit?"

Jermys frowned. "I assure you it must be impassable. There has been no upkeep in that mine for over one-hundred years. If it did remain intact, which I doubt, we could follow it all the way to the mountains before returning to ground level, but really it is not..."

The dwarf was cut off as Schram stepped through the wall. "This will be our passage."

The remaining companions looked at each other and with a subsequent shrug or sigh, all fell in behind their leader, Maldor bringing up the rear with sword drawn still distrusting the Antaagian dwarves after their previous encounter. When he was satisfied that nobody was going to follow, he replaced his sword and caught up with the others. He was breathing slightly heavy when he caught them and immediately broke the silence. "Was not Kapmann expecting us?"

Schram answered as though he expected the question while the dwarf stared uncomfortably back towards him. "Yes, but I feel the fewer who know of our plans, the better chance of success we carry with us."

None could argue with his reasoning, but as they repeatedly had to stop to move wooden beams and large rocks from their path, all wondered exactly what they had agreed to undertake. Besides the obstructions across the passage itself, the beams holding what was left of the walls were rotten and decayed. The question of how far they would actually be able to travel came to each of their minds.

They continued at a slow pace for some time until they came to an open cavern with several side tunnels leaving it. In the center sat a circle of rocks and a small pile of coals. "I thought you said these passages were abandoned," stated Krirtie kicking at the coals. "This fire is old, but I would estimate that is closer to one year than one-hundred."

Jermys went over and stood by the girl. "It was probably just a wanderer who got lost in the mines. We will probably cross his body if we continue."

"I don't think so," stated Maldor. "Everything is too neat to be from a lost soul. There are no messages left in the sand of any appearance that they remained here to search down each corridor. There has been only one fire. No, I think whoever it was knew where they were, and more importantly, where they were going."

The dwarf frowned but before he could speak in rebuttal Schram broke in. "Jermys, come here and look at this." All the companions walked over to Schram who stood inspecting the ground around a large boulder. "What do you make of it?"

The dwarf knelt down and peered at the spot on the ground. "I believe it is dwarven. I can't distinguish between Feldschlosschen, Antaagian, or even Dark Dwarven for that matter, but it appears to be blood from a dwarf."

"Look," said Stepha. "See how the rock is chipped away around the back. Whoever it was, they were tied up here and that blood is probably from their wrists.

Jermys leaped up and began to inspect the entire area much more closely. Schram went over to the dwarf. "Relax old friend, I know what you are thinking and we don't know anything for sure yet."

"I do," he stated. "I know my brother was here, and I intend to find out why and who had him at bay."

Schram shook his head. "If that is true, we will all find those answers." He patted the dwarf on the back, and although Jermys did not notice the human's expression, it was clear Schram did not feel certain about what they had just discovered.

The others fell in beside the two and Maldor said, "we have looked the whole place over and other than some well cleaned bones of some sort of rat," Fehr frowned while Maldor carried a bit of pleasure in his speech, "there is nothing else out of the ordinary. However, Stepha found some light footprints in that tunnel," he pointed to a corridor opposite the one they had come through, "but due to the absence of any wind, it is impossible to determine when they were made. Also, their were two sets, both appearing to be made by dwarven boots, but that was concluded by only looking at their size."

Jermys darted to the corridor Maldor had identified and excitedly hollered for the others to follow. "Look, I told you!"

They all stared at the cavern floor where Jermys stood with his foot placed perfectly into one of the footprints. "Bretten was here. This is his print and I am going to follow them until I find him."

Schram again placed his hand on the dwarf. "Come on, let's get some food and then continue. He has waited over a year, he can wait another few minutes."

The expression of urgency faded from Jermys' face as he too felt the pains within his stomach. The group returned to the open cavern where Maldor quickly prepared a fire and the six sat around as the dwarf began to reminisce about his brother. "I remember when we were much younger, only about seventy-five or eighty years, and Bretten had gotten separated from me in the forest. That was the only other time I can remember ever being separated from the bearded imbecile." Jermys grabbed a glowing twig from the fire and used it to light his pipe.

"What happened?" asked the smiling Krirtie who had become amused at the dwarf's jovial behavior since finding a possible sign of his lost brother.

Jermys leaned back and expelled a huge burst of smoke. "It is the strangest thing. Bretten knew the forest even better than I, but somehow he had gotten lost. For days I searched until one day, he just walked back up to me." Schram had sat up and become intrigued as well with the tale the dwarf was telling. "All he said was he had been lost and fallen into a goblin trap. The trap had been intended to drop whoever was caught hundreds of feet into a pit where they would greet the pointed ends of several rear-planted spears. Somehow he had managed to grab onto a nearby twig as he fell and there he hung suspended in the air. If he had let go, he would have plummeted to his death, and if he tried to climb the smooth sides of the trap using the small twig for leverage, he was sure it would break and the result be the same."

"How did he get out?" asked Krirtie biting into her share of a section of bread.

The dwarf smiled. "It was by the magic of one of the white canoks."

Now Schram had become especially interested, but held his tongue for the moment. Jermys continued. "With some simple words, Bretten was lifted up to safety."

"That's amazing, and lucky," stated Maldor.

"Yes, but even more amazing was that after he was free, the canok vanished and Bretten's mind was completely clear. He knew exactly where he was and in less than an hour had joined up with me."

"Wow," stated Krirtie as she moved toward Maldor. "That story at least had a happy ending. All were smiling except Schram who stared long at the dwarf with an expression of disbelief which went unnoticed by Jermys but not by Stepha.

The elf whispered, "Schram, what is it?"

The human jumped when she placed her hand over his. "Nothing, don't worry yourself. It just is that several of those actions are not characteristic of canoks. Jermys is lying but I don't think he knows it. I think his brother lied to him."

He looked saddened before leaning over and kissing his beloved lightly on the cheek causing her large green eyes to close. She smiled and slightly raised her voice so all would know she was talking. "Come on, let's get ready to go. That was in the past and nothing to bother lost thought on now."

Schram began gathering his packs. He motioned to the others to get ready, but Stepha could see that his mind was focused on the dwarf's story, and it was not as cut and dry as he was trying to let on.

The companions laboriously pushed onward, walking for several hours in the damp, dark caverns beneath the forests surrounding Antaag. Their passage was lit only by the last torch which burned in

Jermys' hand. They had come to no intersecting tunnels since they left the open chamber, and there had been no more signs of Jermys' brother or the one who held him captive. However, the light, dim as it was, did show much more activity in this cavern than in the ones before the chamber. The tunnel was clean and support poles had been placed on the weakened cross boards to secure tunnel sides. The last flicker of light diminished causing the group to halt.

"Ic-ayre" recited Schram as the words he had first recited in Taiju's domain now came to him without thought. The ring burst into a deep array of light illuminating the entire area. "Sorry, with my newly discovered elven sight, I almost forgot the darkness would blind many of you."

The group stared at him and then around their surroundings as for the first time they were able to see extremely well into every possible corner of the corridor. All were stunned by what they saw. Not a flake of dust or one loose rock littered the floor. In its place was a smooth, shiny surface which was polished so clear as to cast a reflection back at them. Maldor, spoke, his voice and tone devoid of any sense of security and confidence regarding their current situation. "I don't care what you believe dwarf, this corridor has been well preserved and seen a lot of recent activity."

The dwarf's voice was strained but the words still came. "I don't understand. Who would be mining this cavern and why be so secretive. We would gladly allow any interested party to mine here, there are few mineral deposits left and even less possibilities for easy access. No dwarf would be fool enough to even attempt such a useless task."

"What if mining wasn't the intention?" interjected Schram.

"What do you mean, Schram?" asked the dwarf turning to face the human. "What other reason would there be?"

Maldor excitedly put forward, "an attack! The first part of the tunnel was full of debris, but its pillars were well supported, somewhat unnaturally supported with all the loose wood laying around."

"That's right," interrupted Schram. "It gave the appearance that the mine was undisturbed but it was well-supported. It is in a condition to be used as a possible route for a surprise attack. That is why they only toy with the other mine entrances. They are waiting for the right moment to move a large force undetected through here."

The dwarf's eyes brightened and then narrowed. "That must be what happened to Bretten. He must have discovered the plan and been captured."

Schram looked dismayed. "Perhaps," he stated in a voice which told Stepha that he didn't believe that, but if it satisfied Jermys, then he would let it go for now.

"What do we do?" asked Stepha. "If you are right, Feldschlosschen and Antaag must be warned. Do we go back?"

Schram began to appear puzzled as he fought with the question. He knelt down to better face Jermys. "Is this the only tunnel which leads to the open chamber and to the outside?"

The dwarf looked blankly back at the human while he fought hard to remember the maze of passages the dwarves had used over the years. He had only been in the southern-most mines a couple of times, but as a boy, he was required to learn all the tunnels and all possible exits if the time should arise that he needed to use them. This time appeared to have arrived as his confident voice answered the question. "Yes. Many of the others connect among themselves and through a few hidden doors that we have already passed to this one, but this tunnel is the only one to reach the outside directly. All others in this end of the caverns have to cross into this one to get to the forest."

Schram nodded and then rose to face the others. "Maldor, use your club and knock out those two pillars, then step back." The maneth didn't hesitate and with two smooth thrusts the large, foot-inch-diameter pillars shattered under his swings. A cracking could be heard up and down the tunnel. A force seemed to shake rock which had been happily stationary for hundreds of years. Schram motioned for everyone to move behind him as he raised his hand bearing the Ku Ring and began to recite some words. At first, only a faint rumbling could be heard, but the sound steadily grew and was accompanied by enough shaking to send Krirtie to her knees nearly crushing Fehr as she fell. Rock and dust exploded into the air and the ceiling came crashing down upon itself. The imploding tunnel kicked up a storm of debris which caused all in the group to begin coughing and fighting for clear air. Schram stood firm however, only chanting words that he knew not their origin, but simply spoke them as if he were reading them from a tablet before him. After several minutes, the roaring thunder of falling rock ended and with it the accompanying dust and haze seemed to settle. The magician's face calmed and he turned back to face his friends. He was about to speak to the group when he noticed their faces. All looked as if they were no longer looking at their friend, but rather some ghost or devil which was about to thrust his wrath upon them. Even Stepha appeared to be fighting off what she saw. All had fallen to the ground as the air had become so thin even Maldor was looking up to the human. Schram gathered himself together. "What is it? I only sealed the corridor, now no attack is possible."

Stepha rose and in a hesitant soft voice said, "its nothing."

"Don't hide your words, Stepha," stated Maldor fiercely. "You saw it too."

"Saw what?" exclaimed Schram.

The maneth looked toward Stepha and realizing she was not going to speak anymore, he continued still in the same tone. "When you used your magic, you no longer looked... human."

Schram's face relaxed slightly. "I gained my magic through the ancient works of a great elf, that is why I appeared more elven as I use it and as I stand before you now."

The companions did not share Schram's calming expression. "We know your now elven heritage," stated Maldor, "but it was not an elf you appeared as."

Schram's large eyes narrowed and he stepped closer. "What then?"

The maneth looked around waiting for any of the others to speak but only received their eyes turning to him. He faced Schram and in a hard, but confident voice said, "A dragon. You became a large, silver-green dragon, as clear as Slayne was when we faced him outside Draag."

Schram's head turned and confusion was evident on his face. Stepha moved to stand beside him and took his arm when he began to pace. He jerked his hand aside and in a pleading voice asked, "Was their anything else you saw or anything else I could have been?"

All shook their heads negatively drawing a sad expression to meet with their response. Fehr's little voice broke the brief silence which had ominously began following the massive destruction Schram had just created. "I saw something, Schram."

"What did you see?" he responded, not sure how serious the rat was.

Fehr jumped out of Krirtie's pouch and approached the magician. "You no longer wore your ring. In fact, you could have even been holding a pole of some kind."

The others looked towards each other and then Stepha's expression changed. "He's right. I would never have noticed but that is true."

Schram looked at the ring which still rested on his finger emitting a brilliant light. "I don't know what it all means, but the only way to remove this ring is to cut off my hand. It could simply be something the Great Ku faced in the past which was brought out as I summoned the Ring's power, but the answer lies with him. I am still Prince Schram of Toopek though many of you seem like you are finding that more difficult to believe lately."

Maldor said, "No disrespect was intended Schram, I just spoke what I saw. I know who you are and would never doubt your actions."

Schram bowed his head. "It is I who should apologize. I did not mean to accuse. There is much about this Ring which is still hidden within me. I do not know how I use its power, I just know that I use it. Please forgive me and don't hesitate to speak if this silver dragon within me appears again."

All nodded and the tension on their faces gradually seemed to disappear. Schram moved over and scooped up the little rodent lifting him into the air. "And a special thanks to you again Fehr, for. . ."

His voice trailed off and Fehr winked showing that he understood. "I will keep my eyes open Schram. After all, being nosy comes somewhat naturally to my kind."

Schram scratched the little guy between his ears and then released him back to the ground where he returned with a leap to Krirtie's arms and then to her pouch. "Jermys, how much farther is it to the outside?"

"My best estimation is about another hours walk," replied the dwarf skeptically. "But remember, I have never traveled this way and am simply going by memory of various charts and tables."

About an hour later the group arrived at the mouth of the mine entrance. "When it comes to tunnels, I've learned to trust your estimated guess more than most men's certainties," stated Schram to Jermys as they peered through the brush covering the entrance.

"Where are we?" asked Maldor, pushing his head through the group, "And what's that smell?"

Schram had not noticed the odor at first, but now the scent seemed to grab hold of his senses not willing to let go. "Death," he stated softly. He paused and searched the darkness with his elven sight. "I don't see any movement but I think it would be smarter to remain here throughout the rest of the night. Let's get what sleep we can and continue ahead at first light." He nodded to Maldor who moved to stand guard as the others began fixing themselves a place to rest farther down into the corridor clear of the odor.

The companions woke the next morning to the smell of Schram's morning meal, a much more appetizing scent than that of the unknown outside. They sat around the fire as the cool mountain air typical with dawn rushed down the mine shaft. Schram spoke when the last of the group joined the circle. "It appears completely peaceful on the mountainside, but I have not investigated beyond the gate. The source of the odor still remains unknown, but I feel we should inspect it as soon as we are ready."

Each nodded wearily and when each of their stomachs was satisfied, they gathered their equipment and met at the entrance. The smell was still present and the heavy morning dew seemed only to intensify its wrath. Maldor and Schram began removing the branches of the temporary barrier and soon a clear doorway was opened and the group pushed through. The mine exit was obviously several miles into the mountains as the surrounding trees were tall and long-needled whose branches rose hundreds of feet into the air. The ground was at a steep angle and with the position of the sun, they knew they stood on the eastern slope of a huge mountain. The group split up into pairs and began inspecting the nearby grounds, but it was Jermys, who was alone, that hollered when he found the body. The others rushed over but had to cover their noses as they grew near. "It's as if the gods won't accept it, but they won't let it dissolve into the ground either. It must simply sit and rot for how many more lifetimes."

"Do you know him?" asked Schram.

"Yes," replied the dwarf. "He is Lyl-Brown, Den-Hrube's commander."

Stepha frowned as Jermys used both of the deceased names but did not interrupt the dwarf's statement. "An equally untrustworthy dwarf of the dark path, but one who would also not take arms against Feldschlosschen or Antaag. He must truly have done evil to be sentenced to this permanent resting place."

Schram looked toward Stepha whose face had grown plain and saddened while she witnessed the lifeless mass before them. He stepped forward and rolled the body onto its face revealing the deep cut along its spine encrusted with dried, blackened blood. Maldor stepped forward using his sword to point. "This dwarf was bushwhacked in the back. His prisoner must have escaped by killing his counterpart when his attention was drawn away."

"Perhaps," Schram stated in the same voice as the previous day, again his disbelief was noticed only by the elf.

Jermys stepped forward. "The wound is that of a dwarven battle axe. I knew my brother could not be held long."

"Then where is he now?" asked Schram, a slight smugness carried in his words.

The dwarf did not read his tone as anything out of the ordinary and only revered in his brother's diligence. "He must have fled to the mountains to avoid any other attackers who might expect him to return immediately to Feldschlosschen through the tunnel. That way he could gain a large lead as they searched the mine."

"Perhaps," repeated Schram as he reached into a pouch he carried inside his armor. He dispensed a small amount of dust from within the pouch across the corpse and almost immediately the smell lifted. With a sudden cold gust of wind and a small rumble from the ground, the body slowly passed into oblivion.

"What magic powder is that?" asked Maldor staring in amazement to where the body of the dwarf had laid. "I always see you use it but don't understand."

"No magic," answered Stepha moving next to her husband. "It is ancient elven dust which acts to aid passage to those souls which have become lost. It was originally used only on those believed by the discoverers to be true of heart and was effective as such. However, it has evolved to be of aid to any who are left between lives, although where they are to go is still dependent upon themselves and the life they led. This only aids in acceptance of their fate, not control their destination." She paused and stared down towards Jermys. "However, it should be noted that this dwarf was well accepted for passage."

"What are you saying elf, Lyl-Brown's kidnapping of my brother was a good thing?"

Stepha became increasingly displeased with Jermys' repeated naming of the dead but answered his question hiding her feelings as best she could. "No, only his life was not totally filled with evil intention. We do not know the circumstances surrounding his death."

Jermys shook his head, refusing to believe what the elf was saying but not willing to pursue the conversation further. "Well, may he rest in peace."

Schram rose. "Come on, due to our position we will head to Eltak, the city of the mountain elves. It is only a couple hours west and will make a pleasant resting point before continuing south."

The companions quickly regrouped and behind Schram and Stepha's lead, they were trudging through the thick cover of the mountain forests. It was a strange and quick exit to a situation that was growing with each statement into a confrontation, and each of them felt the new tension in the air about them. What little talk there was proved empty and without overwhelming importance until Krirtie began thinking about their upcoming destination, and with her thoughts came the unabridged question, "Schram, tell me about the Staff of Anbari you seek."

All other conversation and individual thought ceased immediately and all eyes fell on the human who stared back towards his childhood friend and her extremely deep question. His tone was soft and it was clear that he had been caught of guard. "The truth is, I don't know about it. Its existence is only a memory lodged deep inside me. From where this memory came, I do not know, nor do I know how the staff works or even if it will work. I only feel that it is possible, beyond that, I am at a loss."

Several drew long faces at his vague reply. "You mean you are only guessing at its possible power? This very necessary journey could end up only a wild chase for a lost artifact?"

All were astonished at Krirtie's tone, but none were more taken back than Schram who stopped and turned to face the girl. "Do you disagree with my actions Krirtie? Please speak if you feel we are acting incorrectly."

A silence engulfed the travelers and all stopped and locked on the two humans. Krirtie had surprised even herself with what she had said but now she found herself reaching anywhere for support. Her voice cracked and her heart began beating like a fiercely feeding fire. "I don't know what came over me." She looked around as if pleading to the others to help. Maldor put his arm around her while tears began to form in her eyes. She cried profusely, even falling to her knees bringing the maneth down with her as her emotions seemed to be erupting from within her.

"It's the forest!" exclaimed Stepha. "The mountain elves protect their city much like we do, but their enchantment causes trespassers to become emotionally drained until they flee the woods completely, but it should not be affecting Krirtie. She is no threat to the elves unless," she paused, then added worriedly, "something has happened to Eltak."

Schram's worried gaze became deeper with each statement. "I should have realized the enchantment." He rose his hand and mumbled some words which were foreign to any who could hear. An encapsulating glow formed around Krirtie separating her from Maldor and the rest of the forest. Her crying quickly ceased and a peaceful look grew across her face. "This will protect you as we travel, but it should be known that under normal circumstances, I should not so easily be able to block this enchantment. Their magic has been left unattended for some time and I fear Eltak has met with some evil of their own. Maldor, stay near Krirtie and don't let anything penetrate the shell around her."

The maneth nodded and the group continued all drawing their weapons in preparation for the unknowns which lay ahead. Stepha showed an even deeper concern, as she feared that the other elven kingdom might have faced the same fate as Elvinott. All walked with a stoic and locked stare until a small voice from within the protective field Schram had created broke the silence. "Why was only Krirtie affected?" asked Fehr.

Schram's expression did not change. "I do not know. Perhaps her mind was more accepting to the enchantment than ours."

Fehr had not actually cared about the answer and only wanted to join the discussion. As such was the case, he quickly retired within the pouch in the hopes of catching a few winks before they reached Eltak. After all, he had been up for several hours already today.

CHAPTER 21:

ELTAK

Cries could be heard above the sounds of crashing metal as Krirtie's saddened body met the ground. Maldor was on his knees lashing and slashing fiercely at the onslaught of goblins attacking before him. Stepha had taken to the air only to be shot down by a bolt from one of the hooded figure's hands. Now that Krirtie's magical shell had been cracked, Fehr darted free and leaped into the air digging his claws into the face of a goblin standing with its sword over Maldor's back. Jermys helped Stepha to her feet and the two attacked the remaining goblin force while Schram stood before the two hooded humans who had become to be known as Dragon Lords.

The magical display which ensued was as brilliant as any that had ever been witnessed before. Charges of fire and lightning were met with rebuttals of the same, but each time the attacked was protected by an equal feat of magic. The companions had only just entered Eltak when they were ambushed, and as the fighting first favored the goblins, now the tides were slowly being turned. Schram's use of sorcery was exquisite, but still he had little affect against the combined powers of the Dragon Lords other than to keep their wrath away from his friends. A goblin broke free from the fighting and ran at Schram from behind. Before Maldor could holler, a dagger was thrust deep into the magician's back.

For a very short moment barely able to be measured, everything went quiet and deathly still for Maldor as he watched in fear and agony at his error in preventing this attack. The goblin withdrew his knife and stood frozen before the human who had not moved even as the blade had entered. Maldor watched, and then the noise of the fierce battle split his ears and he saw Schram's eyes unaffected.

He turned to face the brunt of three new goblins with a force of his own that severed their heads from their bodies in one swing.

Schram remained focused on the two dragon-men, ignoring the goblin at his back. The attacker arched as if he was about to thrust forward again when a blinding light appeared at the first incision. The goblin dropped his dagger and fell back, grabbing both hands to his face. In violent convulsions of pain he screamed and began pealing the flesh from around his eyes. Seeing this, those goblins who could still run did so and fled to the trees. Those goblins who became locked within the reaches of the gripping light fell down dead beside their comrade, each facing the same violent convulsions of pain as the first. Maldor, slightly stunned by the actions taking place, swung around and beheaded the last remaining goblin whose face was already completely disfigured from Fehr tearing at its flesh.

All stood stoic before the raspy laughter from the Dragon Lords bit their ears. Their attacks ceased but a magical barrier remained to ward off any further attacks from Schram. All quickly grew quiet except for the muffled cries of Krirtie's frail and fallen body. Schram withdrew his attacks and saying some words seemingly to the sky, a cloud burst over the forest and a downpour of rain fell soaking the company of people. The shower struck quickly and hard but in its wake sat a calmness which enveloped the city and surrounding forest with a long lost peace and tranquility despite the ominous confrontation still occurring in its heart. Krirtie dried her eyes and rose to stand beside her friends who all had moved behind their leader. Schram was cold and hard, his eyes were locked on the two robed figures before him who had acted slightly taken by the magic of the young human. The two looked at each other and again one began to laugh in an indistinguishable and sour tone. With the smooth gentle movement of one of his hands, the laughing Dragon Lord removed his hood.

"That's the one I fought before outside Draag," yelled Jermys pointing toward the magician with his face revealed.

Schram didn't flinch as he and the mysterious creature before him seemed entranced by the other's existence. The two stared at each other a long time before Schram turned and spoke to the dwarf. "Then you have met my father."

His voice was callous and carried little recognition of being from Schram's body. Although Stepha and Krirtie both immediately recognized the figure of King Keith Starland before them, Maldor, Fehr, and Jermys all were caught completely by surprise as was depicted in their expressions and dropped jaws. Schram turned back and again faced his father, or whatever his father had become. "You have changed much since I last saw you father. What evil has done this to you, but more importantly, how could you be so weak as to let it?"

Laughter jolted from both of the figures. "As you have changed too, my son, but my changes are for the good of the land. It is you that carry evil in your path. Just look at the death you have brought about only now." The king motioned to the bodies of dead goblins surrounding the area.

"But what of all the elves that used to call this land their home?" replied Schram. "What fate did you sentence to them?"

The other man stepped forward out of the protective barrier and removed his hood as well. He stared into the bright sun letting its heat fall across his face before answering the question. "The mountain elves carried with them a deep evil and hatred for the new age of the land. They too attacked us and had to be dealt with, severely."

Krirtie moved from behind the group with tears again forming in her eyes but this time not from any lost enchantment. She pushed through the group and walked towards the second figure. "Does that mean you killed them all, father?" Her voice cracked and she choked through her statement following the words with tears large enough to call a small river.

Again a shudder fell through the group, but this time it was equaled by a reaction from the dragon magician. His green-tinted face grew pale causing what Schram witnessed as a slight bit of humanness peeking through his shadow. His voice was not the harsh scratching they had just heard, but a much softer caring tone was present. "Krirtie my darling, I did not see you there."

Dragon Lord Starland seemed to become enraged as he too recognized the new caring tone apparent while Derik Wayward looked upon his daughter. The Dragon Lord raised his hand toward the girl.

"Look out!" hollered Schram shooting a barrier out to protect the girl.

The jolt from Schram's father stung Krirtie's arm knocking her to the ground before Schram's protection could reach. However, in one sweeping motion, she recovered and drawing her curved, single-edged scimitar with a fatal swing, she beheaded the man in front of her. Her sword began to hum and glow and a ball of fire appeared around her. Schram's magic barrier was thrust back at the young magician, and the force sent him to his back. The ringing of the sword had become unbearable but it seemed only to be affecting Schram's father, the one remaining dragon evil in the city. He twitched and turned as a redness grew over his enraged face. Several magical bolts dissolved carelessly into the ball of flame emanating from the scimitar's movements and the confused and frustrated Dragon Lord, seeing the motionless corpse of his comrade, formed into a large glowing ball and then disappeared, silencing the sword as he vanished.

The entire area was devoid of sound and motion. All stood frozen, totally bewildered by what they had witnessed. With the absence of the evil dragon soldiers, the enchantment Schram had guided to return to the mountain city began to gain in strength. Its magical power seemed to soothe the minds of the companions and nurture them back to reality. Schram had used his magic several times since he left his Master of the Ring at Black Isle but never before had it taken so much energy out of him. He wondered if he would really be strong enough to accomplish all that he knew he had to. The young man rose and stepped toward the fallen Krirtie, but then his own legs gave to the strain and he fell only to have a supportive tug from Maldor, the big maneth catching the human's arm in mid-flight. Jermys and Stepha remained motionless, the fear they had felt still etched deep into their minds and showing clearly in their eyes. Fehr did not move and it was Maldor who first noticed the blood protruding from the rat's old wound. This small emergency brought Stepha to her senses, and she slowly moved from where her feet had become rooted to the soil. Maldor lifted his friend until Schram could again stand on his own, and while sweat still beaded down the tired magician's face, he motioned for the two of them to approach Krirtie, who now sat over the body of the beheaded dragon magician, her father.

Bright red blood flowed unhindered along the ground. Krirtie remained on her knees fighting through her tears while she frantically tried to push the spilling insides of her father back within his body. The scaly dragon tail and other malformations accompanying the changed man had vanished leaving only the fifty-plus year old body of the human. Schram closed his eyes at the sight in sadness and respect. Maldor, still holding his sword so tight as to cause his white knuckles to bleed, quickly replaced it and knelt beside the woman reaching around and grabbing her arms tightly. She struggled to break free of his hold screaming through her tears. Maldor pulled her close and whispered, "he's dead Krirtie. Let him go peacefully to his passage."

The girl's spastic muscles relaxed and she fell into the big maneth's chest with her eyes filled with tears. He reached one arm underneath her and carried her over to where Stepha had started a small fire leaving Schram alone with the corpse. Jermys had stirred only slightly, moving from where he had stood to now sit staring blankly into the flickering flames of the fire. His face remained ghostly white giving himself the appearance of being without life. Fehr's injury had been properly bandaged and the small rodent sat cleaning himself next to where Maldor had rested Krirtie. A cold brisk wind passed quickly through the group dousing the fire momentarily and then returning it to its brilliant flame.

Schram returned shortly thereafter wearing an expression of deep peace. His only statement, "Your father has made his passage and is free of the evil which had entwined his body. You freed him, and you should be proud."

Krirtie, who had not moved since being taken from her father's side, looked up toward Schram but could muster no expression as her loss of strength could not even hold her head in the air. Her body fell limp and Maldor adjusted her coiled formation to lie flat with her head resting softly on his crossed legs.

The group remained silent for hours, all simply staring helplessly into the rolling flames of their fire consumed totally in their own thoughts. Jermys was the first to speak after a loud pop sent a coal free to land on his leg. "Even the pain of a burning chip embedding into my skin could not compare to what I saw in Krirtie's eyes." All nodded before he added, "and in yours. I am sorry I cannot take some of your pain upon myself Schram."

He looked affectionately toward the small dwarf. "We have all faced great evil since our endeavor began." He turned toward the girl who appeared to somehow have found a deep, motionless sleep. "My thoughts are with her."

Stepha moved next to her beloved husband and placed a comforting arm around his shoulder. "All of our thoughts are together. We will always be with our friends."

They sat together close, each relishing the other's presence. Although it was barely passed noon, nobody moved for the rest of the day. Night came quickly and was a welcomed guest amongst the mountainside. All were awake now and sat silent looking at the stars blanketing the sky. A burst of light was seen as one of the tightly bound specks broke its grip on the universe and ran ablaze across the opaque background gradually losing its brilliance until it finally faded altogether.

"That was for my father," stated Krirtie softly and mostly to herself. "He has been forgiven for his actions. One star waits for your father as well Schram."

Schram rested back against the legs of Stepha with the elf toying with his long, ruffled black hair. Krirtie has found her peace, he thought, also hoping that he would someday be able to find his.

The night proved to be a satisfactory medicine for the group. Their emotions of the previous day had become pacified within their minds. Krirtie remained alone for much of the morning, but gradually, with Maldor always by her side, she fought past her sadness and joined the companions in their search of the city.

Eltak seemed to be completely absent of all life save their own. There were many places where elven bodies had taken their final breaths, but the forest and mountains had already reclaimed their past inhabitants. The companions searched the buildings and trees of the entire city, and although nothing seemed to be damaged or out of order, it had become strikingly apparent that no elves remained, nor did it appear they had been forced out. They had simply vanished. Stepha and Schram were more taken by this knowledge, but both restrained letting their feelings show. They only hoped some of the elves had escaped to the forest, not all meeting the same fate as Eltak, now a city of death.

"Schram," hollered the dwarf's voice from the side.

He and Stepha moved to the building where Jermys stood and were quickly joined by the others. A sign above the doorway in front of them read *BOKLIS*.

"What does it mean?" asked Krirtie pointing.

"It's elven for library," responded Schram. Turning towards the dwarf, he asked, "Did you find something?"

Jermys looked down. "I found no signs of life, but...well?"

"What is it?" he asked again, growing more worried when he took in Jermys deep expression of concern. He could not put into words what his mind wanted to say and Schram's thoughts began to stray for the worse.

Jermys' voice slipped as he spoke. "The library was clean and free from anything out of the ordinary, except my hatchet did not agree. It began humming," he paused seeming to fight with what to say next, "just like Krirtie's sword when she..." he left it at that.

"What do you mean?" he asked.

The dwarf now seemed frustrated as if he was explaining something to someone who didn't speak his language. "I kept walking and the sound got louder and softer depending on where I went. I followed it until it got to its highest pitch and I thought my ears were going to explode. You must have heard it." The others looked at each other with blank expressions before Jermys continued. "I looked around where I stood and this book seemed to be humming back." The dwarf removed a book from under his armor and held it in front of the group. "That is the staff you held when you destroyed the mine and this," he opened the cover, "is the dragon you became. I am sure of both!"

The others nodded remembering what they had seen in the mine, and Schram felt a cold fear as he reached to take the book. He inspected the cover bearing the staff and then looked at the silver dragon on the first page. The staff seemed to be nothing more than a branch from a large oak and the dragon more resembled a child's pet than a fierce creature of magic. "What happened to the humming?"

Jermys looked even more disturbed. "As soon as I touched it, all sound ceased."

Schram tilted his head and seemed to process all that he was hearing. Then, upon further inspection of the book he added, "There is no author. Show me where you found it, and be exact."

The dwarf led the group through the door and down a long spiraling flight of stairs. Talk among them was absent again as nobody knew exactly what was happening or if it was actually important, but they all assumed it had to do with Schram and all the changes he had been experiencing. Maldor motioned that he would remain at the door in case they were being watched and the others disappeared behind the dwarf.

"It was here," stated Jermys pointing to an empty spot on the shelf.

Schram asked, "What is next to where it sat?"

The dwarf strained to read the faded letters and then answered, "A large book called *Epic of the Wood* without an author, and *Time* written by someone called Anders.

Stepha stepped forward. "*Epic of the Wood* was written by Anatilis, the first true King of Elvinott after Ku who was said to have passed to our race the magical ability with the forests and described it in one great work."

Schram smiled showing he was familiar with the story, and he again began to flip through the various passages of the nameless book he held. Krirtie moved next to the young human. "What does it all mean?"

Schram shrugged. "I don't know. The words are simply poems and various spells and riddles. It is written in several languages with no real consistency between them. There are several maps but they do not all appear to be correct." He pointed to one page. "Like this one which puts a large sea across the Plains of Nakton and an even bigger city where the South Sea now sits."

"Perhaps it is simply a look into the future depicting the dragon's plan or even what has been foreseen to be occurring already," stated Stepha.

"Or maybe it is a look at the past," added Fehr somewhat confidently.

Schram looked at the rat. "What do you mean Fehr?"

He jumped from Krirtie's pouch and landed in Schram's free arm. "Nobody has any records of the times before humans, elves, and dwarves first arrived and began charting the lands. We must assume others were here before us. Why couldn't they have made their own maps depicting what was there before we invaded. Perhaps this author dates back several thousand, maybe even hundreds of thousands of years."

"You have a flare for exaggeration and imagination," interrupted the dwarf who still had his eyes fixed on the book's previous location on the shelf.

Schram only smiled at Fehr and after handing him back to Krirtie, turned to Stepha. "Do you think there would be any dishonor in taking this book with us? I would truly like to read more of it as we travel."

The elf looked around the library and then returned to gaze at the young magician who had again began flipping through its pages. "No, I feel nothing bad about removing it since it is done without evil intentions. This library was created to store knowledge temporarily until it was later desired, not to keep it captive forever."

Schram heard the words but gave little expression of understanding as he walked between his friends and back up the stairs never pulling his eyes from the pages. Jermys made a crooked grin. "What do you make of that? I find a peculiar book and don't even get a thank you for it."

"Thanks Jermys," hollered a voice from upstairs. "You did well."

Those remaining smiled and a strange confidence again began to form within them growing stronger with every pleasant sound they heard. The smiles turned to chatter and even some occasional laughter lifting the heavy air that had been about them. Stepha threw her arm around the little dwarf and proudly stated, "Come on you guys, lets go, and Jermys, you may not want to forget about Schram's now elven ears. Hearing is a newfound strength for him."

Jermys shook his head. "Hearing? Just looking at those ears makes them impossible to forget."

Stepha smiled in return and began walking toward the stairs. "I think they are exquisite to look at."

Jermys and Krirtie both smiled broadly before the dwarf added, "I'll catch up in a minute. I want to push the books together so they don't fall and become damaged. I don't want to upset whoever cares for this place."

Stepha grinned in return while she, Krirtie, and Fehr all stepped through the doorway and upstairs to meet Maldor and Schram outside. Jermys moved to where he had gotten the book and reached up to slide the others over to fill the now empty location. To his surprise, the books had already been shifted over and the book end holding them up was firmly in place. His eyes grew wide and before he even drew in another breath, he was up the stairs with the others.

"What is it?" Maldor asked when he saw the white-skinned dwarf panting his way through the door.

"The book is. . ." his voice trailed off as he felt all eyes fall hard upon him. "I am getting too old for this!" he added before lighting his pipe and sucking in a deep breath of tobac. "Put your sword away maneth, you might hurt someone if you're not careful."

Each shrugged and slapped the dwarf on the shoulder with a chuckle except Maldor who only returned a deep and hardened stare on the dwarf. Schram calmly tucked the book away for future reading and motioned for the others to grab their belongings. "Though it is late, we will leave now and travel a short distance to make tomorrow not such a long journey to the coast. There is a valley to the southwest which we can travel along and avoid the rest of the mountains, but it is still over an hour away. I'd like to reach it by nightfall."

The group gathered their equipment and with newfound energy, departed the dismal ghost town of the mountain elves. Stepha and Schram both stared back sadly as they took their first step into the surrounding trees wondering exactly what had happened to their friends and brothers but knowing that possibly time would tell and all may not be as dismal as it seemed. They had no proof that the elves had been killed, no sign at all of any activity, and that unknown by itself allowed them to continue.

Despite the evil they had encountered, the spirits of the entire group seemed to have been lifted to a new level of accomplishment. Krirtie had found peace within the death of her father by her sword, and all realized the significance of that event. They had killed one of the Dragon Lords and put fear into the eyes of another. Although they were certain the goblin armies would be quick to retaliate, this occurrence definitely put a heavy strike against them. Whatever armies Derik Wayward controlled would now have to be redistributed among the other Dragon Lords. Each of the companions realized this was to be no great feat for the evil dragon forces, but still the knowledge of their first successful offensive of the war where they forced the Dragon Lords to retreat gave a satisfaction to each of them, but most of all to Schram. He knew Slayne would not take this action lightly, and although the companions had been in check the entire time, they were still surviving and even possibly slowly beginning to wear the black dragon's defenses down. Schram glanced toward the stoic glare of Krirtie and he knew that she was stronger with all that had happened. She had freed her father from the evil which had wrongly taken him over, and with that freedom came a well-accepted death, a gift which could never be returned.

They walked for nearly two hours until arriving in the valley Schram had described. Talk was minimal while each seemed happy to be deep in their own thoughts. Schram put down the book from the elven library only long enough to eat a few bites and then again became absorbed in its pages. Brightness had begun to form in his elven eyes and his mind became enlightened with what it was learning. That night left Schram and Stepha entwined in each others arms as they had never been before. The love they shared reached new and exciting plateaus every day, and each knew what the other was feeling.

CHAPTER 22

The Book of Anbari

The next morning carried a festive atmosphere as each could begin to feel a new safety and confidence in their leader. After a quick breakfast, they began their journey one more time toward the blue waters of the South Sea. However, as each of the companions began to think more about their destination, they began to realize that they had no idea what they were going to do when they got there. Maldor was particularly disturbed with this fact since, being a warrior by trait, he preferred to have well designed plans laid out in front of him and thus making the success of a mission dependent on how well the troops executed the plans. This situation seemed to him to be more of a random quest, and they would just take things as they came. The more he thought about it, the more he became concerned.

Krirtie, realizing his discomfort, said, "Maldor, what has got your mind so frenzied? We are near the Sea and have seen no sign of trouble."

The maneth ignored the girl and spoke loudly in the direction of Schram. "What will we do when we arrive at the coast? I am not sure of our plans, but moreover, I am not familiar with this part of Troyf. My travels have never brought me any farther south than Eltak."

Schram grinned because he was fairly sure from Maldor's actions the other day in the mountain elf city and his tone now that he had never been farther south than Feldschlosschen, if even that far. He stopped his quick pace and faced the group behind him, except for Stepha who was at his side. His lips still showed a slight crooked smile, but his speech was totally devoid of humor. "After we reach the sea, we will travel westward around the coast and down the peninsula. Somewhere down there is the pirate city of Icly. I have never been to the city, but from what I have heard it is a haven for every villain and scum on Troyf. We must be cautious, but I believe it will be our only choice to find a ship capable of making a journey through the rough southern sea waters."

"A ship! Rough waters! You never said we would be sailing on the Sea," exclaimed Jermys. "Feldschlosschen dwarves are *not* sailors! You got me in that crooked craft on the Ozaky, and I stated then and there it would never happen again. There is no chance I will step one foot on a ship sold to us by thieves whose destination is across the South Sea."

The dwarf stood stubbornly with his lips pressed tightly together giving the appearance of a four-foot, bearded, pipe-smoking statue. Schram chuckled at the sight and responded, "fine Jermys, you can wait for us to return to Icly. You probably will make lots of friends there."

They all smiled at the statement except Jermys who hesitated and then replied, "Fine! I probably will."

Maldor ignored the comment and again addressed Schram with concern as the group began moving again. "Couldn't we head a more south-westerly course now and save time by making it a direct line to Icly rather than heading South to the water and then following it west?"

He shook his head but continued walking while he answered the maneth's question. "We could, but that path would take us through the Canyon of Icly, and with all the dark dwarves roaming the canyon, I would prefer to avoid it. Moreover, with the D.D.s strange behavior of late, there is no telling who may really control the region."

Maldor shook his head satisfied with the thinking.

There was a long silence until Jermys finally spoke up. "Schram, do you think my brother could have gone to find the dark dwarves and see what they were up to, and that is why he hasn't returned?"

Maldor began to erupt allowing his belief to come full front on the dwarf but a raised hand from Schram silenced him. The human looked toward the dwarf who stared back awaiting his response. Schram paused while he weighed what he should say. He knew that if he saved the dwarf's feelings and answered at all positively, then Jermys would want to go investigate in the hope of saving his brother. If he answered a flat out no, then he also would be lying. The fact was Schram did believe that Bretten had gone toward the dragon-held regions, but not to investigate the dark dwarves. He believed the dwarven twin had either joined forces with the dark dwarves or the dragons, or both as the case may be. Whatever the answer, Schram only hoped they never met with the dwarf again, as he had felt the moment Bretten had left, though at the time he didn't know why. He blinked out of his lost thought to see the questioning, almost pleading, eyes of Jermys still staring back at him. In a soft voice, he replied, "no, I don't think even your head strong brother would risk that much, though I suppose he might have. Yet remember, he had a lot of important information to get back to Feldschlosschen and King Krystof. His sense of duty was too strong to let that slide."

The dwarf seemed satisfied with his well-rounded answer so Schram let out a pleased sigh and continued on his way with Stepha tightly gripping his hand. Krirtie had walked alone more the last two days. All believed her thoughts were still with her father, and not even Maldor, felt he should pry. Schram had told the maneth to give her time and space, once she worked things totally out in her mind, she again would be with him seeking his strong arms for support and comfort. Jermys had dropped back beside the big man and together they exchanged idle talk with Maldor always keeping one eye focused on the human woman in front of them.

The day had grown calm when Maldor yelled, "Schram, the dwarf is gone!"

The companions ran to where Maldor's lost gaze greeted them well behind in the trees. The maneth shook his head questionably. "He was beside me a moment ago. I am sure of it."

Schram joined the maneth in the nearby trees but no sign could be seen of the little man. "He has turned toward the canyon," stated the human softly. "I'll bet my life on it. He seeks to find his brother." There was a brief pause before Schram slapped his hands together clearly upset at the new change. "I should have guessed the stubborn dwarf would act as such. I should have kept a closer eye on him. He still sees Bretten as his honorable brother, a feeling I have not held for some time."

Maldor appeared surprised. "Then you do not think his twin has been acting on the level?"

"I am not sure exactly what has happened, but I am certain that something in the whole situation is foul, and I don't like it." He turned back to the others. "Come on back this way. It seems Jermys has gone off on his own, probably in an attempt to locate his brother. We will backtrack a short way and see if we can pick up his trail. If not, we will make our own leading towards the canyon. I believe he heads west."

The rest fell in behind the two large men and it was not long before a slight break could be seen in the underbrush and several small footprints pressed into the ground below it. The companions inspected the area and noticed that he had left at a full sprint trying to put as much distance between them as he could.

"He did not bother to hide his steps?" asked Stepha.

Maldor returned firmly, "He knew it would be of no use. No dwarf could hide from maneth and elven trackers. We could find his trail in the pitch black of the darkest night if we wanted to."

"Yes," replied Schram, "and he made it obvious that his pace would be quick. He is trying to discourage us from following so our lives won't be put at any risk due to his actions. He is truly of good heart."

"Do we follow?" asked the maneth already stepping into the makeshift path.

"Of course we do," began Fehr but stopping as the others had already begun falling in behind the maneth.

Each removed their respective weapons except Schram who only studied what he could about the terrain before them. They followed the trail left by Jermys for several hours, losing it a couple of times only to pick it up again without difficulty. They froze when they came to a clearing littered with blood and debris.

"How many are there?" asked Krirtie entering the glade last.

"Looks to be about three, but it is difficult to tell with all the blood," replied Schram. "And I don't want to unpile the bodies, or what's left of them anyway."

Stepha looked disgusted at the sight. "Could Jermys have done this?"

"I don't think so," he replied. "Not unless he was attacked and was fending for his life. I think he would have simply ducked around the party if he happened upon it. I also don't think he would openly attack the dark dwarves unprovoked, no matter what he believed about his brother. After all, although he may not admit it, D.D.s are kin regardless of how distant. His honor would forbid a mutilation of this sort."

"Schram look!" hollered the maneth peering down a trail leaving the clearing. Schram joined his friend as he continued. "Those appear to be the same tracks we have been following. The ones we thought to be left by Jermys. But those there are slightly larger, and they are placed after the first ones. You can see by where the loose dirt has fallen into Jermys', and the others remain clean and undisturbed."

"Yes, I see," he replied.

Krirtie's eyes narrowed. "What do you mean? Someone is after Jermys?"

Schram turned. "Or at least follows him. Let us hurry. He may need our help, but remain observant, we may be watched as well."

They hurried down the path for several miles not seeing any sign of life about and not even sure which direction they now headed as the trail had twisted back and forth the entire distance. Schram believed they now headed directly west, but with the tall, thick branches of the surrounding trees, it was impossible to see the sun and be sure. Maldor had moved about fifty yards ahead of the others, and it was his wave which caused the rest to dive into some nearby cover. Within seconds they saw the maneth surrounded by dark dwarves and quickly being stripped clean of all his weapons.

Several sword tips were pressed against the large man's armor and skin only slightly piercing deep enough to draw the thick, blue maneth blood but successful in delivering the "no resistance is suggested message" which made him place both his hands on top of his helmet. Krirtie rose as if she was going to attack. Simultaneously Stepha and Schram grabbed her shoulders while Fehr nipped her in the side.

"Not now," whispered Schram. "They want him for something or he would be dead already."

He silenced as they all heard the strong voice of the dwarven leader. "Backtrack the trail and find his friends. This scum wouldn't travel alone."

His speech slurred and spit struck Maldor's face as he spoke. The maneth grimaced at the commander. "You're right, I wouldn't travel alone, the dwarf with me carries a mighty weapon which will soon separate many parts of your pathetic body."

The leader grinned a sadistic smile and removed a shiny hatchet from under his armor. "Do you mean this weapon, maneth?" His laughter only stopped when he raised the axe before the maneth's face. "Tie him down. I believe my first kill with it will be a warrior maneth. It should suit well to begin our attack."

Maldor did not flinch as the dwarf again began to laugh. Slowly, he raised the Hatchet of Claude and with thunderous speed and force brought it down upon the maneth's chest. Krirtie looked away as Schram tried to keep her calm so as not to give away their hiding place. Some dwarven guards were still nearby and the slightest movement would alert them, though their eyes too were fixed on the scene ahead. Schram closed his eyes as he saw the axe begin to drop. However, the strange thud and then onset of silence brought his gaze back towards the two in time to see the completion of the Hatchet bouncing harmlessly off Maldor's armor. Schram turned Krirtie's face so she too could witness the surprising development. It was clear in everyone's eyes that Maldor was the most surprised of all, except maybe the dwarven leader. A disgusted and enraged look crept across his face as the rage within him began to reach a plateau. "What do you know of this?" he shouted at the maneth.

Maldor said nothing as much from his loss of breath as the fact that he had no answer for the question. The jolt from the axe had not cut him, but it had given him the sensation of catching a dragon-sized boulder on his chest. Yet, he had little time to sort through the details as the dwarf interrupted his own question and ordered the maneth's ropes cut. "Take him to the dwarf. Together we'll make one of them talk, or simply kill them the way I prefer to, piece by piece."

The group of about twenty heavily armored dark dwarves reassembled and led the maneth down the narrow trail. Once they were out of sight, the companions rose and began to follow keeping in the trees rather than becoming an easy target on the path. Stepha led the way using her keen sight which was more specialized and well used than Schram's. The human kept his eyes centered on their rear just in case a stray guard or two found their way to return late.

They continued for about a mile until they came to another glade, this one larger than the last with an open trail leading where Schram knew now to be south-westerly toward the Canyon of Icly. At the far side of the clearing could be seen the reddened and bloodied face of Jermys, who appeared to have been severely beaten. Next to him was Maldor who, although tied to a tree and gagged, seemed to be trying to talk to the injured dwarf. Schram surveyed the entire area but said nothing as it was apparent that there was nothing but a suicide mission at hand.

The sun began to fall bringing nighttime to the forest. Nothing regarding the situation had changed over the past three hours other than successive beatings of the prisoners at their refusal to answer any questions. From Schram's perspective, it appeared Jermys would not last the night without care, but with the rage carried in the commanding dark dwarf's eyes, both Maldor and the dwarf would be dead within the hour. Schram still did not have a plan with which he felt confident. However, as five of the dwarves made their way down a far trail out of the glade and several others remained off to the side eating and drinking totally oblivious to the main area of the camp, his plan seemed to grow more plausible.

There had been no talk for over an hour among the companions so when Schram knelt down and whispered softly to Fehr, all attention snapped to alert. The rat disappeared immediately bearing a smile of confidence and Schram motioned for the two girls to come over and gave a quick explanation to what he had just begun. They sat patiently waiting for the sign that would tell them if Fehr was drawing on success. Then, as if spurred by their thoughts, Maldor's eyes opened wider and brightened and Schram knew that Fehr had made it around the camp. A moment later the maneth tilted his head slightly and they knew his hands were free. Stepha had quietly lifted herself into an overhanging branch while Schram had an arrow notched ready to release it at Krirtie's signal. The girl crept over to where the two guards stood closest to Schram and Stepha's sight and she reached around one with her dagger slicing deep into its throat causing a gargled spew of blood to shower forward. The other quickly turned at the sound only to greet Krirtie's curved blade as it cut through its blackened flesh.

With that, Schram and Stepha both let arrows fly dropping five each before others could even move. Maldor sprung with all the energy he had left, and with a dagger Fehr had brought within his pouch, easily overpowered the much smaller dwarves who were only passively guarding him. The commander leaped at Maldor from behind only to grunt as Krirtie's dagger struck him in the back. The maneth swung to meet the noise to witness the dark dwarf falling to his knees. He looked over and gave a nod of gratitude to where Krirtie stood raising her sword before another guard.

Within moments, the activity settled and all was quiet. On the ground were the motionless bodies of nineteen dark dwarves while one slowly moved trying to reach a dropped sword. When his hand was inches from the prize, a cry of pain echoed out beneath Maldor's heavy step across his outstretched fingers. "I don't think you need to be killing yourself just yet," the maneth said, his adrenaline causing his voice to sound hard and without feeling.

Stepha had already moved to help Jermys as she signaled that his situation was not good. Schram walked over to an open spot which appeared to be some sort of council area. At it sat all of Maldor's weapons and the Hatchet. Schram picked it up and felt a sudden surge of energy pulse through his body ending at the finger bearing his magical ring. He moved over to where Jermys, slipping in and out of consciousness, sat motionless. Stepha looked up and by her expression it was clear the dwarf was beyond her ability to save.

Jermys' bloodshot eyes opened and he peered up at the human before him. "I am sorry Schram. I thought I could help Bretten."

Schram used great care to gently place the Hatchet under the dwarf's crossed arms upon his chest. "Save your strength, my friend, for you will need it in the days to come."

The dwarf could muster no more words, and it was apparent he too felt the end was near. He gripped the Hatchet tighter, and a peaceful look grew across his face. All bowed their heads while they watched their friend slowly lose his grip on life. The Hatchet began to glow and hum in a beautiful song which made all who heard become entranced by its melody. The color released formed a rainbow around the glade. The trees and shrubs seemed to be enchanted by musical notes and danced in the gentle breeze spurred by their presence. Even the fallen dark dwarf commander who also barely held onto life gained a certain peace from what he heard, and he fell back completely relaxed at the sound.

Time became frozen. In the midst of this violent evil, one magical hatchet could bring about a rebirth of life. Moments later, there was no motion in the glade and everyone was fast asleep.

"Am I dead?" spoke a weak and disoriented voice.

Schram lifted his head causing one of the swords he had recovered to fall tip first against Jermys' side. The dwarf leaped to his feet and swung his hatchet around to bear down on the groggy human. "Schram? What the?"

"Jermys!" shouted Stepha. "You're alive!"

Everyone was now pulling themselves to consciousness and each wore the exact same look of total confusion. Jermys stood strong for only a moment and then found his knees absent of any strength and with a thump struck the ground hard. The others huddled around him immediately with Krirtie recovering some water to help revive him. Jermys' eyes slowly regained their color and immediately he began speaking without censor. "I had the most wondrous dream." He glanced toward the weapon he held by his side whitening his knuckles as he gripped it tighter. "This is truly a magnificent weapon, perhaps the greatest gift ever given."

Schram smiled and patted the dwarf on his head. "No, but it's in the top five." He changed to a serious tone. "It is good to have you back, Jermys." The dwarf smiled in return wanting to apologize but being interrupted by Schram's raised hand. "We know old friend, we know."

The group sat around a fire they had built in the clearing and talked and ate as night eclipsed the forest. Maldor had taken care to properly remove all the dwarves bodies, and when the commander would tell them nothing, left him tied to the rotting pile to try to change his mind. Occasionally an obscured cry could be heard from the area, but when no answer would come to one of Schram's questions, the cry was ignored.

"What are we going to do with him?" asked the maneth. "If he does not talk, do we kill him like the others?"

"No," Schram replied. "We will let him go tomorrow morning."

Jermys, who had been silent since his ordeal, added roughly, "His honor will force him to take his own life. He lost his entire garrison of troops. He will have no other option."

"Then it is by his hand which he acts, not ours."

The dwarf shook his head at the human. "By my meaning, I think he would feel more honor if it was by our hand, especially if by the blade of my hatchet."

Schram eyed the dwarf and knew these feelings were born deep within his dwarven heritage. He was beginning to understand exactly how similar the two groups of dwarves who were so very different in appearance really were. He could feel a bonding present that he believed even Jermys and their captive did not realize was there. "Perhaps you are right my friend." He turned to where the dark dwarf leader had been securely tied down and hollered, "See-

Hale, if you do not speak now of your business here in the woods, you shall never speak again."

When Schram spoke the name that the dark dwarf had given them, the leader slowly lifted his head. There was a deep cough which brought a mouthful of blood in its wake and caused Stepha to drop her head in sadness before the dwarven leader spit out his last words of defiance. "Kill me then, human who looks like an elf, though I doubt you have the stomach for it."

His voice trailed off when Jermys appeared before him holding the Hatchet of Claude at his side. "It was decided that your death should be by my hand and that of our father, Claude. If you honor him, your passage will be accepted. If not, I pity your path."

As Jermys stepped forward Schram could see the strength and confidence growing in See-Hale's eyes. At that moment, he knew that they had made the right choice. He remembered what Maldor had taught him long ago when they had been approached by a fatally wounded gar. To honor a creature in death was as important as honor in life. The right to be judged in passage was a right entrusted in all creatures. There was an ominous silence across their small glade when Jermys' hatchet found its rest between the dark dwarf's shoulders.

The others bowed their heads in silence until Jermys returned. "It is done. His life honored Claude. He was accepted."

The rest of the companions remained quiet, quite taken by Jermys' sudden knowledge of the afterlife and talk of honor to Claude. Maldor's rough voice was first to breech the night air. "Why didn't the blade harm me?"

"What?" asked the dwarf, surprised. "What blade?"

"Your Hatchet. See-Hale swung it damn hard into my chest, but it didn't even dent my armor." The maneth suddenly realized what he had done in his confusion speaking the name of one who had passed and quickly looked towards Stepha for forgiveness. She saw his concern and lowered her head gently showing she understood that no dishonor was intended.

Jermys had continued completely unaware of the occurrence and unconcerned. "I don't believe it! Schram, is that true?"

All eyes turned to the human who again had begun reading his book. "I'm sorry Jermys, what did you say?"

The dwarf was now standing though he was still at eye level with the maneth who sat leaning back on his hands. "Did the hatchet not hurt Maldor?"

Schram blinked and seemed to come back to his senses giving a slight smile. "No, it didn't harm him, but there was nothing about him which prevented it. If you were to swing it now, quick would you be to section him up."

Maldor leaned forward at this, surprised by the response. "What, are you saying your magic protected me then?"

The human chuckled. "No, not even I would dare any magic that might affect the Hatchet of Claude, or any of the Weapons of the Ring for that matter. That is why I couldn't use any magic to help free you. Magic can be quite random in its defenses and powers. If I had tried to enchant this glade or place a barrier around you for instance, something in that action could have jolted the Hatchet's defenses and that would have been disastrous for me and possibly everyone in the area as well. No, the Hatchet itself protected you from injury."

He stared at the puzzled faces of his friends and knew more explanation was necessary. Closing his book, he continued. "The Hatchet of Claude carries with it immense magic and power, as does Krirtie's sword and Stepha's bow. My Ring is at the heart of this magic and I am only now beginning to understand a fraction of its limits. However, what I do know about the weapons is that their magic may become absent or greatly reduced if they are stolen and even more so, if they are in turn used against one which it knows to be of good heart. Of course this is only a legend, but so is just the existence of the weapons at all, and we know that part is actually true. I believe the Hatchet did not consider the dark dwarf leader to be a suitable wielder of its powers and therefore it acted as an ordinary axe, and we all know that no ordinary axe could ever even come close to denting that steel wall Maldor calls a breast plate."

The maneth smiled briefly at this, but his thoughts, as well as everyone else's, had become lost in what Schram had said. Never before had he referred to Krirtie or Stepha's weapons as being anything special. Sure Stepha had received her bow in an extremely special and magical way, and Krirtie seemed to be able to wield her sword like someone born with it as part of her body, but she had only bought it from a peddler in Gnausanne. There could be no magic carried in its delicate blade. Maldor looked at the woman next to him who had become engrossed with the shiny curved blade she rested on her lap. The sword glowed as it sent the light from the fire dancing off its shiny silver edge to bounce off her face. Stepha too had been caught by surprise. As her mind remembered the moment at the fountain in Elvinott when she had received the golden bow, she barely noticed the worried and confused expression growing on her husband's face as he read the unnamed book of the staff.

Not much was said the remainder of the night. Each of the companions had drifted off to sleep, with the exception of Schram who still remained mystified by the pages. "Put that book down now, Schram. Let's get some rest," whispered Stepha's soft voice. "We both need it dearly."

He did not move from his crouched position not even hearing her voice. Stepha sat up in alarm and grabbing both sides of his waist shook his body lightly. The contact made him nearly jump from his skin and he whirled around to face the now totally surprised and cowering elf.

"What are you doing?" he shouted causing some of the others to stir but not wake. He quickly recognized his tone, and as the color returned to his pale face, he added, "I am sorry. I do not know...the book it..." his voice trailed off.

"That book has seduced you Schram." Her voice was worried. "What is that book and why does it scare you so?"

"It is not that it scares me. It's that it," he paused, "it just doesn't make sense." Her expression showed that she did not understand but she was willing to listen, and would even if it took all night. Schram adjusted his posture to better face her and began again. "Actually, it is not really a book at all. It is more like a diary."

"A diary? Written by who?"

"I'm not sure, but I think it was written by Anbari. It tells of his deal with Ku. A deal that from what he says, Ku did not honor."

Stepha became disturbed. Schram was basically saying that the father to all elves was a dishonored soul. The warrior saw her displeasure but had to continue. "Many of the passages are faded and difficult to read, but I believe I have interpreted them correctly. It says that a great time ago, Ku came to the most powerful magician in all the universe, Anbari, and asked him if he would teach him the magic necessary to form now what the elves take for granted, the enchantment of their forest and their naturally born knowledge of all its inhabitants. Anbari was taken by the elf, and although he refused to pass all the secrets held deep within him, he did create one golden ring and four magical weapons. In them was carried all that Anbari was, all his magic, all his life, all his soul. They made an agreement that when the enchantment of the forest was in place, Ku would return the ring and thus return Anbari's power to him. When this took place, Ku would be rewarded with the receipt of the four magical weapons which he could spread across the land as he wished. However, after Ku gained the power of the Ring, he didn't want to lose it. He became seduced by the power he now wielded at his fingertips. However, this power, fueled by his refusal to return it, grew into a madness. He also wished to possess the weapons. He desired total power and strength. He did go back to meet Anbari, in what the magician thought was to be the planned exchange. However, Ku used the Ring's power against Anbari leaving him helpless and nearly destroyed. Then, without care or fear, he stole the weapons and distributed them as if they were by his fashioning. The bow remained with the elves and the Hatchet was given to Claude of the dwarves who later used it to become the hero over his kingdom. I believe the diary says that the distribution of the sword and hammer was left to an angel of the stars. Until it fell into Krirtie's possession, the sword had never been seen."

"I can't believe it," cried Stepha. "It can't be true. He is the one we have called father for all of our lives. Only because of his great honor and the need to spread such pure honor to those who follow our lives do we speak his name and spread his long lost message of valor. Now to hear such a horrid tale," she paused then added, "if it not be from your mouth I would raise my bow to you this moment. Your words, if they be true, throw immense shame on our entire race."

"I believe them to be true, but still, there is more for you to hear." Schram became lost in thought as he looked back to the pages to find the right words. "It seems Anbari's race was outraged with his actions. Before, they were the only ones with 'the power' about them and now magic was spreading across the entire land. What it is saying is that all the magic that the elves, the dwarves, the humans, and every other creature on Troyf now experiences, originated from this betrayed deal."

Stepha stared at the man over her. "Could you be wrong? Couldn't the diary be false? This seed Ku supposedly planted years ago could not now be our undoing?"

There was a pause as both came to the realization about what she had just said. Schram's eyes were saddened but slowly his stare lifted and he continued. "Anbari was cast out. He had no powers and no life. His passages became distorted over these years until one point. He returned to where he had fashioned the weapons and laid his head down expecting to close his eyes for the last time. However, in the ground beneath him, he felt something, something he had not felt in what equaled the average creature's lifetime. There was a rumbling and out of the ground rose a magnificent oak. He didn't know how it had occurred, but he could feel the life and magic generating within it. He inspected the entire tree and found the place where the magic was focused. With the only thrust left in his tired body, he removed the branch and began working with it. In time, he learned to fashion the magic in the staff as he had worked so much magic in the past, only now he had mastered it to new levels. Under his guidance, the staff became the most powerful artifact known. His strength, life, and soul were returned. . .that ends the last entry."

There was a long pause as Stepha tried to make sense out of all that was said. Her voice depicted her confusion when she asked, "I don't understand then. You said this staff of Anbari was responsible for the evil done unto the canoks. Are you saying that to seek revenge for the wrong doings of Ku, Anbari gave his staff to the dragons to destroy us when they were able?"

Schram drew a long expression. "No, I believe Anbari to be totally with honor. I believe his intent was to spend his life with his staff at his side. However, somehow Slayne learned of its existence and stole it from where he resided, or where his body rested as I feel the case may be."

"Wouldn't he then keep the staff so nobody could reverse the evil he had done?"

"No," he replied. "Slayne knew that to keep the staff for eternity would mean his death. He needed it to start this process and then he returned it to the South Sea, where I believe is Anbari's final resting place. We must recover it and in his name, undo what has been done, then return it to him forever."

Both leaped up as footfalls could be heard approaching. Schram doused the fire as Stepha moved to wake the others. Their recent experiences make breaking sleep easy and the entire group was out of the clearing and safely hidden among the surrounding bushes in only moments. The footsteps grew gradually louder, and although no voices could be heard, all could tell there were many in the party. Slowly, in the distance down the path they had followed to arrive at the glade, several pairs of white eyes could be seen approaching. They arrived into the clearing and the moon's light reflected off their white coats depicting a party of eight canoks of the white reign. Schram recognized all of them by sight but only one of them did he know well. His name was Stoven and he was probably Kirven's closest friend other than the human himself. Stoven had taken well to the human and Schram considered him one of his greatest friends as well.

The party of canoks continued through the clearing towards the large road leading towards the canyon, not taking notice to the companions or any of the remains from the days activities. However, as they reached the far side, Stoven turned back and stared directly towards where the group hid. *Greetings Schram, old friend.* The words were crystal clear and loud to Schram though he was certain his companions were totally oblivious to their existence. *I have censored your presence from those with me, but do not let this disturb you as we all still remain your friends. However, it should be known that many rumors are passed along the winds and your life is every day placed more and more in question.* There was a pause then as the canok turned back to the road ahead. *Remember my friend, when we meet next, keep your head about you and you will keep your head about you.*

Schram smiled and even let out a small chuckle after hearing the old saying the canok would tell him every time he would leave their homeland. He sent a telepathic *I will* in reply just before the white creature disappeared into the forest shadows.

"I thought we were dead," stated Maldor. "That canok looked right at us."

Schram replied, "don't always expect the worst of canoks, for they are inherently good creatures who have been dealt a terrible fate by evil hands. Hopefully, time is about to right itself."

"Or be destroyed trying," added Stepha solemnly so only Schram, who nodded a sad understanding, could hear.

CHAPTER 23

ICLY

The next few hours before dawn gave the weary travelers a final chance to grab a few winks before continuing their journey. They set out by Schram's lead and for the entire reach of the morning did nothing except drive a furious pace down into the base of the Canyon of Icly. Talk amongst them had once again been cheerful despite the recent hardships and although each thought to suggest to waste the day returning to their original course before becoming separated from the dwarf, none spoke up as they could see the determination in their leader's eyes. Schram too toyed with the idea of retracing backwards toward the South Sea Coast, but after the brief run-in with the canoks, his curiosity was sparked. Their presence there was well beyond simple suspicion, but that was not the only reason. Schram remembered the time he spent in Hoangis' map room where the King had said legend dictated the forging of the Ku Ring. He remembered the magical appearance of the weapons of the ring and knowing what it would mean to recover them all, proceeding into the canyon was the clear choice. However, this canyon, and the South Sea Peninsula at its mouth, was a place he had only heard stories about, and the stories were far from pleasant. In truth, the thought of actually traveling through Icly had never occurred to him for its level of danger was just too high. Nobody, especially a prince, would ever consider joining the city of thieves and braggarts which was overrun with every loathsome creature, from goblin to trolls, but was considered the homeland to the dark dwarves. The only humans present would be desperate pirates or lost souls who had little or no other choices to make regarding their life. Schram glanced at Krirtie and worried for her safety before seeing the large maneth a few steps behind.

No, she would be well-protected he thought. Then he looked toward Stepha. An elven princess would surely bring a high price in the slave markets. They would have to be cautious.

Stepha noticed his glance and stepped up beside the large man. "What troubles you this day? Thoughts from the night passed?"

"No, my love, fears for the days ahead. We are entering a land I have never crossed. All knowledge I have of it is based totally on the fears of those who have visited and thought of their leaving not as a pleasant removal to a new place but as an escape from a land that is truly evil. It seems only fitting that this time period should find us traveling through this desolate canyon in search of a best forgotten city."

She appeared saddened as she heard the words he spoke. Her tone was soft and she reached around to pull their bodies close. "Do not worry for our safety, Schramilis. We have become a family and each watches for the other's care. We are all experienced and well tested warriors excelling in every aspect to an unsurpassable strength. Fate has thrown us together to defend the evil before us. You are strong. Strong with a magic none of us can even begin to understand. Do not doubt your abilities. You have harbored powers long since laid to rest on our world to bring them against the evil intentions of one chaotic mind. Fight with no insecurities, for your people will follow you to the depths of each of their hells if your command dictates it, as will your wife."

Schram looked at the fragile face of the elf beside him and he realized the incredible strength hidden behind her delicate eyes. The two embraced causing a small stir in those who traveled behind, and a similar loving glance shared between the human woman and Maldor.

"She speaks the truth," stated the maneth firmly. He took Krirtie's hand and the entire group fell silent. All feelings were expressed as deeply as ever before and not a word was spoken. Even Jermys remained stoic, his eyes locked forward and his thoughts on only his brother.

The time seemed to slip by unnoticed. It was the long forgotten Fehr whose uncomfortable yawn followed by a bounding leap to the ground at the dwarf's feet which broke Jermys from his trance.

His Hatchet was drawn and Fehr's eyes grew wide as the blade brushed his ruffled fur. "Don't you ever sneak up on me like that again, you flee-ridden rodent."

His tensed spine slightly relaxed and a smile even curled between his lips. "I like you Jermys. I wished I had known more dwarves in my life, though sometimes you little guys seem a bit jumpy. It must be in your upbringing, you know, in the caves and all. I'll bet. . ."

The dwarf's grumbling cut Fehr off but caused smiles to grow across everyone's face as he put his axe away.

Stepha and Schram continued walking next to each other admiring the high arching rock of the canyon walls. The canyon took a new steep descent and looking downward from the small trail on which they walked, several small bands of dark figures could be seen in the trees and other ground cover. Schram began to motion to Maldor, but he could see that the maneth's eyes were already focused on the groups.

"We must stick out like a tigon in a village of dwarves against the side of this rock wall," stated the big maneth shaking his head.

"Aye," Schram responded, "but they don't appear to be taking notice. Perhaps they do not expect any visitors."

Maldor appeared astonished. "Your elven eyes are better then mine. Are they dark dwarves?"

"The three groups near the opposite slope are, but the other is a pack of black canoks," he paused a moment then added, "and they do observe us, but also seem not to care."

Maldor drew his sword as all their faces immediately grew concerned. The black shadows below continued to go their respective directions, and it was the hard stare of the maneth which broke first. "They don't seem to be moving to intercept us. If anything, they move away to give us a larger path."

Jermys interrupted. "The trap is there friends. The question is, do we spring it?"

His words were spoken lightly but all knew and understood their significance. Schram answered the dwarf's rhetorical question firmly and directly. "I do not feel that their intentions are directly evil, although their movements are pre-planned. Someone or something wants us to enter the canyon, but an ambush is not their intention, at least not yet. His voice lightened a bit and he let out a sigh. "Come on, we have been invited in, let's see who gives the invitation."

"Hey Schram," started the dwarf. "Have your feelings ever been wrong?"

"All the time."

The response was not what the dwarf, or any of them was expecting, although they all knew he was only being honest and his light tone served only to attempt to lift their spirits. They moved quickly down the grade and arrived at the final base of the Canyon of Icly without a major change in the dark dwarves or the canok's positions, though now, since they were at ground level with them, they could not be traced as easily. The group relied more on sound than sight, and it was apparent to all that since they were at the base, it sounded as if the dwarves were closing in.

The companions increased their pace heading straight south now towards the city of Icly. They heard the bands of dark dwarves falling in behind them and although there was only about a dozen or so in this group, Schram knew that with their obvious size advantage, should a confrontation occur, the dark dwarves could easily be defeated. However, he had no desire to have one. They couldn't determine where the canoks had gone and although he doubted that no evil would bind D.D.s and canoks as allies, in this desperate hour, nothing was being proven impossible.

They managed to put a small distance between themselves and the party behind them, though Schram believed this was as much by the dwarves choosing as by their hurried pace. He continued searching his mind for clues as to what might lay ahead, but something seemed to be blocking his insight. It could possibly be the evil that has reigned here for so long, he thought, or more likely, some barrier erected for the soul purpose of forbidding his prying mind. For the group, it seemed they had only questions. Whether the canyon held the answers was for them to find out, but at this time, searching was beyond anyone's plans. They seemed to be livestock being herded up for some unknown reason but going nonetheless. It was when they reached the figurative corral and saw the branding iron of dark dwarven troops that the group became frenzied.

Ahead of them were nearly three hundred dark dwarves in full battle armor looking on the verge of exploding onto the six travelers. Jermys stood tall, seeming himself ready for the command to charge forward. The others fell back slightly but were frozen by the sounds of those approaching from behind. Furthermore, their numbers no longer depicted of a mere twelve, but moreover, the other half of one large army was completing the sandwich they had entered.

"I may have been incorrect in my assumption of the situation." His voice grew solemn. "It seems I was led to understand exactly what I was suppose to. I have been a fool."

"And now the trap is sprung," added Jermys as he lifted his axe into the air.

Maldor roared, "I will not be held prisoner by these scum again! I will kill fifty before one takes me captive!"

His roar stunned those around and the noise of the approaching troops silenced as they halted in their tracks. Schram seized the opportunity and a bolt shot from his hand toward the wall of the jagged canyon face. A rumbling softly echoed though the air and a few loose pebbles found their way free from their once firm grip. As if they had broken the arms which held the entire framework together, booming explosions and cracks burst across the surface. Entire walls began to shift and move and a thunder never before witnessed marked the beginning of the end. The entire cliff making up the Canyon of Icly began to collapse. Walls of rock and soil fell unrestrained in massive crashes bringing destruction to anything in their path. Screams answered the rock and quickly a few of the closer dwarves were silenced by the boulders' roar. Dust clouded the air creating what seemed to be solid rock in every direction. More and more debris pummeled downward in an endless stream of violence and death.

The stunned companions ran backwards as it was their only option save being crushed in the debris. No longer did they fear the rear army which had formed around them for now all was equal. However, Schram did not move. He stood hard, holding his ground before his quake. The back army had remained frozen for only moments until they too madly drew a retreat fearing the entire canyon was about to collapse upon them. Schram hollered to his friends to remain as the slide was beginning to be quieted. They turned to see their leader's free hand rise and emit a shower of blue which pacified even rushing wind kicked violent by the graphic turn of nature. Suddenly all was silent once again.

Ahead of Schram where the troops had only moments ago stood was a wall of rock larger in mass than most towns. In one breath Schram had created something that would take a life time to clear. A wall of rock dammed the canyon. However, besides the obvious benefit of protection from the dwarven army, it also did one other important thing. It cut off their only root to the South Sea, a drawback which at the time was a fair trade.

"What about those behind?" asked Stepha as they all seemed captivated by the pile of rock now in front of them.

"They will not return for some time. For all they know, their comrades just had a mountain drop on them. They will not risk to meet the same fate."

Maldor moved next to the human and elf but it was Fehr who spoke. "How long till they break through? You know the ones on the other side are madder than a dwarf in front of an empty barrel of ale."

Schram shook his head and smiled a bit at the analogy. Fehr always seemed to tie to his analogies to dwarves, a fact not enjoyed at the same level by Jermys. Schram looked at the dwarf quickly and seeing his angled expression stated, "I have to agree with your assessment of their anger, but I don't think that as long as there is a Troyf, any creature will break through this wall. However, how long until they come over the top is another story. At best I give us one, maybe two or three days."

They moved forward and stared with amazement at the magician who still appeared lost when he witnessed the destruction he had created with a mere motion from his hand. After this pause, Maldor was the first to speak. "That was undoubtedly incredible Schram, truly incredible."

Schram broke from his stare. "Yes, but did I only delay the inevitable? We should not have been down here in the first place. It was the white canoks that..." his voice trailed off.

"No," stated Krirtie pointing. "You did not delay the inevitable, you found that."

"What in all of Troyf is that?" stated Stepha staring toward where rock had been broken free from the canyon face. "A cave?"

The piles of rock still concealed most of it, but it did appear that she was right. Schram's rockslide had broken through revealing what appeared to be a tunnel of some sort. It looked to run lengthwise along the wall of the canyon. Maldor was the first to arrive at the spot, and his muscles bulged as he began to lift the rock from in front of the small, dark hole.

"It will take an hour to clean a hole large enough to even get the girls through, but we can do it, I think." He paused and added, "Unless you want to zap it again?"

The human's pointed ears danced slightly. "No, I would just as easily bring the mountain down upon you sealing the hole forever. This is work to be done by hand."

Maldor grumbled under his breath. He was beginning to like having a little magic guarding his back, but he guessed it couldn't be held accountable for every task that had to be performed. Together the three men began to heave the rocks aside while Stepha and Krirtie prepared a fire and a bit of hot food for a meal, though the portions were small as their supplies were showing signs of running low. Fehr decided he could be most effective overseeing the clearing of the passage and took a perch on a large boulder where he could shout out commands and reprimands as need be.

"Put your back into it you stupid dwarf. I'll feed you to the maneth if you don't get with it," shouted the laughing voice of the rat. The two girls and Schram could only press their lips together tightly to hold their own laughter which would further infuriate

Maldor and Jermys who looked with hatred towards Fehr. "Hey, I don't remember saying break time. Do you remember hearing me say lets all sit down and rest for a while Krirtie. I didn't think so. There is work to be done. The fool magician that got us into this mess is the only one who seems to want to work." Schram joined the glare upward. The rat caught the hard stares but seemed unaffected. "Well fine, all three of you scoundrels can go without food until your job is completed, and that is the final word on the matter."

Maldor turned to Jermys and after saying something softly hoisted the dwarf atop the boulder adjacent to Fehr. With a quick leap, Jermys had the rat in his grips and jumped down to stand next to the maneth. "Well Maldor, did you hear something heckling us?"

Fehr's face cowered downward as he fought to push out an apology. "Take it easy. Don't get your panties all ruffled."

Maldor spoke as if he had not heard the statement from the rat. "Why yes Jermys, I do think I heard some taunting from one who himself was not working entirely too hard."

"Come on guys, you know I was just kidding. Schram, tell them."

All three looked toward the human, but when he only yawned and turned away, Maldor and Jermys cracked smiles that connected their ears. "I have an idea," stated the dwarf still holding Fehr tightly in his arms. "Why doesn't the heckler dig from the inside out?"

Maldor peered at the small hole. "I don't think he'll fit"

"We'll force the varmint in!" exclaimed Jermys. "Trust me, he'll fit."

Fehr screamed for Krirtie who had already been running over when she heard the dwarf's plan. *Fwack!* She slapped the dwarf as she snagged the rat from his arms. In a powerful voice she said, "shame on you both, threatening a poor defenseless creature like that. "A smug grin grew across Fehr's face which bit the two harder than Krirtie's strike had. "And you," she continued turning to Maldor, "why don't you pick on someone your own size. I am sure there is an ale-bellied, toothless minok somewhere nearby. Perhaps you could take him on in battle, for you know it wouldn't be a battle in intellect."

She stormed off. Maldor dropped his jaw and started to reply, "but I..."

Schram walked over and stood beside his friends. "She is a lively one, and don't say I didn't try to warn you." Maldor nodded before Schram added, "but also don't think I have it so easy. Stepha has got a mean streak in her..."

"I heard that you half-witted magician," hollered Stepha hushing Schram as if his mouth had just been corked.

"But I..." he tried to reply then stopped knowing he was in for an ear whipping later as it was and he would prefer that it was in private.

The three shrunken individuals went grumbling back to their work to the delight of the ones who looked on. They eventually had made the hole big enough to pass and after completing their meager meals and having the two deserving individuals receive their respective verbal beatings, the group began its descent into the cavern.

They had thrown a few torches in to give light, but they were no longer necessary as Schram's ring pulsed with brilliant illumination. The tunnel was exactly as what would be expected. Its sides were of rough rock, and the scent down its corridor smelled of musty, dead air much like that of a tomb. The air was full of dust and it seemed to absorb the light emitted from the ring as it passed. The entire tunnel held an ominous presence which worked to physically break down those who walked its corridors.

Schram had motioned that they would head south in the hope of finding that this maze ended at the gates to the city, though even that was not a tremendously appealing thought. Rocks and twigs cracked under their boots, but the crew of travelers slowly pushed onward. Schram assumed this tunnel was known to the dwarves but since they passed no other entrances, there would not be any suspicion that they had entered it and thus no war party would be sent to greet them. His thoughts were quickly vanquished when he saw the faint light ahead of them.

Ic-ayre, he said softly, causing the ring's light to disappear. In its absence the others became aware of what only the elves had been able to see. The light from ahead was steady, not flickering as would a torch. Schram knew that this meant magic was involved, and probably more importantly, that they had been discovered. With a slow motion of his hand which depicted that they had no other choice, he waved the group ahead. As they neared the light which appeared to be coming from a larger chamber, faint, rough voices were heard, and whoever owned those voices appeared to be arguing.

In an ancient dwarven tongue even Schram did not speak fluently, the voice said, "I can't believe we have to sit in here and guard this stupid thing."

"I know the good fighting is going on out there. Whoever the Emperor fears would come for this has no chance of making it here, but still, orders are orders, and I would not wish to be the one to tell him the weapon was stolen in our absence."

The first voice grunted in reply. The companions crept up to the entryway. Schram peered in to see a large open cavern with a lone table and two overweight dark dwarven guards seated involved in some sort of gambling. At the far side was a large door that was held closed by a large tree trunk pushed through large, circular loops on the door and the inside wall making it impossible for anyone to enter from the other side. The thing that puzzled Schram was from where the light was generating. Somewhere along the wall around the corner of the tunnel doorway hidden from his view, a steady beam of light shot out and filled the entire cavern.

Schram whispered, "Well, we have no other choice but to proceed."

Maldor nodded and rose only to be held down by Stepha's arm on his shoulder. "Schram and I can handle these two."

With that, two arrows flew and as their mark was true, both guards fell down showing a shaft protruding from their black hearts. Maldor leaped around the corner to face any hidden guards and whatever was controlling the light. He nearly dropped his sword at what he saw freezing him in his tracks. The others came around ready for anything except what it really was. Nobody moved. They could only stare at the silver hammer sitting peacefully in a small hole dug out of the rock. A slight hum could be heard as the light it gave out seemed to dance across their faces as it passed.

Maldor was first to move, and being drawn to its captivating hum, he slowly approached the magic hammer. He gently reached his hand out and gripped the handle. Suddenly, the humming stopped, and although the light was still present, it was changed somehow.

"Maldor, No!!!" shouted Schram. "Release it now!!!"

But it was too late. There was a flash of green light whose force caused the other companions to be thrown backwards. Maldor turned and faced his fallen friends with the large hammer now in both hands and a look of terror burned across his face. His eyes seemed like red pools, and the hair making up his mane burst into flames. The maneth roared as his catlike face began to melt and become grotesquely deformed. Then, with another flash of light he doubled over but still not able to release the weapon as its handle had grown around his hands and become flesh-like. Blood began seeping from where his mouth used to be until a final flash occurred and a black apparition of a dragon appeared around him. The dragon was transparent but there was no mistaking its presence or identity.

The two holes depicting Maldor's eyes showed an immense horror-like absence which none of the companions had ever witnessed the likes of before, even in their worst nightmares. His arms shook violently trying to free his hands of the hammer that had become woven into his flesh. A loud tearing was heard as one of his hands broke free only to see the other one become more entwined with his own fingers he had left from his now freed arm. A cry sounded as the maneth's blue blood poured onto the cavern floor to the laughter of the dragon ghost.

Schram could feel the life fading from his friend as he rose his ring and began chanting. His spell was halted when the dragon roared and transparent fire blew across the group still huddled on the corridor floor as he, Maldor, the hammer, and all signs of their previous presence disappeared.

The dragon breath had only been a vision, but its heat could still be felt. "Maldor!!!" cried Krirtie running to where the maneth had moments earlier stood. "Schram, what happened to him?" Krirtie screamed with tears beginning to flow.

In a soft voice, he replied, "It was a trap."

Krirtie tried to regain some composure but her success was only limited. "A trap? But why would he want Maldor."

Schram sat back as the pain he had just felt watching his friend's face began to rip at his mind. Softly he chanted a few words to clear his head, then continued. "He didn't want Maldor. He wanted the hammer, for it is the fourth weapon of the Ring."

The others thought about the weapons they held at their sides before Krirtie said, "why didn't he just take it then?"

"He couldn't. Nothing evil could touch it unless it is freely given to them. Maldor was free to take it and use it because his heart was true. I was too slow to realize that Slayne had placed a magical trap across the porthole of the hammer's shelf. That is why it hummed and gave light, because of the presence of magic, evil magic, around it. However, I did not realize the warning in time."

His head fell as all knew the pain he was feeling in blaming himself. Krirtie was lost and beside herself trying to make sense out of the hell she was experiencing. "Where is he now? We have to go and help him for he will die without us."

Schram looked up. "No, he would be dead already if Slayne had not underestimated the power of the hammer. The spell was designed to bring Maldor's death and in the moment of his last breath, fool him that he was giving the hammer to one of us when really it would have been Slayne who was the recipient. However, the hammer's enchantment forced it to protect itself from the evil which meant becoming a part of Maldor." There was a long pause while Schram fought to hold his composure. The loss of their companion was simply another direct hardship against the group and to show weakness now when they needed the confidence of a strong leader would greatly set back their plans, which could not afford to be set back further. He resisted the stress making his voice carry a note of positivity. "Maldor is not dead, the hammer would not allow it. However, nothing like this has ever taken place before in all of history, and his state of being is now in the hands of magic of the past. I do not know what the outcome could hold."

Krirtie fell to her knees and buried her head in her arms. Her body shook as the tears within her flowed from her eyes. Stepha moved over and placed her arms around Schram and her head on his chest. Fehr slumped over next to Jermys who sat silently, and the rat put his head into the dwarf's crossed legs and all simply took a moment.

They sat motionless for a length of time which was out of their hands to determine. "I am sorry for your loss Schram, and to your friends as well."

Schram threw Stepha aside and spun to face who had spoken and was joined at his side by the stern body of Jermys who stood with axe in hand. "Stoven, where?" Schram's words fell off as the canok stepped forward through the large wooden door that now swung freely open.

"Easy Schram," he replied, "do not be alarmed. We felt the evil presence and moved to discover it. However, it is not safe here. Our brethren also felt it and will be here shortly. We will not fight them and I fear you may not be strong enough to defend against all of them, though I was quite taken with your ability in the canyon. If you value your lives, come quickly."

The others had risen and stood beside Schram and the dwarf, and although he did not know if they all had been made to understand, when Schram moved to follow, he was not surprised when they fell in behind. Through the doorway and down a short hall they found themselves opening up into the town of Icly. Desolate and disturbed as it was, each companion felt an improvement over the tomblike caves of before. They followed the pack of white canoks through a series of streets and alleys to a small house made out of a cave in the canyon side. Once they were all inside and a motion of safety had been signaled, Stoven said verbally so everyone could hear in each of their preferred languages simultaneously, "Welcome to Icly."

CHAPTER 24

The Nightstalker

"What are you saying?" exclaimed Schram as he bit into a large piece of meat that the canoks had prepared. "You saved us three hours ago only to kill us now?"

Stoven looked disturbed. "No, I said Kirven sent us to stop you any way we could. If that meant killing you, so be it."

Schram interrupted again. "So as long as we don't proceed, then we will live."

The white coat of the lead canok began to stand on end as the anger of another interruption rose within him. "Hold your tongue boy," he stated sternly, "or I shall turn it into a rock, though I fear to do so could bring repercussions upon myself that I am not prepared for. I said, Kirven sent us, and as you can see we are here, but it is not Kirven's order which brought us here. I have known Kirven for over 230 years, from the day he was born at the hand of an evil rape by the dragon known as Slayne. We," he indicated his seven white reign companions that they had seen in the clearing in the forest, "believed that day that sometime this evil act would turn full circle, and now it seems that the process is at hand. I became one of Kirven's closest friends the day our race was divided, but I had reasons then that were less than honorable."

"You were watching him," chattered Fehr's voice proudly.

There was a flash of light and a giant hairy-legged spider appeared over the rat and immediately began forming a thick web and cocoon around his flailing body. A small scream erupted before the spider and cocoon both vanished as quickly as they had appeared. Stoven said, "I trust you will not interrupt again," to the upside-down body of the panting rodent. He turned back to the group at the table, "I was watching him, for I did not understand what had happened, but

I felt he was at the heart of it. However, in the years that followed, I learned to love him, as did everyone. He was the strongest, proudest canok in all of Troyf, and I became certain he did not have an evil bone in his body. Then, when he brought that sandy-haired boy into our camp against everyone's better judgment, we learned to love and trust him as well. I grew to know the boy well. Strange things I felt in him, but all were still focused with good. Now that I look upon the man, I still sense those strange feelings, and though they remain impossible to understand or know completely, they remain honorable." The canok walked over in front of Schram and added, "So tell me, Schram, why do the two we trusted and loved as no others, now desire each others death?"

Schram stopped eating and peered into his old friend's eyes. His voice carried a new depth as the loss of Maldor had brought a cold reality to their plight. Confidently he said, "Stoven, you were the first canok besides Kirven that I called my friend. I could no more wish Kirven's death than I could yours or my own. However, if our paths cross, and he stands against me, I will do everything within my power and possibly try things which are not, to destroy everything for which he now stands." Schram rose from the table and spoke to the entire pack. "Kirven told me once that the main body of canoks did not know about what happened two hundred years ago. He said that the ones split to black wanted only to have more and total power, and that the whites, like yourselves, sought only to control the blacks evil and find a cure for the infection thrust upon you." The whites nodded that, although it was oversimplified, it was an accurate definition of their desires. "I am not going to describe what I know, for I don't believe that it is anything that should ever be spoken again. All I will say is Kirven has never in his life acted without honor and nor have I. However, if you follow his lead, your race will forever be condemned to the fate it now faces. I cannot fight all of your combined powers, but believe me now, if you hold me, I will try. I ask a lot. I ask that you trust the man, and elf, that the sandy-haired boy became."

Stoven stood quiet and tilted his head to his companions. It became apparent to Schram that although he heard nothing, they were discussing the matter. The canok's eyes returned to the human and he said, "Kirven warned us to prevent your entrance into the South Sea. Is that your true destination?" Schram nodded. "Could you tell us what it is you seek to find there?"

Schram thought a long moment. "No I cannot."

Stepha and Krirtie both looked surprised at this but did not speak. Jermys remained stoic with one hand resting on his Hatchet and both eyes on the door, the only exit he could see.

Stoven frowned. "Then indeed you do ask a lot, Schram."

I know, he replied telepathically catching the canok by surprise.

"So you can speak without verbal words. I thought I was letting my imagination roam last night. Let me discuss the situation with my companions, while you show yours to the back to rest. We will contact you with our decision."

Schram was unsure of his next action. If he did go to rest, they would be easily trapped and could be held indefinitely. If he declined, Stoven may understand, but the others would grow suspicious. He was sure that Stoven would help him, but it was the others that caused the problem. With a motion to his friends, Schram took the largest gamble of his life. He was betting the future of Troyf on the actions of one canok, and if he was wrong, the world would never be the same again. He gave a nod to Stoven and then led the rest of his friends into the back.

Once they had sat and began letting their large dinners settle, Krirtie said, "Schram, why didn't you tell them why we go to the Sea?"

He looked up from where he sat and saw that the question was actually from all of them, except Fehr who had been lost in himself ever since the ordeal with the spider. Schram replied, "I trust Stoven with my life, but I don't know about the others. If it comes down to it, I will tell them before fighting, but for now, I want to let Stoven do the talking. I sensed many things about the group from distrust to worry, but the one universal thing I felt was the trust they held for Stoven. If anyone can convince them of the necessity of our journey, it will be him, if he trusts me enough that is. He was honest when he said I ask a lot."

They all looked around anxiously and Stepha rose and moved beside Schram. "So now do we just wait?"

"Aye, we have no other choice." He paused then added, "if you can sleep, do so. It might very well be a while."

There was a long silence as they gradually began to make themselves more comfortable. Krirtie stated, "Schram, if they do not allow us to leave, we must fight our way out. Our success could control Maldor's fate. We must help him." She closed her eyes and tossed about as she fought to find sleep only to dream of the maneth she had grown to love.

Schram fell back with Stepha in his arms, though he knew he would not sleep tonight. "Our success controls Troyf's fate, Krirtie," he said softly losing his words to the air. The elf gripped him tightly, and as the old smoke from Jermys' pipe made small clouds on the rock ceiling, the room fell into silence. Schram lay awake until just before dawn when the repetitive snores from his dwarven friend finally lulled him to sleep.

It was less than two hours later when the creak of the door swinging open caused all the companions to jump. "Come on, we must hurry. Blacks have been warned to your presence, and it appears that Kirven or some other power has instructed them to hold you as well."

The tired expressions on their faces instantly vanished and within moments the group was making its way out the door. Schram, by Stoven's side said, "then you convinced the others to help us?"

"Not exactly," he responded as he led them through a secret door that exited where the stove had been the night before. After they were through, Schram heard the door close and the stove be slid back across the floor. They were in another tunnel much like the one from the previous day but this one held the bite of salt water in the air. Schram had several questions but at the pace they were running, he could not even ask them telepathically. He assumed they could wait for a less stressed time.

They ran for over an hour, and as the dwarf began to fall behind, Stoven motioned to stop. "We must wait a moment to be sure it is clear, but be ready."

The travelers looked at each other's tired faces and heavily breathing bodies and each realized that a short rest would be a welcomed guest. The smell of the salt air had grown extremely strong now and Schram's combined senses made him believe that the South Sea was now very near. Stoven had been silent since they had halted, simply sitting concentrating on a spot on the cave wall. Schram knew he was deep in discussion with whoever was helping him, and if they were to escape, it would be by his actions. During this pause, his thoughts went back to what the canok had said. What did *not exactly* mean? If he had not gotten the aid from his friends, then who helped them now, and what would happen to him when the other whites discovered they were gone?

Schram's mind was wiped clean when Stoven leaped forward at the spot he had been staring on the wall passing through it like it was air. *Run! Go down this corridor to the end. My plans have failed, but a friend will meet you at the end. Hurry!*

Stoven's words were spoken telepathically but it was obvious that all of the companions had heard since there was no delay as they all sprinted blindly down the tunnel. Intense fighting could be heard from outside the corridor where Stoven had jumped, but it was not the clashing of metal or the explosions of magic. It was the sounds of two animals violently tearing at each other's flesh with their teeth. It was a clash of canoks, a display which possibly never had taken place before.

It was a short run to the end of the corridor, and as the group arrived they could hear commotion brewing outside. They stopped at the mouth and peered out into the city. Parties of goblins and dark dwarves could be seen scattered randomly across the streets but no apparent friend seemed to be present. Schram assumed more trouble had occurred and it would now fall on them to escape. They no longer could depend on help from others, as it appeared this entire city was corrupt. He was about to motion for the group to follow him when he saw what approached.

"Schram, I presume," said the black canok's raspy voice.

They all froze not knowing what to do. He raised his hand to put up a protective barrier when he noticed something too familiar in the canok's tone. He dropped his hand and said, "friend?"

"Aye, you are truly a well sighted...human?" The canok replied. "Come with me, there is a ship and crew at the ready."

"Who are you?" he asked as they all fell in behind the fast pace of the canok.

"I am Werner, that is all you need to know."

They ran down several twisting streets in the shadows and avoiding all confrontations as their group definitely stuck out among the dark creatures of Icly. When they finally stopped, the canok continued with directions. "Now follow this road to the end and you will come to the ship. It is not much, but the captain has been instructed to follow your command in return for forgetting about certain payments he owes. However, it should be noted that I would make certain that he is well paid from your end as well, and keep a sharp eye on these two." He motioned to the two women. "They would be worth something to the type around here. And hurry, I will remain here and make sure you are not followed, but for the most part, you are now on your own. Finally, never forget what Stoven did for you. He paid a high price for trust, make sure it's worth it." With that he darted into a nearby building.

The companions made no delay as they hurried down the road. It took them slightly south of the city to an area best left forgotten. What houses and buildings there were looked more to be broken down shacks and taverns probably all used to some extent as brothels or the equal. The few they saw on the streets consisted mostly of drunken dark dwarves, goblins, and a few well-traveled humans who appeared to be closer relatives to trolls than humans.

The street turned more into an alley and as the beat-up buildings cast their shadows across it, an eerie feeling began to seduce the group. Schram glanced back and saw that a few goblins had taken notice to them and begun to follow. However, he assumed it was probably due to those he traveled with rather than from any order from a dragon highlord. The desolate place may be filled with a variety of desperate souls, but none would be so desperate as to ally with dragons, unless the price was right, and Schram did not think Slayne would go too far out of his way for these sad recruits. Yet, as more goblins and dwarves joined the small party in their wake, Schram became worried that the alleged boat waiting their arrival had already departed, if it was really ever there in the first place. Then, the alley bent around leaving all the buildings in the shadows behind, and daylight again opened upon the group allowing them to peer across the vast water of the South Sea.

The air was not as clean and fresh as the salt water air Schram was used to in Toopek. Instead, it was filled with a rotten haze of sludge and long-dead fish. The marina Schram had been expecting to see was not more than a single, makeshift dock that was obviously temporary as it sat on large wheels with only frayed ropes holding it in place. Tied to the brittle panels of wood making up the docks floor was a large wooden tub, decked out in several places with big splotches of putty to fill all the holes in its body. Carried on its frame it lifted four sails, all of which were torn and ragged and displayed their deficiencies proudly. Schram knew immediately that this was no normal dock, and it was probably used only for the most important or dangerous smuggling, the kind which wanted to keep an extremely low profile. He only stared at the ship a moment until he heard the growls and grunts of those gaining quickly from behind. Schram glanced back at the increasing numbers and gave an immediate signal to his party and they headed toward the rickety craft at a full sprint.

They all wore expressions of great concern on their faces, but none as grand as that which showed in Jermys' eyes. Their feet pressed deep into the black sand which held a texture more like swamp mud than sand.

They arrived at the wooden plank leading out to the dock and as Schram began to step forward, Jermys stated, "I am not going on that thing. She's a wreck and a half. That decrepit tub couldn't float across a pool, much less the violent waves of the sea."

Schram looked agitated knowing they had little time for this type of discussion. "Jermys, by all the gods, it is our only chance!"

The dwarf stomped his feet stubbornly. "I am not going! That's my final word. I'd as soon stay and fight to the death here than be sentenced to my last breath being that of water."

Schram sighed as he saw the group behind now reaching the far edge of the beach. Fehr poked his head out laughing. "Jermys is afraid of the water." His taunting laughs bit the dwarf's ears.

"Why you foul rodent," answered the dwarf raising his axe locking his eyes on the rat's face.

"You my cargo?" asked a deep voice from behind.

Schram whirled on the plank to stand eye to eye with one of the most disgusting humans he had ever seen. His face was gnarled and scarred, and the patch that Schram figured normally covered his one absent eye, hung limply down due to its broken band. His hair was long and ragged and although he was completely clothed, his garments did little to hide his sloppy rolls of fat that hung in sheets over his belt. However, all of this was tolerable, though it did take Schram by surprise and he was sure it showed in his face. The one thing which nearly brought the human magician to his knees was the rank, deadening, stench which emanated like a green fog from the man standing before him.

Schram's nose twitched and screamed for mercy as he replied in a choking voice, "yes, we must depart in a hurry."

The captain looked over the group, becoming increasingly pleased when eyeing the women and not taking notice to Jermys who stood hidden behind the human arguing with Fehr. "It will be one-hundred. No bargaining!"

Schram removed a bag from his armor. "Here is two-hundred sovereigns. There will be an additional five-hundred when we *all* reach our destination unharmed, if you follow my meaning?" Schram motioned toward the women as he spoke.

The captain laughed and replied, "I do boy, but don't think I won't slit your throat if you double cross me. I don't care how much you pay." He hollered at the goblin and dark dwarves which approached from behind and the motley crew seemed upset but obeyed his word and departed. The captain turned back to his new passengers. "I am Captain Maximus Pete. Call me Pete or Captain Pete. If I hear otherwise, you will never be able to use your tongue again." He paused, then motioned to the group. "Come on, let's…" he froze in mid-sentence as he now saw the dwarf who was still busy arguing and hadn't taken notice of whom was going to be in charge of their sea voyage. "You!" Pete yelled pulling his dagger and raising it towards Jermys. "I killed you already." He paused again. "I'll kill you again you possessed bastard."

Jermys swung his head up startled by the voice being projected at him. His preliminary reaction was one of fright and disgust, but as he drew his axe as quickly and smoothly as always, his confidence returned. "What do you mean sea scum? I have never met you before but will kill you now just the same. This would only do a favor to Troyf to have your presence on it ended."

All were surprised at the dwarf's reaction and statement, but the way his mind was working regarding his fear of the water, it shouldn't have been so unexpected. However, Pete did not show the same surprise as the others almost as if he knew how Jermys would respond. His eyes became infuriated and if Schram had not immediately pulled his dagger and placed it at the Captain's throat, he would have charged at the dwarf madly.

Still with the knife at his throat, Schram said, "This is one of your passengers. You will take him without question and without any harmful action to come."

The captain frowned. "He will not be ridin on me ship unless he swings by his neck from the mast."

The other companions had drawn their weapons as well as they saw many faces of the crew beginning to appear on the deck. Schram looked at them as well and made it plain that he would not hesitate to kill their captain if any should attack. Then, he asked, "what did you mean, you killed him already?"

Pete's eyes were filled with hatred and fear as he began to answer the question. "That bastard nearly caused me to lose me ship. Sent me into the black pool where the stormy sea sought to swallow me boat like a wad of tobac. Only when I cast him overboard and made a quick retreat did we save ourselves. Now he lives again. He's had a deal with Sakton, and he not be setting foot on *The Nightstalker* again."

The dwarf looked up. "Bretten, you killed my bother!" Without another word Jermys let his hatchet fly.

All that could be heard was the whistling drawing in of breath as the big captain saw the rotating blade winding through the air at him. A slap was heard as Schram snagged the handle out of its flight stopping it inches from Pete's white face. However, the captain still cried out in pain as Schram looked down to see an arrow protruding from his leg.

"Goblin attack!" Shouted a voice from the deck.

Schram spun in time to see Stepha's arrow drop the front goblin yet nearly one hundred followed. The painful voice of the captain yelled, "pull anchor and cast off!"

Schram threw the man over his shoulder grunting under the weight. "Stepha, Krirtie, get on board. Jermys, you can stay and fight or come with us now, your choice." He threw the Hatchet back to the dwarf who caught it while still remaining behind his shield. Schram carried the captain up the dock and with one large heave, hucked him over the side of the ship. Schram's eyes lowered, as he knew he could not leave the dwarf behind but they would all be killed if they remained.

The ship rocked sideways as the huge anchor was lifted and with a slow crawling lunge, it began to move from the dock. Jermys swung his head around and watched it start to leave before he felt the brunt of the goblin attack as it began to collapse upon him.

"Wait for me!" he hollered as he turned and busted his short legs like windmills down the dock.

"Stepha, keep those goblins back," shouted Schram as he grabbed a loose rope from the deck and heaved it back at the dock. "Grab the end Jermys and we'll pull you up."

"Schram, I can fly to get him," entered the elf preparing her wings for flight.

"No," he replied sternly. "Jermys chose this situation and I'll not have you be such an easy target when this way will work."

Jermys reached the rope just as it was pulled tight causing the dwarf to be launched into the sea and dragged behind the exiting ship. Schram's muscles exploded beneath his armor, and he fought to pull the rope back. Krirtie had immediately taken to removing Pete's arrow and Stepha was busy returning bow fire so Schram was left on his own. Although Jermys only weighed shy of one hundred pounds, the water seemed to grip his small body like a fist making Schram's efforts near useless.

Just as they were getting clear of the reach of the goblin arrows, one went unseen and struck Schram in the chest plate. His armor threw the arrow harmlessly aside but the force jolted the warrior to his back causing the rope to slide through his fingers. He reached to secure it, but could only grab it with one hand, and he knew this grip would not be firm enough to hold for long. He was pulled to the railing with one hand holding as tight as possible to the rope while the other fought to reach the railing. With the grip of the sea becoming increasingly stronger, the realization came to him that he was about to lose his friend.

Right as his bloodied fingers lost their feel, the rope lost tension and was gone. Schram lifted his sweat covered eyes to see the large arms of the captain firmly wrapping the rope inward. Schram quickly recovered and together they easily hauled the coughing, water-logged body of the dwarf aboard.

The panting captain sat down and stared at the two. "You saved me life human. The dwarf can come, but know you this. One suspicious action from the dwarf or the gods, and he'll be sooner in the water with my dagger than anywhere aboard. Pray not one drop of rain falls this trip."

Schram nodded and motioned to Pete's leg where the arrow had struck. "Are you well?"

His voice grumbled. "Bloody well pissed off I'd say. Bah, one lucky goblin isn't enough but to put a sour taste in me stomach. Clean your crew up below. I'll fetch yeh when we reach," his voice trailed off. "Where is it you be heading?"

Schram stared hard back towards him wondering how he would react to his answer. "The Black Pool."

After a long pause a deep, bellowing laugh echoed back. "Perhaps you not be the land lover I take you for. The Black Pool, you almost had Pete fooled. Now, the crew must be told. Where is it we head?"

There was no humor in his voice when Schram replied, "set course for the heart of the South Sea, the Black Pool. If you do not wish to enter, then we will take your raft in alone. That is our passage." Schram scooped up the unconscious body of the dwarf and motioned to the two girls to follow leaving the reddened face of the captain staring at their backs. Schram knew they would have very little chance of success in the rough waters of the Black Pool in the raft, but he knew they would have no chance if they were cast overboard now, so the choice had been clear.

It was early the next day when Jermys woke for the first time on the ship coughing up a pint or two of sea water in the process. His face had turned a bright green and although he was put in charge of seeing to Krirtie's and Stepha's safety, it was apparent to the girls that if trouble arose, they would be on their own. The only sounds the dwarf made were garbled complaints about every part of his body, but every comment ended with the placement of one or both of his hands across his stomach.

Schram had spent the past day at Pete's side helping prepare the boat for the rougher seas and trying to prove a worthy passenger to gain the captain's respect. Most of the work they performed, Schram could have completed in minutes with his magic, but knowing sailors various superstitions, he could only see trouble arising from that action. Besides, the harder he proved he could work, the better he seemed to be treated by Pete and his crew. He knew that throwing gold around was one thing, but earning a pirate's respect would get him much farther.

The two stood at the helm while Pete spun tales of his various great deeds and conquests. Schram learned that he had been a pirate all his life, and although he now sailed the South Sea, when he was young, he was captain of *The Skelton*, the best pirate ship of all time. He would smuggle everything from furs to people through the North Sea between Drynak and the Far East.

"What happened?" Schram asked, becoming intrigued with the story as it reminded him of his home.

"That bastard King Starland of Toopek. Sent out a fleet to hunt me down, he did. Took me ship and tried to have me hung." Pete smiled his crooked smile. "But I have too many of the right friends to be hung by a mere king." He laughed deeply. "Rumor has it, Starland be dancing his foul dance with Sakton himself now. Heard a dragon done him up right. Wished I'd been watching. Give me some satisfaction watching a man die who be trying to kill me." Again he bellowed a deep laugh.

Schram saved face by trying to join in the captain's good cheer, but all his thoughts went to his father and that he was happy he had not told Pete his full name. "How far is the pool?" he asked after a time.

Pete frowned. "A day. We will reach its outskirts by late afternoon tomorrow." He paused then added, "Why be so interested in the pool? There be nothing there for you. You are good here. You've helped me men with the ship's repairs and you get long with them. Me ship lost many men lately. Good men. I be needin' some new hands. We could let your party go at shore. The Black Pool is a death mission. I don't make this offer to many, so use your head when you think 'bout it."

"What is in it for me to stay with you?"

The captain laughed again. "Yes, you are one of us." However, he could see the determination in Schram's eyes and realized this discussion was ending. "Very well, I'll take you to the pool. After all, you paid twice your way." He paused, then added, "about the 500 sovereigns?"

"If you wait for our return, you will have your money."

"I be waiting a lifetime for your return and not get it. If you have such resources that you are bargaining from, then a new ship would not be out of the question."

Schram heard a crewman yell that mess was about so he returned to his friends to check on the dwarf's condition and bring them some of the food from the galley. Before disappearing below deck, he glanced back to the Captain. "You wait outside the pool, and you'll have your ship."

The food, like the night before, looked as if it had been prepared across Pete's hairy back as the little that was actually cooked had so many unidentifiable substances mixed within it that all the companions were more satisfied with the stale bread they had left in their own packs. After the dinner, Schram explained what he had learned about their upcoming destination and expected time of arrival. Jermys had been sitting up for about an hour and some of the color had returned to his face though the talk of entering a small raft on rougher waters seemed to return him to his previous state.

Later that night, as Krirtie, Fehr, and Stepha all slept, Schram went to Jermys' bunk where he lay awake. "How are you doing, old friend?"

"I am all right Schram. Tomorrow I will be able to avenge my brother's death without your interference."

He frowned. "I felt those were the thoughts that kept you awake this night. That is why I am here now."

Jermys sat up with an intrigued expression on his face. "What is it magician? What have you learned?"

"I have learned that although Pete is a pirate, he is honorable to his debts. He will take us to the Black Pool because he said that he would, though it goes against everything as a captain he believes to be sound. I also think he will wait for our return, nearly indefinitely if that is how long it takes."

"That is all very well," replied the dwarf solemnly, "but that does not change the fact that he admitted to killing my brother."

Schram grew sad. "There is more that I must tell you." He rose and paced shortly before returning with the correct words to continue. "I have not mentioned this to the others, for I wanted you to be the first to hear it. According to everyone I have talked to, and let me say that all their stories match to the letter, your brother was not alone on this voyage. With him were about twenty goblins which held the crew at sword tip by your brother's orders and forced the ship into the rough waters of the pool. It was your brother who drove his message across by slitting the first mate's throat. Pete only seized the opportunity of the rough water to gain an advantage over the party and in the process, cast your brother and his goblin cohorts into the sea."

Jermys now appeared beyond anger. "I do not believe the lies of one who seeks only to save his own life. He killed Bretten, and for that he shall pay. Tomorrow I will go on deck and declare that in my brother's name, Captain Pete must die." He turned his eyes which burnt like glowing coal onto his friend. "If you should stand against me, I will have to take arms against you as well."

Schram rose shaking his head. "I will not allow you to jeopardize our mission out of vengeance. However, I understand your feelings and will not stand against you. I ask only that you reconsider until the facts are known."

"I must act in my brother's honor."

As he walked out of the room shared by the dwarf, Stepha, and Krirtie, Schram stopped and turned back to the dwarf. "What if Bretten lives?"

The next morning brought the normal hustle about the ship that always accompanied a new day. Schram went up and joined the captain who had been at the helm since before dawn. The two chatted calmly until a voice sounded from behind. "Captain Pete."

Pete peered his head around grimacing as his one eye caught sight of the dwarf. "Ah, the fish has come up from the deep."

A spray of laughter and jeers followed from the nearby crew who were within earshot of Pete's term for someone better left on dry land. Jermys ignored the comment and in a deep voice even for a dwarf stated, "I will refrain from any further attacks until I can determine the fate of my brother. But rest assured, if I find you to be the agent of his death, I will not let you live."

All grew silent and Schram became worried that Pete's reaction might be one of malice resulting in only further squabbles. Now that they were within half a day of the pool, Schram wanted nothing to stand in their way. He was about to speak when Pete sternly cut him off. "A decision of honor, dwarf. I be right here should you determine me to be false, but you be certain of your findings before you come back."

The rest of the day went smoothly, in fact, Pete became uneasy as the waters and winds seemed to be pulling the creaking vessel towards the pool with never before seen speed. The waves were dividing lightly before them and regardless of their direction, the winds were always at their backs. Schram could tell that the captain would be much happier when his passengers were off his ship and he could anchor with an ale in some friendly, or at least familiar, port.

A sound from the mate in the crow's nest alerted the magician though he had not understood what had been said. Pete jolted to the railing and peered back to the sky and water in their wake. "Well I'll be a... What in all of hell be that?" he hollered back to the crewman.

"Dun know, Cap'n. Looks to be bout six of 'em though," shouted the reply, this time clear enough to all.

Schram joined the captain's side to peer at the set of black dots spotting the horizon. "What do you make of those?" Pete asked.

Schram squinted his elven eyes and then turned ghostly white as he realized what approached. "Dragons!"

CHAPTER 25

The Attack

The deck seemed alive with activity as the crew took to oars and prepared new sails to gain any speck of speed so far as yet unfound. The rickety ship cut through the waves much better than any of the passengers would have first thought, but each also knew that it would never be enough. Still, the men on board fought like it was to be their final breath to blow.

"Can you git any more out a her, men?" shouted Captain Pete.

"The hulls 'bout to split as it is Cap'n," returned a voice from the deck.

"Where away?" he hollered towards the crow's nest.

"Still closing Pete. Them bastards will be on us in under an hour."

"Blast it!" exclaimed Pete. "Sakton be wanting my ass bad!" He turned to Schram, "or might it be you, mate?"

"If you are suggesting hucking me over to greet Sakton, I assure you he would spit me back. I think he would welcome either you or me, and not care about which."

Pete laughed. "Yes, I suppose he would at that. I don't know where you be from Schram, but there be a pirate hidden beneath that half human-half elf exterior, I be sure of it."

Schram nodded but kept to the problem at hand. "How long till we reach the Black Pool?"

"Damn it all man," Pete shouted back. "We be cooked long before then. Don't you realize, them there dragons are not here for a friendly visit, and we can't fight 'em, not for long any how."

"How long?" he repeated, now becoming agitated.

The captain fell back surprised by the strength behind his passenger's words. He looked over the water and then to the sun and then replied, "probably less than an hour, but I can't be sure with the way the pool moves. One minute it be near, the next, not."

Schram smiled though it was obvious there was no humor in his mind. "Whatever happens, keep this bucket of rotted boards on course. I will hold the dragons until we can get there."

"Just a minute boy, havin thoughts 'bout me is one thing, but takin' words 'bout me ship is quite another."

Schram turned back and even smiled a bit under his breath though he knew that Pete was deadly serious. "No harm intended, this ship has amazed me more than I would have ever guessed. I am just comparing it in my mind to the new ship you will have if we succeed."

That seemed to pacify Pete for a moment but it wasn't long before the next question bit the air. "Just what you be doin' to stop the dragons. We should make wind towards Valis. Its port will give us some protection, if we can make it that is."

"No," Schram stated, stepping towards the captain now. "You have been paid to take us to the Black Pool, and you will."

Pete pulled his dagger and placed it to Schram's throat. "Maybe I kill you now, then go to port?"

His eyes locked on Pete's stare. "I wouldn't."

"Blast it!" he said releasing his hold on the human. "What is at that pool that is worth so much to you? Dayton, hold course to the pool. The rest of you, take arms. We'll fight those flying bastards and send 'em back to hell."

The men looked around at each other and then let out a powerful yell in unison. Schram shook his head. "You made a wise choice."

"I had better get that ship."

A scream was heard as a crewman was lifted in the blue dragon's talons squeezing his body so tight as to separate it in two. Krirtie ducked behind her shield as the fire breath from one of the red dragons ignited the air around her into a violent rage of flame. Schram had, unbeknownst to everyone else, enchanted the ship making in completely impervious to fire, at least for a short time. The flames from the dragons harmlessly struck the ship's wooden frame and were instantly smothered. None of the crew understood why, but they were quick to avoid arguing and accept their gift from the gods.

Altogether there were six dragons, three red and three blue. Schram had wanted to keep his magical powers hidden, so he was refraining from using them for as long as he could. He was relieved to see that these dragons were very young and had not mastered magic on their own despite some use of energy bolts and defensive shields. Their main attack was with flight and fire, but now they had to rely on their strength, as it became apparent that the ship was not going to simply burn into the sea. After witnessing the success of the first attack, the other dragons began to fly in close to attempt to grab those on board and toss them dead into the choppy waters.

A blue came at Krirtie while she was still avoiding the fire breath from the first. It swooped down at water level trying to suddenly appear over the deck and grab those it could. It landed on the ship's rail causing the entire vessel to rock violently forward. This in itself saved the woman as Krirtie lost her balance and went tumbling out of the dragon's reach. The blue seemed surprised by the shifting of the ship and took a moment to gain its own secure footing.

That was the only opening Jermys needed. The small dwarf leaped at the creature that stood over thirty times his size. He wrapped his arms around the beast's neck much to the displeasure of the dragon. It reared its body back trying to shake the dwarf's hold but only succeeded in further rocking the boat. Jermys grabbed his hatchet and drove it deep into the dragon's long throat. The blue roared as its blue blood seeped from the wound spilling like waves across the beaten deck. The dragon panicked and started flapping its wings wildly lifting its huge body off the ship and causing the dwarf to lose his grip sending him tumbling downward. He landed with a thud but his momentum and the ship's unsteadiness carried him towards the railing. Krirtie had gained a stationary position and used it to grab the dwarf just before he tumbled to a watery grave.

Jermys quickly rose with the hope of finishing off his prey, but instead watched as its body crashed hard into the water bearing several of Stepha's arrows. A cheer rang out from the crew as they watched the dragon fall dead into the water and the others fly higher to a safe retreat.

"We've won! They flee!" shouted a voice from the deck, but Schram and the other companions knew better.

Krirtie and Jermys ran towards Stepha who stood near the center of the deck. Schram remained next to Pete who had taken the helm as his crewman had moved to the killed man's position. "Ahoy ahead, the Black Pool," hollered a voice from a crewman hanging high on one of the nets running down the mast.

"Where away?" answered Pete, as both he and Schram pierced their eyes down to the water and off of the dragons.

"Dead ahead, Cap'n," the crewman replied.

Schram stared across their path and then his eyes hit the oblique, gray cloud over distant water. "There it is! Pete, ahead quickly."

"She be movin' as fast as she can, elf. Perhaps you would like to get out and push her a bit?"

"The dragons, they're coming back."

Schram was not certain who had spotted the flying beasts movements, but he did clearly recognize Jeremy's next statement. "They mean to ram us."

The group looked up to see the five remaining dragons flying at a fierce speed directly for the hull of the ship. Fire shot from the lead dragon's mouth with incredible power and accuracy. The flames drove a narrow beam nearly five hundred feet to strike the crewman in the crow's nest and send his flailing and flaming body plummeting to the water. His cries were heard in the ship's wake before they struck a watery silence.

They had reached the outskirts of the Black Pool as the rough waves of the water began to toss the beaten craft about without care. Pete turned the wheel beginning to bring the ship about. "No!" cried Schram who had moved to aid his friends against the assault. "Enter the storm, it is our only chance. The dragons would be torn apart by the winds if they dared follow after us."

Pete grimaced. "Forget it boy. I'd face them beasts any day before matching wits with that damn storm of wind and sea. It nearly killed me ship once already."

His delay proved too much and the dragon attack struck a second time. Rolls of flame blanketed the ship sending more crewmen overboard only to be swallowed by the sea. The vessel lunged sideways in the smoke nearly capsizing as one of the dragons flew headlong into its starboard bow. Pete was jolted from the wheel and struck hard against the railing to stop at the feet of the lead red dragon. The beast rocked his head back about to release a deadly strike of fire when Jermys leaped overboard to grab it as he had the other.

The surprise of the attack was only momentary as this beast was still airborne and not landed as the first one. It reared its neck but instead of a panicked shaking, this dragon stretched its wings and soared high into the air carrying the tiny dwarf with it.

The stunned captain recovered and quickly ran back to the wheel to steady the ship's course. "The big red one has the dwarf," he shouted.

Schram turned to see the dragon flying with incredible speed in a completely random path trying to free Jermys from his neck and send the dwarf to his immediate watery death. Jermys seemed to be trying to get hold of his axe but couldn't risk freeing a hand to retrieve it.

Schram shook his head in anger. "Damn it, Pete!" He stated firmly under his breath. "Our only chance is the pool, but not until the dwarf is back with us."

He shouted his command but with all the commotion there was no way to be sure if Pete had heard. He began to move back towards the wheel, when his next statement was cut short. A large blue raced over the ship striking the magician in the back with its talons but not able to grab a firm hold. Krirtie swung her scimitar above her head as it passed and then dove out of the way. She had not even been sure if her sword had made contact until she saw the mass of blue blood spilling into the black water carrying most the dragon's insides with it. Schram looked up from where he had fallen and saw the beast sail blindly into the storm over the sea knowing it had met its death. His helmet had been knocked clear and his long black hair now fell to his sides.

He leaped to his feet and joined Stepha's side where the elf had placed several arrows into a red dragon's side as it sent a barrage of terror driven fire across the ship and its crew. Schram chanted a quick spell that caused a sheet of water to shoot from the sea between the dragon and the ship. As the fierce dragon's breath struck the wall, the molecules of water exploded apart under the immense heat into a cloud of thick fog. Schram and Stepha quickly unloaded repeated bow-fire into the stunned and already injured body of the red and soon it dropped beaten into the waves below.

No cries of joy rang out with this dragon's death. Now, as nearly half the crew was lost and those remaining felt they were not only fighting the dragons but they must also match whatever devil had ignited the sea. The mood on board was one of intense fear, adrenaline, and despair all balled into single individual forces within each of them. Terror shown clearly on all their faces as they saw the largest red still struggling fiercely to throw the dwarf and a single red and blue preparing for a combined attack.

The two dragons roared and arched their wings sailing low along the water in a high speed approach. Krirtie, Schram, and Stepha stood in a line across the deck with the elf woman beginning to send arrows as soon as they flew within the range. However, their approach was jagged and quick this time, each jumping in random directions as they moved taking slightly away from their speed but making it nearly impossible for bow-fire to be accurate. Many arrows made contact, but few struck true.

When they reached the ship, the two dragon's actions became even more obscure. They seemed to forget their fiery attack and primarily focused on a more direct combat centering on the human magician. They reached the boat's edge and then simultaneously lifted their huge bodies upward moving out of reach of Krirtie's outstretched sword. The swinging movement without contact threw the woman off balance and she stumbled slightly towards where the red and blue hovered. Each dragon reached its huge talons out and latched onto the ship's railing. With immeasurable force, they released their entire weight downward rocking the ship so deeply as to bring the deck nearly perpendicular to the water's surface.

Anyone who was not fully secure, struck the railing or simply sailed over it unhindered until they hit the sea.

Schram had hold of a deck pole and could secure Stepha as well, but with Krirtie's failed attack, she could not be reached and tumbled sideways with the ship. However, it was not the railing which she met as she fell, but rather the large red belly of the dragon. She instinctively rose her sword as she fell and with incredible penetrating power plunged it into the beast's belly. The dragon screamed as its red blood seeped over Krirtie's sword hilt, her arms, and into the water. However, with the tilt of the ship, the woman was powerless to push back or remove her sword as the total weight of her body was gravitationally held firm across it.

An echoing roar lit the air as the larger red still fighting Jermys witnessed the turn of events. The large beast seemed to ignore the parasite attached to its back and turned with never before seen speed and agility towards the ship.

"They're mates," cried Stepha seeing the fire in the dragon's eyes as it approached.

Schram's locked on the approaching dragon and knew she was correct. He swung back to the captain who hung swinging from the wheel. "Damn it Pete, get us out of here! The storm might kill us, but it is our only chance!"

The captain's returned grumbles regarding his helplessness was lost in the ear-piercing scream of Krirtie as the blue dragon next to the red released one of its legs from the ship and reached to grab the human woman. The ship began to slowly level with the removal of the dragon's weight but not enough to free Stepha or Schram for a shot. The red with Jermys was still beating a path downward and as the blue gripped the human woman in a death squeeze, roars echoed from all three beasts. Krirtie screamed in pain as she frantically reached for her sword which rested in the panicking red's belly but to no avail as the blue lifted her into the air. The ship crashed down upon the water freeing those who held on for their lives.

Suddenly, Krirtie's shouts were silenced as she was released and plummeted downward onto the deck. Schram looked back to the blue in time to see Fehr removing and replacing the small dirk he carried into what would be the dragon's wrist of its talon. Only a small amount of blue blood squirted from the wound, but it proved effective as the dragon had lost all motor ability in its leg through the accurate and obviously painful placement. One quick jolt sent Fehr sailing behind Krirtie to fall across the ship stopping at Schram's feet. The warrior snagged the unconscious rat and quickly stuffed him below his armor then joined Stepha in the blue's assault.

Krirtie leaped to her feet and in one motion removed her sword from the belly of the red which seemed to be frozen not knowing what if anything it could do to save its own life. With one sweeping swing she severed the talons of the beast as they remained bit into the railing, and its body fell spilling red blood into the water.

A wave crashed over the vessel and as the last blue struck the water dead, Schram knew they were entering the storm. "No, we must save Jermys," he shouted. However, when he turned to see why they suddenly had changed course into the pool, he quickly realized that the wheel was now unmanned.

He ran to the helm trying to steady the wildly tossing ship as he searched for the absent captain. Stepha and Krirtie joined several crewmen in secure positions but still trying to bring down what was left of the sail. As the ship entered the opaque cloud of the storm over the Black Pool, all sight of Jermys and the lead red dragon vanished.

Schram looked to the base of the post which held the wheel and noticed a large rope tied in an unbreakable knot about it. He followed the rope's path with his eyes and discovered that it disappeared over the side. Immediately, from somewhere deep within his mind, a spell appeared and with a quick recitation, the rope began to glow slightly then faded back to normal. Schram face relaxed and he focused his attention to the wheel and the vicious and violent sea that had them in its grips.

They were tossed carelessly about, having many times what seemed to be more water above them than below. Schram never removed his eyes from the sea ahead, but from the sounds around him, he knew that the main mast had snapped along with probably the majority of every fiber keeping this bucket afloat. The cloud around them became even thicker making his actions on the wheel totally by feel as he only could answer what the waves asked. With undo force, a huge wave struck starboard nearly capsizing the vessel once and for all, but the human turned elf-magician quickly responded turning the ship head on into the onslaught of terror. Schram realized exactly what Pete had meant when he said he would rather face the dragons than this sea again. A fool would enter this place only once. A fool's fool would go back. At least the dragons fought fairly, he thought as another jolt rocked them perpendicular.

Schram several times tried to incant calming spells but something seemed to confuse him just before finishing and the spell would be lost. He realized that this legendary Black Pool and storm were created by magical means and as such, had some sort of enchantment working to protect their existence.

He fought the unrelenting sea for what seemed to be several hours, but in the blackness he had no way of judging time. He repeatedly heard cries from people on board as they lost their footings or that which they had held on to suddenly would break free under the stress, but he could only hope that none ended up sliding free of the ship altogether. His muscles ached and blood showed below the cracked and strained knuckles on his hands. His long, black hair had become soaked with water and blood and the waves continually slammed against his body often nearly knocking him clear of the wheel, but his stubborn grip always held true. Several times he wished he could let go and end this journey through hell letting Sakton give him the kiss of death this suicide mission deserved, but still he held fast knowing it was not his decision to sentence his companions and the others on board to the same fate.

Suddenly, light exploded through the black cloud blinding Schram and everyone remaining on board. The sea became a gentle pond of blue water and the brilliant sun shown downward beating much relished heat upon the deck. Schram wheeled around to see a small amount of movement from those behind him. Stepha and

Krirtie both lifted their heads from where they both sat tightly clasped to the base of the broken mast two feet below where it had snapped. Their wet hair was matted and pressed against their respective faces and their bodies fell back to lie exhausted on the soggy boards. Schram followed the length of the ship and could make out the beginning movements of a half dozen crewmen, then quickly spun as he remembered the rope.

He ran to the railing still panting from his own exhaustion and looked over to see what they had dragged behind them and if it had remained tied. Expecting to see the end of the rope or even in the back of his mind Captain Pete, Schram was quite surprised when he saw nothing but more rope. In fact, when his eyes followed its length and he realized it disappeared into the black cloud behind them, a worry grew across his face and all through his mind.

"Quick, any who can help pull, get here on the double. Someone is tied to us and they are still in the storm." The ship jerked back towards the black cloud as the rope became instantly tensed. "The storm grips them firm and threatens to pull us back."

Two crewmen came groggily over. "Just cut it free elf. Then there is no danger."

"I think it is your captain man!"

"All the more reason to cut it free," the other crewman stated.

Schram glared as his tired arms pulled at the rope. "Damn it, grab the rope or you'll be swimming back out of the storm!"

The second crewman frowned drawing a dagger and placing it to Schram's throat. "Cut the rope or I will, first by passing through you to reach it."

Schram returned with a broad smile, not showing a motion or flinch in his stare. There was only a strange recitation flowing between his lips before the crewman slipped on the deck. A shocked look crossed his face as his flailing arms moved to break his fall causing the full weight of his body to land on the point of his own dagger. Without another question, the other crewman shoved his bloodied comrade aside, joined Schram's side, and the two heaved on the huge rope pulling it slowly backwards.

Stepha pointed to others now slowly making their way back to the deck and they moved to help her drop the huge anchor overboard. Then, when a third man joined their pull, the storm seemed to open its clenched fist allowing the ships cargo to break through the cloud's barrier. With a burst, those pulling landed flat on their backs and the dead body of the large red dragon Krirtie had dropped from the ship's rail entered the calm waters in the center pool. Then, tied to its back holding his old bent sword was the long haired, fat-bodied figure of Captain Pete. He spun in terror as the storm released him showing absolute disbelief in his one good eye.

Schram shook his head. "Well, I'd never have thought it was possible.

"Damn canok won't bloody die," added one of the crewmen.

"Sakton probably wouldn't take him," stated another causing those within earshot to nod in agreement.

It was obvious that a huge amount of relief had been taken from their backs. They all knew in the back of their minds that they were now inside some vicious storm, but they were in calm water and the dragons that were upon them were now absent. To the crewmen, that added up to good news. However, all Schram's thoughts were tied to Jermys, now the second of his party to be taken and possibly killed. He bowed his head and both Stepha and Krirtie knew where his thoughts lie. They moved over to stand beside him when a screech like none they had heard before blew from over the floating dragon and Pete.

The fabulous red dragon carrying Jermys shot wildly through the cloud as if it had been swallowed and then violently rejected. Upon entering the calm air, it quickly gained its bounds but made no motion to attack as the new environment left it bewildered and confused. Jermys glanced up and in one motion plunged his hatchet into the small of the beast's neck and then leaped to the water splashing next to the captain. The dragon roared in pain but it also was apparent that the storm and its flight through it had taken more out of the creature than it was willing to give. It fell to the water with a deep crash not dead, but completely physically and mentally lost. Red blood oozed from the gash in its neck and the near death expression on its face made Schram drop his drawn bow in sadness. He signaled to Stepha to do the same as the gargled coughs of the dwarf could be heard as Pete lifted him from the drink.

The captain stood on the back of the red. "Yo mates, bring us aboard."

Those who remained alive were all five companions, though Fehr was still unconscious, and seven of the crew including the captain. The lead red dragon sat bobbing on the water over the dead body of the other with a calmed and peaceful expression on its face. The ragged group sat on the now dry deck with their bodies stretched randomly about munching on what food they could find in the galley that appeared edible.

Captain Pete sat forward. "Damn, I thought I was drowned for sure. All of a sudden the blasted dragon carcass began floating nice and high on the water. I rode it easier than if I was on me boat." Schram smiled but wondered where in his mind the enchantment for buoyancy had come from. His bewildered look was changed to a question when he asked, "what were you doing out there anyway?"

Pete laughed his deep bellowing chuckle and slapped Jermys, who was still white as a ghost, on his back. "I figured we was dead anyway and when you said the big one," he pointed toward the dragon, "was in cahoots with the dead one, I thought the only way he be following us in was if we brought his mate with us. That blasted dwarf saved me skin only to end up on the beast's back, the least I could do was let him die with us in the storm and not be a simple snack when he lost his grip. I never thought we'd be makin it through to... wherever Sakton has brought us." He struck the dwarf's back again almost knocking his zombie-like body over. "Hell of a ride, wasn't it dwarf?"

Jermys said nothing, showing no signs of consciousness other than his movement taking dry and stale bread rolls to his mouth. Pete smiled, "I know what'll wake 'em." He rose and left to return moments later with a small pouch and a crooked pipe. "His brother left this in his cabin before I...he left the ship." Pete stuffed the tobac and lit the pipe, taking a deep suck himself before placing it between the dwarf's lips. Immediately his face grew relaxed causing the tightened muscles in his cheeks and neck to drop. He arched his head back as if to speak but all his words were carried in his actions as smoke encircled the short fellow's bald crown of his head.

Fehr sat near the dwarf's feet. When the water began to drain from Jermys' spongy beard running across Fehr's nose, the rat began to cough out profanity in three different languages ending up with one that Pete knew well causing his belly to shake so hard with laughter that he lost his balance and rolled over. Then everyone found the humor, either in the words or the sight of the laughing captain, but gaining a lost moment of good cheer nonetheless.

When the laughter subsided, one of the crewmen turned to Schram and said, "you did well to get the ship through. A good captain you would make."

Schram nodded as the others showed their agreement. Pete reached over and slapped him even harder than he had been slapping the dwarf. "I told you that there be some sea blood in you elf."

Schram returned the smile. "If there is sea blood in me, it has much company." He paused and looked towards Stepha before continuing. "As you have referred to me this entire journey, I am elven. However, the two wisest people I have ever known both told me to never forget my heritage, and it is one of which I am proud to hold." He turned back to Pete. "My name is Schram Starland, born Prince of Toopek under my father, King Keith Starland and mother Queen Suzanne."

Pete again laughed deeply. "Well, you be the damndest looking human I ever did see."

"And the ugliest," mumbled Fehr as if he had been part of the conversation all along.

Pete turned to his crew almost unable to speak. "Imagine, the son of the man I hate most, now sitting aboard me ship after saving me life. Indeed Sakton likes to laugh at my ass." Schram let out a small sigh as it became apparent that Pete's hatred of the man responsible for his banishment to the South Sea was all but forgotten in his son's case.

Schram rose, staring at the black storm which encircled them like a wreath. "Captain Pete, if you make it out of this storm and then back to Toopek, I will have your name added to the list of Captains under my father's army and award you with his best ship, if the thought appeals to you?"

Pete looked struck. "You mean I could sail the North again, without fear of being plucked from me sails?"

"If you wish it, yes."

"But working for a king man, within the confines of the law?" he sounded a bit uncertain. "I don't think me body would allow such a thing."

"Then just take the ship and hope that I don't catch you on the sea," Schram returned smiling.

"Aye lad, now that be a plan I can handle." All the men seemed to agree with the preference towards the second plan and were on the verge of a cheer when Pete added, "but might I ask, you said first I had to get out of here. Where pray tell are we and would you not be coming with us when we leave?"

Schram became fixed on a mark near the center of the peaceful pool in which they had anchored. "We are in the heart of the South Sea, the Pool of Anbari." Everyone's face grew long and showed variations of not knowing what the hell that meant but not liking the sound of it. Schram shook his head in understanding but then went on to the second question. "And no, my companions and I will be taking your raft, if it still remains, and we will be going there." He pointed to where his eyes had become fixed. Rising out of the pool were the long, outstretched arms of the top branches of a huge oak tree. Its immense size below water to be growing from the sea bottom meant that it had been only an acorn probably over two or three thousand years ago.

Jermys woke from his relaxing trance to join everyone around in the surprise which was displayed on their faces. "What? We came here to climb a tree?"

Schram looked back, "that statement is grossly oversimplified, but actually it is what we are going to do." The dwarf fell back in disbelief. Worried looks grew across each of the companion's faces including Fehr who still had said nothing but curses and insults, and Schram's last statement had done nothing to clean his speech other than change the more choice words to elven tongue.

Pete rose and removed an extra patch from his pocket and much to the appreciation of all around though none would ever mention it, he placed it over his missing eye. "I will not stand in your way, Schram, but I do wish you could award me that ship now, for even if I make it out, I can't see you informing the court from the bottom of the sea."

Schram only shrugged a short smile as he stared back at the tree, a certain aura appearing around it noticeable to only his powerful eyes.

CHAPTER 26

Anbari's Dominion

The companions sat together on the deck after they had what should have been a solid nights' rest but by some twist of fate darkness never fell so the sky remained bright all night long. However, due to their fatigue, none had any trouble sleeping in what appeared to be daytime as their bodies graphically told them it was time to do everything except die. Schram felt a great power surrounding the large oak. He believed that it was responsible for everything regarding the Black Pool and the storm not to mention the permanent sunshine they now were experiencing, though whatever magic controlling its existence was now absent and this power now thrived on its own. Schram did not feel evil, at least in the tree itself, but the good within it seemed to be fading, as if its heart had been lost long ago and slowly all that this heart affected had grown weaker over time.

The companions discussed their plans, and although Schram had no specifics or even reasons, he said to find the Staff of Anbari, they had to go to the tree. He did not know what they would find there or even what purpose it might serve, but it was the only choice they had besides heading back into the storm and when given the choice, even those of Pete's crew were willing to join. When Schram told them they must all remain on the ship however, none seemed too distressed.

The group had become almost hauntingly silent when Pete appeared over them. "I see the dwarf and rat are looking a might bit sea worthy again."

The two looked up at the fat captain but their expressions did not show Pete's good humor. Fehr simply raised one of his paws and made a jester that any language would understand clearly.

Pete just answered with his deep chuckle. "I think the big red is about to die, if he be not already gone. His head has been motionless for a time. He just sits it across the other's back. I hope when he dies, they both will sink. Otherwise, the stink may drive me men crazy."

Schram rose. "I forgot about him." A saddened look grew across his face overshadowed only by a sudden sense of urgency. "We must make leave at once. Is the raft ready?"

"Yes, me boys replaced the broken boards with some from our hull. She'll not take many waves, but she'll sail this pond without sinkin'."

"Good," stated Schram motioning to the others to get ready. "Drop her in and we'll prepare to leave at once."

The group gathered their belongings and although none of them really seemed overly excited about their upcoming journey, they all did seem to be a slight bit relieved about not staying on the ship any longer. The anxiety of not doing anything seemed to disturb them more than the possible mission they were about to embark on. Even Jermys, who hated everything to do with the idea of entering a smaller and more decrepit boat, did not protest the thought at all. However, he was seen putting some special pinch of tobac into his pipe which, when he smoked it, emitted a strange, sweet odor and relaxed the dwarf as if he was submerged in a warm bath of dwarven ale and not entering the hole-ridden raft at the center of a black storm. The dwarf's only comment to Schram as he climbed in next to the large man was, "I feel pretty good. This was a nice idea". Schram only shook his head.

Fehr on the other hand quickly slid over beside the dwarf. "Might I have a puff of your tobac Jermys?"

The dwarf grinned. "Sorry old friend, I gave the rest to Pete. He seemed really glad to get it. You know, it was my best tobac."

As Schram pushed the oars deep into the water, the companions all looked up to meet the overly smiling face of Captain Pete whose head was already encircled with the same strange blue-green haze from his pipe that they had seen earlier around Jermys.

"Schram?" asked Stepha. "Why are we going towards the dragons?"

He answered flatly. "I enchanted the rope Pete had which made anything tied to it become buoyant. I need to touch the dragon's body to let nature take its course. That dragon deserves that much. He was only acting under the misguided ideas of his teacher."

Stepha nodded. "Yes, I hoped that was what you were doing. But, does the big one live?"

"Yes he does, but I feel nothing but despair and loss within him. He will know we come in peace, though I doubt he would attack regardless. He has lost all which gave him life."

They reached where the two dragons floated, the live one only opening one eye to acknowledge their presence. Schram reached over and placed his hand over the large one's head and said some soft words in a language which was even foreign to Fehr. The dragon's huge red head rose and although his entire body was wet from the water of the sea, Stepha could swear she saw a tear in the beast's eye. Schram moved closer to the dead floating body of the dragon and after incanting a short spell, he sprinkled a small amount of dust across it. A short gust of cool wind burst by and then vanished taking the passed dragon in its wake. The large red roared and then bowed its head to the group. Jermys moved towards the beast he had ridden across the sky and then brought on the verge of its own death with his Hatchet. He reached his arm to the dragon who moved closer so the dwarf could touch its head. As the two made contact, the dwarf's hatchet began to glow and hum as never before. The companions, Schram included, gripped their ears in an attempt to block the overwhelming sound, but the dwarf and dragon seemed unaffected. Jermys lifted his magical axe from his side and slowly placed it up against the wound it had inflicted on the dragon's neck and belly. The red's eyes became pools of peaceful song and the red blood which still spilled from his neck into the sea suddenly vanquished. The deep cut running the length of his throat disappeared and the life which seemed to be quickly draining from him as quickly returned. When the dragon's head rose magnificently over the small raft, the humming and glowing emitting from the Hatchet ceased and the group sat spell bound. The dragon peered at the five travelers before it, and with only a nod dove downward disappearing below the water's surface.

"What happened?" asked Krirtie directing her question to the dwarf who still stood with his axe outstretched.

"I don't know," he replied. "I just knew what to do. He, well he was truly good and I could feel it or something. He loved the one we killed, loved her like nothing else." The dwarf paused and his voice grew extremely soft. "He loved her very much."

Schram said, "I think we are only beginning to understand the power stored within the weapons and this Ring. Come, we have work to do."

The group remained silent as Schram reversed direction and rowed towards the giant tree. Those on board the ship had witnessed all that had taken place, and although Captain Pete and the remaining crew had taken well to their company, Schram believed they were probably subconsciously glad to be rid of the group especially after what they saw occurring with the dragons.

The hustle and bustle around the ship was still clearly in view as they drew near their target. Schram knew that *The Nightstalker* was as beat-up as any tub on the water in all of Troyf, but he had a feeling that Captain Maximus Pete would somehow find a way to navigate the storm once more. Furthermore, he would probably leave tomorrow since he really had nothing to repair all the damage with anyway. Schram made a silent prayer for their safety and then returned his attention to the tree.

As they drew nearer, Schram could feel the strange magic of the area growing stronger. He did not know what they were going to do when they arrived, but he assumed their destiny would unfold before them. As was expected, the tree's mystery did begin to turn full circle.

When they drifted under the shade of the most outstretched branches, a faint rumbling was heard beneath the water's surface causing a series of large waves to move outward from the tree's center. Hollers bounced off the water as the crew and captain left aboard the ship saw the tiny raft taking such a violent beating.

Suddenly, a loud crack broke through the increasing rumbling and a large branch broke free from the center stump and came crashing down upon the raft crushing it when it struck. The companions split in opposite directions to avoid the branch which meant instant death for anything in its path. More shouts rang from the ship but went unheard as the five companions fought the waves. They swam hard for the tree. Fehr was the first to reach it, as he was the least hindered having only his small dirk to contend with. Schram was finding exactly how difficult staying above the water's surface was when carrying fifty pounds of armor on top of his sword and bow. Yet, something foreign seemed to keep him afloat, and it was not any power from him or his Ring. He reached the furthest branches and used them to pull his body forward to the larger ones. He quickly scanned the area trying to locate the others. Krirtie and Stepha had jumped the other direction and when they had safely climbed onto equally large branches, they signaled that they were all right. Fehr ran around several branches and stopped at the branch where Schram sat. His little voice depicted great worry when he said, "Jermys can't swim!"

Schram's eyes swung and began to search the water surrounding where the raft had been hit. Noises could again be heard from below the surface but the waves had stopped. Their raft was shattered and pieces of the wood floated randomly away from the tree but there was no sign of the dwarf. Faint shouts could be heard from the ship and when Schram looked up, he could see it being lifted up and down as the huge waves which they had faced had only grown larger and more dangerous as they moved outward. Captain Pete's ship was now being tossed to lengths which threatened to tear the ship apart. Schram focused his mind in an attempt to calm the waters. He knew he could not stop such a powerful force but if he could just slow it or even add strength to the ship's hull, maybe it could still be saved.

He concentrated, trying to pull some of the hidden enchantments out from his clouded mind. Suddenly, just as the words began to form, all his thoughts went black. He heard the voices of his friends, but as he turned to locate them, the entire environment seemed to melt away. He fought to clear his mind but whatever power he had woken now had him and was unrelenting in its hold. He reached deep into the power of the Ring, but his Ring seemed to be powerless acting like nothing more than a band of metal twisted around his finger. As the power continued, the voices of his companions faded and Schram's head fell while his mind seemed to shut off.

There was no way of knowing what had happened, where they were, or how long they had been there when Stepha lightly began to shake Schram attempting to wake the magician. As he groggily sat up, he remembered all that had taken place. With his memory came the knowledge of the missing dwarf. He swung forward quickly surveying their environment. The room they were in was a large circular chamber with the walls appearing to be of well-polished marble and the ceiling was in an oval dome above them. There were several intricate paintings on the wall which would call for further investigation later. Schram turned from the room to discover the worried and confused faces of his friends answering his gaze. Even Fehr, who rarely showed any kind of fear, looked as if this final journey through the unknown had been too much. His body was pressed against Krirtie who rested wearily on the floor with her arms crossed tightly around the rat so only his head and face peeked outward. Stepha remained next to her husband and nobody spoke as they all seemed to be realizing that Jermys was no where to be found.

It was several hours before anyone moved save to more comfortably adjust their heads or contract and relax muscles so as not to stiffen too much. Schram had been lost in thought remembering each event they had faced, but knowing that regardless of how difficult and trying each one was, they made it through without question. However, when their guard was down and the times were not as serious, that was when they were most vulnerable and struck with hardship. When they began, there were six, and now two were gone, their fate a question of their own abilities. Schram felt a new level of sadness as he took blame for their losses and whatever they were now facing alone. He remembered his feeling as he steered *The Nightstalker* through the black storm. How he wanted to just let the wheel go and end his hell quickly without pain. He hoped Jermys and Maldor had been able to have that choice. However, although he did not know the conditions the dwarf faced, he knew that would not be an option for the maneth, being alone at the hands of the black dragon.

A tear formed in the warrior's eye but was quickly dried by the soft touch of the elf. Stepha whispered, "Do not fret any longer, Schramilis. We are very close to what you seek; you know that and must lead us. Though we are few, we still require your leadership and will follow you anywhere. Krirtie is showing great signs of fatigue, for she has lost everything except you and Fehr on this journey. Don't show her you are fading too."

Schram ran his fingers through the elf's long golden hair. "Do not leave yourself out Stephanatilantilis. Krirtie has grown to rely much on you as well as have I." Without additional words in that moment, they exchanged deep understanding.

Schram broke their contact abruptly and rose before the others. "Krirtie, Fehr, Stepha, we have work to do. I only have roughly enough food for two meals for each of us and they will be divided now to be eaten when you most need it." He walked over to the large painting which appeared between what seemed to be the only two exits out of the room each turning away from each other immediately. "What do any of you make of this?"

Stepha moved next to him. "It is extremely beautiful. The color combinations are like none I have ever seen. Look here," she pointed to a spot in the painting. "If you tied your hair in a braid, it would look just like that."

Schram stared at the picture then grabbed his long black hair in his hands. Shrugging, he said, "I have been meaning to cut this off since I noticed it after my training. It is not the black I mind, but the length is really an annoyance. As for the painting, I don't see any resemblance, and I could never wage magic against that dragon." He shifted his gaze to the large silver dragon that the longhaired man in the painting was raging a vicious magic war against.

Krirtie joined them with Fehr and she added, "I see the resemblance as well, but there is no Ring on the finger of the figure in the painting."

Stepha and Schram both acknowledged her comment which actually soothed Schram's mind as he too saw the mysterious likeness. Though the painting was of a human, there were minor discrepancies. The ears were slightly raised and gave the notion that they went into a point at the top although the long black hair was pulled back over them. Also the skin color was slightly off that of a human, and much resembled elven skin tones though that was probably due to the age of this great work. But Schram did find comfort in the fact that this magician did not wear the Ring of Ku, and he knew, as he looked at his own hand, his Ring would always remain in its place.

Stepha broke Schram's revelry and bypassing Krirtie's comment said, "Your statement made it seem that you know this dragon?"

He nodded and pulled out his book from the mountain elf library. Opening it to the inside cover, he stated, "The dragon in the painting is the same one who wrote this book and the same one who forged the Ring. He is Anbari and this is his dominion." He paused a moment and then continued, "Come on, I have no idea what way to go or what I expect to find, but we should be on our way. If this is like the enchanted mines of the dwarves, we could be searching for quite a while."

The three fell in behind their leader with both Stepha and Krirtie drawing their weapons. Fehr sat in Krirtie's back pouch watching the passage behind while Schram walked with his arms to his sides almost nonchalantly ahead. They continued down the passage for some time keeping a steady pace but not really coming across anything unusual. Occasionally they came to a new room, but ever since the painting room which they began in, these rooms had only one exit other than the one they had entered. The walls of every corridor were of the same smooth marble, and although there were no lanterns hanging about the hallways, all was well lit. It was this fact that made Schram freeze and reach for his book and frantically begin flipping pages.

Stepha stood next to him. "Schram, what is it?"

He returned, "I don't know, but something is not right."

Just then footfalls could be heard in the corridor ahead of them gradually growing in intensity with each step. Schram replaced the book to his pouch and signaled that his magic would handle any intruder, though Stepha saw the concern in his face and continued placing an arrow to her bow. The footsteps grew louder and whatever approached cast a shadow making it look enormous. As the creature caught up to its shadow and came into sight of the companions, it roared a greeting that shook the marble walls as if they were made of broken wood panels. Everything about the greeting told clearly that it was not one to be taken pleasantly.

Schram's surprise and awe over the strength of the roar caused him to fall back a step which was matched by his companions. For a moment, neither the creature nor the stunned group moved, as each seemed to be sizing its opponent. The creature was reptilian-like but had a much more rounded and pudgier body structure than any reptile. Its skin appeared smooth, and with all the slime sliding from it, it was obvious that it was a creature much more at home in the water than out. It had four limbs with its legs being nearly five times the size of its arms giving the impression that their strength must be immense. Its head was large and rounded with lips stretching across its length and the absence of any sort of neck made it appear as a giant ball of slop.

None of the companions moved as the creature slowly took one step forward. Stepha whispered, though she was unsure if any could hear. "What is it? I have never seen the like before."

The creature turned its head as if it had heard the elf's words but not understood. It seemed disturbed and roared again taking a step back to its original position. The three companions stood side by side now nearly stretching across the width of the corridor. Krirtie, who still had her sword drawn, took a small step forward. The creature's bulbous eyes turned from the group and focused only on her. Its head arched awkwardly a moment and then like the snapping of a rubber band, its mouth opened propelling a long pink tongue forward wrapping it around the girl and slowly drawing her towards it. The contact knocked her sword free and pinned her arms to her sides as well as Fehr into his pouch. Schram immediately rose the Ring and began incanting a spell and suddenly his mind grew black again. He halted his spell and fell to his knees totally disoriented with a sharp pain rising in his head. He tried to draw his sword, but his strength was gone. He looked to the Ring which now seemed to glow with a new sparkle he had never seen before. He reached his other hand over in an attempt to remove the ring nearly pulling his finger off before he fell forward unconscious.

Stepha watched Schram fall to his knees knowing something powerful had grabbed hold of him. Without hesitation, she began launching arrows into the belly of the creature before them but although they struck deeply into their mark, they seemed to only be lost in the creature's insides, not injuring it in the least. She turned her attention to its tongue which was continually pulling the girl forward. With precise aim, she sent an arrow directly into the creature's outstretched tongue. However, again it was to no avail as the arrow simply passed through as if only air broke its path. Stepha looked back to Schram and saw him motionless on the floor with blood running from the finger bearing the magical ring he had frantically been trying to remove. She replaced her bow and ran towards Krirtie drawing her dagger as she moved. The girl was only about five feet from the creature's mouth now, and although she fought hard against the pull, it would only be moments before she was overwhelmed. Stepha reached Krirtie and with one quick motion sliced deep into the creature's rubbery tongue. Green and yellow blood oozed from the wound as it quickly released the girl and drew its tongue back into its enraged mouth. It roared the most violent roar yet but seemed confused about how it had been attacked so deeply. Leaping backward, it stared at the elf woman and then quickly vanished back into the dark corridor.

Krirtie fell to her knees being stopped from striking her full body to the ground by the gentle arms of the elf. She looked to Stepha, "See to Schram, I am fine."

The elf smiled and then, after resting Krirtie's head against the wall and removing the battered rat from its pouch, moved to see to the condition of their leader. He had begun moving slightly but no noticeable recollection of the environment had yet come within his grasp. Stepha stroked his soft hair giving him a sense of safety with her presence. Slowly, his senses began to return in full and he sat up, putting both hands around his head trying to stop the war that was taking place within it.

"What happened?" he asked, fighting to make the words form between his lips.

Stepha continued to stroke his hair as she replied, "none of our magic weapons could touch it. I attacked it with my dagger and seemed to hurt it greatly though the wound was only superficial."

Schram's eyes seemed to ignite as she retold the ordeal, and forgetting the pain in his head, he reached into his pouch and removed the book he carried. He tore through the pages as if he was looking for something he knew had to be there. Stepha leaned back slightly even becoming a bit worried by his sudden passion he found in the pages. She was about to grab the book from him and demand that he relax when his eyes grew wide and she realized he had found what he was seeking.

"Here it is," he began, pointing to a poetic passage next to another picture of the dragon Schram was calling Anbari. "I knew when I could not feel the magic giving these corridors light that something wasn't right. After Ku returned and used the Ring to steal the weapons, Anbari then found magic in the staff. He incanted a spell depicting that nobody but he could ever summon the Ring's power while within the confines of his dominion again, and to do so would be fatal if the spell was not extinguished." He rose his eyes from the book and faced the elf who had just finished putting his hair in a long braid to match the one in the previous painting. "Indeed we are close to the staff, and though I can not feel its presence, it can feel mine."

Stepha said nothing as she only stared at the now nearly fully recovered man who seemed to be totally free of the pain he had just endured. Her eyes spoke of total amazement and when Schram swung his head to Krirtie and Fehr, they greeted him with the same response.

"You are the one in the painting."

CHAPTER 27

KIRVEN'S DESTINY

The companions festered about a bit, each using the break to grab a bite of food before they continued their trip. Schram frequently glanced up to catch the eyes of the others upon him only to look quickly away when they were discovered. Schram was as lost as the others in finding any significance in the resemblance, and though he had no way of seeing exactly how he appeared now, he knew by the expression from his friends that the likeness must be unnerving.

Even though he was not convinced that the painting was of him, his thoughts worked on the assumption that it was. He wondered why and how then he was using the Ring's power against the dragon he knew to be Anbari. Could it be that Anbari had succumbed to the evil and joined Slayne in the attempt to rule the country? Yet, if this was so, why was there a painting to give warning? The last thought he had centered on the length of time that the painting had been there. Stepha was correct in commenting on the brilliant colors it displayed, but there was a dullness to their brilliance that depicted of time's effects upon it. In addition, much of the paint had become cracked in places, and with the incredibly smooth surface of the rock wall, it was apparent that only an uncountable number of years must have passed. Finally, Schram thought about his double's hand. If it was truly Schram, where was the Ring of Ku? He could not wield magic without it and moreover he had just proved it could not be removed from his hand. However, the painting was clear in its description that the magician used some powerful magic of his own creation to strike against a huge dragon. Schram knew he was not capable of such a feat.

As they continued through the vast hallways, Schram's troubled mind continually turned over all possibilities. The slow pace at which they had been moving worked to calm the warrior, but did little to shorten the distance he believed may lie ahead. He signaled to the others that they should increase their steps if they were ever going to reach their destination, wherever that might be. Krirtie nudged her pouch to wake Fehr causing him to moan slightly.

Stepha moved several quick steps to catch Schram and continued by his side. She was grinning softly when she stood on her toes to whisper, "you mentioned before you wished to cut your hair. Don't, I find it quite grand."

Schram chuckled and pulled the elf in close being careful not to press her delicate wings. "You never cease to amaze me, love. You can make my heart smile even at my most trying times."

She returned his embrace with an equally strong hold and then they pushed apart knowing they needed to be on their way but thankful for the brief return to their true reality. Schram drew his sword and waved to Krirtie and the three walked down the hallway with the rat still only seeing their path after they had already passed it. However, he felt that his careful watch down the back hallway was an important job so that kept his attention focused and freed the others from listening to his constant chatter.

Once again, little out of the ordinary greeted them as they walked. Each room they came to was empty and only had one exit. It was impossible for them to determine their direction as the hallways wound with turn after turn. Schram believed that they had been walking for nearly twenty miles and if there wasn't magic at work here, then this structure was the largest on all of Troyf. Even the dwarven mines, though made up of hundreds of miles of caverns, were simply carved into existing rock and not created by the forming of marble into a cavern. The time and workmanship that must have gone into this creation was truly phenomenal, though he was certain that magic had held a strong hand in its creation. Schram tried to refrain from dwelling too much on what he was seeing and concentrated solely on what lingered ahead of them. Yet, he couldn't shake a feeling which continually crept into his mind. Kirven is near, he thought, the discomfort clear on his face.

It had been nearly four hours since they had left from where the reptile creature had attacked and Schram knew from the feelings, or the lack there of, in his legs that it was now deep into the night.

He stopped in the next room they came to and said, "let's hold up here for the night." That was all that was needed to be said, for the others simply looked around taking notice to the light that filled the room then collapsed onto the floor. Schram shook his head and added, "I realize we have no way of determining the true time, but by the fatigue I feel and see in your eyes, I think we will be able to sleep without problem this night. I will take first watch."

The others nodded agreement each realizing exactly how tired they really felt. What seemed to be only moments later, Stepha, Krirtie, and Fehr were fast asleep and Schram leaned back against the opposite wall of the room. All remained quiet and calm for about an hour until Schram began to hear a faint humming. He turned to where his friends slept peacefully and realized that they did not hear the noise. He swung his head around the room and almost fell over when he greeted himself before him. The wall on the other side of the room had transformed into a giant mirror. He walked towards the mirror and realized the humming he heard was coming from somewhere on him. He dug through his pouches and discovered the diamond stone which had been included in Hoangis' life pouch for him. The stone looked to be an ordinary piece of granite or similar rock but now it glowed and hummed with a peaceful aura. He looked back to the mirror and saw in its reflection that he did appear exactly as what was depicted in the painting. However, he also discovered that this rock he held did not cast any reflection. He moved closer to the magnificent mirror to further inspect its incredibly perfect glass. He reached out and touched it remembering the only place he had seen its like before. Suddenly, the humming from the rock ceased and when he looked back to the hand that held it, he saw it now appeared as it has before, an ordinary piece of stone, well carved but with no other redeeming qualities. Schram looked back to the mirror and was taken when he now saw the rock's reflection in his hand.

"Schram, wake up. Some guard you are," said Krirtie laughing. "But don't worry, your snores were loud enough to scare any intruder away."

He rose quickly, swinging his head to greet the marble wall where the mirror had been. He dug through his pouches, much to the surprise and even concern of Krirtie, until he found the deeply packed diamond stone. He gripped the stone in his hand seeing that it didn't glow or hum. He stared blankly up to the girl above him. "I guess I dozed off, sorry."

She smiled, "don't worry about it, no harm done." There was a pause then she added softly, "are you all right?"

Color began returning to his face. "Yes, fine. I guess I was dreaming or something."

Krirtie put her hand on his shoulder. "Go get some real sleep, it is my turn to keep watch."

Schram woke early the next morning to join Stepha as she sat over him taking her turn guarding the group. She smiled as he approached and made room for him to sit next to her. The two leaned against each other for a few moments until Schram asked, "did you dream at all last night?"

The elf looked surprised by the question. "No, not that I recall. I think I was so exhausted that every one of my muscles relaxed so immediately that I slept as soundly as could be possible. Did you have a dream, my love?"

I think I did, but it was so real. I could have sworn I was awake acting out what I thought."

She put her arm around him. "I used to hear my father say those same words."

"Your father? Please, tell me."

She smiled when she thought of the Elven King. "He would be sitting alone in the Great Hall just staring into the fire. I could enter completely unnoticed if I wanted to, but I always made some noise so as not to startle him. When he would greet me, it was obvious he had been deep in thought. When I asked him what was troubling him so, all he would answer was that it was nothing to bother my young mind with. When I asked Madeiris about it, he told me that often people strong with magic have dreams which are sent from other magic sources. When this happens, the dreams do not occur as dreams but as a reality to those involved. However, he also said that was just an old tale told by the storytellers to help the children get to sleep. If the children were to dream, they would think magic was strong with them, a thought they found exciting. Yet, with all stories, it probably originally had been based on some sort of truth, though what has been long since forgotten. My father never would tell me what troubled him and his times alone seemed to become more frequent with each passing year."

Schram looked saddened. "I do feel magic was at the core of this dream, but as for what it meant or what magic was behind it, I am at a loss. For all I know, it was a message from your father." Her eyes grew wide and he knew he had to continue for she would never allow it to stop there. "It was something he gave me upon his death that was at the dream's focus. I had all but forgotten about its existence, and it was not my mind which brought it back to me in my sleep."

She hugged him tightly. "I am always here. If you discover its meaning, will you tell me?"

"I will," he returned hugging her back.

The two leaned back and for the next hour said nothing but just sat pondering their situation. Krirtie began stirring soon after and when she was up and around she woke Fehr by stuffing him back into her pouch once more. He responded with a grumbling of displeasure but quickly found his senses returned and with a bite from his remaining food was ready to take his position as rear guard. Stepha and Schram had gathered their belongings and once again the group headed out, Schram taking one last look at the now bare wall before leaving.

They traveled a short distance, passing several small rooms and more of the same hallway when Schram spoke. "Wait, we have been here before. We are traveling the wrong direction."

The others looked at him suspiciously but it was Krirtie who spoke first. "How can you say we have been here before? We left from the opposite door we entered, I am sure of it."

Schram replied, "I am certain we did as well, but that does not change the fact that we have been here before. We must go back."

"I do not wish to walk all day long with no food only to end up back where we began this fool journey yesterday, at the painting room. Nor do I wish to meet that creature again, though I don't know where he disappeared to."

Schram looked disturbed and his tone told of his strong belief to return. "Please come back with me. We have not gone far. If you find that you still do not trust me after we go a short ways, then we will turn back this direction."

Krirtie was not satisfied with his compromise and looked to Stepha for support on her point but quickly realized she would find no such assistance there. She grudgingly nodded and the group turned back. In no time they were back to the room where they had slept, and although Schram wanted to inspect the wall more carefully, he didn't want to further Krirtie's aggravation. He did however pull the small stone from his pouch and stare deep into its carved face. It again sat silently, not humming, not glowing. He placed it back in his pouch and began to move forward.

They exited back out the doorway that they all believed they had entered the night before but were soon aware that they had never been in this hallway before. The walls were no longer smooth marble but appeared as rough, jagged rock much like some of the caverns they had seen in the older, unused dwarven mines. The light that had been present before now was much dimmer and Schram decided to join his companions in drawing his sword. Krirtie did not mention anything about the past disagreement as it was clear that wherever they had been, they now were in a new system of tunnels.

They continued cautiously forward at a much slower pace than they had previously been moving. The atmosphere of this new cave leant a feeling of uncertainty and threat which created a much higher tension level among the travelers than they were used to.

Frequently, they jumped at the sound of the other's footsteps on the now loose gravel floor of the corridor. Schram motioned to the others to join him on both sides thinking that if each could see and feel the other's presence, perhaps they could find a slight bit more comfort.

Unfortunately, this help was only minimal. It became very apparent that all the companions were reaching a new level of intensity. They came to the first chamber since entering the new corridor and Schram said nothing but immediately sat on a large rock that rested near the center of the room. As he sat, he could feel the large drips of sweat rolling down his back not to mention those which appeared on the sides of his face. He looked into the blank expressions of his friends and although their cheeks did not show the same beads of sweat, their discomfort and worry was not well hidden. Schram's voice cracked as he spoke. "I do not know what power it is that we approach, but whatever it is I feel that it must be tremendous to be able to strike such fear into my mind before I even greet it."

Krirtie moved forward, her tone also displaying the blind terror she was feeling. "I have been walking calmly for the past hundred or so yards, but with each step it seemed that something was making my feet heavier as if my feet were telling me not to continue."

Stepha interrupted, "and my wings have been randomly twitching making my entire body near spastic and uncomfortable. I feel danger lies ahead, and my mind is telling me to run. If I did not have all of you with me, I would never have made it this far down this evil cavern."

All nodded, except Fehr who had disappeared into the pouch, that they shared Stepha's evaluation, but all also knew that they could not turn back, for they really had no where else to go. No matter what danger they felt lied ahead, they knew they must continue to greet it.

Schram took another quick bite of bread and then rose to again begin his cautious walk down the ominous cavern. Each of the companions held weapons at the ready, with Krirtie holding both a dagger and her scimitar in case her sword proved powerless. Schram led the three in a single line as the corridor in which they traveled at times became alarmingly narrow.

They passed through room after room and down hall after hall, but nothing suspicious occurred at any time. This in itself made Schram worry even greater. Though his sensing ability granted him through his magic was now absent, he still had a human little voice that was telling him trouble lay ahead. It was just a feeling probably originating from the intense fear he was experiencing in this unknown place, but nonetheless, he believed in his mind that they were very near something which they were not going to happen on in surprise. No, whatever it was sat patiently waiting for them, enjoying every moment as their troubled minds became even more challenged.

Schram swung up his arms to halt those behind as he inspected what blocked their path. A huge wooden door, probably four inches thick resting on hinges the size of human thighs, stood closed fit flush against the narrow shape of the corridor. He turned to the girls. "Even if it is unlocked, I doubt I could budge this huge thing. It must weigh five hundred pounds and those hinges are as rusty as Pete's beard. Without my magic, I don't think this door will even consider moving."

As if it was a feather and a gentle breeze had just gusted to push it through the air, the door suddenly swung silently open. The hinges sounded as if they were brand new metal, well-oiled to ensure smooth mechanics. The entire motion was without sound until the large door struck the cavern wall at its side.

Stepha's shaking voice broke the puff of dust that had been kicked upward. "Do you think someone is inviting us in?"

Schram peered ahead into the room beyond the door responding, "well, I think whoever controls this area wants to be damn sure we know that they are aware of our approach, and that we are scared to do it."

With a motion back to the others, he led the group of four slowly into the large room through the massive doorway. The new chamber was much more poorly lit than the previous hall and it took a few moments for their eyes to adjust, including the elves who both were uncomfortable with the occurrence. Fehr had again risen from his traveling pouch, and the rat's gulp echoed off the red rock walls as the large door slammed shut behind them. All four spun in time to see the now blocked and double-latched portal suddenly vanish leaving solid rock in its place. After a blink, none could even tell where it had been.

Fehr climbed up Krirtie's back and joined her stare back towards the former tunnel. "Well," started the rat smugly, "we won't be leaving by that door."

His attempt to lighten the mood was lost in the obvious fear which was carried in his tone. Schram turned his attention from the now missing exit to see where they had ended up. The room was larger than any of the others they had seen but it was still much less than anything magnificent. Its walls seemed to be of a different rock, red in color and their texture more resembled a hardened clay than actual rock. Besides that, the room had little to offer. The absence of any smells or any other sensory stimulants was noticed by the two elves, but Krirtie and Fehr only found a deeper feeling of discomfort, not putting a finger on its source.

Schram gently shrugged and pointed towards the only apparent exit. "I guess we go this way."

The others said nothing but simply fell in behind their leader. They traveled down another long hallway until its winding pattern straightened, and the group could see nearly fifty yards ahead of their path. The tunnel they were in gradually grew larger for the stretch and then emptied into a much larger room which appeared to be well lit and containing many different rock configurations. However, more important than that was a fact Schram knew from the silent, frozen faces of his friends, all had seen the same thing he saw. A shadow cast against one of the rocks moved. Something in that room was alive and waiting for them.

The last fifty yards were the longest of the day. All the fear and terror that had been generated reached its apex and the companions now moved on adrenaline alone. Step after step they walked, reaching the doorway with legs that resembled brittle sticks. They pushed into the room without losing a step, all uncertain about what might lay ahead.

Schram's eyes peered around the huge room. The ceiling rose nearly thirty feet with stalactites dropping downward, some gripping the tips of stalagmites from the floor forming pillars of the red clay. A large fire burned in a hole cut into the far wall giving the added light to the room. One large exit appeared adjacent to it and was held in black shadow as none of the fire's light seemed able to penetrate its barrier. Schram's eyes moved forward from the blackness and stopped on the figure standing only about twenty feet in front of him.

"Greetings Schram, it has been a long time," said the canok.

"Indeed it has Kirven," Schram responded, wanting to say more but not knowing exactly what.

"And greetings to you two as well," Kirven nodded to Stepha and Krirtie. "I am glad to see you again Krirtie, and you as well Stephanatilantilis, you both look well." The two girls returned his nod with one of their own as Kirven turned back to face Schram. "You have changed greatly old friend. I see I was correct in my belief of your abilities, your mother would be proud."

Schram was surprised at the reference to his mother but passed it quickly as many thoughts were filling his mind. "Yes, you were correct," he responded confidently, "but my strength exceeded even your estimations."

Kirven laughed slightly. His voice was hard and cold with a twist of intrigue. "The moment to test our strengths is near, but not yet at our door. We have much to discuss."

Schram looked slightly lost as the fear he had felt was replaced with anxiety and uncertainty thrust against the aura of confidence he was trying to show. His tone displayed all these emotions as he replied, "the time for talk has long since left us, Kirven. Though I have no disrespect for you or any of your actions, I cannot let them continue unchallenged. I know your honor brought you to

Slayne's side, and now my honor for you must try to strip you from that position."

"Well said old friend, but you cannot defeat me. I have the power of two other great sorcerers working in hand with my own. You have no chance against us." He sent out a bolt of energy which Schram began to block with the rings power, then remembering what happens when he used the ring in Anbari's dominion, he dropped his arm and let the bolt strike sending him against the far wall.

"Good," continued Kirven. "You have already realized the Ring's powers are lost here, as are yours. You are no more than human now. Why do you think we brought you here?"

Schram rose from where he sat with pain erupting across his chest. "You are wrong old friend. I am as elven as human now, and you would not have chosen me if I only needed to master the Ring, many could have accomplished that feat."

"Do not underestimate what you did to gain control of the Ring of Ku. I chose you because you could do just what you believe to be no great thing." He was about to continue when he saw Schram look to his friends and seeing their lost stare at the wall behind him, turned to follow their gaze.

The canok remained silent while he watched Schram freeze on what had gone unobserved as he entered because it had been to their backs. In actuality, it was no wall at all, but rather a huge, rounded cave. What Schram's body had struck was not the soft clay making up the cavern facing, but the large silver belly of a motionless dragon. It was the largest creature Schram had ever seen, easily filling the entire cave with its belly touching both the floor and the ceiling. He looked to its closed eyes and nostrils but could see that he still breathed, no matter how weakly it may be. Softly, he whispered, "Anbari."

"Yes," returned Kirven. "The great Anbari, perhaps the greatest, most powerful magician ever, but also the most foolish. Due to his actions so many years ago, Ku was able to gain power that his people were not ready for. Then, when times were about to restore themselves to their natural order, Slayne obtained Anbari's last grip onto the world, his magic staff, possibly the most powerful focus of immeasurable power ever constructed. How Anbari created it from his weakened condition, I do not know, but why the fool allowed Slayne to gain control of it, truly brought his undoing. You came here to seek Anbari's staff; however, he has not had it for over two hundred and thirty years. The same staff which divided my people has sat here under Slayne's control raking its magic over its own creator." He stopped and stared hard at the human before him, taking on a tone more serious than Schram had ever heard the canok utter. "When the master of the Ku Ring is dead, so shall be Anbari. Then no power will ever defeat us. We brought you here because Slayne knew you would be powerless in Anbari's dominion, and now you will fall prey to our wrath."

With the decrepit sight of the dragon, Schram felt the little hope he still had quickly begin to fade. There was no way to attack Kirven with any magic, and he knew they would be twice dead before any physical attack would meet with success. His options seemed limited to totally absent thinking only now to buy some time to maybe gain a break for his friends to flee, though he was confident they would not.

"I knew from the first day I met you Kirven, you could never harm me. I do not think you can kill me now regardless of any deal you made in the past."

Kirven said nothing, only jumped up to a large broken stalagmite in the center of the room and bowing his head downward, he created a life-size and life-like hologram before all those watching. The scene they saw was horrid, complete with sounds and smells as if it were taking place at their feet. Their companion, the huge maneth they had longed to know was still safe, was slowly being repeatedly lowered into pools of bubbling hot lava. The maneth screamed as his legs burned from his body. Krirtie became fierce with fear and charged blindly through the image attacking where the canok rested. Without hesitation or losing the vision, Kirven fired another bolt of energy grabbing the girl and lifting her over his head to crash into the far wall. Her body fell limp and blood began to trickle from her mouth. Fehr had been thrown clear before the crash and went unnoticed by the canok as he hid behind a rock near the fire pit. Rage grew in Schram's eyes as he continued to see Maldor being lifted from the flames only to be doused right back without care or concern. Finally, the maneth was cast aside on the ground where he began to spastically roll in agony. Surprisingly however, his legs showed no signs of burns or injuries. Schram appeared puzzled and his stare turned back to his old friend.

Kirven shook his head. "Of course these tortures are in his mind, though trust in that Maldor believes them to be real. He will wake to find his skin blistered and bleeding, but in actuality he will be protected by the Hammer. He has convinced his mind to believe what he is seeing. For him, this is reality. I suspect he will be able to withstand over a year of this before finally one of them kills him outright. Imagine the pride he will feel being killed by an illusion. Yet, we will kill him tomorrow when we have the Hammer. With the full power of the Staff at our command and the Ring no longer a threat, obtaining the Hammer will be little more trouble than picking up a loose stone. Do not think I will not kill you Schram, for I knew Maldor's father long before I knew you. You and your friends are as good as dead already."

Another bolt shot from the canok, this time causing Schram to reflexively put up his other hand to break the beam's path. There was a flash of brilliant light and his head was struck with a sharp but temporary throbbing pain. He hit the floor and suddenly realized that the attack had already subsided, and he did not feel as if he had even been struck badly. He swung his head up to see the ragged body of his old friend struggling to regain his footing. Kirven looked completely taken by the blow, and although Schram had no idea what had happened, he did what anyone in that position would do, he faked it.

"A little too confident in your actions, were you not old friend?"

"Aye Schram," he said hesitantly, "but my confusion is matched only by what I feel of your own. However, very few have ever sent me such a jolt, I shall not underestimate you again."

The canok again sent a bolt to which Schram in turn lifted his free hand to greet. The same pain erupted in his head, and he realized that it was his mind silently working a spell. A bolt of equal intensity to his first propelled from his hand and intercepted that which Kirven sent. Again there was a flash as the two conflicting energies struck one another. As before, Schram fell to the ground and felt the strength behind Kirven's power. A plate of blue and white light formed at the contact point and slowly moved back and forth as one of the magicians mounted an attack and then withdrew.

Light filled the room sending what seemed to be red hot liquid droplets of fire in random directions, one striking at Krirtie's feet only to be quickly buried in the dirt from the cavern floor as it melted through the clay base. Stepha moved slowly, drawing her sword she rarely used but not wanting to risk her bow in case its magic was also affected here. If she could make it safely beyond the explosions of fire from the brilliant war before her, she aimed to attack Kirven while his attention was drawn to Schram. She had her shield held high as she ran past. She felt the burning pain of fire erupting on her back and she could smell the scorched flesh. However, the adrenaline in her elven blood quickly shoved these out of her thoughts and she charged at the four-legged magician now only feet from her. Kirven reacted at the last minute turning a fierce attack on the elf as she moved. Stepha took the brunt of the jolt swinging her sword as she was thrust away. She felt the tension in her attack as the sword tore through Kirven's flesh. The canok yelped and was sent sailing to the wall by the now unprotected magic of his opponent. Schram regained his footing and stepped forward, ready to send another jolt towards the bleeding figure slowly turning back to face him. Suddenly, a bolt of energy of incredible magnitude struck him in his side and sent him to the ground with a thud.

For a moment, all was still and Schram could only hear soft voices from the far wall. His head was a violent storm. He fought to regain his composure to attempt to mount some defense against whatever force had now attacked him but his confusion and pain was overwhelming. He lifted his head and tried to focus on where Kirven had laid. His vision was blurry, but he could make out the outline of a short figure beside the white canok. Kirven stood but it was apparent that his injury was not superficial. Schram immediately thought about Stepha but could not turn his head to check the elf's condition. He held his eyes fixed on the two ahead of him, now seeing something long in the new one's hand. Slowly, his eyes began to clear and Schram looked lost when he softly said, "Jermys?"

The dwarf laughed slightly but Kirven was the one to speak. "In most wars of magic, one only must worry for the magic of his opponent. Stepha's charge was unexpected. That is twice I have underestimated you and your companion's abilities, trust that it will not happen again." He paused and stepped forward a few steps with the dwarf by his side. His face remained calm, but the pool of white blood beneath him clearly showed that the canok was in great pain, though his magic would protect him from feeling it. "I believe you know Bretten already."

Schram's eyes grew saddened. "It has been a long while, but we have met before, though I believe that I am closer with his brother."

Kirven smiled. "Yes, the infamous Jermys Ironshield, the one who wheels the Hatchet of Claude and has caused multiple deaths of Slayne's young dragons." He directed his attention to the dwarf. "Why not tell what happens to you each time your brother kills one of our dragons."

The dwarf looked angered. "I was whipped until my beard was soaked full with my own blood from the floor." He cringed, almost reliving the harsh memories as he spoke.

"Tell me Schram," Kirven began after a short silence, "where is the twin dwarf? We had expected him with you so to rid both of you with one stroke."

"He is feared drowned in the Black Sea," he replied coldly, however somewhat surprised when he witnessed the momentary sadness in the other twin's eyes.

Kirven continued intrigued as well, but for other reasons not noticing Bretten's expression. "I feel we would have known had the dwarf perished, however, if it was the gods who took him, it is best left as such." His tone quickly changed, "and as you see, I will not be the one to kill you. Bretten here has mastered what is available in the staff, and it will have little trouble with your magic, no matter how strong you have become."

Schram rose and as he stood he gave a powerful appearance towering over the two before him. His voice was stoic, sensing that this would be his final battle. A final test of strength between his powers of the past matched against the immense new magic in the staff. His tone was hard with his lips cracking slightly as he spoke. "Kirven, I believe that you have become truly evil. The honor which took you to Slayne's side is now all but absent. You have become totally seduced by one's distorted mind and all I can do is pray that the gods remember what you gave up."

Kirven bowed his head, as did Schram, before fire shot from the end of the staff. Schram quickly mounted his defense but the power attacking him was immense. He was quickly on his knees even leaning his muscular body forward trying to fight the onslaught of energy. The explosion of light depicting where the two magical forces were meeting was only inches from Schram's hand. He knew if the energy from the staff touched him directly, the most likely result would give him enough time to take one final breath before finding his destiny. He thought about his entire life centering on all that had happened in the past years. However, most of all, he thought about the elf he loved so much. He longed to look to her but knew he must remain focused. All the feelings in his head were pushed clear by the deep ache that was beginning to form. He knew his time was near and as he looked towards Kirven, it was obvious that the canok realized the same.

A feeling suddenly burst into Schram's mind and he knew Kirven was attempting to speak with him telepathically, but the magic clouding his mind was blocking the message. Schram fought to clear his head but knew to do so would give only seconds before his death. He weighed the options and decided the situation was hopeless.

He cleared his mind and heard, *You will always be my greatest friend.*

Pain struck the magician in the wake of the message. Schram was thrown backwards and a reflex brought both arms up to shield himself from the ensuing power. His hand bearing the Ring of Ku crossed the staff's beam and an enormous explosion commenced. Schram's mind began to darken and he fell completely limp having only minimal sensing ability. However, he was clear enough to realize the attack had ceased and there was someone or something by him. Slowly, feeling began to return to him and the only thing he sensed was an overwhelming pain in his hand. He looked down to see the Ring of Ku sliding loosely as he moved his hand. Pain shot to his head and he knew he was about to black out. He reached his free hand over and removed the Ring which slid off as easily as if it had be placed on a finger half its size.

When the Ring which had given him so much power cleared his finger, a mass of uninhibited knowledge exploded within his head. The faintness he had felt vanished instantly to be replaced with a wave of strength and confidence. He now understood all which needed to be done, beginning with the meaning in the painting.

Kirven's voice broke the revelations taking place in his mind. "So, the other twin lives."

Schram remembered the figure next to him, turning to see the hard face of Jermys guiding a piercing gaze in the direction of his brother. Schram sat up but did not speak as the two brothers seemed locked in a deep conversation completely void of words.

The canok tilted his head slightly and then continued where his past comment had ended. "Finish the magician and then kill your brother as well. It is the least you can do for all the pain he has caused you."

Bretten aimed the staff towards Schram and although he seemed to have doubt in his actions, a fierce beam exploded from its tip. Schram was on his knees, but still mustered an adequate defense as again an explosion erupted between the two.

With one hand defending the attack, Schram swung his free hand around and directed it towards the still motionless dragon. A second bolt erupted from this hand and struck the huge creature as it slept creating a huge silver aura around it.

All noise in the chamber was absent from Schram as he fought to focus his mind in the defense against the staff, and his magic used upon Anbari. He did not hear Fehr attack Bretten from behind, but was thankful for the relief from the wrath of the staff. Kirven quickly incanted a spell which sent the rat plummeting into the wall but Bretten did not immediately resume the attack since Jermys had moved in his path. Schram halted his magic on Anbari and turned to fully prepare for the expected power to again be thrust upon him. However, he was greeted with an indecisive expression from the dwarf and a threatening tone from Kirven.

"Kill the dwarf now, then finish the prince. You swore your allegiance to me and that is my word."

Bretten stared toward his brother and Schram could feel the conflict within him. He was strong with honor, and by some quirk of fate he had come to honor an agreement with Kirven that meant obeying his command. But before any deal, there was the bond between two brothers. Schram remembered his words from the first time they all walked together under the Ozaky River. *He is my brother. I could no longer kill him than I could kill myself.* His statement meant in jest so long ago now haunted him into a winless situation. Bretten's eyes were pleading with any in the room for answers, until suddenly his face took on a new light. He aimed the staff at his brother and as a smile grew over Kirven's face, dwarven blood began to cover the floor.

Another explosion erupted on the wall sending a shower of rocks outward from where the energy beam struck beside Jermys. A tapping was heard as the staff fell from Bretten's hands and rolled between the two magicians, the dwarf falling backwards gripping the handle of his brother's old mining axe as it lodged deep into his chest. Immediately, Schram and Kirven reached out their magical hands and clasped onto the staff in a fierce, ropeless tug of war.

Schram used his mind to pull with incredible force while sending attacks with his free hand onto his opponent. Kirven created a shield around him concentrating solely on recovering the staff, forgetting any idea of an attack. Schram believed that if he recovered the staff, Kirven would use his power to export back to Draag to wait for another day to fight.

Schram's power was strong, but he was having no effect on Kirven's protective shield, and the canok was slowly gaining ground in their battle of wills. Jermys had been thrown clear when the wall exploded and the location and condition of the dwarf was unknown to Schram. That is why it was such a surprise when the dwarf ran forward and grabbed the staff from where it hung suspended between the two magicians. A boom of light shook the cavern and equally strong bolts struck both Kirven and Schram sending the magicians to their backs. Jermys went soaring backwards as the total power of the staff was unleashed in his hands. It pointed out of control randomly shooting bolts into whatever happened to fall in its path. Two strikes struck above where the unconscious bodies of Stepha and Krirtie rested, but the jumping pattern as the staff wildly threw Jermys around quickly moved from the girls to begin an assault on the opposite wall.

Schram saw the dwarf out of control but knew his main concern must lie with Kirven. He turned to face the canok in time to defend the flame of his commencing magic. The two locked wills once again as the destruction caused by the staff seemed to be bringing the cavern down on top of them. Large rocks continually fell from above landing on or near those locked in mortal combat. Neither had saved anything for their own protection but now were concentrating on the most fearsome attack they could muster.

Both beings bled profusely as they fought to gain any advantage, but as time dragged on, it became obvious that Schram was winning. The two were so tightly focused that neither noticed that the explosions about the room had ceased. Schram stood and began to drive fierce blows onto his old companion until the canok's total attack had ended and Kirven fell bleeding and near death before him.

Schram looked at the once brilliant creature who had been brought to the lowest point he had ever believed possible. Tears flowed across his cheeks when he said, "I cannot kill you my friend."

A pool of white liquid was forming around the canok's body when he replied, "I know, but you do not have to."

Schram noticed a presence beside him in the form of Jermys, and something else. He turned to see the hand of Anbari resting on the dwarf's shoulder. The dragon had shrunk to near half his previous size, and it was clear from the expressions on both their faces that the dwarf and dragon were acting together in control of the Staff. Schram heard a message from somewhere he could not determine. The voice was feminine and familiar, but something was blocking his recognition right before it came to him. Schram bowed his head as the staff fired its final bolt into the near lifeless canok body. The message he heard was, *it is his destiny*, while the message he sent was, *you will always be my greatest friend.*

CHAPTER 28

The Silver Oak

Schram felt a cool sensation on his forehead and stirred slightly before suddenly regaining his senses and thrusting his body upward nearly knocking Stepha to her back as she leaned over her husband. She ran her fingers through his long, black hair and softly whispered, "easy Schram, you have been through much. Take it slow at first, for we are free of danger."

The magician seemed to be fighting his mind trying to remember all that had taken place, how long before he could not be sure. From his position on the floor, it appeared that he had fallen unconscious right where he had stood in his final battle against his closest friend. His head swung to where the canok had laid as he remembered the ordeal. All his eyes were met with was a large open area of the chamber, devoid of any signs of being out of order and totally absent of any debris from the previous war.

A deep voice sounded from behind causing Schram to jump at the sound. "His body disappeared right after the battle concluded. Several minutes later this returned in its place. I believe it is meant for you."

Schram looked deeply into the silver dragon's powerful eyes as he reached out his hand and took the small pouch he held outward. His entire physical strength was absent but he still mustered a nod in thanks as he put the sack safely inside his armor.

Anbari nodded in return then continued. "If you are able, there is other business which calls for your attendance. I would not ask this of you so soon, but I believe there is little time left for the one involved."

Schram looked into the deeply saddened eyes of Stepha and then peered around to greet Krirtie's gaze who, although she seemed pleased to realize Schram's improved condition, showed the same misery in her eyes that he saw in the elf's. He swept around the room until he too saw what had touched the others so deeply. "Bretten," was all he could whisper.

With Stepha's help, Schram picked himself up and moved over to where Jermys sat with his brother's head resting in his lap. Bretten remained motionless but as Schram drew near, the little dwarf's eyes opened and gazed towards him. Blood flowed around the dwarf's body, and by the appearance and amount, Bretten had only moments left of life. He began to speak ignoring Schram's motion to remain quiet. His words were soft and gargled as more blood was flowing from his mouth than sound. Schram knelt down to hear what Bretten had remained alive to tell him. "I didn't want to do it, but I was bound." He stopped as a fit of painful coughs broke between his words.

"I know old friend," replied Schram softly. "You acted with nothing but honor, you should be proud."

The dwarf's shaky voice continued and whether he had understood Schram's words was unknown. "I wanted to say I was sorry for any betrayal you might have felt at my hand, but also thank you for giving me a way out." With that his eyes rolled back in his head and Bretten was dead.

All bowed their heads in a moment of silence followed by Schram's whispered chant and spreading of the elven dust across the dwarf's body. He turned to Jermys who sat with tears on both cheeks still holding his brother's head. "Bretten acted admirably. He will be well-accepted by your Princess. You taking his life as such gave him his only escape to die with honor."

Jermys looked up, tears still covering his face. "But his bolt would have missed me anyway. I did not need to kill him. He missed on purpose."

Schram pulled the dwarf against his broad chest. "That is how you returned his honor to him. He knew you would never kill him for his treachery, only forgive him. That forgiveness in his mind was not enough, but if he killed himself, that would only satisfy his conscious, not restore his honor. You gave him what he thought he would never be able to have when he left us so long ago. You gave him life, in his death."

Jermys pushed himself back, now regaining some composure. "You did as well. He told me the idea was placed in his head magically. Though he said the voice seemed unfamiliar and somewhat feminine, he felt you were at its core. We both thank you." He looked down at his limp brother's body and dug into his pack to remove a small cloth to place over his face.

Schram placed his hand on Jermys' shoulder. "I am truly glad that he found his peace before he died, but I was not at its heart. I believe that same voice spoke to me, though I recognized its sound, its source leaves me amiss." He turned to Anbari who had been silent for some time. "Do you know of what I speak?"

The dragon replied, "many voices and powers overlook my domain, each with their own resolve and various reasons for their actions, most of which are independent from anything I know or control. If one spoke to you as such, take it only as a star in the midst of blackness and that there is a hidden force on your side, for you will need the help."

Krirtie spoke, her voice showing surprise and exhaustion. "What do you mean? We have recovered the Staff. Is the war not over?"

Anbari gave a deep echoing chuckle and then stared at the girl. "No child, this war has only begun." His expression changed and the dragon moved to stand beside Jermys. Anbari still towered over the small dwarf even in his shrunken state, but his voice displayed only the deepest sympathy and care. "Young warrior, these caverns making my home hold great power and many secrets. With the protection given your brother by the elven dust he will be well cared for here until your time to join him draws near. I would be honored if you allowed him to remain."

Jermys placed his hand over his brother's heart and felt the peace within him. He gave a responsive nod to the dragon and with the movement of Anbari's staff over the still dwarf's body, a cool gust of wind blew passed and the body vanished.

"From the day he was lost in the forest, he has never had the peace he now feels, and only now do I understand."

Anbari nodded and bowed slightly before stating, "he has found peace." There was another responsive silence and then he continued. "Come now, lets eat in the memory of those we have lost, for we still have much to discuss."

The dragon turned, holding his staff at his side and disappeared into the blackness denoting the only exit next to the still blazing fire. The companions all looked to Schram who still had not had a chance to check on their condition or really inspect himself for injuries. Seeing the comforting replies in their stares, he climbed to his feet and joining hands with all, vanished behind the dragon's tail.

Schram was expecting to walk into darkness and his consciousness had already begun adjusting his eyes. However, to his surprise as well as those with him, the next room they came to was even more brightly lit than the previous one. Also, its walls were not the dull red clay that they had seen since entering this section of the caverns. Moreover, they shined with a brilliant glow with silver vines entwined along every face. The chamber was tremendous in size, giving the impression that they had just walked out into a beautiful garden rather than a cavern chamber. Flowers were randomly growing throughout the surface split only by the small stream which flowed from a gentle outbreak of falls and the white sand they now walked upon. The air was fragrant and although no other creatures seemed to be there at that time, Schram felt that any would always be welcome. They continued through the wondrous room until they saw Anbari stop at a huge table, which looked as if it adjusted its shape to accurately fit all of the companions comfortably despite their grossly different sizes. An enormous wooden wall appeared next to the table laden with food and Anbari leaned against it letting a peaceful expression grow across his face. Schram sat back in amazement as he followed the wall upward to see that the huge silver-leafed branches broke off of the trunk and formed the ceiling above them.

"The great oak we saw above the water's surface," Schram said in a soft, questioning voice while taking a seat at the table.

Anbari smiled. "The very one, Schram. For over three thousand years this tree has grown. Great power is stored within its branches, power capable of tremendous good or horrendous evil depending upon who taps its source. No human has ever seen The Silver Oak from its base, though you are far more than human. In fact, only recently was I awarded with its presence. For most of my life, I had no knowledge of its existence." He paused and studied the magician. "What do you feel from it?"

The dragon's eyes were inquisitive but Schram believed Anbari knew exactly what he felt. He stared long at the awesome site but a lost expression was all he showed. Hesitantly, he said, "I feel sensations I have never felt before. Warmth, cold, fear, confidence, almost something like pure energy but not anything so physical. It seems like it is right ahead, able to be captured and completely understood, but for some reason it is just out of my reach." Anbari looked stunned by this evaluation but silently listened to the rest of the boy's statements. Schram stopped, thought a moment and then added, "perhaps this is what blocks my vision." He dug into one of his pouches and pulled out the ring which had given him all his power, the Ring of Ku. Reaching out, he placed it in front of the dragon. "I believe this was meant for you, over two thousand years ago, please forgive my tardiness."

Anbari appeared completely lost and confused. He reached a long talon out which functioned as a hand and lifted the ring from the table. Showers of light shot from the touch and with a fabulous flash the Ring and its brilliance vanished. Anbari fell back as a silver aura appeared around him. His eyes filled with strength as his power from long ago returned to his body. The Ring of Ku was no longer in existence, for it had returned from whence it came, Anbari.

The magnificent dragon sat forward, a new look about him as he gazed toward the human-elf. "You have truly given a gift I never thought would be returned, I thank you Prince Schram of Toopek, for I am whole again."

Schram nodded politely then continued where he had left off, "and now I too understand that which flows within the Silver Oak's branches."

"I know you do," the dragon replied deeply. "This staff is meant for you. It is given to you by the Oak, not by me. Any misdoing associated with its use will be treated severely by the Oak itself, not by me. As the Staff is part of the whole, its actions are subject to its controls. Any evil done with it now, will result in the users immediate penalty, remember that Schram, remember that well."

"I will, and I understand completely my friend."

"Aye Schram, great friend indeed. You will all always be welcome here. Now, lets settle our empty bellies and feast for the wonders that have occurred today."

None of the companions felt like celebrating after all that had happened, but in the environment they were now in, all trouble seemed to be pushed away, almost as if being within a sanctuary specific to each of them. With that, each found refuge in a new peace within their own self, and with the magic flowing about their minds, they were being aided in understanding. All ate heartily and although little was said during the meal, much was felt.

Once finished, the table magically vanished and the weary travelers found themselves resting comfortably on the soft grass making up the ground surrounding the Oak's trunk. "Now child," stated Anbari looking towards Krirtie. "Much troubles you. Let your mind be free to ask all that it desires."

Krirtie was stunned by the address but his evaluation was correct. She started slow at first, then became more confident as she spoke. "I do not know what happened. I saw you," she motioned to the great dragon, "seemingly dead in the cave. Then Maldor? And now all this including Bretten," she placed her arm on the dwarf as he sat next to her gaining strength from each other. "I do not understand."

Both Schram and Stepha bowed their head at the mention of Jermys' brother's name but did not speak as they too realized the confusion and pain she was feeling. Anbari appeared calm and at peace and began slowly so as not to overwhelm the girl. However, then he stopped and turned to Schram. "You should be the one to tell them, for they followed your lead the entire journey. Do not now let it be passed."

All eyes fell on their leader who shared the same peaceful expression carried by the dragon as he held what appeared to be an ordinary piece of wood across his legs. He sounded extremely confident and secure when he spoke with his voice also carrying a deep note of care and love as well. "I do not have very many answers, but I will say that which I know. Since seeing the painting which resembled me, I had been struggling with its meaning. During the battle, when Bretten used the Staff upon a power equal to it, meaning the Ring of Ku, or more rightly, the Ring of Anbari, it was forced from my hand. This freed my mind and the true meaning of the painting became clear. In it, I was not attacking Anbari, but somehow with a power from deep inside me, I was restoring the power that Slayne had stripped away through the use of the Staff. I do not know where this power within me originated, but it seems to have been awakened by the Ring and once the Ring was removed, it was unleashed at my disposal. The ensuing battle left both my greatest friend, the canok, and our former dwarf companion dead, both dying as their destiny dictated, and both dying with honor."

Stepha had moved over and placed her arm around him when he looked back to Anbari. She wanted to speak but quickly realized that Schram still had many questions. He stared toward the silver dragon for several moments locked in silence, then finally with a strong but still young voice, he asked. "Do you know about this power within me? I can tell it is not of the Ring, for it is a completely different magic I feel."

Anbari nodded and grinned. "Trust your feelings. You have much to learn with the Staff. Eventually, it will provide the answers you desire. All involved were wise to not tell you yet, for your mind was not ready to handle it. You have much left to accomplish. We have much left to do."

Schram was about to speak again when Krirtie interrupted. "You said before the war was not over, but we have the staff that Schram was seeking."

The silver dragon rose and spread his wings stretching in a statue of magnificence. "Child, the Staff is a powerful tool, never forget that. However, Slayne too is powerful. He has had the Staff in his possession for two hundred years; much of its power had been converted within him. He also has armies of those you call goblins, dark dwarves, and trolls not to mention his ever-growing army of young dragons. Let us also not forget what your companion holds in his clutches. Maldor carries my silver hammer. If that object falls under Slayne's command, it will make his next plan well within his grasp."

Krirtie cringed at the sound of Maldor's name but this time it was Schram who spoke. "Next plan, what do you mean?"

Anbari replied. "Never think Slayne is ignorant or over-confident. He can often see how futures can unravel and will always prepare for the worst should it come to pass. This time, for him, it did, but he is not through. That is all I will tell you now. Tomorrow you should leave to do what you have planned to do. Seek out Werner, for he will help you."

Schram nodded appreciatively as the dragon suddenly began to become transparent. "Wait, Anbari, one more question. I believe this is yours also." Schram dug through his largest pouch and pulled out the book he had taken from the elven library. As the dragon totally vanished, so did the book.

Nobody knew exactly when they fell asleep, only that they had. They woke in front of the fire pit of the room where the battle the previous day had taken place. Despite all the excitement and occurrences of late, all in the group looked quite refreshed this day. Perhaps it was the first true restful nights sleep they had gotten in some time, or the knowledge that today they were beginning their journey back to Toopek. Whatever the reason, as they ate the large plates of food that appeared before them, the atmosphere was definitely full of cheer. However, after their quick breakfast, it became apparent that they really had no idea how to go about leaving.

"So, where to now?" broke in Fehr in his usual good humored voice.

Schram looked down at where he sat in Krirtie's pouch. "Well, Anbari said if we sacrifice a rodent into the fire, all our answers will be discovered. Do you want us to throw you in or will you jump?"

Fehr looked worried for a split second, then relaxed when he saw the human's lips begin to curl upward. "Ah, you didn't fool me."

"Sure I didn't," he replied laughing. Then, rising and beginning to turn, he added, "I think we shall find our answers at the tree. However, even if we can make it back to the water, our wondrous ship is long since gone. Good ol' Captain Pete was ready to leave before we even were off his battered tub."

All shrugged as they were brought to the memory of their situation. With a final nod from Schram, he stepped back through the dark portal marking the gateway to the garden room. His foot crashed downward striking water rather than the expected ground. The waves were violent as again the rumbling was heard echoing from the trunk beneath the surface. Schram looked up to the branch to see his friends appearing out of the mist and spray being kicked up by the water. Their first step proved as desperate as it did for Schram and soon all had plummeted into the tossing waves. They were lifted up and down as Jermys' yells punctured each of their ears. Schram swam to steady the dwarf when there was an explosion upward lifting Jermys from the water. A great red dragon carried the small man through the air dropping him on the wooden planks of a decrepit old ship whose name across the bow read *The Nightstalker*.

"Good to have ye back, dwarf. I be needin' someone to scrub me decks." Laughter filled the background as Pete opened his arms to the dwarf whose stunned expression brought out more cheers.

The red quickly moved and carried the others over to join Jermys on the ship. Equal greetings were met for each of the returning passengers and although the sight of the dragon that had attacked them days before astounded the crewmen, none showed any signs of fear. With a brief word to Schram, the red nodded and quickly disappeared beneath the surface.

"Bly me man, what did that beastie say to you?"

Schram turned to his companions and the bewildered captain. "He said, Anbari sends his greetings and told me of a new plan that he had to slow Slayne's movements. He will incant the dragon eggs so those not hatched will not for another year or so. He is giving us a little time. However, the red, whose name is Draketon, says there are already over one hundred dragons ready to fight. He asked that we use care in our defenses and only kill those we have to. He says if we can kill Slayne, he believes he can make those still living see the truth behind his brainwashing. I told him we would. He also gave a special praise of care for you Jermys. He thanks you again for all you have done and tells you that your brother is well."

The companions seemed pleased with the encounter until Pete's voice again burst through. "What the hell are you talking about, boy? Not kill the dragons? Unhatched eggs? Slayne? I wait here for you who I thought was dead just in case you might return. I risked me own life to save yours, and you feed me rubbish!"

"Cap'n," came a small voice from a crewman to the side. "You know our anchor was stuck until this morning. We couldn't have left anyway."

Schram smiled and said, "Don't say that mate. I know Pete and if he had wanted to leave, no anchor would have kept him here."

Pete smiled a crooked smile and handed a large slab of meat to the group before him. "Here, eat up and enjoy. All the food just appeared on the deck. Its mighty tasty."

"No thanks," stated Jermys, "our bellies are already filled."

Schram continued his thought. "And now it is time to go home."

Pete looked slightly worried. "I don't want to sound concerned, but me ship is not in its prime anymore, mate. It could," he stopped in mid-sentence as Schram lifted his hand holding the ordinary looking staff.

A silver beam shot from the staff's end and drew a line directly into the heart of the black storm surrounding them. A swirling wind began to bend the clouds until a peaceful hallway separated them into two black walls. "Your not in you prime either Pete," stated Schram, "but I trust you can keep it in the middle."

"By Sakton's hand himself!"

The captain looked amazed but didn't hesitate to give the order to push ahead. Slowly they moved through the storm, the ship not even rocking because the water was so smooth. The crewmen and passengers stared into the clouds able to see the violently churning winds and waves wondering how they ever made it through before.

After several hours, they broke through the outskirts of the black pool and the water turned the deep blue of the open sea. A sigh could be heard and several were seen making their praises to the various sailor gods whom had protected their journey. However, it was Pete's expression that was most surprising. Schram approached the old sea dog who stood motionless staring off across the water. For in the distance a small island could barely be made out and the captain's eye seemed focused on that point.

Schram put his hand on the old man's shoulder and asked, "how long till we can reach Icly? I need to reach a friend there."

The captain turned and the normal dirt brown and red color always present in his well-traveled face had been replaced by a white paleness which gave him the look of death. He appeared as if he had just stepped into Sakton's domain and sat down for dinner with the devil himself. His voice shook when he answered, "I be thinkin it will take about forty to fifty days."

Schram almost fell over. "We don't have that much time. Is there anyway to make this bucket move any faster?"

Pete still looked lost. "No, Icly would mean sailing completely round the eastern peninsula. I would prefer, with your permission of course, to make port straight ahead. We could reach it by nightfall."

Schram peered across the sea but even his elven sight could barely make out anything but a dot. "What, or where, is it? That port of Valis you spoke of?"

"No boy, that would be Toopek, you're home."

CHAPTER 29

The Return

"What is it Alan?"

"I'm not sure Geoff," replied the ex-third lieutenant of Toopek who had since been promoted to first in command over the human armies. "It looks like some sort of ship, but the distance is too great to see any specifics."

"Blast it!" Geoff scowled. "I knew things had been too quiet for too long. Do we have a ship ready?"

"Aye sir, we have a whole fleet. I'd say twenty-five ships or so could leave port today, though their crews would be little more than makeshift guardsmen — a far cry from strong sailors. We could possibly even add to that number by tomorrow should it be deemed necessary."

Geoff thought a moment, then said, "no, send only one heavily armored ship to intercept, but keep a close eye on it with others at the ready. Also, prepare two garrisons to move to the southeast and southwest fronts and send a message to Reynolds in Empor."

"Aye, aye sir," replied Alan, his voice becoming raised in anticipation at the new turn of events which had brought a splash of excitement to what had become calm and eventless days. "You think the ship is a decoy, eh?"

Geoff only shrugged as the commander ran to relay the orders. Since the war began, Toopek more than any other city had seen the most destruction. Geoff, being the head of the maneth Batt Line for so long before becoming King, was well prepared to serve as an efficient and powerful leader. Under his rule for the past fifteen months, Toopek had become one giant fortress. Huge stone walls had been erected around the entire city with gates facing the mountains, Empor, and the large harbor open to the island with the destroyed Tower of Council and the King and Queen's castle. Of all the exits, Geoff knew the harbor was the most difficult to defend, however he had also established a separate detachment of maneth troops on the small island to attack the rear should the harbor fall prey to dragon forces. Though he had only been able to defend and not go the offensive himself, except pursuing the attacking goblin forces, the human and maneth losses over the past year had been minimal. This was in part due to his cunning skill in leadership during wartime added with the strong bonds which had been created between all the Toopekian residents who had been thrown together as one. However, it also was due to the greatly reduced number of attacks which they had been forced to face.

In the past six months, though they heard of the major offensive against the elves, they had only seen three attacks upon themselves, two of which were totally goblin and troll forces resulting in no Toopekian casualties while the rebels suffered heavy losses. The third attack had only been two weeks ago and it involved two Dragon Lords, an army of goblin foot soldiers, and nearly fifteen dragons. The losses suffered during that battle were indeed heavy by Geoff's standards, but they could have been much worse. The attack lasted only two days and the forces attacking Toopek, though they were slowly wearing down the defenders, suddenly retreated. It was the next day the news reached regarding the state of Elvinott. When it had happened was not clear, but the fact was that the elves had fled their homeland. Whatever had drawn the dragons away from Toopek probably saved the city from siege. The troops could have held for one week, maybe two, but the end result would have been the same. The maneth and human forces would have had no where to run, defeat was inevitable. Now Geoff saw the approaching ship and wondered if it was the preliminary stages of the next attack, the one that would prove to be their final battle and possibly finish them. He peered across the water. A worried look slowly grew across his already aged face while he watched the Toopekian battle ship hoisting its sails and with a small crowd forming around its dock pushing slowly out towards the open sea to intercept.

"Cap'n Pete! Warship approaching!"

"Where away?" hollered Pete back towards the crewman who sat straddling their make-shift crows nest they had built.

"Dead ahead, Cap'n. She be riding to our eyes."

Schram ran to the railing and looked across the sea. He saw the approaching vessel and knew immediately from where it had come. Also, by its direction Schram gathered that the crewman's second statement had meant that its course was directly across their path and destruction was its intent. "She's one of mine, Pete. She'll sink us faster than that storm would have if we don't signal to her."

"Bly me!" he hollered. "Ram me by me own passenger's country. I knew this blasted sea be cursed. Do you have any signal to use?"

"If I use magic, I would only scare them into thinking dragons are behind it. Then we could have a fleet of ships upon us. By the time they figured out who we were, we'd be kissing the sea floor."

"Huck the dwarf over Cap'n," hollered the crewman laughing. "His bloody screaming would scare those basta. . ." A loud thump was heard as the crewman, the makeshift mast and the basket all crashed across the deck shattering wood planks upon impact. Jermys only knocked a few wood chips from his hatchet before replacing it.

A deep bellowing laugh rose from Pete's fat belly. "Dwarf," he began through his chuckles, "you be more pirate every day. I think you should," his voice froze as his eyes stared blankly into the sky. He faltered when he continued. "By Sakton himself, I have never seen the like."

Schram spun his head to witness Stepha's golden hair blowing in the wind as she flew towards the oncoming boat. Her flight was awkward as she had not used her wings in some time, and they had sustained a slight burn during the encounter with Kirven. However, as the muscles began to regain their feel for the air, the grace and beauty she was capable of began to show through. She glided through the air as if it were her true home and walking was but a past time. The men on the approaching ship stirred wildly. All drew arms about the ship's rail and prepared for the first of the dragon's attack.

Some had already drawn their bows and were beading a path towards the approaching beast when one yelled, "hold your arms. It is Princess Stepha!

Suddenly all recognized the beautiful flyer elf who had spent most of the past year with them. A cheer with the strength to reach clear to Empor, echoed across the water. Stepha landed on the deck to the pleased and excited greetings of the Toopekian troops. Immediately full sails were lifted and the large warship pushed quickly along towards the near stagnant movement of *the Nightstalker*. Those on land saw the two ships meet without the appearance of any hostilities and as Pete's ship was brought into the harbor he had been forever forbidden from, a series of loud echoing cheers rang out from the length of the coast and those on board. There had been times the crewmen assumed they would never see land again, much less find port as heroes in the largest human sea port city in all of Troyf, let alone the North Sea. Schram had repeatedly wondered if he would ever see his home again, but now with Stepha, Krirtie, Fehr, and Jermys by his side, he was about to do just that.

Geoff and Alan Grove both waited on the first pier and as eyes met, a deep comfort fell over all. However, Schram saw something in the large maneth's eyes as he looked across their decrepit ship that showed of deep worry. Then, Schram remembered Maldor. He looked to Krirtie whose stoic expression told that she too had been suddenly confronted with memories and no longer felt the excitement of the festivities. She seemed to be staring at Geoff, but only seeing the horrible vision Kirven had showed them.

Schram walked to her side. "When we land, I will bring the others along. Tonight we will spend together among our close friends, and tomorrow we can spread the word of our success."

Krirtie nodded with small beads of water forming in her eyes, and as the ropes were tied down securing the boat to land, the travelers walked down the plank leading to the docks of the harbor of Toopek. Geoff stood with arms wide as Schram fell into them. The maneth no longer dwarfed Schram as much as he had but there still lingered a shy foot difference in actual height. Geoff stood broad shouldered at about seven and a half feet while Schram rose about six feet eight inches off the ground. Either way, the sight of Jermys receiving the next maneth embrace almost brought the onlookers to their knees.

After all the companions had received proper greeting, Geoff said, "I'm almost fearful to ask as I saw the answer in Krirtie's face before she left. Maldor is. . ?

"Maldor lives," replied Schram to a relieved sigh from the maneth king. "But he has been captured by Slayne and his condition grows steadily worse with each passing day. I will explain more, if you will join me later, for we are hungry and tired and wish to rest a spell."

He was going to continue when Pete broke in from behind. "Well tar me back and throw me to them dragons, I thought I had seen it all. From what part of Sakton's home would you be of, lion man?"

Geoff and the other nearby maneths looked stunned by the comment but Schram quickly interjected. "Geoff, King of the Maneths and acting ruler of Toopek, may I present Captain Maximus Pete of the forever banished Pirates of the North Sea. We owe him much, and though he rarely mixes words and may seem outright rude and inconsiderate, he is a good man."

Geoff nodded appreciatively but refrained from the big hug he had been giving as he took in the captain's somewhat disgusting physique. He smiled and said, "Welcome to Toopek Captain. If your men desire bath houses there is one ready by the ale house at the end of this pier, and trust all food and drink tonight will be counted for by us, for tonight, the city celebrates the return of its prince.

Pete pretty much ignored Geoff's comment till he came to the part about the free ale, then a rousing cheer from the crew and all those within earshot backed his smile. Pete motioned to his men and then turned back to Geoff and Schram. "A might bit of washin' would do me men some good, especially since this night now might be a long one."

As he led his five remaining men away, Schram smiled and whispered to the maneth, "good, maybe tomorrow I can stand next to him without sending my elven scent into chaos." The two laughed and throwing his arms around Stepha and Geoff, the three departed down the pier with Jermys arguing heartily with Fehr in their wake, though with the noise of the crowd, nobody but those two involved, could hear.

The group walked into the small cabin where Krirtie had started a small fire and had been joined by another who had witnessed their return from the crowded streets. When the group pushed into the single room, it was Stepha who was first to see the new visitor. "Madeiris!" she yelled running into the outstretched arms of her brother, now King of the Elves.

Even Geoff was surprised at the elf's presence though nothing about elves really caught him off guard. The big maneth king said, "well, I guess we will have to tighten our defenses. Somehow I keep finding that elves have an uncanny way of sneaking past them."

Madeiris loosened his grip on his sister. "On the contrary, I was stopped three times." He winked towards Stepha, "by your guards. Only because of my position as son to my father did they let me pass."

Geoff simply grumbled as everyone laughed knowing that not only had the elf not met any Toopekian guards, but he could have brought nearly an army of elves through with him. The maneth approached his old friend. "I am pleased to see you well, regardless of how you show the weakness in my," he turned to Schram, "our defenses."

Madeiris took Geoff's hand in a tight grip that was joined by Schram as the three leaders of drastically different people showed the depth of their alliance. The handshake turned into an embrace which gave a refreshing security among all in the room. Noises of celebration could be heard in the streets nearby but the cabin was well back away from the main city and unless you happened to be an over-observant elf, none in Toopek paid heed to the whereabouts of their leaders.

Fehr had made his home on the end of a large table which sat in the center of the room. By sure chance, he happened to be on the end nearest the fire where Krirtie could softly stroke his soft fur. The rat sat up as he felt the greetings had gone on long enough. "Okay, enough already. What happened to the belief to eat and be merry. This just being merry is getting out of hand."

The three leaders broke, all turning wearing broad smiles as Madeiris and Schram took places at the table and Geoff exited briefly and then returned. Shortly thereafter, several maneth guards brought in large trays of food then stood watch outside the door.

The meal was festive much like the atmosphere of the entire city. The companions decided to indulge Fehr as the rat was about to burst from his excitement of finally having an audience. He relived the entire journey for all to hear, with Schram or Jermys adding a bit of information that somehow, in all his wordiness, Fehr seemed to leave out. All in all, his tale took nearly four hours, and it would have gone longer but Jermys had begun sharpening his hatchet in front of the rat's seat and coincidentally the story quickly found its end. However, regardless of its excess, the adventure was well-explained and those who had not lived it sat spell-bound with both Madeiris and Geoff showing an added sadness at the news of Kirven's death and understanding for the dwarf's loss.

The mood had become somber until Schram spoke to the Elf King. "Madeiris, might I now inquire about the reason for your presence here? Your people and the dwarves have not fallen under attack have they?"

All leaned forward at this since most had forgotten about the unexpected presence of the elf. Jermys looked extremely interested as it was his homeland that Schram had referred to.

Madeiris rose and paced a bit before replying. "Completely the opposite, and now I am beginning to understand why. Feldschlosschen fell under heavy siege following our escape to the mines, but the combined dwarven and elven forces held strong. However, shortly after your groups leave," he nodded to Schram, "the attacks became minimal and our scouts found that the only dragon army force left was a large unit numbering nearly eight or nine hundred goblins between Feldschlosschen and Elvinott. I assumed that force was left to prevent our return to our forests and the three other equally sized armies had moved to smother you and whatever trouble you were stirring up. However, now it seems they returned to wherever Slayne's secret base is to begin preparations for this new plan of attack Fehr said Anbari spoke of. I had originally come here to see if Geoff could send some troops down the goblins back while my forces sandwiched them from the front in an attempt to return my people to the lands we call our home. However, I do realize the importance of discovering the heart of our enemies new attack and will lend my forces to aid you in your quest to restore the canoks to their life of long ago and find the one called Werner."

Schram rose, his face hard but his voice was soft and well-spoken. He held his staff close to his side and the jet black hair he had acquired during his transformation with Ku still hung down his back in a long braid. "Thank you Madeiris, but I will not require any aid in what I have planned next. I believe your idea to return to Elvinott is sound and should be done. Your father's last wish was to make Elvinott strong again with magic, and he was successful. Do not spare anything to return, for its boundaries are now nearly impenetrable. Our people will be safe there as well as its ability to act as a strong base for future offensives. I must go eastward to the canok homelands, where hopefully Werner will have returned there as well. If not, I will move to the last place I saw him, the peninsula city of Icly. Depending on what I learn, I will then either return or continue onward to attempt to face Slayne and rescue Maldor."

Geoff rose, his expression showing the seriousness that the current conversation had generated. "I will be more than willing to aid you in anyway that I can Madeiris." He turned to Schram, "and anything you require is at your disposal as well, though I would like to add that I would stress that you do not face Slayne alone, even if it means forfeiting Maldor's life. He is as honorable as any I know. He would not want, nor willfully allow, any lives lost in attempts to save his, especially if it jeopardized what he fought for."

Madeiris began to speak in agreement with Geoff's comment but was cut off by his sister. "I believe his advice to be sound, Schram, and I hope you are including me in your upcoming journey."

Jermys also stood, "and me and the rat as well, though as you can tell by his snores, he will thankfully not answer on his own."

Schram shook his head but couldn't speak due to Krirtie's strong input. "If there is a chance you will go to rescue Maldor, nothing will keep me away."

Schram now held up his hand to quiet the room. "Dear friends," he carried more in his eyes as he looked deeply towards Stepha, "I must go to the canok lands alone. Only I know their whereabouts and I made a promise long ago to a friend I shall never forget that it would remain as such. Geoff, I thank you as well for your offer of aid, but none will be necessary as you have already given too much of yourself in the protection of my father's city. Also," he turned to Madeiris, "my path will take me through Elvinott so leading an attack on the forces sealing off your forests from you should be at our forefront. The magic which now flows freely at my command will be a strong asset to you." He took both of Stepha's hands in his as he continued. "Your presence, and yours with your people," he added nodding to Jermys, "would be best used in Elvinott. Your father used his entire being to return the power to the forest. The elves, our people, will need your strength to help lead them. Your brother is extremely wise, but in these times of great evil, it is possible that he could ask too much of himself. Your presence will aid him in more ways than just in the leadership on the battlefield. You will lend him the support he needs as he makes some of the most difficult decisions he has ever made. I have had a friend to lean on my entire life, and when that friend was taken from me, I turned to you for support. Now its time to forget my greed and let your brother, now King of Elvinott, use his sister's strength to aid him. You are truly a powerful and wonderful elf, and wife, and I shall return to once again be greedy."

Stepha fell into his arms to the sad but proud gazes of those looking on. Schram peered over her shoulder towards Jermys, who stood quietly with his head lowered. "And Jermys, you will be needed at Feldschlosschen. When Madeiris leads his elves back to Elvinott, your support with the Hatchet of Claude at your side will be immeasurable."

Jermys lifted his eyes and stepped over to face the human who now stood with one arm around the elven princess with soft tears forming in her eyes. "It was an honor serving with you Schram. Your abilities as a leader are incomparable, but that does not begin to speak of your abilities as a friend. You will always be welcome in the dwarven lands, and if you ever require assistance in the future, I hope you will not hesitate to seek me out. I thank you, from me and from my brother, and know that I will always be your friend."

Schram's face began to darken as the emotions in the room began to overwhelm him as well as the others. He knew that those words did not come easy for the dwarf as emotions were never something his people discussed. He reached his hand down and placed it on the little man's shoulder. Softly he added, "And may you know that never have I learned to trust any as I do you. Many times you risked your own life to save others, and it was because of you we were successful in our attempt to recover the Staff. You are a powerful dwarf Jermys Ironshield. Your brother would be very proud. You also will always be my friend and ally. Should you ever need a magic hand at your side, you know who to ask."

Schram knelt down and the two embraced, the dwarf showing signs in his color that he too was feeling the tight control over his emotions faltering. He looked back towards the others and stated, "I wish all of you gathered here to know that the dwarves will cooperate with whatever you decide to be the best plan of action. We are strong in numbers and control many very sensitive areas. Use us as you need and come to us for help, for we will be waiting to stand by your side." He lowered his head and it was clear that he was fighting back the tears. "Now, as the aches in my body seem to be screaming at me, I must find a room at the nearest inn and find a nights rest with one more mug of ale."

Krirtie nodded and said, "May Fehr's snoring accompany you to your inn, Jermys? I believe he would prefer to share that ale with you."

The dwarf nodded and the two left the small cabin to the smiles of those remaining at the table. Madeiris spoke, "in all my life, I never thought I would see a dwarf and bandicoot become friends."

All laughed heartily but it had become apparent to everyone that the time to retire for the night was near. Geoff and Madeiris left the room with the big maneth's arm loosely over the elf's shoulder like brothers after a bar fight. Schram could still hear Geoff mumbling something about elves sneaking into his city and the elf king returning with the idea of joining the still roaring festivities with a few more mugs of ale. Krirtie gave Schram a long, loving hug whispering a welcome home before she left only to head to the harbor to look over the water, consumed by the thoughts for the maneth she loved.

Stepha turned to Schram with a peaceful expression full of the strong feelings she felt for this human that had changed so much over the last two years. Softly she said, "shall we continue with the festivities tonight or may we find some time together?"

He smiled, pulling her close. "I think together would be my choice."

Standing on her tip toes, she gave him a small kiss. "Come on, I am sure the Inn has an open room for the Prince of the City."

Schram said, "You go ahead. I have one more thing I must do first."

She was surprised by his comment but something in his voice told her not to question him. What he had planned was of utmost importance and something that was just between him and whoever it involved. She kissed him again and then disappeared out the door.

Schram sat back on the table and dug into one of his large pouches beneath his now magically shiny elven armor. Withdrawing his hand slowly and carefully, he removed the small sack which had appeared when Kirven's body had vanished. Sitting alone, he let a large tear roll down his cheek as he began to think about his old friend. He almost felt a slight fear as he reached hesitantly into the pouch. He moved his hand around the bag finding only an odd feeling substance in the bottom. He pulled it out to see a small tuft of brilliant, red-colored, canok fur. A sudden chill swept through the room causing Schram to shiver a bit before the gust burst through his hand sending the fur about the room. However, instead of falling randomly across the floor, the hair began to swirl magically in front of him until it suddenly vanished.

He smiled and began to get up to leave when he heard the voice of his lost friend. *Thank you Schram. You have given me what Jermys gave his brother, the honor that I thought lost. You have done well.*

He bowed his head in one last prayer for his friend before leaving to join Stepha. He knew he would not hear from Kirven again until possibly when his own time to pass had come. However, he felt Kirven was safe, and if he could be successful in defeating Slayne, as Kirven had believed he could, then the canok would not mind waiting, though now that he lived by elven years, it could be quite some time.

View other Black Rose Writing titles at www.blackrosewriting/books and use promo code **PRINT** to recieve a **20% discount when purchasing.**

BLACK ROSE writing™